END AS AN ASSASSIN

ANDRÉ WARNER, MANHUNTER
BOOK 1

LEX LANDER

ROUGH
EDGES
PRESS

End as an Assassin
Paperback Edition
Copyright © 2022 (As Revised) Lex Lander

Rough Edges Press
An Imprint of Wolfpack Publishing
9850 S. Maryland Parkway, Suite A-5 #323
Las Vegas, Nevada 89183

roughedgespress.com

Paperback ISBN 978-1-68549-191-8
eBook ISBN 978-1-68549-190-1

END AS AN ASSASSIN

PART 1

LAST HIT?

CHAPTER ONE

A CONTRACT TO KILL, perhaps for obvious reasons, is not a document. It's not even sealed with a handshake, that reputed currency between men of honor. Surprising as it may be to those for whom the printed word and a handshake are all, the so-called hard contract is no more than a verbal understanding that, in return for payment by the contractor of a specified sum of money, the contractee will—not to mince words—commit murder.

In my case at least, the terms hardly ever vary. Fifty percent of the fee is paid up front. From that point, it's binding on both parties, and reneging is out of the question. If the assassin fails to deliver, the word will travel and he will never find employment again. Worse, he may himself be hunted down by the defrauded party. Conversely, if the contractor defaults on the balance of the fee, he in turn becomes a legitimate target for the assassin who, for the sake of his reputation, cannot forgive the default. For him, retribution is not a matter of ego, it's a commercial imperative.

A contract to kill might therefore be considered the perfect covenant. A win-win scenario.

Except, that is, for the victim.

———

THE WARBLE OF my cell phone dragged me from my afternoon doze. Initially disorientated, I rolled from my side onto my back and forced my eyes open. It was a bleary world out there. I blinked once or twice to clear my vision. The balloon of confusion popped and the walls of the hotel room swam into focus. I reached for the trilling, annoying, indispensable piece of plastic on the night table. Who said cell phones were smart? Not smart enough to leave me in peace.

UNKNOWN CALLER the green screen announced. I swiped the response icon.

"Yes?" I snapped, letting my irritation hang out.

"Townsend, *c'est bien vous?*" my unknown caller—male, French— queried. He was using my current alias, so it could only be one of two people. In any case, I recognized the Parisian accent of my paymaster.

I confirmed it was *bien moi.*

"Bonhomme here," he said.

Bonhomme translates as Goodman in English. Was it his real name? I guessed not. Same as mine wasn't Townsend. In the world where I did business, pseudonyms were the rule.

"You received the transfer?" he asked. His voice had an edge to it. I wondered why.

"Yes." The second stage instalment of two hundred thousand American dollars, minus a precise two thousand two hundred of extortionate bank charges, had shown up in my Swiss account this very morning. "Have you got the arrival time yet?"

"That is my reason for calling. They will land at München at eighteen-fifty. From there it is about an hour by car."

The fog of sleep was rudely dispersed. I sat up and swung my legs off the edge of the bed.

"Whoa there, just a minute. What do you mean, *they?*"

"The woman will be with him." No wonder he was edgy. The woman wasn't part of the program.

"Look, Bonhomme," I said, a growl creeping into my voice. "She's not supposed to be here until the day after tomorrow. If she's around tomorrow night, it will totally fuck up the job."

A short silence, then, "Do not worry. She is expendable."

"Expendable! That's big of you. You mean you expect me to take her out, too?"

"If she's there, you'll have no choice."

He was wrong there. I could pull out, citing breach of contract. It was tempting. I didn't kill women—period. For now though, self-interest ruled, and it suited me to play along.

"The price just went up," I told him.

"Don't try to blackmail me, Townsend. You'll be sorry if you do."

"And don't try to get two jobs done for the price of one," I countered. I gave him a couple of beats to think about it. "Another hundred thousand or it's off."

To my surprise he didn't go volcanic, he just sighed.

"But it will not reach your account until tomorrow."

The connection was cut, leaving me glowering at my reflection in the cell phone's screen. The additional hundred grand was a *malus* not a bonus. I didn't need the money, and I especially didn't need more blood on my conscience.

Fuming, I flopped back on my pillow. The job had just been transformed from straightforward low-risk, to complicated and tricky, with my neck on the chopping block if it went awry. Human collateral damage was anathema, professional and personal. Killing an innocent party transgressed a private code; that the party in this instance was female just added to the anguish. Too late now to make new arrangements. The venue—their secret love nest—was custom built for my purpose, and none of the alternatives came even close. Whatever heart-searching was involved, I was not about to compromise the outcome.

Another negative factor was the identity of the woman. The hit's mistress was the free-ranging wife of a prominent German politician and business mogul. This mean that she, through the husband, could bring influence to bear. The ability to get things done, such as mobilizing the police, organizing road blocks, before I could cross the border back into Switzerland.

Aside from the nuisance element of potentially leaving a witness to my crime, only the escape route was causing me the odd twinge of concern: a narrow, twisting track without a single exit—a good three minutes' driving and nowhere to hide. Meeting an oncoming vehicle would mean pulling over, backing up, and God knows what else. Plenty of opportunity for the other driver to make a mental note of my car and my license plate and wonder what the hell I was doing on a road that led only to one place. The risk of such an encounter was slight, but I'd lived to a ripe thirty-eight and a few months by keeping such risks to a minimum.

By now I was thoroughly awake if not refreshed. I slid off the bed. Outside it was grey, damp and dismal; November in Bavaria. It didn't make poetry. It didn't chime with sunshine and trees in blossom and a glass of wine on the terrace. Beneath saturnine skies, mist hung motionless in cobwebs, with incessant rain varying only in its intensity. It hadn't let up since I set foot in Oberpframmern, on the outskirts of München, two days ago.

From the window of my functional, plastic-veneered hotel cubicle, I looked out over the Höhenkirchenwald, a roller-coaster landscape coated with black conifers, broken here and by a farm. On the other side of the rolling hills, this time tomorrow give or take an hour, I would enter the house where the hit would be staying, and place two, maybe three, bullets where they would do lethal harm. As far as the guy was concerned, no qualms on my part, and no regrets. As for the woman, I had serious doubts that I was ruthless enough to do the deed.

The complication of the woman apart, I was fairly chilled about the job. It was just another contract, latest in a decade of contracts. Just another hit.

Simple, yes?

Actually, as it turned out, simple, no.

———

ON THE OBSERVATION deck of the Olympiaturm, I met up with Wolfgang. From that eyrie in the sky, five hundred feet up, you can see clear across to the Bavarian Alps, their peaks white under the dipping sun. In the opposite direction, looking straight down, is a bomber pilot's view of the BMW plant, dominated by a twenty-story cloverleaf building.

Despite the distant sunshine, it was wet and windy at the top of the tower, and consequently pretty much deserted. That suited me. The business I was there to transact was not for the eyes and ears of the general public.

Wolfgang was ill-at-ease, unusual for him. We shook hands routinely. His clasp was sweaty.

"*Grüss Gott*, Herr Black." God greets, statutory Bavarian hello.

To him I was Black, not Townsend. Sometimes even I got confused over my real identity.

"Good to see you again, Wolfgang," I said in English, not wishing to confuse him with my German, which was derived mostly from Hollywood-produced war movies.

He bobbed his head like a nervous hen. He was of diminutive build with thick black hair. Very un-master race. His coat was exquisitely tailored, with an expanse of astrakhan collar.

"Got the merchandise?" I asked.

"*Ja*...er, yes, but there was a little difficulty."

His little difficulties seldom caused a blip of my graph of worries. The price would be adjusted to compensate, and we would all live happily ever after.

Even so. "How little is little?"

"How...? Ah, I understand. It is the firearm. The short barrel was not available. I have only the long barrel model for you."

His failure to supply the merchandise as ordered was only a minor irritant. Still, it wouldn't hurt my reputation as a hard case to let him think I was seriously put out. While he sweated, I rested my arms on the parapet and gazed out over the Munich rooftops. Apart from the twin domed towers of the Frauenkirche and a scattering of lesser spires, it was not inspiring. Too many blocks and cubes deformed the skyline. The rain didn't improve it, either.

I decided he had sweated enough. "Did you know the Colt Python is the most numerous handgun in the world?"

As an arms expert, he would be more familiar with that statistic than I. His bobbing head confirmed it. "Not only that," I went on, my tone casual, "but the four-inch barrel is the most popular size. And you, a professional dealer, are telling me you couldn't obtain this particular gun in two weeks?"

"It is not my fault." He gave an audible gulp as he said it. "A shipment from Algeria...it was by the police inter...inter..."

"Intercepted?"

"*Ja, richtig*. If you can wait until next week..." The suggestion tapered off. The little turd knew I couldn't wait until next week.

"Well now, Wolfgang," I said, grinning disarmingly to put him at ease and dry the sweat on his brow. "If that's the way it's got to be I can live with it. Just don't let it happen again. All right?"

If my plans jelled as expected, I wouldn't need his services again, but he wasn't to know that.

"*Jawohl.*" He managed not to click his heels. "You must understand, Mr. Black, here in Germany is very difficult for the arms business now. Many new laws from Brussels, many new controls. Many immigrants coming, so much more crimes. It makes everything for all of us difficult."

He was breaking my heart. I considered offering him a handkerchief.

"Prices increase every day," he threw in as a makeweight.

The punch line was coming up.

"You know how much I must for this one charge?" he went on, softening the impact by making it a question.

"No," I said, my grin sardonic now. "Just how much must you for this one charge?"

He leaned toward me, his manner conspiratorial. "Two thousand three hundred euros."

I whistled. It was expensive all right. In the States you can buy it over the counter for less than fifteen hundred US.

"Wolfgang, inflation in Germany was only two percent last year. Now here you are, trying to stick me with a price hike of fifty."

"Inflation, hah!" He dismissed the retail price indicator with a flicking of his pianist's fingers. "This has nothing to do with inflation. It is the importers. I tell you, the police have put a big squeeze on illegal guns. The importers are scared, so a bigger profit they expect." His nervousness seemed to have evaporated. Maybe I was letting him off too lightly. I decided to give the screw of my displeasure a couple of turns. I crowded him back against the parapet. From here, the outlook was straight down the sheer concrete side of the tower.

"Listen to me, my good *wurst*-eating friend," I said, still pitching it mild. "When I order a gun from you, I expect to get what I ordered, at the *agreed* price. I don't expect to have to pay extra for five centimeters of gunmetal I didn't ask for and don't need."

"*Versteht.*" His head jiggled as if it were no longer attached to his spinal cord. "I have done my best." He breathed schnapps fumes over me.

An elderly couple meandered past, sliding apprehensive glances in our direction. The man wore a Tyrolean feathered hat, and she was in blue mink with a matching rinse. Their presence bought Wolfgang a reprieve.

I stepped away from him, patted his cheek.

"The merchandise," I said, snapping my fingers.

"*Ja.*" His face was the color of putty and shiny with sweat. From inside his coat he withdrew a rectangular package measuring about ten inches by six, wrapped in multi-hued gift paper; standard trade camouflage. It fitted the pocket of my quilted waterproof jacket, projecting five centimeters over the top: the unwanted length of barrel so thoughtfully supplied by Wolfgang. From the technical aspect, the extra length mattered hardly at all. The increased range and accuracy that went with a longer barrel were not attributes I could capitalize on, since this particular contract called for point blank delivery.

What really riled me about the substitution were the principle and its portents. I depended on Wolfgang and others of his ilk for the tools of my trade; not only firearms, but also false papers, transport, and inside information. The underworld bush telegraph travels fast. Let just one of the clan shortchange you, the rest would conclude you were becoming a soft touch. It was lucky for Wolfgang that this was to be my last hit.

"So, how much do I owe you altogether, Wolfgang?"

As usual, he put on a deprecating air, as if the subject of money were distasteful to him. Like honey is distasteful to a bee.

"Already, you have one thousand euros paid. Normally, I would only ask for five hundred more, but as I explained, it is two thousand three hundred for the gun, plus the ammunition and my services, as I explained..."

"You'll explain yourself into an early grave one of these days."

That was altogether too subtle for him.

"The balance you must pay..." He pretended to do a complicated mental calculation. It was all show. He would know the total to the exact cent. Rounded up, of course. "You must pay one thousand three hundred and twenty-two euros." He swallowed hard.

"So you expect me to finance your expensive tastes?" I rubbed the astrakhan collar between finger and thumb. "Your fancy outfits and your new Maybach. Oh, yes, I saw you trying to park it out of sight."

"Mr. Black!" He drew himself up. Since there wasn't much of him to draw up, he still had to bend his neck to look me in the eye. "I have always been correct with you. My profit on this job is very small."

"And your bullshit is very large." I reached into my inside pocket, drew out an envelope, handed it to him. "There's another eight hundred. That's all you get, Wolfgang, and this..." I glanced around to make sure we were alone.

He had been peering inside the envelope; now he looked up. "*Ja?*"

Most of my strength went into the punch. It connected just below the belt. For him, doll-sized but flabby, one punch was more than enough. He jackknifed at the waist and his legs buckled. Down he went on his knees, coughing and dry retching over my shoes.

I crouched beside him, my mouth to his ear.

He was still clutching the envelope, money-grubbing instincts unimpaired.

"Don't ever try to screw me again, Wolfgang, because it just makes me mad."

I left him on his knees, head bowed, gurgling and gasping, and rode the free falling elevator to earth, with the attendant and the blue rinse couple for company.

———

THE LIGHT WAS FADING when I pulled the VW Golf—that most ubiquitous and therefore most anonymous set of wheels—off the *Bundestrasse* into the secondary road that snaked down into the village of Guntering. The rain had eased off in favor of a fine drizzle. Through it, I glimpsed ragged clouds clinging to the hillsides like grey cotton candy. A Porsche swished past, flinging arcs of spray from its wide wheels. I held piously to my fifty kph. Confrontation with the police, notorious in Germany for enforcement of urban speed limits with instant fines, was to be avoided. For today, I was a model motorist.

The radio was on. A female singer was belting out a rendering of the old Dietrich number, 'Falling in Love Again'. In German, naturally. I chanted along with her. In English, naturally. Happy-go-lucky as any commuter on his way home. Happier, even. No rush hour traffic to stress me out.

I was through Guntering, the houses and other buildings just houses and buildings. The next hamlet, Wasach, more of the same. From there it was open road, a grade above dirt track. No other vehicles sharing it in either direction.

The turnoff was a couple of kilometers beyond Wasach, announced by a shiny metal signpost: Schloss Thomashoff—Thomashoff Castle—3km. The pretentiousness of it had amused me yesterday, seeing it for the first time. Admittedly, the place occupied an elevated site with views over the Ammersee, a large lake shaped like a prawn. Admittedly, too, it was made of stone: a grey, granite-like stone, but the resemblance to a castle went no further. It was a single-story building, with a dormer window in the steep roof, a portico entrance, and a cupola at one corner. Nothing to inspire awe.

Rain had made the dirt surface of the track treacherous. It forced me to go easy on the gas pedal. Among the trees, the light was poor, and I flicked the headlights to full beam, sending white shafts to investigate the gloom. A pair of yellow eyes sparkled—fox or badger. Then they were gone, and I was slithering onward, holding the car in third, the trees seeming to press in on me, looming in the headlights then whipping past.

The road was climbing now, a succession of increasingly acute bends. Raindrops dripped from overhanging branches, making little explosions on the windshield. I slowed and dropped down into second gear. An accident on this no-exit road would be as disastrous as a brush with the law.

The dashboard clock showed 15:26. Night was already draping its shroud across Bavaria. Darkness was always welcome—the best natural protection going. Nosy neighbors and inconvenient passersby posed less of a threat after nightfall. I had other codes of conduct, other axioms, whose observance had helped me stay in business. Enabling me to cross borders anywhere in the world without let or hindrance, like it says on my red British passport and my navy-blue Canadian one. Not so much as an unpaid parking fine besmirched my real name.

Lake Ammersee came into sight on my right, a glossy gunmetal glint below the cliffs. No wind, eddies, or currents ruffled its glossy surface. The car skated on a patch of mud and the front end slewed toward the shoulder, only spitting distance from a sheer hundred-foot drop. My grip on the wheel tightened as I lifted my foot off the gas pedal, slowing to a walking pace. At this point, I dispensed with the headlights.

A hundred meters or so farther on, a rectangle of light glimmered between the trees at ground-floor level. Above it, a smaller rectangle represented the bedroom. Lamps mounted on the gateway pillars and along the short driveway diffused yellow pools over a graveled surface. An expensive-looking hunk of Milan-built iron squatted in front of the entrance.

I rolled to a standstill short of the gateway, reversing into a space between the trees, and killed the parking lights. It was a spot I had pre-selected for this purpose. The dark green paintwork of the Golf would be virtually invisible from the track. As an extra precaution, I draped an olive green groundsheet over the windshield, the hood, and the indiscreet, reflective license plate, weighting it with two dead branches. The car now became part of its surroundings.

It was a few minutes to four. Under the trees, it was dark as midnight. The sheen of the Ammersee was visible through the pencil-straight trunks. No moon to reflect, only charcoal-grey clouds, their bellies bulging with more unshed rain.

I zipped my waterproof jacket up to my chin and pulled the hood over my head, listening to the intermittent tap of raindrops on the car and foliage. It was the only sound in that cathedral stillness, except music from the house. So faint I couldn't identify the tune. I was still straining my ears when the dormer light was extinguished and the darkness became darker.

For a while I stood there, the dampness climbing my legs and permeating my body. I stomped my feet, but the bed of pine needles offered no resistance; it was like stomping on Jell-O. The minutes crawled by. Waiting was the worst part of a contract kill. But wait I must. My arrival had been timed to ensure I was off the road during the evening rush, when the country dwellers streamed out of Munich to their neat, synthetic, dormitory towns. The getaway was subject to similar criteria. By then, the job behind me, all but the tail-end workaholics would be settled in front of their TV sets. Every motorist had to be considered a potential witness. It takes more than just a killer instinct to make a successful assassin. Blending in with the law-abiding majority is just as crucial.

The drizzle was petering out. I strolled across the track to stand on the bare cliff top and gaze out over the Ammersee. The far shore was black and shapeless, only relieved by a constellation of lights round the towns of Diessen and another, smaller, community. In the daytime it was a million-euro panorama, and explained why Thomashoff had built his self-styled castle here.

In deadly boredom I whiled away the next two hours. My sauntering about left plenty of footprints to excite the police forensic team. I had bought my shoes from a market trader in Dar es Salaam, where I was hunting down a Portuguese drug trafficker. Along with the waterproof jacket and gun, they would be disposed of when I left. Just as I had already discarded the brown hairpiece, the matching stick-on moustache, and the brown contact lenses. I had no more need to hide my yellow-blond hair and my—some say piercing—blue eyes. In the Master Plan (revised), the hit and his mistress didn't survive to assist the police making up photo-fit pictures after the event. From here on, Roger Townsend ceased to exist; just one of many dead-end false identities. I would leave Germany under my real name of André Warner, Anglo-Québecois, respectable citizen and businessman.

At half-past six I got ready to move. I pulled on a pair of surgical gloves and loaded six .357 magnum rounds into the Colt Python, stowing the gun in my coat's side pocket. The extra two unwanted inches of barrel made it too long for the pocket, but I had cut a hole in the lining to accommodate them, binding insulating tape round the shallow triangular sight to smooth the profile and stop it snagging on the material. A small detail, but no less significant than all the other details.

Here at Schloss Thomashoff, it would be no use my going up to the front door and thumbing the bell push. The hefty door restraint was bolt-cutter proof, and I expected it to be in place. I would therefore enter via the back door, the same as yesterday when I broke in to carry out my final reconnaissance of the empty building. The lock was of the deadbolt type, and I had a skeleton key that fit. The only complication had been the surface-mounted bolt, thick as a man's finger, at the top of the door. I had neutralized it by sawing most of the way through it, masking the cut with dirt, and clearing up the few metal filings. Now, all it would take to snap it was a nudge against the door.

Silent as a drifting snowflake, I crossed the open ground between the wood and the knee-high hedge that bordered the yard, past the cupola. The drapes of the lighted rectangular window of the living room were open, necessitating a wide detour. The TV set, a Bang & Olufson in a rosewood cabinet, flickered in a corner of the room. A dark head was visible over the back of an armchair. It could only be him; *she* was a blonde. No sign of her though. The dormer window above was lit up again, meaning she was back in her natural environment—the bedroom. Suiting up for more erotic games, I bet. The stuff I'd come across up there told its own tale: leather corsets, thigh boots with twelve-centimeter heels, dildoes of many shapes and sizes—you get the picture. Maybe they performed for the Net.

The kitchen was in darkness. The door was locked as expected and the key had been left in the lock on the inside. Keys left in locks were a commonplace, and I had the means to deal with them. With the aid of my pencil flashlight and some long-nosed pliers of a pattern not found in any tool store, that obstacle was soon removed. The key made no sound when it hit the doormat.

I was putting the flashlight and pliers away when the kitchen light came on.

The vast window, with its outlook over the lake, was fitted with Venetian blinds. They were lowered, but the slats were open. The

light bathed the lush lawn in white stripes, picking out drops of moisture on the grass. Pressed flat against the wall and in shadow, I would
be invisible from inside. The only small worry was the key lying on the
doormat. If spotted, it might arouse suspicion. Then again, it might be
assumed it had fallen out of the lock. Then again...

The person in the kitchen was whistling out of tune. Cabinet
doors were slammed and an object fell with a metallic clatter, followed
by a muttered *"Merde!"*—it was the Frenchman, Fabrice Tillou
himself. More doors banged, then a triumphant, "Ah...*vous voila.*"
Seconds later, the pop of a cork. Footsteps approached the door.

I flattened myself against the wall, the elongated Colt Python at
the ready. Kill him now, or five minutes from now, it was all the same
to me.

A clatter of metal to metal. The footsteps receded and the light
went out.

My breathing resumed. It was raining again with renewed vigor. I
glowered at the heavens to no effect. I gave the Frenchman a minute or
so to settle down with his bottle of plonk, then leaned my shoulder
against the door while depressing the handle slowly. It opened
without effort on my part, meaning it wasn't bolted, and my sabotage
had been unnecessary. I stepped inside the palatial kitchen, all black
tiles and stainless steel, with mechanical aids in abundance. A mutter
of male voices filtered through the open door between the kitchen and
the inner hall. Did they have company? I remained motionless, my
head cocked toward the doorway. A police siren sounded, overlaid by
a yelp of brakes and a ripple of gunfire. I remembered the flickering
TV screen and grinned at nothing in my relief.

The Python was in my hand now, hammer cocked, ready to
deliver its lethal load. I crossed the kitchen, detouring round an island
counter, and wedged myself into the corner behind the door. A spoor
of wet footprints gave away my presence. No matter. Nobody would
see them until it was too late.

"Liebling?" the Frenchman called in his accented German. He
was in the hall, just a few feet away. Then, again in German, a question. He sounded impatient.

The answer was inaudible; I guessed she was still upstairs. The
verbal exchange ended and the yammer of the TV took over again.

Water dripped from my hair, coursing down my face in rivulets.

Presently, I took a cautious peep around the edge of the door. All was clear. I emerged from the kitchen into the carpeted hall. The carpet pile was thick, and I battled through it soundlessly, the TV noise removing any need for caution. The living room door stood ajar. I widened the gap with my toe and went in.

The room was as plush as money could make it: a cornfield-deep cream carpet, the furniture all in rosewood to match the TV, the walls paneled in contrasting pale pine. Not forgetting the hi-fi with its library of CDs I could have played nonstop for a month without hearing the same one twice. A rack of vinyl LPs suggested Thomashoff was a serious collector. Shelves behind the mini-bar sagged under a profusion of designer label booze.

The drapes, tasteful brown velvet, were now drawn; one less precaution for me to take.

Tillou was back in his armchair, which was positioned sideways to the doorway. He didn't notice me at once.

Raising my voice above the grating cops-and-robbers dialogue, I announced myself. "*Bonsoir*, Monsieur Tillou."

His self-control was impressive. The glass of white wine that was halfway to his mouth slowed only momentarily before resuming its journey. He drank in generous gulps that I could see travelling down his throat, and then his head slowly swung toward me.

He was just past his thirtieth birthday, according to the dossier provided by Bonhomme. Pretty boy looks, with dark hair, not too long, dark hooded eyes, and full lips that a lipstick advertiser could have put to good use. Well groomed, dark blue pants and vest, shirt whiter than white. I knew him to be tall, an inch over six feet, about my own height. He was married, no children.

"*Qui êtes vous?*" he asked finally, reverting to his native tongue. He was still composed, disdainful even.

It's funny how they always want to know who I am. As if it made any difference to the outcome.

"A messenger," I said. Thanks to my Québecoise mother, my French was fluent, and I proceeded to tell him, as instructed, who had sent me.

His control slipped, face darkening, lips contorting. "So, he finally declares himself," he snarled. "And you? You are English? American?"

"Neither, if it matters."

He continued to smile, still more angry than afraid. "Have you come to kill me?"

I answered with a nod.

"How much is he paying you?"

I waved the question away as an irrelevancy. In this business, you don't negotiate with your victims.

"He just asked me to wish you a pleasant stay in Hell."

His jaw tightened and his eyes flashed. For sure, he wouldn't just sit there and let me finish him off. He knew he was confronting his quietus, so he had nothing to lose by trying to save himself.

For me, the squeezing of the trigger, had always been a psychological fence, a hurdle to be cleared before the irrevocable ending of a life. I was bracing myself for the leap when I heard the tattoo of high heels on wooden stairs.

Still cool, still in control, I sidestepped to get clear of the doorway and was backed against the wall by the time she came in, a whirling flurry of pale flesh and black accessories. The sight startled me into jaw-dropping inertia.

Tillou wasn't slow to exploit my divided attentions. The gun he whipped from inside his vest was a slim automatic—its slimness explaining why I hadn't spotted it—and his actions were fast and fluid.

Not quite fast and fluid enough to save him. My three slugs, squeezed off as fast as I could work my trigger finger, punched holes in his chest and knocked him clean out of the chair before he could flip the safety.

"*Was machen Sie!*" the woman screamed, and that was when I noticed another accessory she was sporting—a tiny, shiny revolver, now pointing at me, her hand trembling so much that her first and only shot went right by me. Survival instinct kicked in, and I fired just once without aiming. The bullet entered and left her throat, travelling on through the doorway to be stopped by woodwork, with a noise like a hammer striking a nail. Her gaze was on me as she collapsed without a whimper to spread-eagle on the carpet, face up, the baby pistol jolted from her hand. Blood bubbled around the bullet hole. I had encountered enough gunshot wounds to diagnose the outcome of this one: without immediate treatment she was going to bleed her life into the pile. Exsang-something was the medical term for it.

I flicked her gun out of reach with my toe. I felt bad about shooting her, even though, technically, it was self-defense. If only she had turned up the following day, as expected...

As for the Frenchman, he was already a goner and then some. Perfectionist that I was, I checked him out just the same. He had come to rest sprawled sideways over the chair arm, eyes still open, mouth agape. No longer such a suave and handsome fellow, just another corpse; just another dead lowlife, and a particularly low lowlife at that.

The job was done, contract executed. Half a million dollars' worth of death supplied according to my client's small print. No evidence to implicate him—he was many hundreds of kilometers away and would have solid witnesses to testify to it—and no evidence to implicate me. My tracks would be covered as cleanly as the incoming surf wipes footprints from a beach.

Tillou's gun was still attached to his limp hand. I prized it free and inspected it. A Walther PPQ-SC, the truncated version of the PPQ, designed for concealment. The grip plates had been modified to slim it down to two centimeters across. I stuck it in my spare pocket. Unlike dead men, guns have a habit of telling tales. Let the police scratch their heads over the different calibers of cartridge they would dig out of the corpse and wall. Let them try and figure out who killed whom and with what. It would all add to the confusion.

To leave the room, I had to step over the woman. I frowned down at her. Even dead, she could still foul up the operation. Her name was Ingeborg Thomashoff, wife of Erich Thomashoff, a chemicals magnate and junior minister in the Christian Democrat Government. She was thirty-four, crowned with fluffy blonde hair, her features blurred under a whore's make-up. A pole-dancer figure, her breasts incorporated the best that plastic surgery could sculpt. Her skin was pale, almost white, which made for a dramatic contrast with the black thigh-length boots and black garter belt.

I bent over her. Her eyes were shut tight, her breathing rapid and shallow. The purple-fringed hole in her throat still dribbled blood; a scarlet rivulet meandered down toward her armpit, like a thin shoulder strap. I suppressed an impulse to reach down and touch her, to caress that soft white body.

Shooting her hadn't been a pre-meditated act after all, and I was thankful for that. Thankful that my code and my conscience, feeble though it was, could rest easy. If merely planning to kill her had caused me such heartache, how could I ever have gone ahead and killed her in cold blood, dressed as she was? In the event, I'd been spared that moment of truth and self-discovery.

Without notice, a wave of nausea hit me, siphoning off my strength, sending me to reel against the wall for support. My breath came in gasps as I fought the revulsion that was wringing my guts.

Minutes passed. I gradually won the battle to keep the contents of my stomach off the carpet. The spasm slowly loosened its grip, leaving me clammy and cold. When at last I felt capable of moving, I went at a shuffle, bent like a fishing rod with a fat pike on the hook. It was a reaction without precedent. I had never been squeamish. Blood and bodies were routine, just part of my trade, the same as a butcher's—until this moment.

Switching off all the lights, I left the way I came, bent and hugging my rebellious guts with one arm. I locked the door and tossed the key into the bushes. Before my handiwork was discovered, I would be long gone, back home in Geneva, the evening's events no more than a memory among many others. Soon to fade.

The rain was still doing its thing, descending in vertical stripes from a matt black sky. Recovering fast now, I returned to the car. There I changed my shoes, put the discarded pair, the waterproof jacket, the Python, the Walther, and the ladies pistol—all wiped clean of prints—into a tough polythene bag that already contained several lumps of rock. The bag was destined for the muddy bottom of the Starnbergersee, the Ammersee's neighboring lake.

I tore the identification pages from Roger Townsend's impeccably-forged American passport, later to be flushed down the lavatory at Munich airport. The rest of the passport joined the stuff in the bag. Of the items to be junked, that left only the surgical gloves. I was still wearing them but would dispose of them in a public trash bin, far from here.

I ran a comb through my dripping hair, stripped the groundsheet from the car, and drove out of the forest and back down the slippery track without meeting a soul.

Three hours or so later, I was sipping champagne and exercising my charm on a suntanned stewardess on a Lufthansa Airbus bound for Paris.

And retirement.

CHAPTER TWO

THE EVENING after returning to Geneva, my home of the past seven years, I dined at Le Bateau, a floating restaurant moored on the banks of the lake. Alone, alas. My choice of fare was *filets de perche meunière*, with a demi of Carabiniers Lunar 2017 to swill it down. The cuisine in Francophone Geneva is very French.

Being mid-week, other diners were thin on the ground. No lonely females on the lookout for lonely males, worse luck. For want of distractions, as I chewed and drank and viewed the boat traffic passing under the Pont du Mont-Blanc, my thoughts meandered of their own volition down corridors of the past, back to my Secret Service era.

It needs to be stated that the license to kill is a myth. In the British Secret Intelligence Service, no operative is sanctioned to pull the trigger on another human being. A very select few officers get to carry a handgun and *de facto* are authorized to use it. That's it. I was one of them. The rules allowed me to shoot in defense of self and a third party, but even then, not deliberately to kill. To deter, to wound, to disable, those were the options.

The year I quit, I fired my Walther P99 automatic for the third and last time. It led to my dismissal and almost my incarceration. It was the day after Easter Monday. Tony Dimeloe and I arrived at Gatwick airport, having travelled by an RAF Hercules from

Afghanistan. Tony was a case officer like me, but a few years older and, by longevity of service, my nominal superior. We shared a taxi. My home was an apartment in Egham, a half-hour drive from the airport.

When we pulled up outside the apartment house in Lynwood Avenue, overlooking the Royal Holloway campus, it was 9:05PM by the taxi's digital clock.

Tony and I shook hands.

"See you Thursday?" I said.

"Expect so. Say hello to Marion."

"Right. You say hello to Spooky."

Marion was my wife; Spooky was Tony's Siamese cat. No wife awaited him at home, not since his divorce the previous year. I gave him a parting high five, and backed out of the taxi onto the sidewalk. I stood there, watching the taxi's taillights dwindle, savoring the good old English drizzle. It felt clean on my face, scouring the dust and battle smoke of Afghanistan from my pores. Then, bag over shoulder, valise in hand, I turned to walk up the path. The building was four stories high. Marion and I lived on the top floor. No lights showed, which wasn't unusual, because the living room and kitchen were at the side of the building, out of sight from the street.

In the lobby, everything looked normal. The elevator door stood open, like an invitation, which I accepted. Using the stairs would have been twice as quick, but I was too travel-worn. Just standing was a strain.

The corridor from the elevator to my front door was short and carpeted in green. My door was green, too. Not our choice. Our landlord—the Government—had chosen the decor in all the building's communal areas.

Normality ended at the entrance to my apartment. The door was open. Only a tiny fraction, meaning that I didn't notice until I poked at the lock with my key. When it swung inwards under the light pressure, my first reaction was puzzlement. Then the training manual took over. I backed away, creating space to maneuver. Being the wife of a government agent, security consciousness was second nature to Marion. All spouses of operatives were considered potential targets. It wouldn't have been cost effective to provide individual protection, so they were schooled in how to look after themselves and turn their homes into mini-fortresses. Leaving the door open would count as an eighth deadly sin.

My Walther was in my overnight bag. As I crouched, putting my ear to a two-inch gap between door and jamb, I noiselessly unzipped the bag and drew the automatic from the internal pocket. Cocking it would have made a recognizable noise, so I left it uncocked. If an intruder was lurking inside, it might make the difference between winning and losing a shootout, but the risk of alerting him—or her— was greater.

The Service procedure for entering potentially hostile premises is to stand to the hinged side of the doorway and push the door slowly inwards with an extended arm, until it's at right angles to the doorway. An armed intruder has no visible target at which to shoot. His next move is either to shoot anyway as a deterrent, or retreat farther inside. Either option gives away his presence.

No gunfire, no commotion.

If anyone was in the entrance hall, he was lying doggo.

Now to test his firepower, if any. The SIS training manual requires one to crouch and spring—literally—across the doorway to the other side, like a frog. The object of this procedure is to encourage the hostile party to fire. By diving from a crouch, you're below the normal level of a pointing gun. Even if the assailant can react fast enough, the bullet will pass over you. On the other hand, if he doesn't fire, odds are he isn't armed. The theory was tried and tested, and probably reliable. You're offering yourself as a sacrificial lamb. No choice, anyhow. So I didn't think about it, I just sprang.

Still no bullets flew. A door at the far end of the communal corridor opened as I was straightening up. Mrs. Ogilvy, the elderly widow who lived there, came out, umbrella in hand. She stopped dead, stared at me, then at the gun.

"Mr. *Warner!*" she exclaimed. Fortunately, she had a rather hoarse, low-pitched voice, only an octave above a whisper.

I placed my forefinger crosswise over my lips, then waggled my hand to indicate that all was not well in my apartment. Finally, I pantomimed that she should call the police. She may have been ancient, but she was very lucid. Also, her deceased husband had been a brigadier with the Royal Tank Corps. Army wives understood things like emergencies. She nodded and scuttled back into her apartment.

Whether speed was of the essence or not, I had no means of telling. Now that my path was clear, I intended to move fast. I was in my hallway and up against the living room door in seconds, my left hand curved over the Walther's slide, ready to pump a round into the chamber. My next move would ordinarily have been to repeat the earlier procedure with the door, but at that point, I lost the initiative. The living room door opened and a flashlight beam hit me in the face.

Hard to say who was more surprised. Him probably, as I was expecting an interloper, whereas he probably figured he had the place to himself.

By pure reflex, I operated the slide and fired at a point just above the flashlight. The dark shape gave a grunt of pain. The flashlight spun away and he crashed to the floor. No answering fire. If he was carrying a gun, it must have been in a holster or pocket. Careless of him. But then he'd assumed he only had Marion to worry about.

I reached out and switched on the light. He was starfished on his back, on the Afghan rug that was a souvenir of an earlier tour of duty there. His eyes stared into mine, unblinking. Blood was spreading from underneath him. His heart had pumped its last.

Not that I cared about any of it. All I cared about was Marion.

"Marion!" I yelled. Perhaps she was hiding in another room. "Marion, it's André. It's safe, you can come out."

Only then, belatedly, did I consider that the intruder might not be working solo, that Marion might have a gun at her head, or was perhaps bound and gagged.

I crossed to the kitchen, which was open to the living room, in case she was behind the counter. And she was. Curly blonde locks splayed out on the tiles, her blue eyes wide, just like the dead guy, though hers were wide with terror. A kitchen carving knife lay nearby, tipped with blood.

Not bound, not gagged. Just dead.

———

MARION'S FUNERAL was delayed by an inquest into her death and that of her murderer. He was of Middle Eastern origin and carried no identifying documents. This much I learned at the tribunal held a week after the event.

In the so-called Interview Room at the Vauxhall Cross headquarters of the SIS, I faced a panel of three men, jocularly known as the hanging judges: Colonel Sewell, Middle East Controller; Lt. Colonel de l'Isle, MC, Deputy Controller; and Julian Vansittart, Permanent Secretary from the Ministry of Defense. This triumvirate was ranged behind a long table. At their backs, three tall windows overlooked the Thames and the Vauxhall Bridge. The space between two of the windows was occupied by a NO SMOKING sign. Slanting shafts of afternoon sunlight glinted on Sewell's and Vansittart's bald craniums. Those same shafts also put me in the spotlight.

The police had ascertained that the intruder gained entry by picking the lock, and that Marion attacked him with a knife, inflicting a shallow wound to his midriff, and that he shot her twice using a silenced automatic. The purpose of the break-in was unclear. His clothes yielded no clues, only a scrap of paper with a rudimentary sketch of the layout of my apartment. An assassination attempt on me seemed the likeliest intention. I hadn't realized I was so important, though I had without question made enemies in the Middle East.

After a succinct résumé of the incident, Sewell moved into the realm of speculation by stating, "With no identity and nothing even to prove his nationality, the unofficial conclusion is that your activities in Iraq over the past two years have made you a target."

"I'm the target, but my wife gets killed," I said bitterly.

Vansittart, the MoD man, cleared his throat self-consciously. As a civilian, he might be expected to show some compassion. "Most unfortunate."

"You've been with the department, what, four years, Warner?" Sewell said, his glaring eyes set in a perfect pink sphere from which his ears protruded unevenly. "Collateral damage is a fact of life."

"Collateral *damage*?" I echoed, quashing a powerful urge to punch him on the snout. "My wife's not a bloody commodity...sir."

"Just so. But we'll have to leave the mourning to you, Captain. Other issues must be addressed. You shot and killed this man, which means we can't interrogate him. According to your record..." He flipped through a few pages in a folder. "You've previously been in two shooting incidents. The first of these two years ago, resulted in the death of an Iraqi police officer—"

"A *bent* Iraqi police officer," I interrupted.

"The second incident..." more shuffling of papers, "...in December last year, resulted in serious wounding of an Iraqi civilian."

"Self-defense in both cases, sir," I said, while privately acknowledging that it looked damning on paper. "Kill or be killed. There was a full inquiry both times, and I was vindicated."

"So I see. But let me give you some statistics, Warner. Since the war, the average number of violent deaths attributable to each Secret Service operative throughout their entire careers is zero point six. In other words, one death for every two officers over the entire period of their service. In your case, we have *two* deaths for one officer over four years. Plus one serious wounding."

I said nothing. No use arguing with statistics.

De l'Isle spoke for the first time. "Do you wish to comment, Warner?" Plummy accent, haughty aristocratic features, he was old-school officer class, happily a moribund breed.

"It was kill or be killed, sir. It was dark and I had only a flashlight to aim at." I let my gaze travel across the lugubrious threesome. "I rest my case."

Suddenly, I was sick of it all; sick of them, sick of the Service, sick of being subject to this rule and that regulation. Not only that, Marion's death had left me devastated. They say you don't know what you've gotten till it's gone. That was never truer than the effect of her loss on me.

In my next breath, I quit. Of course, nobody leaves the Secret Service simply by announcing the intent. Protocols and procedures had to be observed. You write a letter of resignation. It's rubber-stamped by the Director of the Service, and counter-rubber stamped by the MoD. It never takes less than a month. Meanwhile, you can still be posted abroad, to a war zone, still put in harm's way.

In the end, I left after four days, having been granted a month's compassionate leave. In a manner of speaking, my wife gave her life for the British Secret Service. They owed me for that.

At twenty-seven years of age, I was now a free man. A civilian. No wife, no home—the apartment went with the job—and no prospects. And there was still the bill for the funeral to pay.

———

IN HER WILL, Marion had stipulated cremation. The deed was done at the crematorium in her hometown of Nailsworth near Bristol. Naturally her parents, Derek and Margaret, attended. So did her younger sister Susan, and a bevy of lesser relatives and friends. On my side, there were my parents, my sister Julia and her fiancé Willie. Tony Dimeloe, friend and one-time mentor, showed up, which surprised and pleased me. The service was short and simple, and the halting eulogy by Susan incredibly moving. Tears pricked my eyes. Fact was, though, by then, I was all cried out.

After the funeral, family and close friends gathered at Derek and Margaret's cottage on the edge of town, where Marion spent her childhood. Up to that point, my future was as uncertain as tomorrow's weather. It was launched on its next phase that first Saturday in May when Tony accosted me in the kitchen, as guests were starting to drift away. He was due to leave for foreign pastures in the small hours of the next day.

"A word of warning, chum, because I know you're pissed off at the Department. Don't ever be tempted to breach Official Secrets, not even by so much as an apostrophe."

The Official Secrets Act, rulebook of the British Government defense and security departments, was held in reverence. It was rumored that the penalty for breaching the vow of silence was a bullet in the back of the head. One disgruntled ex-operative, who had let off steam to the press back in the nineties, was never seen again. 'Went abroad' was the official line at the time. This piece of folklore was now enshrined in the annals of Secret Service history and served as a useful caveat to those with itchy tongues.

An untimely demise held no appeal for me. Marion's death had left me miserable, not suicidal.

"Don't worry, mate." My reassuring backslap jerked his cup-holding hand, and coffee surged over the rim into the saucer. "That warning's already been issued, in copperplate with a brass band accompaniment."

He nodded and, setting down his cup, dipped two fingers inside the breast pocket of his jacket. They emerged pinching a standard-size business card.

"You know my phone number and email address and phone number," he said, setting the card face down among the crumbs on the kitchen counter. My father passed through the kitchen just then, wriggling his eyebrows and nodding to indicate that my presence was required in another part of the house. I affected an air of sufferance, as if Tony had cornered me and I couldn't escape. Dad grinned sympathetically.

Tony was scrawling on the reverse side of the card. "You might care to look up this fellow."

It was gloomy in the kitchen, and I had to tilt the card toward the light to see.

"Karim Mahfouz? *Cairo*, for fuck's sake!" A woman I didn't recognize, standing over the electric kettle, darted a disapproving glance at me. I smiled an apology at her. "It's a long way to go to look somebody up."

"He needs a man," Tony said, inscrutable as a waxwork.

"Needs a man? Are they scarce in Cairo?" I tucked the card in my wallet. "What sort of man?"

Tony tossed back the dregs of his coffee. "A man with a gun."

———

MY MEAL at Le Bateau was inside me, all five courses of it, and I hadn't tasted a morsel. I paid with my AmEx card, left a generous tip for Sergio, the Italian waiter, and went back to the apartment on foot.

Oh, yes, the apartment. On the fifth and top floor of a small, exclusive block on the Route de Frontenex, with a fine panorama of the lake, taking in the Jet d'Eau fountain, nowadays only switched on intermittently. Economy or ecology, I wasn't privy to the reasons.

Nobody was waiting for me when I shut the door on the outside world, only my possessions: several nineteenth-century brass clocks and a handful of antique pieces of sculpture, including a bronze female in chains by Leigh Heppell. Occupying a prized place before the grand *fausse cheminée* was a Bengal tiger skin rug, gaping jaws and all. Politically correct I was not.

A cream carpet and a pale green lounge suite relieved dark woodwork. The walls were much obscured by shelves of books, including some rare first editions. What wall space remained was taken up by paintings. All originals, and every one—apart from a Manet—were bright modern watercolors by little known and usually struggling artists. On the whole, I collected *ars gratia artis*, not reputations.

So much for the living room. The kitchen, where I strove to whip up nourishing meals, creating heaps of detritus in the process, was clean and sparkling, thanks to the dour Swiss widow who kept house for me twice a week to supplement her state pension and relieve her straitened circumstances.

As for the rest of the accommodation, I had two bedrooms: the master with an en-suite washroom, the other for guests, and rarely occupied. A second washroom, a tiny entrance hall just big enough to absorb a coat stand and visitors in single file; and finally the balcony where, on dry summer days, I usually breakfasted.

It was home. And it was about as cozy and cheerful as a cell on Death Row.

———

AT THE INTERNATIONAL news dealer in Place Neuve I bought copies of three leading German newspapers: *Die Welt, Allgemeine Zeitung,* and the Bavarian *Suddeutsche Zeitung.* I stood under the broad awning at the front of the store, out of the rain, whipping through the pages for reports on the Tillou-Thomashoff killings. A flood tide of whey-faced Swiss swirled around me like a sluggish stream around an island.

Nothing in the papers. Eight days gone by, and no mention of a double murder. It was inconceivable that the bodies still lay undiscovered. Apart from the certainty that Thomashoff would have launched inquiries into his wife's whereabouts, a cleaning woman visited the house every Friday, and it was now Monday.

Conclusion: the story was being suppressed, possibly on account of Frau Thomashoff's status as a government minister's wife. The police might even suspect *she* was the target, not Tillou, and the killing politically inspired. So much the better. It would be a handy red herring, tending to divert suspicion away from hired assassins and toward terrorist factions.

A passing trolley car deposited a quantity of dirty rainwater on my feet. I glared after it and set off at a brisk pace for more congenial surroundings.

CHAPTER THREE

AS A RULE, in Geneva, May Day signals the advent of summer. It makes its appearance as an abrupt transition from freezing squalls straight off the Alps, interspersed with snowfalls, to days of warm sunshine, soft breezes, and chestnut trees in blossom. Cafés, *brasseries*, and restaurants free their chairs and tables from storage and arrange them on sidewalks and in the squares and, often as not, it's warm enough to take morning coffee outside.

Not this year. This was the year of the never-ending winter. Less snow had fallen than usual, but the rain more than compensated for the shortfall. What was more, it showed no inclination to change for the better. The sun continued to skulk behind clouds that ranged in hue from battleship grey to indigo. Global warming had somehow bypassed this corner of the globe.

The gloomy weather conformed to my mood. In the near-six months since my retirement I had worked hard at becoming a playboy: frantic parties where animal behavior was not merely tolerated but expected; gambling to the point of recklessness; two weeks' solo vacation in Venice, even damper and more depressing than Geneva; a week in Majorca with a new and, as it turned out, strictly transient girlfriend, still seeking the sun and still failing. My jaunts farther afield—Mauritius, too hot and deadly boring; Tokyo, exhausting for all the wrong reasons, and Cape Town, world-beating scenery but dangerous—gave no fulfilment. Lastly, disillusioned with the exotic, I took a long-deferred trip to the UK to visit my sister Julia. Sickeningly content at thirty-six, with a hardworking successful husband and two quite likeable daughters. There at least, when it rained, I could be philosophical about it.

Otherwise, it was day after day of unceasing monotony and no relief in prospect.

Or so it appeared that mid-May morning, sitting in the wash room with my pants around my ankles, a ceremony during which I usually planned the day ahead. More and more often nowadays, I would rise from my throne with those plans still unmade, the day a yawning void. In short, retirement was not proving to be the panacea I had foreseen, to the extent that I was even beginning to hanker for a return to the hazards and excitement of the hit game. Insanity. That phase of my life was dead and buried. Never to be exhumed. No, I had to find other means of filling the empty hollows.

That was as far as I got in my ponderings that morning. I needed inspiration, and in that area I was bankrupt. Mooching around the apartment was never likely to generate original ideas either, so I sallied forth to search for the answer in the dregs at the bottom of a coffee cup, like a fortuneteller reading tealeaves.

It was only a few minutes' walk to the Comedie, my local *brasserie*, on the Quai Gustave Ador. I stepped out between the automatic sliding doors of my apartment block, umbrella held aloft. Most other pedestrians were similarly armed, the street resembling a forest of bobbing mushrooms. Rain descended in vertical lines, and the cloud base hooded the tops of the taller tower blocks. I walked, or rather splashed my way toward sanctuary.

Thanks to the weather, few tables were taken at the Comedie, and I was able to secure a seat by the window. I sat staring across the wind-swept, rain-swept lake until the *patron* came to serve me.

We shook hands.

"*Comment allez-vous*, Monsieur Warner?" he asked, always formal, despite an acquaintanceship of several years. De Galle was a Parisian, known to Geneva's Anglo-American community as 'Charlie', after his near-namesake, the former President of France.

"*Ca va*," I responded without enthusiasm before ordering a *noisette*, a small coffee with a dab of cream.

Charlie bustled away. The coffee would be served before I could blink twice. Nobody ever waited long for service at the Comedie, except when Charlie took his annual vacation.

A fusillade of rain rattled against the plate glass window, driven by the wind coming off the lake, gathering momentum as it travels from the west end to the east end. An old man with an umbrella the size of a parachute, zigzagged past, the wind slamming him this way and that.

The coffee came, conveyed by a young redheaded waitress I hadn't seen before. I sweetened it with a rock of brown sugar. Like his service, Charlie's coffee was consistently excellent. The swing entrance door squeaked, announcing a new arrival. Lacking other distractions, I glanced that way. The newcomer was my next-door-but-one neighbor, a balding man of sixty-plus, not very tall and carrying more paunch than was healthy for him. He had taken up residence a few weeks earlier, since when we had exchanged the odd pleasantry in the corridor. His last name was Schelling; his first name, equally Germanic, momentarily escaped me.

He recognized me, nodded and, after a moment's indecision, shambled over to my table.

"Good morning," he said, his English inflected with a guttural intonation. "May I join you?"

"Why not?" I waved my hand at a vacant chair opposite. Any company was better than solitude in my present dark mood.

The chair squealed on the tiles as he pulled it away from the table. He sat down heavily, slightly out of breath. His narrow face was at odds with his overweight condition, and his blotchy complexion hinted at some internal disorder. I hadn't noticed before, but his eyes were ice-blue, almost colorless. In days gone by he had probably been as blond as I was, and indeed there was still the odd yellow streak in what remained of his white hair. His clothes were from a bygone era but well-tailored: dark blue blazer with shiny buttons, light blue pants, though the mustard-colored vest blighted the effect.

"You are Mr. Warner, yes?" he said with a stiff sitting-down bow.

Giving my name to strangers was a courtesy I usually tried to avoid. Difficult with neighbors, though. In any case, if you live in an

apartment block it's easy enough to check the names of other occupants from the mail boxes in the vestibule. Why worry, anyway? I was
now retired. A little loosening up was overdue.

So I replied with an affable, "That's my name."

"It is pleasant to meet you somewhere else than waiting for the
elevator," he said, a half-smile creasing his face. "You are in Number
52, are you not?"

I inclined my head. "Can I offer you a coffee?"

"Yes...please. You are most kind."

I flagged Charlie and he came twirling across. Schelling ordered
white coffee in a mutilated French that made our host cringe visibly.

"How do you like it here?" I asked, just making small talk.

"Geneva? It is very agreeable, except for the weather."

"You can say that again. I've lived here seven years and I've never
known rain like it."

"I, too, have been many years in Switzerland. Since 1999, in fact,
when I left Germany. But until I came here in March, I always lived
in the east. First in Zurich, later in Winterthur."

"Is that so?" Out of politesse, I yawned with my mouth closed.

Just as I was protective of my own background, I only ever pried
into others' for professional reasons. But Herr Schelling seemed willing, even eager, to be forthcoming, so I said, "You're German then."

"Yes." He confirmed it with pride, a glow lighting up his
unhealthy pallor.

"Retired?"

"For many years." His coffee and my repeat order were delivered,
courtesy of the redhead. He thanked her, his gaze on her buttocks as
she withdrew. My own gaze, naturally, was directed finer things. "I
haven't worked since I came to Switzerland," he went on, "although I
dabble in this and that. My family is quite wealthy, you see. When my
father died, he left me enough to keep—how do you say it—the wolf
from the door?"

In contrast to his lousy French, his grasp of idiomatic English was
above average. I congratulated him on it.

"Thank you," he said, seeming pleased. "And you, Mr. Warner, an
Englishman living in Geneva. What is the nature of your business?"

"Like you, I'm retired," I said and didn't elaborate.

"You are young to be retired."

We eyed each other over our coffee cups, like fencers assuming an *en garde* stance.

"You remind me of a man I used to do business with in West Berlin, long ago before reunification," he remarked. "An ex-SS man. Not a nice man to know, but he was making a fortune transporting refugees across into the West, and we did good business together."

I stirred my second *noisette* and sampled it.

"I thought all the ex-SS were rounded up and either strung up or put in prison."

"Not exactly. My father was..." He toyed with his spoon again, not looking at me. "You are not, by any chance, Jewish, are you?"

The question was so unexpected, so out of context, that I gaped at him. "Jewish? No, I'm not Jewish." Perhaps the slight concavity of my nose had confused him.

"Good. Then you will not be disturbed when I tell you my father was also in the SS. A *Stürmführer*."

"*Stürmführer*?" I wasn't familiar with the SS pecking order.

"Equal to an army rank of Lieutenant. That was at the end of the war, of course. He joined as a recruit in 1944."

It was nothing to me that his father had been in the SS. The SS were just common criminals. Hey, no different from me, except I didn't advertise it by wearing a black uniform.

I was beginning to wonder where all this soul-baring was leading.

He sighed deeply. "In a perfect world, we would all be perfect people, would we not? No crime, no injustice, no jail. Have you ever been in jail, Mr. Warner? As a punishment, I mean, not as a visitor." He gave a nervous giggle.

This was a baring too far.

"If I had," I said, fixing him with a hard stare, "do you think I would confess to you, a stranger?"

"*Scheisse*, man. Does it matter? I was in jail once. It was a long time ago..." A shrug. "I paid for my crimes."

"Yeah, well, I wouldn't broadcast it if I were you. The residents in our apartment block are boringly law-abiding. I don't think you'd be very popular if it got around that you were a criminal. Even an ex-criminal."

He took the hint. Conversation was suspended while I finished my coffee.

Outside, the clouds were breaking up, a dirty white peeping through the cracks. A boy on a bike went past, swerving to avoid two doddery old women crossing the street where they shouldn't, hanging on to each other for support.

At a streetcar stop on the far side of the street, people waited in a glum line; sober Swiss faces, sober Swiss clothing. A dour, unexcitable race, the Swiss. Adept at providing secret bank accounts, storage facilities for Nazi gold, and keeping out of world wars. Outside of the tennis world, you had to go back to William Tell for a Swiss of international prestige. Not that I had anything against them.

"Well, Mr. Warner," Schelling resumed, his voice a few octaves lower. "I have told you about my past. I spent five years in prison for my so-called crimes. I have nothing to fear from the police any longer. But what of you? Is *your* past so pure and white?" He sat back, smiling now, a thumb hooked in the armhole of that sickly vest. "Have you been a good boy all your life?"

What was his agenda? Was he just being funny, or was he naturally nosy, or did he have a veiled motive for entering the realm of my personal history? I didn't rise to the bait.

He chuckled. "Don't be so...how do you say? Reticent? You know, Mr. Warner, you have the look of a man who could be ruthless. If I am right, I might have some work for you."

So that was it. The bastard sounding me out for some doubtless tricky operation, like gun running or smuggling illegals.

"I'm not in the market for work," I said, playing along when I should have walked out and left him with the bill. Now why was I reluctant to do that?

"Not even for a large sum of money?" He studied me. "Excuse me if I am mistaken, but I was wondering if perhaps you are some kind of mercenary."

"Not in my line, Schelling. I'm as mercenary as the next man, but not in the sense you mean, a gun for hire."

Cue for hollow laughter.

"It was just an impression you gave me. You have a certain...air. I have encountered it before in men with no scruples."

Like a dog with his favorite bone, he wasn't ready to let it go.

"Look, friend, keep your impressions to yourself if you want us to stay on good terms. I'm just an ordinary guy who made a buck or two in stocks and shares, and is enjoying spending it."

"In Geneva? It is not exactly the Cote d'Azur, is it? Or even the Costa del Sol."

There, he had a point. The rich only live in Geneva if their income depends on it. No retiree with money would make the place his base through choice. Too staid, too wet.

"Have you ever visited my country, Germany?" he said then, in an apparent switch of subject.

This was safer ground. So I thought.

"Once or twice," I said grudgingly, still wary of his personal probing.

"You know München—Munich, you call it—perhaps?"

"A little. Why?"

"I was born near there. I often go back, although my family are all dead now." After another sip, he blotted his lips on the paper napkin that was delivered with every drink at the Comedie. "Bavaria is at its most beautiful in autumn, in my opinion. It is often warm and sunny—even in November."

I had let my guard down; now it was back in place. Munich... November...just a place and a time. Separately meaningless. Even together, they didn't necessarily amount to more than coincidence.

Now and again, I played poker. It helps in the exercise of facial control. Right now, those attributes were being tested to the limit.

"I'm sure it's close to paradise," I said distantly. Enough was enough. I signaled Charlie to bring the bill.

"*Have* you ever been there in November?" Schelling persisted, the words coming hurried now. "In Munich? The lakes are so beautiful. The Ammersee, for instance."

That Schelling should hit on the exact location and date of my last hit was a coincidence beyond the pale. My cup was empty and so was my stock of prevarication. I flicked Schelling a tight smile. "I have to leave you, Mr. Schelling. An appointment with my dentist."

De Galle loomed up. I took the bill, winced, and parted with a

twenty-euro note. "Thanks, Charlie," I said over a farewell handshake.
"*A bientôt.*"

"*J'espère bien.* Have a nice day, Monsieur Warner."

"Thanks for the chat." I flipped a hand at Schelling. "It's been...instructive."

I walked to the door, standing aside for a young couple escaping the latest downpour, hair plastered flat to their scalps. In the doorway, I put up my umbrella, cast a departing glance at Schelling.

He was watching me with a cat-that-got-the-cream smirk that did nothing at all to allay my fears.

———

CLASSICAL MUSIC WAS a potent form of relaxation for me. Returning home, a little after 10:00PM from a meal at the Parc des Eaux Vives, I settled in my reclining armchair and fired up the iPod. The second movement of Dvorak's New World Symphony swirled from the speakers as I sipped a bourbon and soda. On such occasions, I usually emptied my mind of all distractions, content to wallow in the wail of the strings, the mournful bleat of the bass clarinet, and the leap of massed brass. But this evening, I was still gnawing away at my bizarre conversation with Schelling. I had set aside my initial disquiet. After all, why should I worry about some old guy playing guessing games? The Ammersee in November. A coincidence? Why not? And the lakes *were* beautiful, a major tourist draw.

Yet, whenever I dismissed his maddening presence from my mind, it boomeranged right back, unwanted and unbidden. A black cloud darkening my tranquil, albeit dreary, skies. He was an itch I couldn't scratch away.

As the second movement entered its closing phase, the bleat of a French horn leading into a string finale, my thoughts travelled south, to Monaco, to my boat. The summer season was still weeks off, but if nothing else I would be able to do some maintenance work on it and share a bottle or two of *vin du pays* with Jean-Pierre, of an evening. Watch the Monaco Grand Prix from the balcony of an old friend's apartment in the Avenue d'Ostende. Then maybe sail *Seamist* down to Corsica, or along the coast to Marseille or Barcelona.

Barring habit and a classy über-whore called Evelyne, there were no attractions to keep me in rain-soaked Geneva. I was a free agent now. Instead of a two-month summer layoff, I had twelve months, year in, year out. Better prospects, too, of decent weather down there on the Côte d'Azur than here among the mountains, whose peaks were still crowned with white.

Fired at last with a sense of purpose, I quit biting my nails over Schelling and went into the bedroom to sort out my luggage. It's funny, but bedrooms have a curious effect on me that has nothing to do with sleep. I stood at the foot of the bed, succumbing to those age-old primitive urges. The packing was postponed. I skimmed through the contact index on my cell phone, and tapped the number.

"*Allo, oui?*" Her high, almost childlike voice called forth visions of never-ending legs, dark velvety skin, and nipples the size of cherries.

"*C'est moi*—André," I announced.

She squealed with what I interpreted as venal delight. "André, *mon cher!*" Then, switching to English, "'Ow are you?"

"Just fine, Evelyne. But I'll be even more fine when you get here. Are you available?"

"For you, *chéri*, always. But first I must tell you, I 'ave to make a tiny adjustment to my prices."

"Screw that, Evelyne, you get over here. We'll discuss inflation afterwards."

She giggled, flirty, pseudo-guileless. "I shall be zere in thirty minutes. You can chill ze wine and warm ze bed while you wait."

We said our so longs and cut the connection.

Evelyne was a well-integrated Somali immigrant, lighter skinned than most. Her real name sounded like 'fish and chips' but her prices were more caviar and champagne. Her skill, her enthusiasm and inventiveness and, perhaps most of all, her personal hygiene, entitled her to command the sort of fees that most prostitutes only fantasize about. She also ran her own company—exotic lingerie online. This enabled me to pay for my pleasure with my AmEx card. A little refinement that somehow made the whole business much less sordid.

CHAPTER FOUR

THE ASTON—A month-old DB11—was drawn up at the curbside, fresh from the high-priced ministrations of the local dealer, its black coachwork polished to the brilliance of patent leather. As always, the chief mechanic had returned it to me. As I emerged the apartment block, he was flicking imaginary specks of dust from the car's long, drooping snout.

I slipped him the customary twenty Swiss franc note, which he pocketed with an appreciative grin.

"*Merci, patron. Bonnes vacances là-bas.*" He patted the hood. "Watch your speed, hey?"

He took off back to the garage on foot. Into the Aston's trunk went two large valises, an overnight bag, and a shoulder bag. I reached inside the trunk under the section between its front lip and rear window, into the narrow padded compartment that didn't figure on the manufacturer's blueprint. Reassuring myself that the Korth NXR revolver with the four-inch barrel was securely clamped in place.

Transporting arms, even a modest handgun, across the border into another country was a risk. Slight enough since the Schengen Agreement relaxed border controls across Western Europe, but nevertheless a risk—especially with recent moves to reintroduce passport checks in the wake of terrorist attacks and mass immigration from the Middle

East. I ran that risk because I'd grown accustomed to going every-where with the principal tool of my trade, unless one happened to be waiting for me at my destination. It was a habit that would die hard, for my potential enemies were numerous and varied and kept me on permanent alert.

Because of the gun, I intended to cross into France at Ambilly, one of the lesser points of entry. Passport control officers are stationed there on a random basis at infrequent intervals. Their presence can be observed at a distance, before making the commitment to cross.

Some compulsion made me glance up at the apartment before getting into the car. Not sentiment—I had no such feelings about my home—just instinct. Two balconies along from mine, leaning on the steel rail and staring down at me, was my nosy neighbor, Herr Schelling. He saluted me with a raised forearm, almost Hitleresque. I nodded brusquely in return and ducked inside the car. I wouldn't pine for *him* while I was away.

I made myself comfortable in the hip-hugging seat. Only the thick-ness of my hair separated my head from the low coupe roof. I surveyed the maze of dials, switches, screens, and other impedimenta of modern luxury transportation. In the six months I had owned the car I still hadn't learned to use all its features. I programmed Quai Antoine 1e, Monaco, into the GPS and thumbed what I hoped was the right button. Its guidance wasn't necessary, but it amused me to watch my progress on the little screen and its frequent corrections of my choice of route. The high-class female voice of the computer ordered me to get my ass and my car into gear and hit the road. Well, that was the gist of it. Oh, and to respect the speed limits. Sure I would.

The sun was making an effort to break through, patches of blue prizing apart the sullen clouds. I settled a pair of Ray-Ban sunglasses on my nose to give it some encouragement. I thumbed the starter button. The engine broke into an indolent rumble: the quadruple tailpipes chugging, the tachometer needle steady on 400 rpm, eight cylinders and 590 bhp of raw power literally at my fingertips.

A feather-light touch on the accelerator, and I pulled away from the curb behind a garbage collection truck. Another tap of the toe and I was past it and half way down the street.

Goodbye, Geneva. Hello sun, fun and Mediterranean girls.

———

THE FIRST STAGE of my trip, destination Grenoble, was fast; *autoroute* most of the way, only slowing down for the tollbooths, those blights on the otherwise superb French highway system. The weather conditions remained good for high-speed driving. I cruised at a lazy 150 kph, with the occasional faster burst on straight stretches where the police couldn't sneak up on me unseen.

By five o'clock, I was in Grenoble and registering at a modest hotel on the north side of the river under the ramparts of the Fort de la Bastille.

Came the morning, I left early. It was sunny, just the odd ball of cumulus hovering above the mountains. I opted for the slow but pretty route south via the Col de Croix Haute, no matter that Miss Hoity-Toity on the GPS took a dim view of my decision.

To Digne, my next stopover, was a leisurely one hundred and eighty kilometers. Speed was not a priority. I dawdled through the curves, letting the Aston off the leash on the infrequent straights, generally taking it easy and making halts whenever the panorama merited a longer scrutiny. At these high altitudes snow still lay picturesquely in the fields on either side of the road and in the folds and creases of the mountainsides.

The mountains stayed with me all along the route, sometimes only a blue-brown smear away to the east, sometimes closing in. Occasionally, depending on the twists and turns of the road, they lay directly ahead, giving the illusion of blocking my route. Just beyond Aspres, I lunched at a quaint terraced *auberge* with a roof shaped like a witch's hat.

As the kilometers unwound and Geneva receded into the past, so my worries over Schelling receded. I even began to toy with the idea of quitting Geneva altogether and moving to sunnier climes: Sardinia, perhaps, or southern Spain. After all, my residence in Switzerland had been governed by professional criteria that were no longer relevant.

Two girl hitchhikers, laden with rucksacks and becomingly attired in designer-ripped denim shorts and halter tops, stuck out hopeful thumbs on the far side of the old stone bridge coming into the village of Montrand. I was tempted but the Aston was short on space, aside from which, three's a crowd in a mixed-sex scenario.

Farther on, out of purely altruistic motives, I did take pity on a woebegone motorist standing by an old Peugeot with a collapsed front suspension. He was, I learned, a schoolmaster at Sisteron, a town along my route. I took him as far as the next village, which boasted a small motor repair outfit.

Then I was alone again in my computerized cockpit, hands positioned on the wheel rim at a quarter-to-three, eyes occasionally swiveling to the rear-view mirror. Now and again catching a glimpse of a dark blue BMW 3-Series as it rounded each bend behind me. How many dark blue BMW 3s would there be in the whole of France? A thousand? Five thousand? Not so many as that, surely. And what were the odds against seeing a car of that description purely by chance on no less than four separate occasions within two days of driving? Always pacing me no matter what my speed. Occasionally dropping back or out of sight altogether. Never passing me, even when I slowed.

My survival antennae were bleeping. If—and it was still a biggish 'if'—I was being shadowed, by whom, and with what purpose? Not the police. They wouldn't tag along after me halfway across France; they'd haul me in for a cozy grilling. Conclusion? A private enterprise operation. It still didn't tell me who or why? Schelling came to mind for no obvious reason other than his weird attempt at interrogation at the Comedie. Too old for a regular cop, he could be private fuzz acting under instruction.

It led me to consider another, far more serious aspect. The BMW only appeared at intervals. It had not followed me constantly; I was sure of that. This pointed to a team of cars, working in relays. To maintain a tail of such sophistication for two days, using two or more vehicles, takes money and organization. That conclusion still didn't shed light on who or why.

At Chateau Amoux the road forks, the N.96 swinging southwest to Aix, and the N.85, the old Route Napoléon, southeast to Digne. There I passed under the railway, the sudden gloom inside the short tunnel bringing a curtain down over my vision, and searched again in the mirror for the BMW. The road was empty. It stayed like that for several kilometers until a motorcyclist came out of a side turning, exercising his *priorité à droite,* and nearly became another accident statistic in the process. He rode ahead of me, rarely out of sight on this relatively bend-free section, and in due course I began to get ideas about him, too.

In a spasm of pique, I wrenched the wheel over, pulling off the road onto a flat piece of ground that served as an unofficial turnout. Dust spewed up in a choking cloud, rolling over the car. Geneva's monsoon weather obviously hadn't penetrated this corner of France.

I switched off the engine, berating blue BMWs, motorcyclists, and my own ragged nerves. As I got out, an ancient truck clattered past, spilling gravel. I cursed it too, for good measure.

I lifted a can of Kronenberg beer from the chiller pack behind the passenger seat and sat on the hood, sipping the brew and watching the traffic go by. The two girl hitchhikers passed in the back of a station wagon. One poked her tongue out at me. I saluted them with the can to show no hard feelings. The motorcyclist didn't come back to look for me, and after a while I felt slightly ridiculous.

All was quiet and traffic-free for a minute or so, then came a small Peugeot, tailgated by a Total tanker with squealing brakes. After another lengthy gap between vehicles, a garish green Citroen Dyane buzzed into sight, going at a crawl with a predictable fuming procession in its wake. No Beamers, blue or otherwise. My phobia receded a touch.

After polishing off my beer I resumed my road trip at the same unhurried pace, the engine barely ticking over. It was almost hot now, even up here in the foothills, yet I still drove with the window open, rather than be sealed in with the air-conditioning. I enjoyed the play of wind on my face, the contact with the elements.

The railway ran parallel to the road for part of the way on the last leg before Digne. An orange-and-silver SNCF express swished by, decelerating for the station. I trailed after it into town, pulling up for a red light by the first of two bridges spanning the River Bleone.

I glanced in my offside mirror and my heart gave a tiny skip. Sitting squarely in the center of the mirror was a motorcyclist. It was impossible to be sure that this motorcyclist was the one I almost sideswiped back along the route. The bike was the right color, blue, a

Harley Sportster. Nice set of wheels. I studied the rider. His head was mostly helmet, but the visor was raised and I took note of a big moustache with curly points and a stubbled chin. I also noted the expensive motorcycle gear: black, one-piece leather suit, *de rigueur* attire for all discerning bikers. No use at all though for future identification—too easily discarded. Clothes maketh not the man.

The lights went to green and the line of vehicles jerked forward. I said goodbye to the *route nationale* and went round the traffic circle into Boulevard Thiers, past the park and the Municipal Swimming Pool. The motorcycle clung to me all along the boulevard. Until I swung left into the pillared gateway of the courtyard of the Hotel Grand Paris, Digne's biggest and finest, where he accelerated away, continuing on down the road.

In an evil mood I strode into the hotel lobby, carrying the smaller of my two valise, now convinced that I was under surveillance. I was short with the charming woman desk clerk who managed to rise above my boorishness and smiled endlessly, no doubt regarding me as a typical Anglo-Saxon. I also forgot to tip the flunkey who hauled my valise up to my room. It was a double on the second floor, with all the usual trimmings, even satellite TV with BBC 1 and 2 and a DVD player, still comparative luxuries in traditional French hotels outside of the cities.

After a shower and a nap my humor improved. I went for a saunter around the town, pausing ostensibly to window-shop every few minutes, checking behind, ahead, and opposite, for persons of hostile intent. Pointless really. All they had to do was keep a watch on the hotel. They could be sure I wasn't going to abandon the Aston.

Out of my walkabout came a resolve to bite back. To provoke a showdown on the road tomorrow, and extract a few answers by the tried and tested gun-barrel-in-the-teeth method. The mere prospect of action made me feel better.

It was warm enough to eat outside that evening and several tables had been set on the terrace at the rear of the hotel. I declined the unspoken invitation. It would be ten o'clock or later before I finished. Digne being about two thousand feet above sea level, and with midsummer's day still over a month ahead, it tends to get chilly there once the sun drops out of sight.

Three quarters of the way through my dinner, as I was making inroads into the cheeseboard, a girl entered. A sandy blonde, five feet seven or thereabouts, she was dressed in a lemon shirt with a matching skirt that swirled about her knees. A nice line in hip rolls, too. To my deprived eyes she was an oasis in a desert. Sadly, she didn't toss so much as a sidelong glance my way as the waiter showed her to a table at the far side of the restaurant. She then rubbed salt in my wounded ego by sitting down with her back to me. I resumed my attack on the bleu d'Auvergne, meditatively now, my mind not on the sustenance but on how to break the ice with the sandy blonde. To leave such a gorgeous girl to her own devices for an entire evening amounted would be nothing short of sacrilege.

Opening a conversation with a female as poised and classy as Ms. Sandy Blonde wasn't like picking up some bimbo in a bar. It called for bucketloads of finesse. On this occasion it also called for haste. If her stay in Digne was an overnighter, it would leave me only a couple of hours at best in which to go from a zero base to a full-on relationship. Mission improbable.

Barging in as she was about to dine would earn me no merit points. Restraint and patience were the watchwords. Resigned to holding my impulses in check, I eked out the wait with cognac-laced coffee and much piteous sighing and the occasional yawn. The restaurant, with its Napoleonic decor, contained little to divert, least of all the other diners. Sharing a table by the window were two tanned elderly couples; next to them a young sales representative type demolishing a steak as though he'd just ended a year's fast; and occupying a large circular table near the double doors, a family of six: harassed-looking father with a mop of unruly hair, mother pretty and plump and laughing a lot, their brood, ages ranging from about three to early teens. All squeals and chatter. The way it might have been for me if Marion...

I closed the compartment of my mind where Marion resided with a slam. Such reminiscence brought only pain. Purging the memories and the images for now, I devoted my full attention to the view of the girl's hair. It tumbled to well below shoulder level. It was abundant and rebellious, and looked as if she'd forgotten to brush it—a sort of unstyled style. Maybe it defined her. I hoped to find out.

When the waiter removed her plate, I observed she hadn't eaten much of the main course. She passed on the dessert too. No wine either, just mineral water. Maybe she was a health fiend.

Finally, she got to her coffee. Now to make my move. There was a wide expanse of floor to cover and I felt a mite self-conscious as I homed in on her left flank.

"*Bonsoir, mademoiselle...j'espère que je ne vous dérange pas.*"

Now, you couldn't get politer than that.

She looked up, no surprise registering at the sight of me standing there instead of the waiter. Maybe she couldn't tell us apart. Her eyebrows climbed inquiringly.

"Please speak English," she said, to the tinkling of icicles. She had an American New England accent, whereas I had assumed her to be French. Mistake number one. Whatever her nationality, she was, as I had judged from afar, stunning, with her lazy-lidded, slanting green eyes. There was a catlike quality about them and they were disturbingly worldly-wise, sizing me up almost cynically. Nose dead straight, mouth well-endowed with lips, hair parted off-center, framing her loveliness to artistic perfection. Age around twenty-five.

"I was apologizing for the intrusion," I said, fixing her with an ingratiating smile. "May I introduce myself? My name's Warner, same as in the movie company..."

While I was still speaking, the green eyes narrowed and a frown line formed above the bridge of her nose.

She cut into my opening gambit with scalpel-like efficiency.

"How do you do, Mr. Warner as in the movie company? I'm sure you're aware you're an attractive man. I expect lots of bimbos regularly shower you with compliments. As far as I'm concerned, however, you're just a nonentity forcing his attention on me. I am not, emphatically not, interested in talking to you, sharing a drink with you, or sharing a bed with you. So will you kindly fuck off and find some other victim to pester."

All this, thankfully, was delivered in an undertone and I was therefore able to hold on to some external semblance of dignity. My grin became fixed. I didn't take offence—you can't win 'em all. Nor did I persist in my overtures. Whenever a girl gives me the cold shoulder, I accept it with good grace and move on to the next in line.

To my chagrin there was no visible next-in-line stopping over at the Hotel Grand Paris this night. I managed a stiff nod at Ms. Put-me-down and murmured an apology. Even in adversity, I always tried to behave like a gentleman.

I signed the restaurant bill and went up to my room, where I switched on the TV. It was a French quiz show. Within minutes I was bored stiff by its inanities and wandered into the palatial Louis XIV bathroom with its exposed pipes and cranky plumbing, there to release the evening's intake of liquid. Afterward, I examined my features in the mirror through a critical lens. At least she said I was attractive. My hair was my best asset, being a cornfield yellow with a few kinks that looked man-made, but weren't. At thirty-eight, my jaw was still lean, no jowls or extra chins developing, teeth all my own, slightly crooked but still in good shape and in no need of artificial whitener. I was tall, slim, fit, with no hint of a potbelly. In all modesty I had no quibble with my appearance.

Giving up on Ms. Put-me-down left worry space to resurrect visions of blue BMWs and big-mustached bikers. What with a mysterious organization tailing me through France and a girl slapping me down harder than I've been slapped since my teens, my sabbatical was off to an inauspicious start.

———

TO A RINGING, "*BONNE ROUTE, MONSIEUR!*" from the smiling female desk clerk, I hauled my overnight luggage across the vestibule and down the stone steps, out into the morning sunlight.

The Aston was half-in, half-out of some shade thrown by a row of beech trees in the hotel courtyard. The trunk lid was already hot to the touch. I stowed my valise, discreetly removed the Korth from its place of concealment and transplanted it in another, still secret, but more accessible compartment under the glove box in readiness for the planned confrontation.

My preparations complete, I was poised with one leg in the foot well when a voice hailed me from several cars down.

"Say, Mr. Movie Company. Could you lend a hand here?"

It was the sandy blonde with the nice line in brush-offs. Dressed in a white cheesecloth shirt with short sleeves and skinny jeans custom-made for a shape like hers. I was tempted to repay her in her own coin and drive off, leaving her to choke in the fumes of my exhaust. I didn't, due to a serious character defect that prevents me from saying "no" to a pretty face. And this girl's face was more than just pretty.

"Are you speaking to me?" I said, as though the courtyard were full of people.

"Sure I am. Go figure. There's nobody else here!"

"Yes, right...well, since you ask so nicely..." I shut the door of the Aston and walked over to her Peugeot. Not hurrying; making a point. She stood there, hands resting languidly on her rather boyish hips, that same little frown as last night marring the otherwise flawless space between her eyebrows.

I stopped in front of her. "Well?"

"It's my car. It won't go in gear."

"Is that a fact?" No mechanical wizard, I wasn't sure what she expected me to do about it.

"Well, don't just stand there," she said tartly.

"All right." I turned to go, back to my car.

She grabbed my arm, her cool fingers clasping my elbow. Her grip was surprisingly strong.

"Hey, look, I know you're sore at me about last night." She stared down at her feet, presenting the top of her tousled mane to me. Her parting was crooked and somehow that tiny defect touched off a protective feeling toward her. "I'm sorry. I was kind of—"

"Rude?" I prompted. "Yes, you were. But now that your car's broken, you're prepared to forgive and forget. Have I got it right?"

Her mouth formed an O.

"Because, if so," I ground on remorselessly, "how did that line go? I insist that we talk, share a drink, and share a bed, before I take a look at it."

The O grew bigger and rounder, and the eyes were lazy-lidded no more. Until I gave the game away by laughing. After a flicker of uncertainty, she burst into a splutter, and there we were, two strangers convulsed with mirth in the courtyard of the Hotel Grand Paris. So undignified. The German-Dutch couple strolled past, eyeing us with disapproval, and this restored a degree of sanity. It wasn't all that funny, anyway. If she but knew it, I was deadly serious.

In my dreams.

"I'm Georgina Gregg." She stuck out a hand as a peace offering. "And you're Mr. Warner. Have I got that right?"

"André Warner at your service, Miss Gregg. Okay, now that we're bosom friends, let's take a look at your car."

The clutch pedal proved to have plenty of resistance, so the hydraulics were good. But when I ran the engine and tried to engage gear, the lever wouldn't go through the gate and horrible grating noises issued from it.

"It's got to be some sort of internal fault in the clutch unit," I diagnosed.

She was leaning on the open door, her arms resting along the top edge, the cheesecloth pulled taut against her breasts. One notices these small details. My announcement brought her out in a rash of anxiety.

"Is that serious?"

"Serious enough to keep you in Digne for a day or more is my guess. The clutch will most likely have to come out for repair or even replacement."

"Oh, shit. I can't wait a day. I have to be in Monaco this evening."

How about that for a lucky break? Opportunity was knocking again, much louder and more persistently now. In a studiedly flat voice I mentioned that Monaco was also my destination.

"I'd be happy to give you a ride," I added, in case a casual hint wasn't enough.

"A ride? Thanks, but there's no need. I'll get the hotel to call Hertz or whoever does car rentals in this town."

"Your decision," I said with a shrug. "If you don't mind spending the money."

"Well...I suppose it *would* be quicker to go with you. No filling in forms and all that jazz." She directed those heat-ray eyes on me then, boosting them to maximum wattage. "Do you think you can get me there in time? I have to meet my boss for a high-powered business conference at five o'clock. He'll kill me if I miss it, or even if I'm late."

"No promises, but I'll do my best."

"Oh, thanks. I really am grateful." Her hand was resting on my forearm now. It brought me out in goose bumps. "I'll just pop into the hotel and get them to phone for a repair outfit."

"Do you want any help?"

"With the language, you mean?" She shook her very attractive head. "I've lived in France for the past eight years."

"But last night you told me to—"

"Speak in English?" She smiled, arching a coquettish eyebrow. "That was to give you the brush-off. I thought *you* were French."

How ironic was that?

She trotted off, very elegantly, up the steps. I went around the back of the Peugeot, opened the trunk and lifted out her luggage, which consisted of two pigskin valises and a capacious shoulder bag.

Waiting for her to reappear, I mulled over the turn of events. The future was suddenly looking brighter—on the romantic front, at any rate. No chance of an overnight stop en route to Monaco, more was the pity. She had to be there this evening, and I wasn't such a heel as to engineer an opportunistic breakdown. No, far better to strike up an *entente cordiale* during the seven hours' drive in the hope of an eventual night of bliss on board my boat. I wasn't greedy. I didn't seek a long-lasting meaningful commitment. Just a few hours in a double bed would suffice, with perhaps a follow-up or two until the novelty wore off, as it invariably did these dissipated days.

She emerged from the swing door, ran down the steps. She moved with the flowing ease of an athlete. From whichever angle you viewed her, she was a knockout.

"Your three pieces of luggage are in my car," I told her. "Are there any bits and pieces you want to take?"

"No, thank you." She looked quite pleased with herself.

"Did you organize a breakdown truck?"

"A what?" Her frown was followed by a snort of mirth. "Sorry, I've gotten other stuff on my mind. Yes, it's all organized. They'll be here in half an hour."

"You want to wait for them?"

An emphatic headshake. "I daren't. We need to get moving." She tossed me an uncertain look. "If you don't mind, that is."

"I'm ready when you are."

We took our leave of the Hotel Grand Paris, Digne, and trundled out of town.

"Lovely car," she remarked, caressing the soft hide upholstery. "I'd love an Aston Martin. Unfortunately, PAs don't earn that kind of money."

"A PA? Is that what you are?" I slowed down for the always-red lights by the bridge, accelerating when they changed unexpectedly.

"Mm. My boss owns a company called Sud-Marine. They import diesel motors and marine equipment."

I was stuck behind a horse-box, the oncoming traffic inconveniently spaced to rule out passing. During this enforced crawl I did a rapid scan of all rear-view and door mirrors for unwanted adherents. Several cars were forming a line behind me, but none of them stood out. In any case, with the Gregg girl on board, my planned showdown with the enemy would have to be postponed. Instead, I'd try to use the Aston's speed and acceleration to shake them off. Also, as a bonus, to make Georgina Gregg melt into my arms.

The road cleared. I fed serious gas to the Aston's eight cylinders and darted past the horse-box and a garbage truck, blasting through the gears to 150 kph in the space of half a kilometer. The first bend spoiled that bit of fun, though I still negotiated it fast enough to make the tires howl their anguish.

"Wow!" Miss Gregg gasped. "Nice demo. Maybe I should have mentioned I need to get to Monaco in one piece."

I tucked in behind an Alfa with Torino plates to wait for an opening. "That was just to whet your appetite," I chuckled and passed the Italian without effort. A white sedan followed through after me but couldn't keep up, and was soon a diminishing dot in the mirror.

"Speed doesn't frighten you, does it, Miss Gregg?"

"Not a bit." She didn't add, "It makes me amorous," which dashed that particular hope.

After maybe a minute's silence, she said, "By the way, my friends call me Gina."

"Not George?"

"Are you serious?" she said, but her tone told me she knew I wasn't.

I grinned. "Not really. Gina it is. I'm André."

"Not Andy?" she came back at me, tongue well tucked in cheek.

"Hell, no. Give me a break."

"Okay. Hi again, André." She pronounced it slightly incorrectly as ahndré rather than orndré. I forgave her. In fact, I'd forgive her almost anything. "How come the French name?"

"I'm half English, half-Quebecer, raised and schooled in Montreal and Toronto."

"Hence the accent, I guess. You sound almost like one of us North Americans." A proverbial pregnant pause followed, then she said, "I bet I can guess what your first love is."

"You can? You mean my car?"

"Your car?" She went off into a spasm of laughter. "No, no, not your car. Your *self*."

A comeback momentarily failed me, an unusual event.

"You have a nice line in compliments," I remarked finally and not a little resentfully. "For a hitchhiker, that is."

"Oops, *touché*." If she was embarrassed she covered up well. "Hey, I was only kidding. So tell me, André, what do you do when you're not using the highways of France as a race track?"

We were bowling into a set of bends and I was obliged to reduce speed to a 100 kph crawl. I had my answer ready. In fact, I had answers ready for a whole set of routine questions. She was far from being the first inquisitive young lady to warm the Aston's front passenger seat with a comely bottom.

"Essentially, I'm retired," I said. No lie, that. "I made a pile in currency speculation. I still dabble from time to time but the opportunities aren't there anymore. The recession and all the uncertainty took the fun out of it."

She made no comment, just stared pensively ahead. I had my work cut out holding a respectable speed on these bends, so I was content to let the dialogue lapse.

We drove on like that for some distance, making desultory conversation, remarking on this gorge or that mountain. My mind was still partly on blue BMWs and suchlike. In that respect my racing tactics seemed to have paid off. Towns and villages came and went: Chateauredon, Barrême, La Tuilière, then the murderous bends before Castellane, one loop after another...

We were through La Garde before she renewed her not-so-subtle probing. "You live in Switzerland, in Geneva." It wasn't framed as an inquiry. She was observant enough to have checked out the license plate.

"You've found me out."

"Unless your license plates are phony. Do you like it there? Geneva is a rather un-Swiss town, I've always thought."

"If it wasn't, I wouldn't live there." I whipped the Aston past a dawdling mail van, which entailed illegally crossing a continuous white line.

"Naughty, naughty," Gina chided. "Just because you've gotten Swiss plates, don't think you can get away with murder."

Get away with murder. Nice choice of words. After all, I'd been doing literally that for more than a decade.

North of the perfume town of Grasse we lunched at the Auberge La Mirande. The restaurant part is converted from an old water mill, hemmed in by mountains with their evergreen-clad slopes and grey soaring summits. At this latitude, snow was history. Peering at the handwritten menu together, our hands came into accidental contact. When she didn't pull away I experienced a tingle of pleasure, like a teenager on his first date.

"I'm going to have the trout," she decided after perusing the *à la carte* section. "But I'll skip the starter."

"I'll join you."

"Not that I think we should be stopping at all. Are you sure we'll still make it by five?"

"Quit worrying. They're quick here. We'll be on our way in an hour at the most."

Over tomato juice aperitifs I was tempted to fire a ranging shot across her bows, test her reaction to a tenuous hint about sleeping arrangements. But instinct warned me it would be premature. For all her raunchy language this woman was more than a cut above my usual conquests. So I held back, with what was for me commendable restraint.

"You must have thought me a bitch last night," she said as we tucked into our fish. "I was pretty pissed off with myself afterward."

"Were you?" I speared a morsel of flesh. "No need, I deserved it. I was hitting on you, and you didn't want to be hit on. You were right to put me in my place."

Big-hearted Warner. I could afford to be magnanimous now.

She left off munching and regarded me with a frown. "I ought to explain...I was married until...well, until recently. It wasn't an agreeable experience. I've been kind of off other men."

I expected her to elaborate. She didn't, so as a gentle prompt I said, "Divorced?" Once my curiosity is aroused it has to be satiated; like my lust.

She didn't respond, just chewed at her lip.

I drew my own conclusions. I tried to catch her eye, without success. "I'm sorry...for you, that is." For me, it was good news.

"Oh, I'm getting over it." A quick on-off smile, the kind that signals sadness, not joy. "You're helping, too, in a small way. Do you know, you're the first man I've so much as shared a meal with since...since it happened?" She sniffed, and covered up her embarrassment by rummaging in the depths of her purse from where, with a triumphant "Ah!" she produced a crumpled handkerchief.

I pretended not to notice her upset, focusing on my food.

"Gee, this trout is good," she said a moment later. "How's yours?"

"No complaints."

"I must come here again." She wiped round her plate, French-style, with a hunk of bread, looked at me with the bread poised before her mouth. "How old are you, André?"

"Thirty-eight." What with her being so young, I discovered I didn't much like admitting it.

"And married?"

"Was. My wife died." It still hurt to say it out loud.

"Oh."

"It was a long time ago."

She nodded jerkily as she munched bread. "Since then?"

"You want me to bare my soul?" I joked. "There was another serious relationship. It ended in disaster." And was best forgotten.

"It doesn't seem to have harmed you physically," she remarked. "You've kept in good shape by the look of you. I wouldn't have put you at much over thirty."

"Generous of you to say so. I work out most mornings when I'm at home and improvise when I'm away, but I'm not fanatical about it. Come to that, you don't look so bad yourself. What are you—twenty-five?"

She fluttered her eyelashes in mock-humility. "My, my, the compliments shoh are flyin'," she said in a parodied Scarlett O'Hara accent. "If you must know, I'll be thirty this year."

This exchange of compliments led her to talk about her life, starting with her education at an exclusive and expensive school in Baltimore before going on to study French and Spanish at Columbia University and later at the Sorbonne in Paris. During the Sorbonne period, she met and fell in love with her husband, who was French. They got married while she was still studying, to the disapproval of her very middle-class parents. She was twenty at the time, he a year older.

She managed to spin the yarn without an emotional relapse, sticking to the bones and leaving out the meat. I didn't ask for more. It was enough that she was available. I didn't care whether she climbed into my bed on the rebound from her ex-husband or because she was genuinely attracted to me. That's the beauty of physical desire: it makes no demands at all on the soul.

"When you get to Monaco, what are your plans?" This, I felt, was an innocuous enough question. It didn't smack of ulterior motives. I could be very devious when it suited me.

She drained the last dregs of Fouilly Puissé from her glass before replying.

"As I said, my appointment is at five PM at the Hermitage Hotel. I should be through there by eight. I'll be staying overnight and driving home in the morning in a rental car."

"Staying at the hotel?"

"That's right."

The peach was ripe and ready to drop. My mouth was opening to utter the words I had marshalled in my head, when our waitress popped up between us to clear the table. She piled dishes and debris into her arms, chatting to us nonstop, wanting to know if we had enjoyed our meal and managing to give the impression that she genuinely cared.

When at last we were alone again, I cast my die.

"Have you any commitments for dinner?" I said, making it a casual inquiry. My heart, of its own accord, was thudding away fit to induce a coronary. Wow. It wasn't like me to get so wound up about a prospective date.

She didn't reply at once. She subjected me to a scrutiny so intense I found myself coloring up. Finally, she admitted she had no commitments for dinner.

"Your cue to make one for me, I presume," she added, her eyes crinkling at the corners in amusement.

"Such cynicism," I sighed. "But you've rumbled me, of course. I generally eat at the Hotel de Paris my first night in Monaco." Not true, but I hoped to impress her by name-dropping that most exclusive of Monegasque establishments. "Will you join me?"

She appeared to consider the proposition, her head tilted sideways. "No strings?"

"No strings," I said with as much solemnity as I could muster. "Just eat and talk and get to know each other. Afterward, you go to your bed, and I go to mine." And if that was how the evening really ended, I'd give up chasing girls and take a vow of celibacy.

"Yes, well, I'm sorry, but I guess it's still no thanks."

"Come on," I said, keeping it light to mask my irritation. "Think of it as further therapy."

This served only to prompt a gust of merriment. "Therapy? Oh, André, you should listen to yourself. With somebody like you, therapy doesn't come into it. The reverse, if anything."

"Somebody like me?" I repeated blankly.

She hedged. "I mean...oh, damn it, André, it's not that I've gotten anything against you. I'm enjoying your company. I don't want to hurt your feelings, but ... I think you know what I'm getting at. That comment I made about your first love was a compliment really. You're a very good-looking man."

"Look, Gina, all I'm doing is inviting you to have dinner with me. It doesn't have to lead to anything. It takes two, and I'm no master seducer, believe me."

"I don't believe you and it's still no thanks."

With that, I decided to let it drop for now. Our coffees arrived, and between sips, Gina asked where I would be staying in Monaco.

"On my boat, as always."

She frowned. "You have a boat? You didn't mention it before." She made it sound like an accusation.

"I thought I had," I said, knowing I hadn't. "She's no big deal, just a forty-foot sloop. Goes by the name of *Seamist*. She's my best girl."

"*Seamist*." She pronounced it slowly and kind of reverently, as if savoring the word. "What a romantic name."

"Do you like boats?"

"Love them. I've a little dinghy of my own, only three-and-a-half meters. Where have you sailed yours?"

"Most places in the Med: Corsica, Sicily, Malta, North Africa, the Greek Islands. The Canaries too."

"You don't sail alone, do you? She'd be quite a handful, a forty-footer."

I poured more coffee for us both. "No. A Frenchman called Pradelou crews for me and takes care of the boat while I'm away. In his teens, he crewed for some of the big French names, including Loïck Peyron, so his credentials are top notch."

"I'd love to see her—your boat."

This was more like it. Hopes flickered in the ashes of my disappointment.

"You're welcome aboard any time." Not wishing to invite another rejection I held off suggesting a sailing date. I had my pride to consider. Disappointingly, she didn't pursue it.

After the coffee came the bill, which was modest in comparison with Geneva's restaurant prices.

"Bet you can't get me to Monaco by quarter to five," Gina dared me as we walked to the car.

It was just after 3:45PM and Monaco at least sixty minutes safe driving away. But my ego, once stimulated, is a potent force. Ditto, my testosterone.

"Hang on to your nerves," I grinned.

———

WE CROSSED the nominal frontier of the three kilometer-by-three hundred-meter piece of real estate that constitutes Monaco with five minutes in hand, so technically I made good my boast. Until Gina announced that her challenge was for me to deliver her to the hotel, not the frontier.

"You can't change the rules just like that," I said.

My protest cut no ice.

"It's a woman's privilege. Don't be a wuss."

After that, what could I do but try for it? In the end, road repairs in the Boulevard de Suisse and a dithering Belgian tourist conspired to erode my slim margin, and it was twelve minutes to the hour when we rolled up before the Hermitage's grandiose entrance. The blue-uniformed doorman snapped as smartly to attention as any Buckingham Palace sentry.

"Nice try," Gina consoled.

I took it on the chin, made no excuses. "Good thing for me we didn't lay bets."

We both got out and the doorman came to unload Gina's luggage. All that remained now were the adieus.

"So..." Gina smiled brightly, stuck out a hand. "Thank you so much, and...goodbye."

"*Au revoir* is preferable," I said, my schemes for the evening and beyond crumbling faster than a sandcastle at high tide. "Still, you know where to find me if you ever need another ride."

She flushed at that mean-spirited barb. "Thank you, André. It's been swell knowing you."

She turned and clacked on her skinny heels in the wake of her luggage, leaving me out there in the hard sunlight, feeling foolish and frustrated.

That was to be the last I saw of her for six weeks.

CHAPTER FIVE

I DROVE down into the Port de Monaco and parked the Aston opposite the Automobile Club offices. *Seamist* was moored three-quarters of the way along the Quai Antoine 1, where most of the English and American-owned craft lie. Even from up here on the promenade I could pick her out by her distinctive deep-blue hull. She looked good: sleek and racy, and the silver-anodized mast sparkled as though coated in frost. I had bought her three years ago and she was still as new. This was mostly thanks to Jean-Pierre Pradelou who, for a yearly twenty thousand euro retainer, plus an extra five hundred a week when he crewed for me, kept her shipshape.

I passed the Bar-Restaurant du Port, exchanging handshakes with Victor Jamail who ran the place. From the edge of his terrace he was peering about anxiously for hungry customers. With June still a week away, he would be pressed to cover his overheads.

"I'll be along later," I promised, to add a little sunshine to his morning.

"*D'accord*, André. I'll be expecting you."

I plodded along the quay, trailing luggage, glancing at each jetty in turn out of professional interest. I was still several berths short of *Seamist* when, with a squeal of delight, a slight, jeans-clad boy exploded from the cockpit on to the quayside and was all over me while my hands were still full of bags.

The French hugs-and-kisses greeting is alien to most Anglo-Saxons, even those with Quebec in their blood. The years I had spent in France had long since converted me though, and I gave Pascal the full treatment. He was on the cusp of his tenth birthday, the only son of Jean-Pierre. His mother had died giving him birth, and Jean-Pierre had raised the boy alone. The result was a credit to him.

"Did you have a pleasant journey, André?" the boy asked, so formal, so solemn, that I laughed. His father drilled him relentlessly in protocol in readiness for my arrival.

"Excellent, Pascal, thank you."

We conversed in French, the lingua franca onboard *Seamist*, though Jean-Pierre and I were teaching the boy everyday English phrases. Some he picked up without our input, not all of them appropriate for a boy his age.

"How's your father?" I asked him as we walked to the boat. At his own insistence, he was towing the smaller of my two valises. "I hope you've been looking after him properly."

This was a standing joke between us. Jean-Pierre was that comparative rarity among Frenchmen: he had no culinary skills. Even such an elementary process as heating a can of soup usually ended in disaster. Conversely, Pascal showed signs of becoming a true *cordon bleu*. During his vacation periods he catered for the two of them.

"Yes. Last night, I did *moules marinières* and *veau escalope*."

"I hope he appreciated it," I said gravely, impressed.

He flashed me an engaging grin. "But, of course."

He was a fine-looking boy, typically Mediterranean, with straight dark hair, olive complexion, and huge brown eyes. Tall for his age and bright, his ambition was to be a merchant seaman, ultimately to captain his own vessel. He was already taking steps toward that goal, understudying as crew on *Seamist*.

As we transferred from the gangplank into the cockpit with its teak seats, Jean-Pierre came out through the companionway, massaging oily hands around an equally oily rag. He was clad in a pair of blue overalls open to the waist, his barrel-shaped chest a V of black curls.

Our handclasp was warm, born of genuine mutual affection.

"*Comment vas-tu*, André?" His grin was as broad as the horizon, teeth flashing in a bronze visage, an adult replica of Pascal. He was shorter than me, but more than made up for it in other directions. Stripped to his trunks, he was all bulges and rippling flesh. Fortunately, his pugilist physique contained a mild manner.

"Good, Jean-Pierre. And you?"

"Also. The boat is fine, too," he added, anticipating the inquiry.

I made a noise to indicate satisfaction. "You can take me over her tomorrow. Meanwhile, I could use a cold drink."

Pascal's voice floated up the companionway, informing me that my valises were installed in the so-called master suite, and would I like a beer. I ordered a six-pack.

Jean-Pierre and I killed an hour and more than one beer apiece, lounging in the cockpit, yarning about our respective doings since the end of the last season. From where we sat we could see clear across the harbor and its surrounding crescent of buildings. The famous Monte Carlo Casino dominated the scene on the east side, while the sheer flanks of the Tête de Chien *massif* frowned down on the concrete and glass towers clustered on its lower slopes. The orange parasols that lined the Boulevard Albert during the summer months were not yet in evidence, and the harbor promenade looked curiously undressed without them.

"It's early for you to come here," Jean-Pierre commented, slurping his third beer. "I was surprised when you telephoned me on Friday."

"It was a spur of the moment decision. The weather's been lousy in Geneva. Nothing but rain, rain, and more bloody rain."

"Hah! The same here until ten days ago. Now, I think the sun is here to stay." He drank thirstily in great gulps, emptying the can. "So, *patron*...where shall we sail this year? I have some new charts for Corsica and Sardinia."

I gave a small chuckle. "That's an unsubtle hint you'd like to visit your brother."

"Well..." He looked sheepish. "If you decide to go to Corsica, it is true that I would like to call on him. But, of course, the decision is entirely yours."

He knew damn well we would be going to Corsica. I was a soft touch.

Pascal came aft. He had been testing the radio-controlled model yacht I brought him. Now, it was tucked possessively under his arm and his face was lit up brighter than Monaco by night.

"It goes very well," he announced. "I can control it from more than a hundred meters. Thank you very much, André."

I ruffled his hair. He evoked pleasure and regret in equal proportions. Pleasure from his simple presence, regret for a son that never was and never likely to be, barring a seismic shift in my lifestyle.

"You can give me a demonstration in the morning," I said. "Right now, I'm going to shower and then we'll go and eat." I glanced at Jean-Pierre who was eyeing his son fondly. A lucky man. Uncomplicated, undemanding, content with his lot. All he lacked was a wife, but then, like me, he preferred to play the field. And how. He never went short of female companionship.

We dined at the Restaurant du Port, washing down oysters, king-sized langoustines, and other sundry shellfish with a magnum of Moet '99. Our first and last meals of the season were always in the nature of a celebration. In between those extremities we scraped by on wine.

That night I slept badly, invariably the case on my first night on board until I grew used to the gentle undulation of the deck and the slap-slap of water against the hull, not to mention the chatter of halyards all around. On top of that, I had to contend with the encroaching image of a certain Georgina Gregg and what might-have-been. The sense of frustration was strong. Overnight, she'd come to represent a lot more than just another convenient lay.

As a result of my restless night, I rose sometime after nine next morning in below-par humor. Jean-Pierre showed up and, after a breakfast of *cappuccino* and a mountain of hot croissants, we did our customary inspection tour.

Seamist was an Océanis 40 Bermuda-rigged yacht, built in France by Beneteau. Below decks it was partially customized with a single master bedroom forward instead of the two cramped doubles provided as standard. She was a fin-keeler, with wheel steering in the cockpit and a second position in the wheelhouse-cum-saloon for control in bad weather.

Her equipment included an inflatable tender, Raymarine Autohelm steering, echo sounder and repeater, transceiver, gas detector, radar reflector, beaching legs to keep her upright when stranded at low tide, and all that my blood-soaked earnings could provide. We were a sail-anywhere outfit.

That afternoon we made ready for sea, just Jean-Pierre and me. Pascal had been consigned to the care of an aunt in Menton. It was to be one of those jaunts that could be described as "unsuitable for children". The destination of the first leg of our voyage was Bastia, in Corsica, where we'd spend a day or two in port for Jean-Pierre's annual fraternal reunion. For the second phase, we'd continue down the western side of the island to take advantage of the nor' westerly airflow to neighboring Sardinia, my first visit to that island.

A short burst of the beefy Perkins auxiliary motor kicked us clear of our berth when we cast off in the blush of early evening. We puttered out of the harbor, trading greetings with an incoming catamaran. As soon as we reached open water, we hoisted the sails. A sharp gust hit us while we were turning to leeward, and *Seamist* heeled over, sails crackling, a small bow-wave forming. Jean-Pierre switched off the engine and its clamor was replaced by the creak of the boom, the hum of the rigging, and the restful rush and chuckle of water along the hull.

"Next stop, Bastia," I said to Jean-Pierre as he joined me at the helm.

He winked. It wasn't only his sibling he intended to look up over there. In a recent letter, his brother had spoken of a blonde divorcee, awash with generous alimony payments and ripe for plucking.

Good for Jean-Pierre. Good for me too. The blonde divorcee had a younger sister, also blonde, also divorced, and also—by repute at least —ripe.

———

THIRTY-SIX EVENTFUL DAYS later we sailed back into Monaco harbor under a molten sunset. Thirty-six days in which we had battled with force-ten gales, been intercepted by an Italian Coast Guard cutter on suspicion of smuggling heroin, and run aground off Naples— to mention but a few of the trials that had beset us. We had also fought battles of another kind. My most memorable had concluded with a drainpipe descent at dawn from the boudoir of a voluptuous Italian *contessa*, whose husband, renowned for his violent temper and the pearl-handled pistol he toted, returned home early.

As for Jean-Pierre, his tangle with the private property of an over-protective Sicilian pimp was resolved satisfactorily. The greasy little sleazebag was left dangling upside-down by his fancy suspenders over the toilet pan in an evil-smelling washroom at the 2000 Club in Palermo.

Having debauched our way around the western half of the Mediterranean, we were coming back to recover from our excesses and escapades. Berthing was carried out with a shade less diligence than usual, Jean-Pierre being keen to take off for his home in Roquebrune. The deck received a perfunctory hosing down. High fives were exchanged and off he went. I stumbled below and hit the sack.

The next day was the last Saturday of June, and I awoke sufficiently restored to do a hundred press-ups and sit-ups on deck before breakfast. A modern motor yacht had entered harbor overnight and was riding at anchor, her white thoroughbred profile mirrored in the still surface of the water. Elsewhere, there was the usual hustle and bustle. A cabin cruiser was being lifted onto the opposite quay, her bottom festooned with streamers of weeds and clusters of barnacles.

After breakfasting off defrosted *croissants* I went to see the Harbormaster. I was crossing the road by the police station when squealing rubber on asphalt drowned the buzz of traffic. The assault on my eardrums lasted no more than a second, was punctuated by a crunch of metal and the dainty tinkle of shattered glass. Like everyone else within earshot I swung round, casting about for the source of the accident. A scruffy, once-yellow VW Beetle had rammed the rear of a black limousine with dark-tinted windows, and the drivers of both vehicles were getting out for ritual remonstrations. All in a day's routine. I clicked my tongue sympathetically. I was about to resume my walk when a glimpse of the car at the head of a line forming behind the VW made me do a double-take. It was a dark blue BMW 3-Series.

The weeks of high seas and low dives had exorcised my BMW phobia and I'd thought no more of it since arriving in Monaco. Even the driver's droopy moustache, redolent of a certain Harley rider in

Digne, didn't pluck an immediate memory chord. No, it was the guy beside him who raised the hairs on the back of my neck—no less than Herr Schelling: neighbor, self-confessed criminal and ex-convict, with an unhealthy interest in my travel experiences.

He was looking straight at me with some anxiety, and while I was doing my imitation of still life, his nerve broke. He spoke to Harley Boy. The BMW reversed hastily and crunched into the car behind it. Pure slapstick. They didn't hang around to fill in accident reports for their insurers. To outraged horn blasts from the damaged car, Schelling and his driver U-turned out of the line. This maneuver caused more rubber-squealing as traffic travelling in the opposite direction was brought to a halt. Leaving chaos in its backwash, the BMW tore off up the hill toward the Casino.

The duo's panicky departure confirmed that they were in Monaco because I was in Monaco. It all hung together—Schelling, references to Munich and November on that morning at the Comedie, the blue BMW 3-Series, the mustachioed biker...Too many coincidences. Somebody was interested in me and I didn't kid myself the origin of the interest was a Hollywood talent scout. I was back to square one, back to where I had been in Digne: puzzled and angry. Maybe a little worried, too.

Prior to being waylaid by the delectable Miss Gregg, my proposed solution had been to force a showdown. No other means of getting some answers occurred to me then, nor did it now. Only now, here in Monaco, I had no means of tracing Schelling and co. They held all the cards.

After my meeting with the Harbormaster about new mooring regulations I returned to the boat. When I first came aboard I'd trans-ferred the Korth from the Aston to a space behind the false back of the closet in my cabin. As I hefted the weapon in my hand, I was forced into a reappraisal. To use it, to actually fire it in Monaco, would be to court disaster. It was one thing to provoke a confrontation at gunpoint on some lonely road, where witnesses were sparse. To do so in the most crowded piece of real estate in Europe was not an option. The local police would be all over me before the echo died. A silenced weapon would lessen the risk—if I had such a thing to hand. The nearest underground dealer in my network was in Marseille.

Common sense prevailed. I put the Korth back behind the panel. All was not lost. The gun shared its hiding place with a switchblade knife. It was a brute of a weapon, with a fifteen-centimeter blade. I thumbed the cutting edge: it was well honed but spotted with rust, and I decided to give it a few licks with a file.

My maintenance work on the knife done, I spent the rest of the day on deck, restless and disguised under a multi-hued baseball cap and a pair of aviator sunglasses. At intervals I used binoculars to scan the harbor and the adjacent streets, like an army commander surveying enemy positions—a fruitless exercise. These particular enemies were keeping their heads well down.

When darkness began to close in and the lights along the quay sprang into life I called off my vigil. Changing into a lightweight dove-grey suit, I went at an easy stroll for a session at the baccarat tables of Monte Carlo's casino. Midnight found me comfortably settled at the table by the main door of the *salon privé*, plaques to the value of fifteen thousand-plus euros stacked before me, a profit of five thousand on my original stake. A rotund Italian with the jowls of a bloodhound and a neck with more folds than a concertina, held the bank. He was making sweat the way a squeezed lemon makes juice. With good reason: his bank was showing a loss of fifty thousand or more, mostly due to his own inept play, which consisted of brinkmanship alternating with over-caution.

There were two *tableaux*. I was in the left with seven others, more winners than losers. The most successful player of the evening sat opposite me, a woman around my own age, raven hair drawn severely off her unlined forehead into a serpentine coil that snaked down her back. Her figure was all good old-fashioned curves. When she walked in, she had set the salon alight with her sashaying motion. Her slinky black dress, which had the sheen of silk but wasn't—it didn't crease— clung to her like a skin diver's outfit. Her French was basic and distorted by a North American twang the croupier had difficulty understanding.

As is more or less inevitable when facing someone across a baccarat table, glances had passed between us now and again while the game progressed. Mostly, she looked away quickly, taking refuge behind her e-cigarette. A sign of lack of interest, or just coquettishness? So far, she represented the best prospect in my line of sight for a satisfactory finale to the evening.

"*Un banco de cinquante mille,*" the croupier was chanting, and I realized with a start that the player on my left had passed and it was my call.

I gave a small nod. "*Banco.*"

The Italian mopped anew at his glistening brow. Good. Anxiety makes for bad judgment.

The dimpled hand that delivered my two cards was trembling. I hid my contempt and frowned at a pair of deuces that added up to four points. On a count of less than five, one always drew a third card. I received an ace, which brought me up to five points. Mediocre. The Italian flipped his cards over, beamed down at an eight and a queen. At baccarat, court cards have no value, therefore his total was eight. He won. His mouth was a crescent of triumph as the croupier shoveled five of my plaques across the table into no man's land.

The dark-haired treasure cast a sympathetic eye in my direction while exhaling vapor from her e-cigarette. I responded with a wry smile and a shrug to match. Contact established. Possibilities evolving.

On the green baize in the center of the table stood a hundred thousand euros—a useful pot.

"*Un banco de cent mil,*" the croupier droned.

At this point, I could either pass or commit the rest of my plaques. The sweaty Italian was watching me closely under lowered eyelids, the wide, flabby shoulders hunched with tension. Smoke from the cigarette in the ashtray by his arm rose in a spiral toward the hooded shades that illuminated the table; the no smoking rules were very relaxed in Monte's casinos. Around us floated a murmur of voices from other tables and the imperious cry of a croupier, "*Rien ne va plus!*"

"*Suivi.*" The word tripped spontaneously off my tongue. I couldn't back down before the woman in black. Even losing my stake was better than losing face.

The cards flicked across the baize. They lay there, pieces of pasteboard, inoffensive, yet deadly. Men have paid with their lives on a show of cards. I picked them up slowly and fanned them behind my hand: four and three made seven, a respectable tally, no more than that.

Fatso Italiano revealed his hand: six and an ace, also seven. Equal to mine. Unlike *vingt-et-un*, a draw at baccarat does not result in a win for the bank, so I could let it ride. The other players would expect it.

Ordinarily, I would have done just that.

The lady across the table was twiddling with a wayward tendril of hair. Her gaze was on me, and there was no flinching now when I held it. Then, as I was about to settle for the hand I had and lay my cards face down on the baize, her chin rose a fraction and her lips puckered ever so slightly in a blown kiss.

In a sudden rush of madness, incited by that tiny gesture, I went for broke.

"A card," I said to the Italian. His eyebrows did a vertical ascent. He couldn't believe I would be so rash. He shot out the requested card, flicking it across. His expression said he was convinced I was making a mistake, big-time. I faced the card—a two! A total of nine, the maximum count. An unbeatable hand. The Italian would likewise have to draw a deuce to save himself and his stake.

His card slid out of the shoe and it was a nine, giving him sixteen, less the ten, since only the final digit counts at baccarat; a final total of six. It was over and he was busted. My heart nearly went out to the guy. Sweat was soaking his jet-black hair and he looked like a fat wet cat. He regarded me stonily and without warmth. I hoped he wasn't a big wheel in the Cosa Nostra; you never could be sure with Italians in Monte.

A huge mound of plaques was shoveled across to me. I tossed five hundred euros to the croupier, who signaled a *huissier* to wheel my small fortune off to the *caisse*. For me the game was over. This game at any rate. If I was not mistaken another, altogether more old-fashioned game, was about to commence.

"*Bonsoir, monsieur*," the croupier said effusively. "*Merci, à bientôt*."

"*Je vous en prie*," I responded.

The dark-haired dish was on her feet too, murmuring in the ear of a *huissier*. He glanced sharply at me and responded in an undertone.

I circled the table as she vacated her place, leaving the *huissier* in charge of her quite respectable pile of plaques.

"Mr. Warner, I presume?" she said, beating me to the introductions. At close quarters I still couldn't fault her looks, though the make-up had been laid on thick as oil paint on a portrait. Her low-cut bodice exposed most of the suntanned uplands of her breasts. No artificial uplift was detectable. Down in my private jungle the tom-toms were pounding.

"And you'll be Dr. Livingstone," I rejoined, taking her arm. She let me steer her across the prairie of red carpet to the nearest bar. As we walked past walls adorned with tapestries and paintings that symbolized the splendor of a bygone era, I couldn't resist a sidelong peek down the front of her dress. All was in shadow, mysterious and exciting.

"What do I really call you?" I enquired, once we were installed on the high padded bar stools.

"Mrs. Folkov," was what it sounded like. She spelt it out for me. "That's V-o-l-k-o-w."

I wagged my finger censoriously. "Mrs. Is a title I don't recognize."

"All right." She gave in without a song and dance, an excellent omen. "Drucilla, then—or Dru, if you prefer."

"Hello, Dru. I'm André."

She didn't ask about my French first name in conjunction with my Anglo-Saxon family name. Didn't care, was my guess. If I read her correctly, she was looking for a stud, a foil for her sexual appetite. No problem. I had years of experience playing the lead in that cameo.

The dry Martinis I had ordered appeared. We raised our glasses, eyes exchanging signals over the rims.

"Where's Mr. Volkow?" I said, for the sake of form, not curiosity.

"On the yacht."

"The yacht? Would that be the big job with the yellow funnel that sailed in last night?"

She nodded.

"So-o-o," I said thoughtfully, privately impressed. "You're not short of a dollar or two. Which means, I don't have to offer you any to get you where I want you."

Some women might have been insulted. Not this one.

"I never refuse money," she said brazenly. "And where might you want to get me?"

"I believe in showing, not telling." I swallowed the rest of my drink. "Your place or mine?"

"I have a room at the Hotel de Paris across the road, if that's any use to you."

Convenient anyhow. "You don't sleep on the yacht then?" I said innocently.

She gurgled into her glass. "Sure, I *sleep* on the yacht."

The penny dropped.

"Oh...and I thought I was being forward."

She took my hand, squeezed it. "You know, you're the best looking man I've met in a long time."

"Thank you."

"I wonder though...is that all you are? Just a handsome poser. Or do you have something special between your legs."

"If size matters to you, Mrs. Volkow—Dru—I don't think you'll have any complaints. The question is, will you be able to accommodate me?"

"If I can't," she breathed, "you'll be the first."

A pink arrowhead of a tongue wormed around the outside of her lips, a come-on of such blatancy, it gave me an instant boner.

"We'd better go," she murmured. "Talking about it is making me all wet."

I blinked and was about to counter with some equally debauched patter when she said, "Do you *know* that man?" She was staring toward the wide corridor that led to the *salon privé*.

"What man?" Right then I wasn't interested in men, but I dutifully twisted my neck round for a look-see.

"He's been watching us ever since we came into the bar."

Had my mind not been full of Mrs. Drucilla Volkow, I might have reacted a bit faster. The man in question, lurking by a square pillar in the center of the corridor, dressed in an ill-fitting tuxedo, was Harley Boy, mustachioed motorbiker, in league with Herr Schelling. While recognition was still dawning on me he took off as if jet-propelled.

"Wait for me in the hotel lobby," I called to Dru over my shoulder as I shot across the bar after him, using my elbows to clear a path through the multitude. Abuse flared in my wake.

I passed the startled commissionaire and burst out of the main entrance into the cool night air. Harley Boy was doing a hundred yard dash across the Place du Casino, past the gleaming ranks of Rolls-Royces, Ferraris, and Maseratis. Heads swiveled to watch him go.

If he hadn't tried to cross the road just as a procession of taxis came sweeping round the central traffic island, I would have lost him. As it was, the cars obstructed his line of flight. He teetered at the curbside like a becalmed sailing boat. I plunged down the casino steps and across the square toward him. Late-night strollers stepped aside, no doubt gawking at the unusual spectacle of a man in a tux pursuing another man in a tux through the tranquil streets of crime-free Monte Carlo.

With me closing on him fast, Harley Boy discarded the idea of crossing the road. Instead, he accelerated toward the Café de Paris via the central island, plunging into the jungle of luxurious vegetation that sprouted there. But he had dithered too long and I was right on his heels. With a flying tackle that would have won me a standing ovation at Montreal's football stadium, I brought him down.

We rolled over in the lush grass, screened from spectators by shrubs and bushes, and fetched up against a fan palm. I tried to put an arm-lock on him but he was as slippery as a bar of wet soap. No sooner had I got a firm grip on a skinny wrist when it dissolved and left me clutching at air. His knee homed in on my groin, and I doubled up to protect myself. Wriggling free, he staggered to his feet. A slim-bladed stiletto leapt into his hand, as neat a conjuring trick as I ever witnessed. A savage grin illuminated his features. The slick, smooth way he'd summoned up that foot of steel, now flashing and winking at me as it caught the casino lights, warned me that it wasn't just window dressing.

"Not such a big man now, *hein?*" he said in the lilting accent of the Midi. He was right. I wasn't eager to rush in and mix it with that overgrown knitting needle even with the switchblade in my inside pocket.

If I wasn't quite as slick on the draw as Harley Boy, I was still fast enough to wipe away his smirk. The newly-sharpened blade came out with a businesslike clunk. Now we were equal, or at any rate less unequal. Not since my Secret Service days had I used a knife in anger. My technique was bound to be rusty.

"Now listen," I said in French, making soothing gestures. "I'm not looking for a fight. Just tell me why you're following me, that's all. Who's paying you?"

His teeth bared like the fangs of a rabid dog.

"Fuck you, *conard!*"

To reinforce the insult, he feinted with the knife, the tip of the blade at throat height. It occurred to me that I might have picked the wrong man to cross blades with. He handled that sticker as if he was born clutching it.

Outside the traffic island, life was still going on as normal. Car tires swished incessantly round the tight bend of the Avenue de Monte Carlo. A few feet away, there were voices of passersby. I could have bolted, throwing pride to the winds. On the other hand, I had been angling for a confrontation. The opportunity might not occur again.

I decided to see it through. At arm's-length, we circled each other, searching for an opening.

"*Allons-y, mon brave,*" he taunted. "I'm going to cut you into little pieces and feed you to the fish in the harbor."

Teeth bared, he feinted again, then lunged for real, missing my rib cage by no more than a couple of centimeters; another feint and lunge combination. He knew his business all right. At the third lunge, I deflected his weapon with a crude sidelong slash, turning the blade aside and almost disarming him in the process. Luck, not skill, but it proved he wasn't unbeatable. He came at me once more, and I made the only evasive move open to me—a backward hop to get out of range. He swore as I slashed defensively, a blur of crisscross swipes, no finesse at all. Now he had me on the run. A succession of thrusts followed while I hopped and skipped, all the while giving ground, staying just ahead of that lethal length of steel, until my back thudded against the fan palm and I could retreat no more.

"*Enfin, mon petit,*" he purred as he closed in.

The needle-thin point lanced at my gut, a vicious thrust that would have gone clean through me had it connected. I saved myself by sidestepping, lifting my knife to deflect his. The stiletto went through my jacket under the armpit, missing my sacred flesh and pinning me to the tree by my sleeve. My own knife was still on the descent and it didn't stop until it cleaved into his right bicep, up as far as the hilt. His yodel of pain brought a hush down on the square.

He wrenched free and the switchblade went with him. With his good arm, he lashed out. His fist smashed into my cheekbone and sent me stumbling, my sleeve still attached to the tree. I landed in an aggressive cactus plant. Multiple spines pierced my backside, doing more damage with that wild blow than all his previous efforts put together. To avoid drawing attention to our fracas, I converted a howl to a hiss of breath through clenched teeth.

Then Harley Boy was gone, abandoning his stiletto, which protruded at right angles from the tree, pinning my torn sleeve. Impaled on the cactus, still groggy from his fluky punch, I let him go.

His noisy exit had attracted a lot of interest from the folks in the vicinity. Excited chatter close by spurred me on. I wrenched my sleeve free of the blade, followed by my backside free of the cactus. Heading away from the rising hubbub, I emerged on the far side of the island into a deserted part of the square. The stiletto I left in the tree. It bore no incriminating evidence. No Warner prints, and—thank God—no Warner blood for the forensic experts to analyze.

I brushed loose dirt and other nameless adhesions from my clothing and transferred wallet and keys from jacket to pants pockets. I bundled up the ruined jacket and deposited it in a garbage bin and made off toward the Hotel de Paris where hopefully, Mrs. Drucilla Volkow still lay in wait. It took more than a duel with knives and a few spines in the butt to douse my ardor. At the hotel entrance the commissionaire in his smart beige outfit, bedecked with braid and brass buttons, paced back and forth. He gaped at my disheveled appearance, stuttered a belated, "*Bonsoir, monsieur.*"

"*Un accident,*" I muttered to avert embarrassing questions. "I'm visiting Madame Volkow."

To explain more would have been to explain too much. I swept regally past him into the hotel foyer. It was all but deserted. No Dru anxiously awaited my return. My desirable wanton had run out on me.

A rotund, uniformed figure popped up from a doorway behind the front desk.

"Monsieur Varnair?"

"*Oui*," I barked, letting my displeasure show. He took a backward step in alarm.

"Er...I am the night porter," he said, round-eyed. "Mrs. Volkow asks that you join her in Room 202."

It was one of those times when I was happy to be proved wrong. In my haste to rejoin Dru, I gave the porter a euro note without even checking the denomination. By his incredulous reaction, I had erred on the side of profligacy. I spurned the elevator and mounted the wide, curving staircase in bounds. The cactus had left a few souvenirs in my flesh, and my exertions reminded me of it. Maybe I could get Dru to play nurse.

Room 202 had a mahogany-stained door with a large buzzer set in the center. I thumbed it.

"Enter," came an immediate invitation from the other side.

I did as I was bid, passing through a short vestibule into the day room. And there she was, disappointingly still clothed in that black dress, though her hair was uncoiled and hung to her narrow waist in a shimmering cataract.

"You took your time," she accused, her eyes roving over my tux-less top half. "And just look at you. Have you been mugged or something?"

"Sort of. I did the mugging myself. That guy I went after has been tailing me and I wanted to ask him why."

"It doesn't look as if you asked very nicely." She held a glass half full of green liquid: *crème de menthe*. "You want something to put the zest and zing back into you?"

"Don't mind if I do. Scotch and soda, if you've got it."

"What happened?" she said as she poured an unstinting snifter. "Did he get away?"

I touched my bruised cheekbone. "Yes, but not intact."

"You don't say. Better not tell me more. I don't want to be an accessory after the fact, or whatever."

"Maybe we ought to do something besides talk."

"Now you're talking," she said, grinning.

She crooked a finger and went through an open door on my left: the bedroom, naturally. I tagged along obediently. The immediate impression was of light. Lots of it, including some freestanding spotlights placed strategically round the bed. So it was to be that kind of session. I didn't mind. I much preferred to see the goods on offer—in particular, a landscape as scenic as Mrs. Drucilla Volkow's.

She set her drink down on a small table at the head of an emperor-sized four-poster bed and faced me—with a knife in her slender white hand.

I'd had my fill of knives for this evening. She might just have wanted me to slice a lemon, but I wasn't staying to find out. I went full astern.

"Don't be stupid!" she exclaimed. "I want you to cut it off!"

That slowed me. "What?" I said weakly, misunderstanding, my hand instinctively shielding my crotch. "Cut what off?"

"My dress, dummy." She reversed the knife so that the black plastic haft pointed toward me. "Cut it off!"

Now she was talking in a language I could understand. I didn't protest about ruining an expensive dress, that was her business and Mr. Volkow's money. With his luxury yacht and all, he could surely afford to have them run up by the dozen.

I deposited my glass next to hers, so it wouldn't feel lonely, and relieved her of the knife. I gathered her in my arms, squeezed some flesh, and got busy with the knife. The tatters of the dress plus some scraps of coordinated underwear accumulated around her ankles. Then things got seriously interesting. I thought I had experienced all the variations on the sexual intercourse theme. I even kidded myself I might teach her a technique or two. Boy, had she got news for me! Compared with Dru Volkow, I was still at the apprentice stage.

When it was all over, I got her to extract the cactus thorns and bristles still embedded in my backside. She was good at it, though her bedside manner left a lot to be desired. Within a few minutes I was pronounced thorn-free. She slathered some antiseptic cream over the wounded zone.

"Nice butt," she remarked, then settled on her back for a cigarette.

"It takes one to know one."

I stretched out beside her, smarting and not yet recovered from post-coital *tristesse*. All was quiet except for the rhythm of our breathing and the muffled throb of the city's night-time pulse.

Cigarette smoked and stubbed, she raised her beautiful head, the raven hair in disorder, the make-up smeared. By God, she was an eyeful. Still hotly desirable. Still ripe for mischief.

"Well?" she said, propping herself up on one elbow. Her finger traced a line down the center of my forehead, over my nose and down my chin.

"Well what?"

"Don't tell me you're a just a one-fuck wonder?"

———

I BREAKFASTED with Dru at a window table from where I could see out over the lavish casino gardens across the point to the sparkling blue vista of the Med. Except it wasn't sparkling this particular morning. A rare sea mist cast a clammy shroud over it, and all was damp and dismal.

Of necessity, I was dressed casually in a shirt and tux pants, the latter not quite restored to their former glory by the hotel's damage control service. Dru was as bright and merry as the weather was dull and gloomy. She wore a jersey dress of blue and white diagonal bands, her hair tied loosely back with a matching ribbon. She had confessed to thirty-six summers, but could have passed for a lot less this morning. Conversely, I felt all of *my* thirty-eight summers, plus a few winters beyond. Sleep had not been on the menu.

"What will Mr. Volkow say?" I asked as I trickled orange juice over my tonsils.

"About?"

"Your all-night absence."

Her eyes flared wickedly as she leaned forward, deliberately to give me an eyeful of the panorama down the loose front of her dress.

"He won't care. He spent all night at the tables."

I spluttered over a mouthful of juice. "You mean...he was in the *casino* all night? Just across the road?" I glanced round furtively. Cuckolded husbands were not high on my list of 'must meet' people. "He isn't here, is he?"

Dru clapped her hands together in delight. "Oh, you're a peach! Of course he isn't here. He went back to the yacht at about six. He'll be sound asleep right now, don't you worry."

"But you haven't been on board. How do you know all this?"

"I have my sources," she said with a wink.

I selected a croissant and tore off a chunk. "Pass the apricot jelly, will you?"

Eyes twinkling, she obliged.

I was spooning out a generous helping when a group of people—three women and two men—entered the breakfast room, talking loudly. I only glanced casually in their direction, as you do, but it was as if I had stepped on a live cable. A tingling sensation travelled from my feet to my scalp.

Lovely as she was, Drucilla Volkow was definitely an also-ran alongside Georgina Gregg, one of three women in the group, and the cause of my temporary paralysis. The sight of her instantly put the clock back six weeks. She was seated now, her profile darkly silhouetted against the big bay window, the firm jaw, straight nose and high forehead all splendidly outlined for my appreciation. As yet, she wasn't aware of me, but my moonstruck gaze raised an acid laugh in Dru.

"I've a rival already, I see," she said. "Somebody you know, or just somebody you'd like to know?"

The jelly spoon was still poised above my plate. The jelly itself had slid off, missing the plate and lay like a red amoeba on the table-cloth. I scooped it up.

"Somebody I know," I replied, dabbing my lips with a napkin. "If you don't mind, Dru, I'll just say hello. Be back before you know it."

She waved her croissant airily. "Don't mind me, lover." The words sounded easy-come, easy-go. Her tone belied them, oozing pure bile.

Gina didn't exactly shout for joy when, tendering apologies to her party, I greeted her in the manner of a long-lost school pal. I asked for a word with her in private, and her friends, all French and all middle-aged, excused us. Conscious of Dru's basilisk glare, I hustled Gina out of the breakfast room.

"Hey, how about this for serendipity," I gushed. "I thought I'd never see you again."

"Really?" She was cool, neutrally polite. No matter. I wasn't about to be brushed off again.

"I won't keep you. I just wondered if you're free tomorrow."

A wary shadow passed across her face. "And what if I were?"

She had a nice feel for the subjunctive mood.

"If you are, or were, you could come sailing with me. Just for the day. We'll leave early, be back before dark, and then you can decide whether you want to put yourself in mortal peril by dining with me."

All this came out a bit garbled in my anxiety to get my proposition over in full, before she could voice a rejection.

The green eyes, with their slumberous lids, ran a tape measure over me and my motives. Me and my motives both. It was like being under a hospital scanner.

"The son of a friend will be coming along, too," I improvised in case she was averse to being alone with me. I only hoped Jean-Pierre didn't have other plans for Pascal. "He's only ten if you're wondering about gang-bangs."

She smiled then, setting off a fireworks display inside me. "You sure don't give up easily, and you have an impressive pitch, Mr., Warner."

"André... remember?"

"Sure. André." She still had me under scrutiny. I smiled encouragement. "I don't know..."

On a hard-to-get scale of 1 equals pushover, to 10 equals lesbian, I rated her a 9.

"What are you afraid of?"

"Strings."

She'd remembered then. She was smiling again, albeit obliquely. The iron curtain was melting.

"Not a string in sight, same as before," I assured her.

"All right, you've sold me." The capitulation was sudden, almost as if she had planned it all along. "Or I should say your boat's sold me. Tomorrow then. The *Seamist*, I believe you said your boat's called?"

"Yes. She's moored on the Quai Antoine."

"Cool. Expect me at nine."

She breezed off and the roll of her *derrière* had me mentally panting.

I hurried back to make my peace with Dru, not quite ready to burn that particular boat just yet.

CHAPTER SIX

JEAN-PIERRE BROUGHT PASCAL aboard shortly after the sun climbed over the top of the harbor wall, and from then on *Seamist* was full of chatter and laughter as he helped make her ready for sea. I put on a carefree show for his benefit, though truthfully, I wasn't in the best of spirits. My second night with Dru—now restored to her obliging spouse—had brought me to a low-water mark in my relationship with the female of the species.

When it came to finer feelings, such as affection, tenderness, and, yes...love, I had spent years living in arid country, irrigated only by copulation. And far from showing signs of flagging as I grew older, I seemed driven by lust to pile depravity on debauchery, collecting sexual exploits like medals. Someplace, somehow, I had mislaid my moral compass.

What made me pause now for such profound reflection was a tiny star that had crept over my dark horizon, its twinkle so feeble it surely could not survive; a star by the name of Georgina. It had moved me to examine my code of behavior. Misbehavior, rather. Seeing Gina again at the Hotel de Paris made me realize that she had rarely been far from my thoughts during my six-week absence. An amorphous figure, lying dormant, waiting to be beckoned into the limelight. Now that figure had acquired depth, color and substance. With this girl it might yet be possible for me to recapture lost emotions and trashed morals.

"Don't be so bloody sentimental," I said aloud, giving a vicious turn to the rigging screw I was tightening.

Pascal, coiling a warp nearby, glanced up. "*Comment?*"

"Nothing," I said with an uneven grin. "I was talking to myself, Pascal. It's a very bad habit."

"Is it? I do it all the time. Especially when I want something very much."

I could see his point. That's how it was with me right now.

My watch told me Gina was due any minute. Sure enough, when I next raised my head, a familiar figure was passing the Customs office. My heart gave a hop, skip, and a jump. Her effect on me was without precedent since Marion.

She was all in white: biker shorts, T-shirt that stuck to her torso like wallpaper, and practical gym shoes. A red-and-white duffel bag was slung over her shoulder.

I hitched up my shorts, pulled on my striped matelot's T-shirt, and went to welcome her aboard. She spotted me and waved. I waved back, but looked beyond her, a swift, uneasy survey of the promenade for Schelling and/or his Harley Boy buddy. Suddenly, I was afraid—not for myself, for Gina. If my enemies got the idea she and I were an item—even if we weren't—what better way to apply pressure than through her? I was used to having only my own skin to worry about. Worrying about someone else's was a whole new box of tricks. Dark memories of Marion's corpse clutched at my heart.

Gina arrived at the gangplank, teeth flashing in that generous mouth, an ad-man's dream. Two guys on a launch called *Sailaway,* occupying the next berth to mine, blatantly ogled her.

My helping hand was politely spurned in a statement of independence. I relieved her of her duffel bag, then stood there, feeling as awkward as a country yokel at a high society ball.

Pascal rescued me, skating along the coaming, nimble as a grasshopper, accosting Gina with a cheerful, "*Bonjour, madame!*"

She bestowed such a radiant smile on him that he was immediately captivated.

"*Bonjour* yourself," she returned, and in French asked him his name.

"Pascal Pradelou," he said. "I live with my father in Roquebrune."

"I'm Gina. I live in Marseille."

The idea of addressing her as Gina would have secretly horrified him. True to his nationality he would insist on addressing her as *madame*.

I'd neglected to prime her about Pascal's family circumstances. Fortunately, she was enough of a diplomat not to ask about his mother. They exchanged a few more pleasantries in French and generally got acquainted, while I checked the rest of the rigging screws.

"You've crewed on a sailboat before, am I right?" I said to Gina when she came over to me.

"Uh-huh. Smaller boats than this, dinghies really, but I guess the principles are the same. My tutor told me dinghies are harder to sail, not easier. Everything happens so fast you need the reflexes of a fighter pilot."

"You'll be able to do your share here then." I twanged the shroud whose tension I was adjusting and gave the screw another quarter turn. "Have you breakfasted? There's coffee in the galley, just needs heating up."

"Thanks, but I'm fine."

"How true."

She absorbed the compliment without letting it go to her head.

"Let's get the show on the road." I slipped into my businesslike skipper's mode. "I thought we'd go along the coast to Villefranche, have lunch there, and come back early evening for dinner."

"Sounds lovely." She moved aside to let me pass. I went across the cockpit to where Pascal was inspecting the lifelines for wear and tear.

"All okay, *chef?*" I asked him, resting a hand on his shoulder.

He made a circle of forefinger and thumb.

I operated the fume detector, let it run for thirty seconds then punched the starter button. The Perkins grumbled awake, settling quickly into the customary diesel clank.

Gina, unasked, was standing by to cast off the two stern mooring ropes. Pascal had grabbed a boathook and was heading for the bow to fend off in case I bungled the operation, a not unknown occurrence.

"Let go aft," I sang out.

Gina unhitched the two lines, her movements economical and assured. I injected some throttle and we eased forward, our fenders barely nudging the yacht moored to port. Pascal's boathook was happily surplus to requirements. Gina flopped down on the cockpit seat next to me, her cheeks flushed, hair swirling in the breeze that pounced on us as we cleared the line of boats.

"A happy coincidence, your being a sailor girl," I remarked.

She just nodded, gazing ahead toward the harbor entrance. We were passing the bows of the Volkow motor yacht by the harbor mouth. Even up close, the yacht was nothing less than immaculate. No tell-tale stains below the anchor hawsehole or the various discharge ports.

The wind was blowing from the northeast, so we would be running before it along the coast until we reached the Cap Ferrat peninsula. Rounding the peninsula would call for several directional changes, gybe-ing from downwind to wind abeam. For the final leg, to Villefranche harbor, we would have to tack or use the engine. No need to decide yet.

As we motored out of the harbor, *Seamist*, even with no canvas set, heeled slightly before the stiff breeze. Gina took the helm while Pascal and I, safety lines attached, raised the mainsail. The boat responded immediately as the canvas whipped and snapped and filled.

"Cut the engine," I shouted to Gina while trimming the sheets.

As she complied, *Seamist*, while in fact losing way, gave the impression of surging forward. Now the motor no longer drowned the rush of the hull through the water and the strum of the wind in the rigging.

The headsail was already on deck in its bag. With Pascal's help, I hooked it onto the forestay, and attached the sheets and halyards to the mast. Up it went, fluttering like a bird with a broken wing, then hardening, the canvas becoming a taut curve. The increase in speed was at once apparent. She was doing six or seven knots, I estimated, and would do better still if the breeze continued to stiffen.

I could now afford to relax and drink in the unique sensation of wind-powered motion. It has a therapeutic quality, soothing and yet sensual—almost a love act. Released from his crewing duties, Pascal went to fetch his fishing gear. I added a notch of tension to the sheets and found a space in the cockpit beside Gina, careful to leave a few virtuous centimeters between us to avoid accusations of making a pass.

"Your boat's lovely," she said, one hand rested lightly on the wheel, the other on her bare thigh. I wished we could swap hands. "You enjoy the good things in life, don't you, André? Boat, flash sports car. What else have you got tucked away, a private jet?"

"No, that's the lot." I had detected a note of censure. "Possessions for their own sake don't appeal to me, if that's what you're thinking. I only want things that give pleasure."

"Spoken like a true lotus eater." Still the reproving tone, not softened by a smile.

Instead of justifying myself further I lapsed into a sulk.

Gina sensed it, I guessed, and tried to make amends.

"I didn't mean to be bitchy, André. You're a likeable guy. I wouldn't be here if you weren't. It's just how I feel about the general trend toward accumulating possessions. Believe me, I'm as guilty in that respect as you are, probably more so. I just don't have the money to indulge my tastes. Let's call it envy and leave it at that."

Though not entirely mollified, I let that line of talk atrophy. We chatted banalities for a while.

The breeze was freshening. I went into the wheelhouse and bent an ear to the radio for the latest weather information. A mistral was building and was expected to hit the area by mid-afternoon. This would swing the wind round from northeast to northwest. Very convenient for us, as we would be able to run before it on the homeward leg.

"If you'd like to take over," Gina said when I got back to my seat, "I'll do my little woman bit and rustle up some coffee."

"You're on. Make it orange juice or a Pepsi for Pascal."

"Leave it to me." She relinquished the helm and went forward, ducking under the hatch and presenting her comely bottom. From this angle the biker shorts bordered on indecent.

The wind was already shifting, veering degree by degree toward the north, forcing me to ease the sheets. It wasn't yet inhibiting our progress, which so far had been rapid. By eleven-thirty we were rounding Cap Ferrat. At that point it was all hands on deck ready to gybe. Gina took the helm again, leaving Pascal and me free to deal with the sails. We commenced our turn to leeward, the canvas flapping and the sheets snaking with the uncertain movement of the boom. Pascal had unhitched the headsail from the starboard cleat and it whipped away like a wild thing, almost wrenching the sheet from his grasp. Tempted as I was to take over, I let him battle on alone. He wouldn't have thanked me for intervening. The crisis quickly passed, with Pascal keeping his cool throughout. Jean-Pierre would have been proud of him.

The rugged shoreline of the Cap Ferrat peninsula, with its toytown of playboy homes, slid by to starboard. In the foreground, sailboards zigzagged, their sails splashing the scene with color; the Côte d'Azur at its most beguiling.

Within a half hour we were tying up at a mooring buoy in Villefranche's tiny port, cuddled up to an overfed cabin cruiser. Pascal opted to stay on board for lunch. I chucked the tender over the side and rowed ashore to fetch him a takeaway meal: hamburgers and French fries with lashings of ketchup. Gina and I left him wolfing this unwholesome repast and I did a second stint at the oars.

We strolled along the cobbled quayside to the Mère Germain restaurant, securing the last vacant outdoor table. From the terrace the port was just in sight around the edge of the Chapelle St. Pierre, lying under the towering walls of the Citadelle.

An orange-and-white gingham tablecloth was spread over our table and places speedily set. Menu, wine, and starters came in quick succession. We ate hungrily and soaked up the sun, the scenery, and the French chatter around us.

"When it comes to cuisine, the French still leave the rest standing," Gina observed, draining the butter sauce from a mussel shell. "I couldn't imagine going back to live in the States."

"Not on account of the food, anyhow," I quipped.

She laughed at that.

"But let's not get drawn into a discussion on the merits of French versus American cooking," I said. "I meant to ask you. What are you doing in Monaco right now, if I'm not being too nosy?"

"Not at all. I'm with my boss. We have a branch office there and he visits it once a month. Now and again, I get to tag along."

I squinted askance at that.

She interpreted the workings of my mind and giggled.

"You couldn't be more wrong. His wife accompanies him more often than not. You saw her at the hotel yesterday morning, the tall woman with auburn hair. Anyway, he's not interested in me in that way."

"You don't say. Looked in a mirror lately?" It was meant as a throwaway, but the tenor of my voice said different.

She gave me a fast, funny look. "André..." She stopped, began concentrating very hard on splitting open a stubborn mussel shell and fumbling it.

To put her at ease, I launched a different subject, relating my first and last participation in the Fastnet race a few years back when a storm blew up. Not as bad as the infamous 1979 disaster, but bad enough. I'd been crewing for Jacques Lalanne on *Le Vainqueur*, and we were forced to batten down the hatches and heave to with bare poles and a sea anchor. It made a dramatic tale and she listened enraptured, the mussels forgotten.

"But what happened to the missing crew member? Wasn't he ever found?"

"No, only a sneaker and a packet of condoms. They were picked up by an Irish trawler off the Lizard Rock."

"A packet of *condoms*? How did you know they were his?"

"We didn't, not for sure. But he used to be a boy scout, so it was a reasonable assumption."

She was slow on the uptake. "A boy scout?" Then her face cleared and she appreciated the joke.

After that, I made a point of avoiding personal comments. We ranged over topics as diverse as my love for classical music to her escapades at the Sorbonne. There, so she claimed, the *concierge* was bribed to let the *fleurs-de-nuit*, as the more adventurous young ladies were christened, back into the building in the early hours in return for a quick grope. Until one day the quick grope became a quick rape, followed by a quick ten-year stretch in the Chateau d'If prison; a salutary experience.

"You steered well clear of all that, of course," I said.

Her eyebrows wriggled indignantly. "Are you implying I'm a prude?"

It had crossed my mind.

"No," I white lied. "It's just that I think I'm beginning to know you better and I don't see you letting some seedy concierge stick...er, get familiar with you. Am I wrong?"

"No, you're not wrong. As a matter of fact..." She hesitated. I kept quiet. "What I was going to say was...I've only ever...you know, made out...with my husband."

A shrewd hands-off-I'm-not-a-pushover ploy. Superfluous. I'd already received that particular message weeks ago.

"Why I should be telling you this, I can't figure." Her frown was for herself, not me. "Normally, I keep my personal stuff personal."

"Must be the effect I'm having on you."

Just then, the main course was placed before us. We dropped the sensitive subjects and tucked into a succulent *bouillabaisse à la Provençale*. As I chewed, however, I mulled over her professed fidelity, and it fueled the fires she had already lit inside me. Sure, the part of me I wasn't proud of still wanted the clothes off that lithe body, still wanted to bed her, only somehow the sexual urge had declined. Or perhaps it was the same as ever and other priorities had superseded it. For instance, I badly wanted to earn her respect, her esteem. Call it what you will. Dragging her off to the bushes caveman-style was not going to win her over.

Toward the end of the meal I happened to glance up at the sky and noticed clouds looming over the Mount Gros observatory that sits atop the mountains behind Nice. Great clumps of stratocumulus with fleecy edges, like tattered flags of truce, were forming. The wind was blowing from the northwest; force four at least. The sea was thrashing against the harbor mouth, the masts of the moored yachts oscillating in the swell.

"Something's brewing up there," I pointed out casually.

She looked up. "Holy crap! We're in for a storm."

"Afraid so. Question is: do we sit it out here or head back home in the hope of outrunning it?"

"I've been at sea in a storm before," she said slowly, considering it. "And in a smaller boat than yours."

A gust lifted the edge of the tablecloth at a recently-vacated table and sent an empty wine glass crashing to the floor in a burst of splinters.

Somebody exclaimed, *"Ooh-la-la!"* and seconds later a waitress emerged, armed with brush and pan.

I called for the bill. "Glad to hear you've been blooded. Okay, then. If you're game, we'll try and run ahead of it."

"Aye, aye, skipper."

Maybe it was the wine, or maybe she was beginning to loosen up naturally. Whatever it was, she swayed against me as she spoke, her hair touching my cheek, the smell of it teasing my nostrils. It smelled clean and fresh, with just a hint of lightly perfumed shampoo. It smelled of woman, too, and it excited me. I craved to make some small intimate gesture of my own. It was a craving so intense it was almost a physical hurt. Then she was sitting upright once more and the psychological opening had slammed shut.

The Harbormaster's office gave me the latest weather report. Wind from the northwest, rising to force five, gusts to force six or seven. Squalls, too, possibly heavy, dying out before nightfall. The good news was that the heart of the storm was expected to pass over Nice, which meant that the coastline between Villefranche and Monaco should escape the brunt of it.

I rowed us back through the choppy green waters of the harbor to *Seamist*, and we made ready for sea. Pascal and I secured the tender to the cabin top. We all donned lifejackets and harnesses, before upping anchor and going astern to get clear of the fat cabin cruiser that bucked alongside us.

Immediately we cleared the harbor mouth, up went the main and headsails. We were running before the wind again, south-by-south west, down the side of the peninsula toward Cap Ferrat point. It pushed us along like a train. In no time at all we were abeam of the Cap lighthouse and preparing to gybe.

Then the sun went out, as if a light had been switched off. One minute, blazing sunshine on our backs, the sails so brilliantly white it hurt to look at them, the spray from our leaping bows bursting over us in rainbows; the next minute a great shadow was draped over everything. We all looked up together and I gasped involuntarily. An enormous purple-black canopy, extending as far as the eye could see, had rushed up behind us, blotting out half the sky. The wind speed had increased too, howling through the rigging, the sails ballooning, the mast flexing like a bow.

"My *God!*" Gina said at last, and she spoke for both of us.

The shore toward Villefranche was already lost behind a wall of rain, which meant the storm was no more than five kilometers away. Since low-pressure systems travel at twenty to twenty-five knots, it would hit us in a matter of minutes.

Lowering the sails became a matter of immediacy. With the wind behind us, this would be a difficult and potentially dangerous undertaking. I went ahead with the gybe and brought *Seamist* round into the wind. Then, with the Autohelm engaged and the motor at low revs, it was all hands to get the canvas off her. The deck was lurching and rolling crazily now and our task was not easy. As the headsail was freed from the restraint of the sheets, the wind took hold of it. We all stood to windward—less chance of becoming entangled in the flailing canvas—and used our combined body weight to suppress it. Even so, I collected a painful knock on the arm from a wayward shackle before the job was finished. The mainsail proved easier. It was down and lashed in half the time, the boom made secure by hitching the sheet round the block.

The sea was no longer blue but slate colored and angry, with curling crests that flung spindrift over us. The hump that was Cap Ferrat was fading, losing shape. It disappeared altogether as the deluge reached it, our last visual contact with land. All that remained now was the heaving, writhing sea and us. We might have been in the middle of the Atlantic. It was in our favor that the shore lay to windward, meaning I had no immediate worries about sea room. The storm would push us southeast, and the next piece of land was Corsica, more than a hundred and sixty kilometers distant. Rocks, not waves, present the greatest threat to small craft.

"Pascal, get below," I ordered, taking over from the Autohelm.

He objected to this banishment. "It's okay, I have my safety line."

"Get below, Pascal," I repeated and signaled to Gina, who was clipping her safety line to a stanchion. Observing the stubborn set of Pascal's jaw, she took firm hold of his skinny brown arm and pulled him toward the companionway.

He grumbled something, a last token protest, and unhitched his safety line. Simultaneously, the storm proper burst upon us: darkness, wind and rain, acting in concert. Except that the rain fell as hailstones the size of walnuts, bouncing off the boat and our bodies alike. Pascal slipped and went sprawling on the cockpit grating. While all three of us were momentarily distracted a rogue wave thumped into *Seamist*'s port bow. It was not gigantic as squall waves go, maybe twenty feet from trough to crest. Just big enough and vicious enough to push the bow sharply round to starboard, presenting our beam to the wind. We took a roll that sent the starboard rail under and tipped Pascal effortlessly out of the cockpit into the water. He didn't even have a chance to shout.

For a few vital seconds, Gina and I were held in thrall by the suddenness of it. Then with one accord we rushed to the side. Pascal was close under the lee of the boat, bobbing in his life jacket. I wrenched a lifebuoy from its seating and tossed it into the water. It was a hasty throw. I made no provision for the wind and it landed well beyond his reach. To add to our difficulties, *Seamist*, her wheel unmanned, was spinning round through one hundred and eighty degrees, and the seas were now breaking astern. She was pitching like a seesaw. Waves crashed aboard and swamped the cockpit, the hull shuddering under the impact. If I didn't get her bows back into the wind all three of us would be swimming in the Med.

"Take the wheel!" I yelled to Gina. "Bring her into the wind!"

Her reactions were fast and positive. I thanked my stars she knew boats. A novice would have been useless, a liability even. As it was, I could devote all my energies to retrieving Pascal. That in itself would be no mean feat. He was already drifting away at a frightening rate. Uppermost in my thoughts was that Jean-Pierre had entrusted his only son to me and I had placed his life in danger. Now, I had to save him. No matter what it cost me.

I unhitched my safety line—it wasn't long enough for me to leave it attached and still reach Pascal—and dived in. It wasn't the smartest way to recover a man overboard. My concern was that he would be lost from sight before I could get a line to him, as visibility was down to about fifty meters and worsening. I also feared that if I had tried to steer *Seamist* toward him and haul him back on board, I might have run him down. Lifesaving him was the best of a lousy set of alternatives.

The windbreak effect of *Seamist's* hull offered some temporary protection from the sea's turbulence and I made the most of it. I swam as I'd never swum before, and to hell with conserving my strength. Every second stroke I shouted encouragement to Pascal. He was doggy paddling toward me, his arm movements made awkward by the lifejacket.

We linked up and clung together, grinning in mixed relief and anxiety. Stage one was accomplished. I glanced back at *Seamist*. She was almost stern on to us now, a rolling cockleshell. The naked pole of her mast was swinging like a metronome against that mad boiling sky. Gina's face was a featureless oval in the murk. I had counted on her maintaining position. In reality she was doing a whole lot better than that, allowing the boat to be pushed steadily stern-first toward us while keeping her bow into the wind. She was quite a sailor.

With Pascal safely in tow, I resolved to save my strength for getting us both back on board. I would need it. It's notoriously difficult to climb over the gunwale of even a small boat from sea level. Hefting Pascal back aboard would be easy enough, with Gina pulling and me pushing. My worry was that, by then, I'd be too weak to save myself.

Seamist continued to slide backward. I could make out Gina's features now, her hair plastered flat to her scalp like a helmet, her eyes huge. But she was keeping her head, side-slipping under minimal power to pass us to port.

Then the bucking hull was looming over me, shutting out the dark sky with its own royal blue darkness. The lower lifeline was already uncoupled ready for our recovery. A safety line came curling over the side. Gina appeared and hung both arms down the side for Pascal to grasp.

With Autohelm engaged *Seamist* was cranky, her stern crabbing to port. I worked fast. I hooked the line to Pascal's harness, breathed in deeply and boosted him up as hard and as far as I could. Having nothing solid under my feet to provide purchase, it was a feeble effort. Nonetheless, it was just enough to launch Pascal into Gina's arms, and, less happily, to immerse me in the green depths.

When I emerged spluttering from my ducking, Pascal's feet were passing from sight over the gunwale. I let out a wet sigh of relief. Up until then, the boy's rescue had been my priority. Now that he was safe, my own survival became paramount. I had nothing to hang on to and staying close to the sleek hull was not easy in the raging seas.

"Gina!" I bawled. "Don't forget me!"

In the howling and crashing of the storm, my shouts sounded puny. Judging by her erratic behavior, *Seamist* was still on Autohelm and still pointing into the wind, climbing the steep white-capped rollers with ease and swooping into the long troughs. I yelled again, paddling closer beside the hull, careful to stay well clear of the spinning propeller that would chop slices out of my hide without missing a beat. A wave lifted me. I made a grab for the pulpit rail, my left hand locking around a stanchion. There I swung, my legs only centimeters from the propeller, unable to lift myself any higher. Waves pounded me almost continuously, salt water filling my nose and mouth. My stamina was dribbling away like sand through an egg timer.

"Gina!" I yelled again, almost a scream. My grip on the stanchion was loosening. Another big wave would rip me from it and that would be the end of me. I was inflating my lungs for a last mighty holler when I spotted the safety line dangling over the side, not half-a-dozen strokes away. It wouldn't lift me back aboard, but it would keep me in umbilical contact while I got my second wind. Somehow, enervated though I was, I had to swim for it. Either that or go under. Either that or die.

I swam, drawing on reserves I thought were all used up, and splashed wildly through the madness of the sea in the driving hail and wind. It was a matter of a few feet. It seemed like half an ocean, but I made it.

Even the action of clipping the line on was almost beyond me. Under the lee of the boat I was protected from the worst of the elements. But my fingers were numb, barely able to respond to the signals my brain sent. I succeeded finally. At the very instant the clip snapped into place, the line was reeled in from the cockpit. As it pulled taut, there was a flurry of impatient tugs, more annoyance than a serious attempt to raise me.

Gina's head rose over the gunwale, peering down. On sighting me, her mouth fell open. "André! Thank God! Wait a minute."

Before I could respond she was gone again, only to return with another safety line, which she lowered. I attached it. Now I was doubly secure, if still no nearer to climbing aboard.

"Can you haul me part of the way up the side?" I called.

"I'll try," she shouted through the strands of hair smeared across her face.

"Wait until she rolls to port." Hardly were the words uttered when *Seamist* did exactly that, pulling me clear of the water. For perhaps a second, the topsides were angled over, and I was sprawled across them, incapable of movement. With precision timing, Gina hauled on the two safety lines. I crashed into the cockpit just as the boat flipped the opposite way, onto her starboard side. If I hadn't clung to the wheel, I would have been tossed smartly back into the sea, almost certainly for good.

When *Seamist* rolled back again to port, I let gravity take me with her into the safety of the narrow space between the wheel binnacle and the seat. There I lay, utterly spent, an untidy squelching heap. Even speech was beyond me.

Presently, the storm moved on. The corkscrew motion of the hull moderated and the hail eased off, then abruptly ceased altogether. Pascal's voice came to me through a fog of exhaustion. I couldn't tell what he was saying, but he sounded all right. That was what counted, that Jean-Pierre's son had survived with nothing worse than a fright and a ducking.

More presently, the sun peeked out, warming me, beating against my closed eyes with a fierce cynical heat. I could almost believe it had never been away, that the storm had only happened in my imagination.

Groaning, I sat up.

There was Gina, sitting coolly behind the wheel, fluffing out her hair to dry it. And Pascal in his undershorts, cross-legged on the cockpit floor. He was the first to speak. "The storm's over, André. Are you all right now?"

"I think so, Pascal." I dredged up a shaky grin to reassure him, then remembered his own scary experience. "How about *you*?"

"Okay." He waved away his near-drowning as of no consequence.

"Thank you for saving me." He looked down and wouldn't meet my eyes, aware of his own culpability.

"Don't be silly. You'd do the same for me."

Gina's voice was strained. "I was sure you'd drowned. I...I ..." Her free hand covered her face.

"What happened after you pulled Pascal on board?" I asked. "Where were you?"

I was trying not to let it show, but I was pretty upset over being left to fend for myself. At least, that's how it had seemed to me when I was being tossed around in the drink.

"I'm sorry," she said, her face drawn. "First, I wanted to get Pascal inside out of danger. Then I...I slipped and fell—I must have stunned myself. The next thing I knew, I was lying on top of a safety line and someone was tugging it. That's when I saw you." She burst into tears and reached out to me. "Thank God you're safe."

Feeling like a heel, I got up to sit by her side, gently prizing her fingers away from the wheel.

"Don't cry, love," I said, holding her against me. Tears made tracks down her already salt-stained cheeks. "It wasn't your fault. I should never have put to sea in such conditions, with a storm forecast. I'm the one who should feel guilty."

She crossed my lips with a silencing finger. "Don't say that. I was just as much a party to it."

"I'm the skipper. I carry the can, for good or ill."

She fell silent but for the snuffles.

The sky overhead was back to standard Côte d'Azur azure, the black band of cloud fast receding to the south. The sea was still choppy though, and the wind shrilled through the yards. By the feel of it the temperature had dropped about ten degrees since we lunched on the quayside in Villefranche.

Pascal had taken up a position on Gina's flank and was making consoling noises, which ultimately raised a tearful smile.

"You're very sweet, Pascal," she said, clutching his hand. "You're both real sweet and I'm just being girly to get upset about it."

"I think you were very brave to handle the boat all alone," Pascal said, some of his father's charm breaking the surface. "It's not easy for a lady. You're not so strong as we men." Overlooking the fact that it was Gina who had hauled him to safety.

"You were bloody marvelous, Gina," I agreed. "And you, Pascal, you were brave for not panicking when you went overboard."

His chest puffed out with pride. "Oh, it was nothing special." His innate modesty would last only until he related the story to his friends, when he would, of course, assume the role of hero and savior.

"While we're all being so complimentary to each other," Gina cut in, wiping her nose with the back of her wrist, "you were the bravest of all, André. When you jumped in like that without your safety line, knowing how difficult it is to get back on board a boat this size, it...it..." She gulped, and the crying restarted. "It was the most courageous, most unselfish act I've ever seen." She finished through a spate of tears, again seeking solace in my arms.

"Make some coffee, will you, Pascal?" I said gruffly. "Then we'll get some canvas on her and make use of this wind."

I had brought *Seamist* back on course, north by northeast, running parallel to the shore. Gina still rested against me, and our two bodies swayed in harmony with the roll of the deck. Except for the steady beat of the diesel beneath us and the cries of a pair of gulls trailing us at masthead height, all was at peace in my world.

It was a strictly temporary state.

————

UNDER FULL SAIL we made it back to Monaco by six and, by prior arrangement, motored over to Roquebrune to restore Pascal to his father. Jean-Pierre had spent the day with another of Pascal's surrogate mothers, a fiery gypsy with copper-hued skin and a red gash of a mouth. She was preparing a light multi-course snack when we trooped in.

Over the meal an account was given of the day's events. Although I deliberately played down the violence of the storm, Jean-Pierre paled noticeably when I told him of Pascal's loss overboard. Afterward, his appetite was not what it had been.

Later in the evening when the feasting was over, he took me unobtrusively aside.

"I'm more grateful than you will ever know for what you did, André," he said, but his expression belied the plaudits. "I think that storm was worse than you say."

I held my tongue. I knew what was coming and, employee or not, he had the right to voice it.

"You know you should not have left Villefranche in the conditions you have described."

As a sailor whose skills surpassed mine, he wasn't asking, he was telling.

I just nodded. I felt lower than a snake's belly.

"I only want to say, I think you made a very serious mistake. Also, that you learned a lot today and you will not repeat this mistake. So if you ever wish to take Pascal sailing again in the future, it will be okay by me." His grin was the Jean-Pierre of old.

Too moved to speak, I gave him a tentative man-to-man hug. He would understand that far better than any words.

We rejoined the party to drink a toast to friendship. Various other toasts followed, until I lost count. We didn't stay late. Jean-Pierre clearly had plans for his gypsy rose. Though he protested as a matter of form when I announced our departure, he couldn't hide an antici-patory smirk.

I wasn't drunk, but my alcohol intake was certainly over the prescribed limit. So I piloted the Aston back through the winding streets as sedately as an undertaker at the wheel of a hearse. Gina sat with her head back and eyes closed.

"A nightcap before we part?" I ventured, expecting a refusal. "It's not yet eleven."

"Sure."

So I was wrong again. I didn't mind.

I squeezed into a space on the Quai Albert, and we mingled with a handful of late night drinkers at Victor Jammais' bar. Victor himself was there, yarning with a couple of regulars and didn't notice us right away. We ordered cognac and nibbled nuts and raisins from a dish on the counter.

"It's been quite a day," I observed.

"Not short on excitement," Gina agreed. She was contemplating the pink reflective tiles with which Victor, in his wisdom and bad taste, had covered selected areas of the wall.

"Don't say it," I chuckled. "Not in Victor's presence, at any rate."

The man himself chose that moment to gatecrash, inserting his long, svelte figure into the space between our stools.

"*Salut*, André," he said, smothering me in whisky fumes. "How goes it?"

"Could be worse. Have you met *Mademoiselle* Gregg?"

Instant charm spilled from Victor like water over a weir.

"I don't believe I've had the pleasure. *Enchanté, mademoiselle*." He bent his lips to Gina's hand. She accepted the gesture gracefully. "May I offer you both a drink?"

Of alcohol we had both had a sufficiency. Gina settled for a tomato juice, I for a non-alcoholic beer. Victor summoned them up, then said, "Someone came here today looking for you, André."

"Is that so?"

He swiveled his eyes toward Gina, an unspoken question.

"You can speak freely in front of *mademoiselle*," I assured him.

"As you wish. This man would not give his name. He asked where you were and I told him you were probably sailing." He knocked back his cognac in one go, running his tongue over thin and rather reptilian lips.

"He didn't say who he was or what he wanted me for?" My suspicions were aroused and multiplying.

"He told me nothing. He was over fifty, running to fat, and with not much hair. Also, he had a German accent."

Schelling. I was no longer surprised, just resigned.

"He offered to pay for information. He asked me where you stay in Monaco. Where you eat, who are your friends. Naturally, I answered none of his questions."

Gina butted in. "Do you know this man, André?"

"Vaguely." I squeezed Victor's shoulder. "Thanks, my friend. Let me know if he shows up again."

"Certainly. Now...if you will excuse me...*mademoiselle*, André." He drifted off, apparently aimlessly, yet when next I looked he was chatting up a lonely redhead at the end of the counter.

"You may find this hard to believe," I said to Gina, "but the guy

Victor just described has been trailing me ever since I left Geneva; him and others. It's beginning to get on my nerves."

"Why should anyone want to follow you? Are you in some kind of trouble?"

"Not as far as I'm aware," I hedged.

She turned to her drink, toying with the straw. I fell to addressing the problem of how to get Schelling and company off my back. When inspiration came, it came from nowhere, or maybe it was alcohol fueled. The idea that took root grew faster than Jack's beanstalk. Wherever I went, so did they. If I left town, if I headed home to Geneva, they would surely dog my footsteps, my tire tracks rather. At some point along the route an opportunity would arise to engineer the long overdue face-to-face showdown. Then again, on reflection, it would perhaps be safer to fly. Let the showdown take place on my home territory, in Geneva itself. Schelling had an apartment there. Our trails were bound to converge.

It was still a long shot. There was no certainty that Schelling or Harley Boy would come after me, or if they did, that either or both would stay at Schelling's apartment. But further brain-racking produced no other solution. Doing nothing was not going to make them go away.

"I have to go back to Geneva," I said decisively. "Tomorrow."

Gina continued to mess with her straw, using it to swirl the ice cubes. "Is it to do with this mystery man?"

"Sort of." I stared moodily into my empty glass. "Well, actually, yes. I'll probably fly, that'll knock a couple of days off the trip."

"How long will you be away?"

Did she care? Or was she just making small talk?

"A week maybe, no more. I'll be back as soon as I can."

"Unlikely I'll still be here when you do. We're returning to Marseille at the weekend."

"That's a pity." I pushed a vacant coaster across to her. "Write your phone number and I'll buzz you from Geneva."

"Give me yours and I'll call you now, so you have mine logged. Oh!" Her eyes widened. "You didn't lose your cell overboard, did you?"

"No. It was in the cabin."

I supplied the number and she keyed it into her smart phone. Mine began to chirp in its belt holster. She cancelled the call.

"We're connected," she said.

"I'll call you over the weekend."

"No, don't. Let me call you. We made some progress today, but I need a breathing space."

I made understanding noises. Her hand rested lightly on my arm, remained just long enough to convey something more than friendship, before she glanced pointedly at her watch.

"Let me run you back to the hotel," I said, taking the hint.

More funereal driving up the hill to the Hermitage. I parked round the corner from the hotel entrance. Its blazing opulence was not designed for amorous farewells.

"I'll say goodbye then," she said as I applied the handbrake.

I drew her to me. She didn't resist, but her body was stiff and unresponsive. I sighed and pecked her on the cheek.

She shivered. "André...don't expect too much...too soon," she said softly, not looking at me. "I'm really not ready to think of anyone else in that way."

"I understand. Believe me, I do." Surprisingly, I really did. For months after Marion's death I hadn't given other women thinking space. It had taken a drunken bar crawl around the ninth *arondisse- ment* of Paris and an accomplished hooker to remind me what I was missing in my celibacy.

As an afterthought and, to some degree, a demonstration of trust I suggested she enter my address in her cell.

"In case you want to write me a love letter," I said.

Managing to restrain a chortle, she recorded the details as I reeled them off.

Our farewells were platonic but warm enough. She went off into the hotel. I drove down to the port to spend the night alone on *Seamist*, in bed but far from asleep. For much of the night I lay listening to the tap-tap of water by my head, my mind a-buzz with the kind of speculation that had been absent for many years. Not about Schelling and his crew dogging my tracks. For the present, that unexplained mystery had faded into the background.

The image that kept me from sliding into oblivion was far more attractive than that of an ageing German with SS connections, yet no less disturbing. Now it was Gina who kept me staring sleeplessly at the ceiling. Staring and wondering, wishing and hoping. My relationship with her had moved into new territory in the past few hours. I sensed it strongly, though I couldn't plant a flag in it.

Several times during our meal with Jean-Pierre and afterward at Victor's bar, I had caught her looking at me with a new tenderness in her expression. In her voice too, a hint of intimacy that had been absent before. Maybe it was on account of my selfless rescue of Pascal, or my near-death by drowning and her inadvertent contribution to it. The thought of having lost me, just as our relationship was showing signs of becoming meaningful, might have released feelings inside her that so far she had kept locked away.

Or maybe it really was nothing more than fantasizing on my part. No more than my vanity being tickled at the prospect of a gorgeous woman falling for me.

As I was falling for her.

Yeah, that's right. Me, André Warner, the original hard man: outlaw, philanderer, cynic, loner, going all mushy over a girl because she flutters her eyelashes at me. Shit, what was the world coming to?

Disgusted with myself, I turned on my side and went to sleep. Well, tried to.

The next morning, hollow eyed and yawning, I drove openly, even ostentatiously, to Nice Airport and flew Air Méditerranée to Geneva.

CHAPTER SEVEN

IT WAS RAINING when we touched down at Geneva airport, the runway awash, the uninspiring terminal cowering under the downpour. Weather-wise, it was as if I had never been away. Then the cheerful taxi driver informed me that today's rain was the first in five weeks.

I might have been tailed from the airport. Then again, I might not. For once, I didn't mind if Schelling, Harley Boy, and the whole crew were tagging along in my wake. On the contrary, I was depending on it.

The apartment was neat and tidy, and as welcoming as Dracula's tomb. I connected the iPod to the speakers, selected Rachmaninoff's *Piano Concerto Number 2*, and prowled about, only half-listening. By and by I discovered I was hungry. I went out to the Italian Bar-Restaurant where I made short work of a *cannelloni* lunch, then retraced my steps in the pale sunshine to which the rain had grudgingly surrendered.

The afternoon dragged by. I played a few more classical albums, exercised with weights and my rowing machine, read half a book, and consumed coffee by the liter.

With the setting of the sun, I prepared to engage the enemy. I stuffed a Glock 36 sub-compact automatic inside the back of the waist-band of my pants, and donned a jacket to hide it.

I poked my head outside my front door to check for loiterers. I wanted no witnesses to my call on Schelling. I scuttled past apartment 53, home of a middle-aged bank executive, and leaned heavily on the bell-push of number 54. Nobody came. I leaned harder and longer. The summons remained unanswered. Cursing under my breath, I snuck back to my apartment.

So much for stoking up the adrenalin. I dumped the Glock on the coffee table and glared at it. It was possible Schelling had expected me to come calling and simply declined to answer the door. A phone call might flush him out; unless he wasn't answering the phone either. Unless he was still in Monaco. Or anywhere.

The Geneva directory wasn't helpful, not a single Schelling listed. So, on to the Information Service. The female who answered was terse and officious. How was the name spelled, *monsieur*? Over the line, I could hear a tapping of keyboard buttons.

"I am sorry. There is no Schelling listed in Geneva."

With a little persistence, I got her to probe deeper. While I waited I poured myself some lukewarm coffee and drank. She finally came back with an imperious, "*Allo, allo!*" that made my ears ring.

"We have a record of Mr. Schelling's application to take over the line formerly allocated to Mr. Spinelli," she informed me. Spinelli was the previous tenant of number 54. "This was in...April. The twentieth to be exact."

"So I can look him up under Spinelli," I said. I should have thought of that sooner.

"Ye-e-s." She sounded doubtful. Then, "It seems that Mr. Schelling cancelled his application on the twenty-second of May. He didn't stay very long," she remarked as an afterthought.

An understatement. He'd packed his bags just two days after my own departure for Monaco.

Thanking the woman, I hung up.

If Schelling had cancelled his telephone, it was safe to assume he'd likewise cancelled his tenancy. In that case, my return to Geneva and my Grand Scheme showed signs of being dead in the water. To make it work had depended on my being tailed here by a person I would recognize—Schelling or Harley Boy. If they had guessed I was headed for home, it would have been easier for them to station some local guy in the street and wait for the lights to come on in my pad, then report back.

While I was pacing the room in simmering frustration, the doorbell went through its musical chime routine. I suspended my pacing to stare at the door. Officially, I was still out of town, and none of my friends and acquaintances were aware of my return. That made it a professional caller. I dithered briefly whether to lie doggo until the caller's thumb got tired, but curiosity won the day. I consigned the Glock to its home, a recess built into the refrigerator under the cocktail bar. Under the pretext of pouring a drink, I could get at it quickly. The peephole revealed a thin face with a chin like Punch of Punch and Judy, and sparse brown hair brushed severely sideways and flat to his head. I engaged the locking bar on the door and opened it a crack.

"Mr. Warner?" my visitor said in English.

My "Yes" was wary.

"Police." He poked an ID card through the gap, pinched between finger and thumb. I relieved him of it and scrutinized the facial shot and physical description of the holder who, it proclaimed, was Inspector Klaus Diethard Engels. "May I come in?"

It was a rule of mine never to make waves with the police. They might come back to drown you. So, as if I were any law-abiding citizen, I cooperated. I disengaged the bar and invited Inspector Klaus Diethard Engels into the entrance hall, exuding what I hoped was a plausible amalgam of puzzlement and innocence.

He snatched his card back from me, as if having his credentials checked was tantamount to an insult. Then the obligatory backup cop came into view, sliding out of the space between my door and number 53: a doughy, heavyset man with even less hair on top than Inspector Engels, and wearing a baggy brown suit. He greeted me with a dip of his head.

"This is Sergeant Maurer." Engels smiled, exposing the whitest set of teeth—too symmetrical to be natural—I had ever been dazzled by.

"What can I do for you gentlemen?" I wasn't yet convinced these guys weren't part of the Schelling crowd. Police ID cards can be forged the same as passports.

"We'd like to ask you a few questions, Mr. Warner." Engels flashed his teeth again, not so much a smile as a grimace. His English was flawless. His body was as thin as his face, and his height was on a par with mine.

"If it's about that parking ticket in March—" I began, but he silenced me with a sideways slash of his hand.

"This has nothing to do with traffic misdemeanors. May we go somewhere more congenial?"

Still, I hesitated.

"Or would you prefer to continue the discussion at Police Head-quarters?" His tone was silky. He knew the answer.

"I thought they only talked like that in B-movies," I grunted and retreated before him. Now I needed to get close to the Glock. If these flatfeet were here to slap the cuffs on me, I wasn't going to let them haul me off meekly to my fate.

"Drink?" I offered, heading for the cocktail bar.

"Why not?" Engels said. A civilized bunch, the Swiss police. None of this antisocial crap about not drinking on duty. "Have you any Scotch whisky?"

I took a bottle of Glenlivet 12 single malt down from the shelf. "Water? Soda?"

"That would be sacrilege, would it not?"

Here was a cop who actually knew a bit about whisky.

"What about you, Sergeant?" I said as I tipped a liberal slug into a cut-glass tumbler.

"The same," Maurer growled in Romansch-accented French; economical of speech, our Sergeant Maurer. No wasted words like "please" or "thank you."

I distributed the drinks and invited them to sit. I returned to the bar and remained standing behind it, tending a modest finger of Scotch. The Glock was less than an arm's reach away.

"Well, gentlemen." I switched on my clean living, eager-to-help smile. "What exactly can I do for you?"

Engels folded one long leg over the other. Despite his self-assured exterior, I had the impression he was slightly uneasy. In my experi-ence, police forces in democratic states are leery of the sensibilities of foreign nationals.

"We are cooperating with the German police, the Kriminalpolizei, in their investigation into a certain...ah...incident."

I maintained an expression of polite inquiry. Inwardly, I was churning, doing a fast mental rewind of all the hits I'd ever made in the Federal Republic. It wasn't quite into double figures.

"It is, in fact, a matter of murder," Engels went on, pausing for maximum impact.

Straining my acting prowess to the limit, I feigned a mystified frown. "Murder? My God. How can I help?" Careful, Warner, don't overdo the gush.

"Do you know a Mr...." Engels pulled a notebook from his pocket, shook it open. "Roger Townsend?"

"Roger Townsend?" My composure, already fragile, began to crumble. How did he know about my bogus identity from the Tillou contract in Munich, my grand exit? What was going on here? First, Schelling with his November in Bavaria travel pitch, now the police chasing a lead from the same job. Somewhere along the line my cover had been compromised big time.

Engels still wore an inquiring stare. Some kind of answer was called for.

"I knew a Bob Townsend in England," I said, holding the frown. "But *Roger* Townsend? No, I'm sure I've never met anyone by that name."

"No matter," Engels said, with outward indifference. "What about a Mr. Black?"

"Black? There must be a million or more Blacks in the world, Inspector."

"Mr. Arnold Black?"

Now I was doubly blown. Arnold Black was one of my regular bogus IDs, known only to selected contacts. I dosed myself liberally with Scotch, for medicinal purposes. Engels was stepping into a mine-field. I slid my hand closer to the hidden Glock.

"Sorry," I said, wagging my head. "Ask me another."

"Oh, I will, Mr. Warner, I will."

My movements screened by the front of the bar, I opened the fridge and extracted an ice tray with my left hand and the Glock with my right. I was confident I could take both of them out if I needed to.

The shots wouldn't carry far either. These top people's apartments had walls as thick as the Bastille's. Not that noise and neighbors were my chief concern. I simply wasn't sure I had the nerve to take out a couple of cops.

"Let's try a different name and a different nationality." Engels focused on me the way a hungry hound focuses on its food dish at mealtime. "Wolfgang Roschinger?"

My network of contacts and false identities was coming apart. My last encounter with the dinky gun dealer had been at the top of the Olympiaturm a few days before I took out Tillou, when we had our disagreement over the product and the price. Surely, he hadn't set the police dogs on me because of a grudge over that?

"Mr. Warner?" Engels nudged gently.

"Sorry, Inspector. I don't know your Mr. Rottweiler."

"Roschinger," he corrected.

"I don't seem to be much help to you."

"Not at all. You will understand that crime detection involves a great deal of routine inquiry work. Many questions must be asked and most of the answers are only useful from the point of view of elimination. It's a negative concept." He picked up his empty glass and examined it against the light.

"Well, then, gentlemen, if that's all..." It wasn't all, of that I was sure.

"Where were you in November last year?" Engels rode roughshod over my attempt to conclude the interview. He continued squinting through the glass, as if angling for a refill.

"Any particular day?"

"Oh..." He set the glass down to consult his notebook. "Let's say the sixteenth."

"The sixteenth, eh? If I kept a diary, I might be able to give you specifics. As it is, all I recall is that I spent most of the month in Geneva."

"So. In Geneva. Not in Germany then? Not at the Hotel Zum Goldenen Adler, in the village of Oberpframmern, near München, by chance? Wearing a brown hairpiece and a stick-on moustache."

Up until now, the news had been merely bad. This was calamitous. It was beginning to look as if he was shaping up to an outright accusation, even an arrest.

The sky was darkening outside and the room with it. To buy a few extra seconds, I switched on the light above the bar. It cast a warm, amber glow over my unwelcome guests.

"No, Inspector," I said heavily. "I was not in Germany at all last year, with or without hairpieces, false moustaches or wooden legs." My fingers were wrapped around the grip of the Glock. It was already primed. I cleared my throat to conceal the click of the safety catch. "Suppose you tell me a bit more about this...this murder you're investigating. Suppose you explain why you've come to question *me* about it."

"You're quite right, Mr. Warner." Engels glanced at his colleague. "Don't you agree, Maurer? We owe him a full explanation."

Maurer cracked his knuckles and stayed mute. His function was primarily decorative, the unspoken threat, to counteract Engels' good cop facade.

"On seventeenth November last year, two people—a man and a woman—were staying at a private vacation residence known as Schloss Thomashoff, near the village of Breitbrunn, on the shore of lake Ammersee, which is about forty kilometers west of München." He was relating this in a bored tone as if he had decided I was guilty, and therefore more familiar with the geography of the crime scene than he was. "Between six PM and eight pm, a person or persons unknown entered Schloss Thomashoff and shot the man three times, probably killing him instantly, and the woman once through the throat, leaving her to die. Nothing was disturbed or damaged, apart from a bolt on the back door, which had been partly sawn through, suggesting the killer had entered the house on a previous occasion."

"What's the world coming to?" My head-shaking and hand-wringing didn't seem to impress my visitors. Maybe they thought I was taking the piss. Maurer's built-in scowl deepened.

"The killing appears to have been the work of a professional. The male victim was Fabrice Tillou, a Frenchman, thirty-one years old and the only son of a certain Bernard Tillou. You have heard of him perhaps? I am informed by the French police that he's a notorious racketeer."

"France has its share of...er...racketeers, I suppose." The term smacked of Chicago bootleggers and G-men raiding illicit whisky stills.

"Possibly. However, this Tillou, the father, controls most of the organized vice and illegal immigration on the Mediterranean coast from Cannes to the Spanish border."

"It sounds like a profitable operation."

"This is not a matter for flippancy, Mr. Warner," Engels admonished. Little did he know how right he was. But a jocular attitude helped camouflage my guilt. "In any case, it is not the son who interests the German police. It may be that there's a gang war between Tillou and a rival organization. If so—I believe you Anglos have an expression—good riddance to bad rubbish?" I nodded, chuckled a bit. "No, the fate of this French gangster does not concern them; it's the woman, Ingeborg Thomashoff." He checked his notes. "Thirty-five, desirable, sexually active, one might almost say *overactive*, and attached to certain...ah...perverted practices. The mistress of Tillou the son; and also the wife of Erich Thomashoff, the German minister. The name will be familiar to you, I expect."

"Sorry, no."

"Really?" Engels said, registering polite disbelief at the extent of my ignorance. "Even so, you can visualize the implications. If the intended victim was Frau Thomashoff, and Tillou was eliminated only because he happened to be there, the matter assumes a different hue, does it not? The crime may have political implications."

What a sick joke. To be questioned over the killing I'd committed in self-defense!

Engels smoothed his already super-smooth hair. "The shooting of a minister's wife might be the work of a terrorist faction. Perhaps part of a scheme to put pressure on the Government." He shrugged. "Who knows what these fiends will try next?"

"You mean you think someone like Al Qaeda or Isis might have done it?"

I would have been delighted for the Islamic militant crazies to get the blame, but couldn't believe the police seriously suspected them. I was right.

"No," Engels snapped. "I was thinking more of the neo-Nazi

groups, such as the NSS. That is a line of enquiry the Kriminalpolizei are themselves pursuing. We are only involved because they have asked us to follow up information received from an apparently reliable source, which implicates..." He gave the impression of having chosen the word with extreme care, "... a certain Roger Townsend who, in turn, has been linked to an Arnold Black, and thence to an André Warner."

Now at last I could let the juices of indignation spurt.

"Me?" I said, manufacturing a stunned tone. "You suspect *me* of being involved in this...this crock of shit?" Just the right degree of outrage, I thought. "So what are you suggesting? That I'm a neo-Nazi?"

"We're not quite sure what you are," Engels said unctuously. "All we know about you is that you hold British and Canadian passports, that you have a Swiss residence permit with two years still to run, that you have no record with Interpol, and apparently have considerable wealth. Perhaps you would care to...ah, fill in the gaps?"

He flashed a phony searchlight smile on and off. If it was meant to be reassuring it fell some distance short.

"What gaps? Why don't you just tell me what you want to know?"

He pondered, then nodded. "Very well."

He proceeded with some skill to extract from me the best part of my life history to date, extensively modified to account for my affluence and lack of gainful pursuits. On his side, it was all straightforward stuff. No obviously loaded questions, no chicanery. Maurer made notes, but otherwise contributed only an occasional grunt or snort according to his opinion on my answers.

This ritual occupied an hour or more, and in the course of it my guests' glasses were twice generously replenished. Regrettably, soaking the bastards in expensive hooch had no noticeable effect, except that Engels' complexion gradually assumed a rosy tint. Maurer was unchanged; he might have been hewn out of granite.

Engels finally seemed satisfied that he had the full picture, down to the dimple on my backside and how often I changed my sheets. His next pronouncement was therefore unexpected.

"Would you object to our searching your apartment?"

"Searching? Don't you need some sort of warrant? How do you call it, a *mandat*?"

He wasn't at all fazed. "Indeed we do. But I'm certain you will wish to cooperate with our inquiries." A smirk pulled his mouth out of shape. "As a law-abiding English gentleman."

Aside from the Glock, my apartment was as clean as the Queen's private washroom at Buck Palace. Even my laptop, sitting open on the dining room table, its screen blank, contained no personal data, coded or otherwise.

"Okay, go ahead, search away," I said with forced nonchalance, preparing to stow the Glock in its refrigerated compartment the minute they got busy.

Engels inclined his head toward the laptop. "Do we need a code to open your computer?"

"Not even. Nothing to hide, Inspector."

His grimace could have been disappointment or it could have been dislike. Or even indigestion. He gestured to Maurer, who got up with an air of resignation. Now that they'd asked for permission, and I had obliged, they had to go through the motions. Maybe Maurer had already figured out that my casual acquiescence meant there would be no glory in rummaging through my things. Aiming a flint-eyed glance at me, he went straight to the master bedroom as if he already knew the layout of the place. It made me wonder if he had been here before, in my absence.

While Maurer did the physical search, and Engels trawled the computer, I hid the Glock under the pretext of getting fresh ice. The whole exercise took them the best part of half an hour. I pretended to read a newspaper. Neither the physical nor the electronic search came up with anything.

As Engels shut down the laptop and left the table, I said with a show of fake asperity, "If you're satisfied, how about filling in a few gaps for me?"

"If I can. If it's not privileged information."

"For a start...this Roger Townsend person. What led you to connect him with me?"

Glances were exchanged between Engels and Maurer. They were clearly unhappy about parting with the source of their information.

"Come on, Inspector," I wheedled, drumming up some fake outrage. "Whatever you might think you know, this is just a great big bloody mystery to me. For Christ's sake, man, I've a right to know what led you to me."

Engels was tugging at his lower lip, looking uncertain. "I would not normally reveal my sources at an inquiry stage. However, being a foreign national, you're something of a special case, so I will break my rule." A grunt of disapproval from Maurer darkened Engels' brow, but didn't deter him. "The Kriminalpolizei were tipped off by an anonymous caller whom they succeeded in tracing. It was the man I mentioned to you: Roschinger."

So the little cocksucker *had* crossed the tracks. I cursed him silently, regretting that I hadn't tossed him off the Olympiaturm when I'd had the chance.

For Engels' benefit, I put on a blank look. "Well, I don't know your Mr. Roschinger, so I can only assume it's a case of mistaken identity. Seriously, Inspector, I wouldn't know how to point a gun in the right direction, let alone kill a person with one. To suggest that I could have murdered..." I shook my head in rejection of the very idea, "two people, especially a *woman*!" I dried up as if words failed me. Again, I privately reminded myself not to overdo the ham.

Engels looked surprised. "You must have misunderstood me, Mr. Warner. I said the man was killed, not the woman. She was shot, yes, and her injuries were life threatening. But thanks to an unexpected visitor to the house, *she* survived!"

———

FAR INTO THE night I stayed up nursing glass after glass of Glenlivet. Still technically a free man, though my two legitimate passports had walked through the door with Engels and Maurer. The duo's less-than-fond farewells included a warning not to leave Geneva without their authority. Just one grade above house arrest.

As I progressed down the bottle, I reviewed my options on how to dig myself out of the dung heap that little prick Wolfgang had deposited me in. He would have told the Kriminalpolizei about the gun and maybe, if they'd given him a thorough going over, about the other guns he supplied me with. They would know about the car, since Wolfgang had hired it for me. The Townsend alias must have come from the hotel. Singly, none of these pointers led to André Warner, respectable resident of Geneva. The gun was lost forever to mankind and police alike, therefore Wolfgang's allegations could not be substantiated. The car rental on its own proved nothing. Even using a false name wasn't a crime, and my false papers, which *were* illegal, were as inaccessible as the weapon.

So far, so circumstantial. To make the charge stick they had to place me at the scene of the killing. That was where the Thomashoff woman came in: the fabled witness for the prosecution. The humane part of me was glad she was alive. However, not only could she provide the police with hard proof of my guilt, but if Engels was telling it straight, she was claiming I shot her in cold blood, rather than in self-defense. And about that, I was not glad at all.

My nerves were jumping even before I arrived at this stage of my conjecturing. I went out onto the balcony to seek inspiration from the night air. The city pulsated with the usual cadence of nightlife traffic: people walking and talking, disco music, a distant siren. Lights still blazed in the tall buildings of the commercial sector. Here and there, neon signs flickered their seductive messages. Sights and sounds I had previously taken for granted. I was unprepared for their removal from my life. Despite my criminal deeds, I had never seriously expected to be condemned to drag out my years within the grey walls of an eight-by-six prison cell. No more *Seamist*, no more women, tropical paradises, or luxury hotels. No more sybaritic lifestyle. Just a monotonous, colorless existence.

I shuddered. I'd sooner take a bullet in the brain than it should come to that.

My options were limited. I could go on the run and seek residence in a country whose extradition laws were more benign. That would make me a fugitive, my movements restricted. Living in perpetual fear of a heavy hand on my shoulder, twitching at every knock on the door, every clamor of the telephone.

No thanks. Defection was the last resort, only to be applied when all other options proved barren. First, I must try to brazen my way out of this mess by every legal tactic at my disposal. Legal tactics meant Jules Victor, my lawyer.

I went inside and sat on the edge of an armchair while I tapped out his home number.

"You *do* know what time it is?" he growled, his voice blurred with sleep.

I hadn't known, but I now saw it was after 2am. I apologized, gave him a potted run-down on my troubles and arranged a lunchtime appointment for that day.

"Now go to bed," was his churlish valediction.

———

FIVE EMPTY DAYS DRAGGED BY, relieved only by my meeting with Jules, who noted the particulars, but felt disinclined to intervene until the police made contact with me again.

"We must play a waiting game for a while," he advised. "It doesn't pay to overreact in a situation like this. There is some truth in the old dictum that only the guilty run to their lawyer when interviewed by the police."

Easy for him to talk.

So I passed the hours at the Comedie, stimulated by caffeine, watching the world go by. I lunched and dined. I gambled a little. I read, watched TV, and listened to music. I worked out frenetically. For once, I stayed clear of women. My appetite for sex, usually as reliable as a Swiss clock, was in limbo. With harassment coming at me from two directions, I couldn't have done justice to the likes of the ever-willing Evelyne, or any of her contemporaries. Not only that, I was surprised to realize that the spiritual presence of Gina deterred me from seeking my pleasure elsewhere.

When I wasn't eating, drinking, gambling, or fretting over my enforced confinement, I wrestled with various, mostly impractical schemes for getting off the hook. The remaining gaps I plugged with thoughts of Gina.

The weekend had come and gone, and she hadn't phoned as promised. I tried calling her but she didn't pick up. The omens were not favorable. If she chose to drop me and disappear below my radar, I was screwed. So here I was, stuck in Geneva on the whim of a policeman called Engels. I had just resolved, on the sixth day—a Monday morning of menacing skies that presaged more wet stuff—to go and create a stink in his office, when the telephone emitted its discreet whirr.

My housekeeper, Madam Segond, had just that minute shown up, so I took the call on the bedroom extension. It was Engels, as unwelcome as rain at a picnic.

"I was going to pay you a visit today," I said. "You can't keep me in Geneva forever. I have some business matters to attend to in France."

"Naturally we regret any inconvenience, Mr. Warner," he purred. "Police investigations cannot be rushed, unfortunately. We have to consult with our counterparts in the Bundesrepublik, you understand."

"Yeah, yeah, my heart bleeds for you. But *you've* got to understand that this shooting is nothing to do with me, and I'm being prevented from leaving Geneva without justification."

"Precisely my reason for telephoning."

"You mean I'm now free to leave?"

Soft laughter trickled from the earpiece. I was glad he found it funny.

"Not quite, but if you would care to call here at police headquarters, I am hopeful that the matter can be cleared up without further delay. You know where to find us?"

"Boulevard Carl-Vogt?" It was the only police station I knew of.

"Correct. No immediate hurry, but in the interest of...ah...justice, the sooner the better."

The interest of justice was what I feared most.

Having little choice, I promised to be there that afternoon or the next morning. I couldn't be more specific since I wasn't going without Jules, and he might well have other commitments.

I had only seconds to brood over my conversation with Engels, when the bleep of my cell phone summoned me, the one reserved strictly for business. It didn't bleep much these days. Slave to habit that I am, I still kept it charged and switched on.

The message on the screen was *pas disponible*. Caller ID not available; a call from outside Switzerland, most probably.

"Monsieur Townsend?" enquired my caller before I could open my mouth.

The use of my old pseudonym froze me rigid.

"Wrong number," I replied and tapped the red End-Call icon. There was sweat on my forehead and on my palms. Mr. Townsend was no more, part of a past that was supposed to be dead, but was increasingly coming back to life.

The cell phone chirped again. Uttering an obscenity, I picked it up with an unsteady hand. My thumb hovered over the End Call icon, but even as I delayed, I knew in my heart I wouldn't tap it. This was a call that had to be answered.

"Yes," I said heavily.

The same voice rapped, "Call me back. I'm in France on this number—zero-four, fifty, seventy-five, zero-nine, sixty-six. *Jusqu'à midi.*" He repeated the number and I jotted it down on a notepad I kept by the bedside.

Then I was listening to the hum of a dead line.

In France, he had said, and I could reach him there until midday. It was a near certainty that the number he gave me was a payphone in a cafe or post office. So I could call him back on my cell phone without fear of the call being traced to him via my cell phone account.

That is, if I wanted to talk to him, and about that I was in two minds.

My caller was no stranger. I had accepted a contract from him nine months before to eliminate a certain Fabrice Tillou. A contract that was currently giving me more heartaches than all its thirty-nine predecessors put together. My caller and I weren't connected socially. So he was phoning about a professional matter, either related to the Tillou hit, or—the alternative struck me like a sonic boom—another contract. During our initial negotiations he had raised the prospect of more work.

Nobody has yet devised a way of randomly tuning in on cell phone calls, so I reckoned it was safe enough to use it. Or was it? If my caller had given me the number of a payphone, fine. Any record of the call wouldn't matter jack shit. But I couldn't be a hundred percent sure the number wasn't private. If it was, and the police traced it via my cell phone provider's records, it could incriminate both of us.

I hadn't consciously taken a single step, but suddenly I was in the street, heading for the payphone rank in the Place de Jargonnant. On the way I bought a newspaper and acquired a pocketful of coins for my call.

He answered with a neutral "*Allo?*" In the background, a murmur of voices.

"Townsend," I said tersely.

"Ah, thank you for calling back." Courteous as ever. The name he had used when we previously did business was Bonhomme, obviously bogus. "You know who this is?"

"I know. I recognized your voice."

"I have been trying to contact you for several weeks. Have you been away?"

"Yes. Was it urgent?"

"It wasn't, but it is now. When and where can we meet? I'm only an hour's drive from Geneva."

Meetings on Swiss soil were ruled out, as far as I was concerned. Switzerland was my home and my sanctuary, and only a cretin fouls his own backyard. Yet I couldn't cross the border until Engels gave me the green light. Gambling on a happy outcome to tomorrow's session at police headquarters, I proposed a rendezvous the day after tomorrow afternoon, in Annemasse, a popular ski resort just across the border in France.

"There's a big square downtown. You know it?"

He didn't, but his GPS would direct him there.

"Outside the BNP building at three. Okay?"

"*Entendu*, Monsieur Townsend."

End of dialogue. Bonhomme hadn't said much, but between the few lines he did say I scented a new contract, causing me to wonder at my sanity for even hearing him out. To take up my former trade again, while the prospect of extradition hovered over me would, at the very least, be ill-advised. And yet, and yet...After seven months of free-wheeling, the prospect of action had the pull of a whirlpool. I would see Bonhomme, always assuming I was allowed to leave Switzerland, talk to him, and then, who knows?

I was like a smoker who, having successfully given up the weed for months, is offered a cigarette out of the blue. Why not? he says to himself. Just one lousy cigarette won't hurt. Before he knows it, he's back on the nicotine treadmill.

I returned to the apartment block and, as was my custom, ascended the stairs at a jog.

I reached the fifth floor landing only slightly out of breath, and was fumbling for my keys when I saw her, perched on an upended valise by the door to my apartment. Hair disheveled, no make-up, blue pants creased. No less lovely though, for all that. No less desirable.

No less Gina.

CHAPTER EIGHT

"TELL ME, love. You are *real*, aren't you? I mean, I'm not dreaming, am I?"

"You want I should pinch you?" she said, girlish and giggly. Interwoven with the wisecrack was a frisson of self-doubt. "Listen, my friend, it took a lot of soul-searching before I could nerve myself to come here. So don't write me off as a figment of your fantasies."

"You sum it up very nicely," I admitted. "How did you know about my fantasies?"

"Hey, cool it, cave man. Let's keep the conversation platonic for now."

The "for now" was encouraging.

A shower, a change of clothes and an impromptu lunch of spaghetti Bolognese had transformed her. Relaxing on a long couch, one foot tucked under her bottom, dressed simply in jeans and one of those short smock things women wear these days, she was a knockout.

"Why didn't you phone? I'd have come to you." With Engels's permission.

"Gee, I don't know." She didn't meet my eyes. "I wanted to. But it wouldn't have meant anything. It's too easy to pick up a phone. I...I guess I needed to prove something to myself." Some of her inner agitation went on display. She was squeezing her interlocked hands together.

"When you left," she carried on, swallowing hard, "I felt sort of... empty, as if a big chunk of my life had just been ripped away. At the same time, I was afraid of you."

I found that hard to believe, and my expression must have said so, for she hurried on, "No ... no, that doesn't sound right. I was afraid to *commit* myself to you, is what I mean." She turned her head toward me, regarded me gravely. "It was easier to just forget you, easier and much safer. Then I could go on feeling sorry for myself, curled up in my shell like a snail, avoiding men, avoiding relationships." She smiled, but not with joy.

It made me want to comfort her, to hold her tight against me, murmuring whatever it took in her ear. It was not a physical longing. For a change, post-Marion, I was thinking of a woman as a person rather than just a means to sexual gratification.

She stared at me, eyes moist, lips slightly parted, waiting for me to utter words that still lodged in my throat.

"I'm glad...I'm glad you came." The sentiment rang trite and hollow, and conveyed about as much warmth as a blizzard. I pressed on, desperate to say things I hadn't said since Marion died and, through lack of practice, not sure how. "In fact, glad doesn't nearly do justice to the way I feel. It's been so long since I formed a...a close relationship with a woman. My emotions are rusted up. I..." As I fumbled over my words, she nodded encouragement. "Like you, I meant to steer clear of involvement. I wanted freedom of choice. Then you came along and loused up all my fine intentions." My laugh was hollow. "Goddamn it, Gina, you've gotten me acting like a teenager!"

My confession ignited a faint titter.

"It's kind of comforting to know it's not just my life that's been turned upside down."

"Upside down, yeah, that sums it up to a T."

She looked at me expectantly, waiting for more.

But I wasn't quite ready to plumb the depths of either of our feelings. I edged the dialogue toward more practical matters.

"Are you going to stay?" I asked flatly.

Her gaze was level. "I've taken three weeks' vacation, so I can do as I please. Would you like me to stay?"

"Would I *like* you to?" I let out a snort. "Does a fish like water?"

She grinned. "I'll take that as a yes."

Easy as that, a pact was made.

Neither of us raised the subject of the sleeping arrangements. I took her valise to the guest room. With this woman I was going to play it in a low, low key. Call it a test of the depth of my feelings, and of hers. Make her want me physically as much as I wanted her but wait until our wantings converged.

These amorous schemes might yet prove to have no substance. The major hurdle of my interview with Engels still lay ahead. The thought prompted me to ask Jules to hold my hand for the occasion. I excused myself and went into the bedroom to use my cell phone. Jules expected to be free from four o'clock and would collect me from the apartment.

I found Gina at the kitchen sink, washing the lunchtime dishes; a domestic scene. A portent?

"Why don't you use the machine?" I indicated the expensive and under-utilized dishwasher at the end of the mile-long counter.

"Not worth it for a few plates and cups," was her crisp response.

In addition to all her visible attributes she was practical.

I stood beside her, hands in pockets. "It grieves me to say it, but I have to go out for a while," I said.

She was scrubbing away at an encrustation of Bolognese sauce on a plate. "Will you be very long?"

"A couple of hours perhaps." And perhaps for good. No profit in telling her that.

"Do I get to come with you?" Her face was hidden behind the curtain of hair that swung forward as she leaned over the sink.

"Best not. It's an appointment with my lawyer. Boring stuff to do with my Swiss residence." Not an out-and-out lie. I sidled closer to her. Our hips brushed. She kept on scrubbing at that same spot on the plate. "I won't be long."

"Oh, swell. The little woman sits at home washing the master's dishes while he goes off doing"—she pantomimed quotation marks—

"important stuff. Have I gotten that right? Is that how man-woman relationships go for you, André?"

I made a pretense of warding her off. "Easy, easy. Look, maybe today really is the first day of the rest of our lives together. Maybe not. I can't just put my old life on hold on the basis of you suddenly showing up here, welcome though you are. Cut me a bit of slack here, love."

Some of the tension went out of her. She flashed me an on-off smile, almost a grimace. "Sorry. You're right. You've got private business with your lawyer and I have no business butting in. I'm being unreasonable and I apologize. Sincerely."

"You're forgiven." I hesitated over sentiments that might be a step too far, but went ahead anyway. "You'll always be forgiven."

Now her smile was genuine. "Thanks. You're sweet."

Me, sweet?

"So what'll you do while I'm gone?" I said. It wouldn't have surprised me if she fled the minute the door closed behind me.

"Oh, watch a DVD, I guess. Don't worry, I'll while away the time somehow."

"Promise me something."

"Sure, if I can'.

"You'll still be here when I get back."

She gave a little start, taking a backward step to study me from a distance.

"You're not just play acting, are you, André? You're not just setting me up for a...oh, hell, for a quick *screw*? Bam, bam, thank you ma'am, and off you go?" She was blinking, fighting tears. "If you are, just say so and we'll go to bed right now and get it over with!"

She read me all too well. But that was yesterday, this was today.

I reached for her, but she backed away, clutching the dish brush like a club, as if to beat me off with it.

"It's not like that," I protested. "Not with you. With other women...yes, I admit that's all it ever amounted to. With you, it's something else. I tell you, love, you've got me so mixed up, I feel like sweet sixteen and never been kissed, all over again."

She expelled a long breath. Her arms fell to her sides.

I stood watching her, uncertain whether to offer comfort or shrug it off. She was a hard act to figure. I would have liked to dig into her past, to know more about her husband and what went wrong between them, but I suspected she wouldn't take kindly to my raking up dying embers.

She expelled a long breath. "I might be doing you an injustice. If I am, I'm truly sorry." She was under control now, quivering behind a veneer as thin as rice paper.

A car horn tooted down at street level.

"That's my lawyer," I said, collecting my jacket from the back of a kitchen chair. "I'll see you later."

I left her toiling away at the sink like a housewife of long-standing.

Going down the stairs three at a time, it struck me that I hadn't even kissed her goodbye.

———

SERGEANT MAURER, predictably taciturn, showed Jules and me into Engels's second floor habitat, a cool and airy office with cream painted walls and steel filing cabinets lining most of them. In the middle reposed a desk, also in steel, like an island fortress.

The man himself was in shirtsleeves. Dapper as he was, he looked ordinary compared to Jules, who was suave and debonair as always, in his pinstripe lawyer's suit, not a straight black hair out of place. The rather disconcerting Hitler moustache bristled with aggressive efficiency and his small brown eyes were like gun-sights behind gold framed spectacles.

If Engels resented Jules's presence, it didn't show.

"Thank you for coming, gentlemen," was his opening line.

Hands were shaken all round. It was all very amiable, very civilized, and very Swiss.

At Engels' invitation, we sat in the two upright armchairs arranged before his desk. Maurer went to a third identical chair strategically positioned at a corner of the desk on Engels' side. We were lined up like opposing armies. Jules flipped open a slim cigarette case that I knew to be solid gold and offered it around.

"No smoking in this building, *Maître*," Engels said mildly.

"Of course. *Veuillez m'excuser*." Jules spirited the case back whence it came. "Now that we're all settled, Inspector," he went on, converting to English for my benefit, though my French was fluent enough, "we're here at your insistence to clear up this misunderstanding over an incident in the Federal Republic. I demand that you now apologize to Mr. Warner for this clear case of mistaken identity, lift the restriction on his movements, and return his passports with immediate effect."

It was an aggressive shot across the bows. Jules was a past master in the art of bluff. His favorite form of relaxation was poker, at which he excelled and, moreover, usefully augmented his already considerable income.

In return, Engels offered a regretful smile. "Alas, I cannot do as you ask. It is not a simple criminal matter, you see, *Maître*. Pressure is being exerted at a political level. As I have already explained to Mr. Warner, the fact that the lady concerned is the wife of a member of the *Bundesregierung* has brought into play considerations other than who killed this Frenchman...this Tillou, and who shot her."

Jules rested his elbows on the chair arms, formed a spire with his hands and commenced tapping his index fingertips in a slow beat. He once confided to me that it kept him calm when confronted with excessive bureaucracy and bullshit.

"But my client was not in Germany at the time of the killing."

"We have evidence to disprove that claim."

Engels proceeded to give Jules a rundown of his evidence. It contained nothing I hadn't already heard.

"This is all circumstantial," Jules said imperturbably, tapping away steadily. "What evidence, what *proof* do you have that this person whom your Herr Roschinger allegedly supplied with a pistol was ever at the Thomashoff residence? That he ever used the pistol? That he used it on these two unfortunate people?" He checked these points off on his slender fingers.

Engels's features drooped. "None, as yet. The police are still continuing their inquiries. They're confident that, given time, they'll come up with hard proof."

"Given time?" Jules was adept at seizing on key phrases. "This crime took place in November last year, Inspector. How much more

time will our German colleagues require? For how long do they expect
my client to put his life on hold?"

A shuffling of feet under the desk betrayed Engels' uncertainty. I
mentally congratulated Jules on herding the policeman into a corner,
though I didn't expect a white flag to be raised quite yet. He was being
squeezed from on high and wouldn't put his job at risk just because
some smart mouthpiece thumped the table.

"I have urgent business to attend to in France," I said, adding a
modest amount of fuel to Jules' inferno. "I have to meet an associate
there tomorrow. If I don't keep the appointment, it could cost me literally hundreds of thousands of dollars. Will you—will the Swiss
government compensate me, Inspector?"

Out of the corner of my eye, I saw Jules' shake of the head. He
knew well enough that such tactics would go nowhere.

Maurer, a non-participant until now, gave off a deep rumble like a
tractor starting up.

"These matters are not interesting us," he began in his basic
English, but Engels silenced him with a glance.

"I understand your difficulty, Mr. Warner," he said, then turned to
Jules. "However, there is a new development. The Germans have
asked us to send Mr. Warner to München to be either identified or
cleared, as the case may be. That will end all debate, will it not?"

It certainly would. It would also be the end of me.

"Under Swiss law, you cannot extradite Mr. Warner without
incontestable proof of his guilt." Jules spoke quietly and authorita-
tively in a no-nonsense tone. "Not unless our country has become a
police state overnight." He fingered his jaw and looked at me. "I think
they will now ask you to go to Germany voluntarily, André."

This was immediately confirmed by Engels. "Will you go?" His
stare was disconcerting. It made me feel he could read my guilt.

Jules, too, was frowning at me. "You don't have to go. They cannot
make you, no matter what the Inspector says."

"It's the only way to clear your name," Engels said sourly. "Otherwise, you'll never be able to enter Germany again. Also, you may..." he
shifted uncomfortably under Jules' glare, "I say *may* be declared
persona non grata in Switzerland."

A scornful "Pah!" summed up Jules' view of that threat.

"Why not simply scan a photograph of Mr. Warner? That would suffice, I would have thought."

"We already did. She was unsure. It seems she only caught a glimpse of him before she was shot." Engels effected an airy gesture. "So you see, a confrontation in person is the only way to clear or condemn Mr. Warner."

I didn't ask where they got the photo. From either or both of my passports, I supposed. They were poor likenesses, fortunately.

Jules grumbled about the lack of difference between my photo and my physical presence

"If I do go," I said, having not the smallest intention of going, "I can't do so right away. As I explained, I have to be in France tomorrow without fail. Possibly, I could go in a week or so." I put on a dubious air. "What do you advise, Jules? Should I go?"

Jules, in his ignorance of my former profession and presumably believing in my innocence, said, "It is not necessary for you to go, if you prefer not to." He pursed his lips. "On the other hand, I assume you'll wish to clear your name and they will, of course, pay all expenses, plus perhaps a modest sum in compensation."

He fixed a legal-eagle eye on Engels, who nodded vigorously.

"What would the Germans want with me?" I asked Engels with a sinking heart.

"The woman, Frau Thomashoff, will simply say, yes, it was you, or no, it was not." He spread his hands, implying there was nothing to it.

"Why can't she come here?" Jules asked. "Why inconvenience my client?"

"For reasons best known to themselves, the German police prefer that Mr. Warner goes to München," Engels said blandly.

It was easy to guess why. If she identified me here in Geneva, the police would still have all the extradition rigmarole to go through, a procedure that could take months and whose outcome would be uncertain.

The cards Engels was holding were all face up on the table now. Either I agreed to go to Germany, and thereby commit hara-kiri, or I refused and risked being held as a material witness, or whatever they called it. Engels would also interpret my refusal as an admission of guilt. A third alternative occurred to me—delay.

"I'm willing to go on the basis that all expenses are paid, but not at once." The initial blatant surprise shown by Engels faded when I added my qualifier, to be replaced by an equally blatant sneer.

"How long before you would consent to go?" he inquired in a civil tone that belied his curled lip.

"A month or so. As soon as I've concluded my negotiations in France." I arched an eyebrow at Jules. "Does that sound unreasonable?"

"Not at all, not at all," he said briskly, taking out his cigarette case. Remembering the no-smoking rule, he put it back unopened with a peevish grunt. "In fact, I think you've been exceptionally tolerant throughout. I'm sure the Inspector appreciates your cooperation."

A door slammed outside in the corridor and somebody shouted, a torrent of vernacular French. Another door banged and the wall shuddered in sympathy before an uneasy peace was restored.

Engels had borne the disturbance with ill grace. A frown was still in place when he said, "If we could set a specific time limit, it would be appreciated. I have to say though, *Maître*, I am not sure whether Mr. Warner should be allowed to go to France. What is to prevent him from breaking his promise?"

"If Mr. Warner so chooses," Jules measured his words, his voice low and even, "that is his prerogative, Inspector. He has no obligation either to the Swiss police or more especially, the German police, other than his own *voluntary* agreement to travel to Germany at some future date, possibly in about one month. If he chooses to remain in France or take a vacation in some other part of the world, that is entirely his affair. Unless..." He fixed a baleful eye on Engels, whose displeasure was unconcealed.

"Yes...unless?" Engels prompted, drumming fingers on his desk.

"Unless you wish to prefer charges against my client."

Christ, Jules, don't put ideas into his head! was my instinctive reaction. I understood though, that it was a stratagem to force Engels to acknowledge the weakness of his case. The form of open arrest already imposed was probably illegal, given the lack of hard evidence and the fact that the crime had been committed in another country. My foreign national status also weakened their right to deprive me of my freedom.

For all I knew though, Engels was just as big a bluffer as Jules.

"Well?" Jules demanded.

The Inspector had seemed to recoil from the suggestion of arrest and was now rolling a badly chewed pencil in his fingers, his lips drawn in a tight line.

"We do not wish to arrest Mr. Warner at this time," he admitted at last, a piece of news that had me sighing inaudibly with relief. "He is free to come and go as he pleases, and to report here for the arrangements to be made with the German authorities as and when he pleases." He looked straight at me, his face as bleak as a winter's morn. "That, Mr. Warner, is the official position. But before you go, I wish to clarify my personal position."

"Careful, Inspector," Jules warned, as if he had an inkling of what was coming.

"I personally am not convinced of your innocence, Mr. Warner," Engels went on without so much as a glance at Jules, his eyes spearing mine. "With your legal representative present, I will not go so far as to say I believe you are guilty. I will only say that, in conjunction with the *Bundespolizei*, who are determined to hunt down the killer, I intend to devote a great deal of time and resource to obtaining the necessary proof." He tilted back his chair, nodding in self-satisfaction. "Do I make myself clear?"

I was about to say "You do" when Jules stepped in. "I shall complain to Commissioner Grünwald about your attitude," he snapped. "An attitude which, I might add, is inconsistent with your position as a senior police officer in a democratic country." He stood up so sharply that his chair rocked and almost tipped over. "I trust I have made *myself* equally clear?"

Engels blinked, but otherwise wasn't noticeably upset by Jules's counter-threat. He would dismiss it as obligatory legal rhetoric, was my guess.

"Now," Jules said, his tone still stern, "if you will kindly return Mr. Warner's passports, we'll leave to let you get on with arresting real criminals."

But Engels wasn't quite ready to set me free to roam where I may. They returned my Canadian passport, having copied it, but hung onto my British one. I would be like a dog on one of those extending leashes, running so far but no farther. Frontiers could still be crossed, but Interpol would be alerted and my status as a murder suspect would be circulated to police forces across Western Europe. The tiniest infraction involving me or my car would be reported back to Interpol HQ, and thence to Engels.

Nobody said *au revoir* when Jules and I stalked out, and nobody escorted us to the exit. We just went, Jules in the lead opening doors and flinging them back with a crash, with me hurrying along at his heels like a faithful servant and closing them quietly in mute apology. I didn't want to get nailed for disturbing the peace or wanton damage to police property.

Driving me back to my apartment through another cloudburst that the wipers of his Merc were barely able to handle, Jules was full of reassurance.

"Legally they can't touch you, so don't worry," he said as he fed a cigarette into his mouth. "I know Engels. He'll soon get tired of chasing a...what do you say...a mare's nest?"

The unlit cigarette waggled as he talked. I thumbed the car's lighter for him.

"Will o' the wisp," I grunted. Overall, I was pleased with what Jules had achieved, less so with my general predicament.

"Always the government here is eager to curry favor with the Germans," he said, puffing smoke. "A great deal of German money is invested in Switzerland, you know, and I don't just mean in Nazi gold, though there is plenty of that still resting in bank vaults. And the Germans haven't changed that much. They may be welcoming to immigrants and tough on Nazi sympathizers, but they still like to flex their muscles with their smaller neighbors. Of course, Engels is a Zurich man and therefore pro-German by instinct and language." He patted my knee. "Be assured, my friend, you're in the clear."

"I'm relieved to hear it."

We stopped at a red light by the Exhibition Centre. Turning his head toward me, Jules said, "On a personal level, I would like to ask you something, and I hope you won't be offended by it."

I lifted my hand to indicate indifference.

"Did you actually do this thing? This shooting?"

Jules's bluntness was legendary and I should have foreseen the question. It was his legal right to ask it. I resorted to prevarication.

"What do you think?"

He chuckled softly. "When in doubt answer a question with another question. Nevertheless, I will tell you what I think. We have known each other for five, no, six years. I know you're quite wealthy. We've never discussed how you came by your wealth, and unless there is a legal reason why I need to know, I don't insist that you tell me." Jules' usual affable tone was hardening. "Yes, I think you probably are involved in this affair. And if you are involved, then I think maybe you did what they say you did."

The lights changed to green. I pointed to it.

"Drive on, my friend. I'll find myself a new lawyer."

He made no immediate comment, just drew agitatedly on his cigarette. He spun the wheel and we turned left up the Route des Arcacias. The rain was as bad as ever, but Jules drove serenely, keeping his distance from the vehicle in front.

"You're too sensitive," he admonished a minute or so later. "You're not merely a client, you are my friend. Friends don't desert each other in times of difficulty. Is that not how it is in your country, whichever your county is?"

I allowed myself a grin. "Thanks, Jules. Thanks, friend."

"We'll speak no more of this matter unless you say so. I'm quite certain you'll not be troubled again by Engels."

I wished I shared his confidence.

Thunder crackled overhead as we arrived outside the apartment. Jules tucked the Merc tidily into a slot between two lesser conveyances and, leaving the engine running, twisted sideways to face me again, an elbow resting languidly on the back of his seat. Ash tumbled from his cigarette onto his knee.

"So, nothing is changed, André, *hein?*"

"Nothing at all. Come up for a drink. There's someone I'd like you to meet."

He shook his head regretfully. "I'm sorry, I cannot. I have an appointment in fifteen minutes." He took off his glasses and polished the lenses vigorously with a Kleenex. "Nellie was asking about you the other day."

Nellie was Jules' second wife, a vivacious thirty to his nudging fifty. She was as frivolous and mercurial as Jules was staid and sober, an amazing contrast in personalities. I liked her a lot and had no designs on her at all. Well, hardly any.

"Come and have dinner tomorrow night." Jules's invitation over-rode a mildly lascivious mirage. "Bring your new friend."

"Okay, thanks. I'll look forward to it. About eight?"

"*Parfait.*"

The rain had abated to a light drizzle, the thunder a resentful mutter backing away across the lake.

I got out. He lowered the passenger window.

"Until tomorrow," I said through the open window and watched him drive off toward the city on twin geysers of spray.

————

IN THE BASEMENT restaurant of the P'tit Vegas Club on the north side of the Rhône, fine dining and fine drinking were the order of the day, albeit at extortionate prices. It wasn't the sort of place where you dined alone, nor where you would expect to pick up some cruising floozy. The P'tit Vegas catered for the rich and the influential, the upper strata of Geneva society. The service was up there with the London Ritz, the atmosphere made for lovers, and there was a discreet gaming room for those with money to burn—hence the 'Vegas'.

I escorted Gina to this playground of the plutocracy on the evening of her first day as my houseguest. She was in good form, displaying a healthy appetite and a talent for silly small talk. With more than half a magnum of Dom Pérignon inside us, we were both relaxed and putting our inhibitions on hold.

Throughout the meal the nine-piece band maintained a stream of background music, subtle and unobtrusive. Once the serious eating was over and the majority of diners were sitting back over coffee and cognac, the musicians pepped up their output. The floor was soon thronged with twirling couples, their movements convulsive under the colored strobe lights.

"Would you like to?" I said to Gina.

"Dance?" She looked out across the floor and nodded. "Sure, love to. It's been ages, so I might get my feet tangled with yours."

"I'll chance it."

I pushed my chair back and went around to take her hand as she rose. She smiled at me, and I saw no sadness there now. Sheathed in an ankle-length simple green dress that rippled as she walked, she drew more than one keen glance from the male contingent. Her hair was loose, caressing her bare back, shimmering with rainbow colors from the lights. I sensed that beneath those heavy, sensuous eyelids, behind that occasional icy composure, lurked an Aladdin's cave of passion. All it would take to open it was the right combination. Get it wrong and the works would jam up solid and stay that way, like a badly blown safe.

As a dancer, she was out of my class. I felt like a clumping yokel as we waltzed and tangoed, bossa nova-ed and jived. And always her body, slender and sinuous with its curves and hollows and legs that went on forever, was close, too close. It was more than flesh and blood could bear. Yet I stiffened my upper lip, stuck out my jaw and held my baser instincts in check.

During a slow, intimate waltz, she let me draw her closer still, and with the melding of our bodies, thigh-to-thigh, chest-to-chest, I became aroused. What was more I sensed a corresponding arousal in her. It took the form of a deep, inner pulsation, steady and regular, and her skin was on fire under my touch.

"Feeling good?" I said.

"Oh, *yes*. Very, very good."

We smooched on a bit longer, then she said in that taunting singsong children often use, "I-know-some-thing-you-don't."

I entered into the spirit of the occasion and singsonged back, "Are-you-go-ing-to-tell me?"

She stopped right there in the middle of the *Dreamcatcher Waltz*, those catlike eyes flickering over the contours of my face, as if she were seeing them clearly as never before.

"What's the matter?" I asked, concerned.

She was tense and still. Around us, the other dancers maneuvered, sliding curious glances our way. She bit her lip, started to speak, checked herself, then it finally came out in a rush. "I'm falling in love with you."

For once my handbook of platitudes failed me. I was caught well and truly wrong-footed. The usual slick rejoinders would have been inappropriate. She had bared her emotions before me. Sincerity was the least I owed her.

"Let's sit down." I took her elbow and we weaved between twirling couples to our table. There, I poured the last of the champagne.

"To us," I proposed. Then, gulping a huge breath, "To our love."

She gave me an uncertain look, her glass raised tentatively. "Do you feel the same then? Truly?"

I was like a man on a ledge at the top of a tall building, bent on suicide, but shrinking from the irrevocable terminal plunge.

"I won't placate you with an outright "yes", but...I think so. I really do think so. I may even have been in love with you since the day we met at the hotel in Digne. Admitting it, even to myself, was something else. I'd had a bellyful of love—so-called love." Here I was thinking particularly of Rebecca, my Jewess lover, whom I courted on the rebound from Marion. "But you...you're special, unique. You're..." I fished around in my storehouse of superlatives for one that conveyed what I felt about her. "You're sensational in every sense of the word."

I held both her hands and leaned across the table to kiss her.

As kisses go it was not earth shattering, a delicate meeting of lips, a tentative sampling as with a vintage wine, an appetizer. But it was no less memorable for that. It marked the end of a beginning and, though neither of us could have foreseen it, the beginning of an end.

"I love you," I said softly, and it was as near true as no longer mattered.

"I love you, my darling," she whispered back with a trace of shyness.

We clinked glasses.

I drank the champagne, but didn't taste it. I tasted only an elation so heady it made me dizzy and lightheaded. She was mine. This stunner of a girl sitting before me, manifestly happy, the lights picking out the planes and angles of her beauty, casting shadows along her jaw line, emphasizing the smooth texture of her skin. All mine.

We talked. Endearing phrases, avowals of love repeated over and over. The exchanges, often trite, but no less meaningful, that bounce back and forth between lovers the world over. From here on, as we saw it, we could only go forward, building on the foundations of our feelings, tightening the knot that already held us in bondage.

I swore to make her happy.

"Oh, darling, I know you will. My only regret is that I didn't give in sooner, that I fought against my feelings." She cupped a hand under her chin, gazing at me with an intensity that was disturbing. "I've been so stupid. So blind to so many things."

I stroked her lips, tracing their outline with my forefinger. She kissed my fingertip, a gesture so simple, yet somehow incredibly moving. I reached back into the past. Was this how it had been with Marion? I couldn't be sure, it was so long ago; a waning memory in a distant pigeonhole of my mind; a fallen leaf, brown and curling at the edges, disintegrating slowly, but necessarily to make way for new life, for a new love. A sense of disloyalty pricked me. I deflected it. It would return, I was sure of that. Somehow I would deal with it, maybe learn to adapt to it.

Later we danced again, touching everywhere now, oblivious of our fellow dancers. We were suspended in a fifth dimension, a make-believe world where no one else existed and nothing else mattered, except that we were together. And for a while, I imagined there would be a happy ending, like in a Mills & Boon romance.

Inevitably, sanity returned to remind me of the quicksand foundation on which my immediate future rested. The afternoon's session with Engels nagged at me still. The business with Schelling remained a festering abscess. Then, too, I was committed to meet Bonhomme, though the temptation to resume my old profession had evaporated. Gina had changed all that. She had changed my whole life.

A more basic need subjugated those worries. I escorted Gina back to the table.

"I have to leave you for a minute," I said.

"Another appointment with your lawyer? Or is it your shrink this time?"

The twinkle in her eyes told me she was joking.

I kissed her lightly on the forehead. "Even we supermen have to visit the washroom."

Her lips sculpted a kiss to speed me there.

I returned it, before heading off toward the discreetly signposted *toilettes*. They were located in the darkest corner of the restaurant, as if bodily functions were beneath the exalted clientele of the P'tit Vegas.

In keeping with the rest of the place, the washroom was immaculate, apart from the odd cigarette butt on the orange-tiled floor. I watered the nearest urinal and was shaking off the drips when the door opened on what I assumed to be another full bladder. My sideways glance took in a pair of dark-suited characters. Some deep down instinct of self-preservation warned me they were bad news. My instinct was reliable; they came straight for me. I just had time enough to zip up before they pounced, and they pounced hard. Both my arms were seized above and below the elbow. I was whirled around and flung against the wide mirror above the washbasins that lined the opposite wall. My nose made violent contact with the glass and blood sprayed. For a moment the three of us were poised staring at our reflections, mine twisted with pain, theirs grim and brutish.

The bigger of my two assailants sported a garish yellow tie to set off his loose-fitting dark blue suit. He had big Bambi eyes, at odds with his general thuggish appearance. The other was black, with wild hair, as if he had just received an electric shock. Bambi Eyes let go with his right hand to fumble inside his jacket. I kicked out backwards, connecting with his shin. It was like kicking a tree trunk. The bastard didn't even grunt, though his grip on my arm loosened fractionally. I consolidated my flimsy gain by thrusting backwards, dragging the black goon along with me. We hit the tiles in a tangle. Blackie came off worst, cracking his skull on the rim of a urinal. The result was his immediate incapacity, leaving me to concentrate on Bambi, physically the more formidable of the pair.

As Bambi and I picked ourselves up, his hirsute fist acquired an extension in the shape of a big, butch automatic. I gave him no chance to use it and kicked out again, aiming for his balls. He was a mile ahead of me, his own foot intercepting mine in mid-flight, catching me on the calf and knocking me off-balance. I went backwards, tripped over the comatose form of Blackie, to finish up sprawled on the tiles in my almost new mohair suit.

While I was still floundering in the cigarette butts, Bambi wagged his abbreviated cannon at me.

"*Ca suffit!*" he barked in a voice reminiscent of crunching gravel.

The muzzle of the gun was ogling me and it didn't look friendly.

"Get up!" The crunched gravel was crunchier, more menacing. I obeyed, groaning as pain stabbed at me from several angles. My nose was dripping blood. Bambi pushed me up against the washbasin counter again, prodding impatiently with the gun. Half-concussed from my fall, I was in no condition to argue. His frisking was swift and practiced, but I wasn't packing so much as a razor blade. If I had been he would have found it, he was that thorough.

"What's this all about?" I demanded, feigning indignation, my arms and legs still spread, my midriff hard against the counter.

"You don't know?" Bambi's tone was incredulous.

"Would I ask if I did? You've got the wrong guy."

"You've been fingered, buddy. No question—it's you we want."

I switched to a different approach. "Who's "we"? Schelling?"

"Who?" Bambi growled.

Noises of revival were issuing from Blackie.

Bambi ripped off a terse command, which roughly translated as "Stop fucking about."

"Are you going to kill me?" I asked, pretty sure now that he wasn't.

He displayed a crowded mouthful of teeth in varying stages of decay. "Kill you, buddy? You should be so lucky. You're going on a little trip to the seaside. I got strict orders about you."

That was all I needed—the all-clear to take him without fear of a lethal bullet.

Blackie was up on his knees now, shaking himself like a dog after a swim. If I was going to move against Bambi, I had to do it before he rejoined the party. Yet still I wavered. Going for an armed man takes a lot of nerve. I wasn't sure I had that much.

Need overruled nerve. I let my legs buckle, as if I were about to collapse from sheer terror. Strong as he was, my hundred and eighty pounds burden put a strain on his muscles.

"Get up, you creep!" He grabbed a lapel of my much-abused suit and tried to haul me back upright. A seam parted under the stress. His balance and concentration were both upset, the gun wandered, and I rose up underneath him. My forehead crunched into his chin, snapping his head backwards. The rest of him went along with it. He fell over Blackie who was in the closing stages of his climb back from the floor, resulting in a pileup that took out both my assailants. Even the gun chose a different trajectory from its owner. It bounced off the mirror, shattering it, and ricocheted off along the tiles.

A multitude of "*Merdes*" and earthier also ricocheted about the place. I didn't stick around to learn new expletives. On my way out of the washroom, I discovered the door had been wedged from the inside to discourage interruptions. I kicked the wedge away and hit the corridor, assuming a sedate stroll and an air of unconcern. As I strolled, I mopped the blood from my upper lip with a handkerchief, and brushed the miscellaneous deposits from my once-immaculate suit. That made two sets of apparel I had ruined in the last few days. Smoothing back my hair, I reentered the restaurant to collide with Gina in the doorway. She stumbled into my arms, her expression a mixture of relief and anxiety.

"Where have you *been*?" she demanded, clinging to me.

"Was I gone long then?" I asked, pecking her on the cheek, oozing insouciance.

"Over ten minutes. And look at the state you're in." She plucked at my sleeve. "Your jacket's torn. You look as if you've been in a fight."

"I have." I steered her back to our table. "We're leaving."

"If you say so."

I retrieved her clutch bag and thrust it into her hand.

"What's going on, André?"

As we headed for the *caisse*, I gave her an edited rundown of my skirmish with the two goons.

"You remember I told you about some guys tailing me everywhere," I said. She nodded worriedly. "Well, I've just bumped into more of the same in the john. It was quite a collision."

I felt her grip tighten on my bicep. "Are you all right? You're not hurt?"

"A bruise or two; nothing a Band-Aid can't fix. Oh, and an expensive suit that'll never be the same again."

"Fuck the suit!" she said crossly.

I had a credit account at the Vegas. A hasty scrawl on a bill, created by a computer gone berserk to judge from the number of digits, and we were out of there. I banked on Bambi and Blackie taking five minutes or more to sort themselves out for another try. Long enough for us to get well clear of the scene.

The doorman rustled up a cab right away. Gina and I huddled together on the back seat in a clinch that allowed me to keep an eye on any following vehicle. Traffic was light and no one showed any interest in us. As we crossed the Rhône by the Mont Blanc Bridge, the road behind was clear.

My heart wasn't really in our necking. Moreover, I was so rattled by the incident at the Vegas that I gave almost no thought to the delights that might await me when we got back to the apartment.

In the event, we slept in our own beds. At the outset anyhow. In the predawn, when darkness still ruled, Gina came to me: her decision, her move. Taking the initiative, not merely submitting to my advances. It was perfect. I was exactly how I had hoped it would be.

The door opened without my hearing it. Only when her warm bare flesh brushed mine did I jerk into wakefulness, tensed for action, the old defensive mechanism sending my hand under the mattress in search of the Glock. A touch of fingers on my stomach, light as fantasy, pulled me back to reality. My nerve ends tingled as I came fully awake and conscious of who and what, and especially why. A breast pressed against my arm, and I put my hand on it. Gently at first, and when I wasn't rebuffed, more firmly, I fondled the nipple, which responded emphatically, becoming pebble-hard.

I kissed her on the mouth and the sweetness of it swept away the debauchery of my past, transporting me back to the days beyond my first love when ideas and ideals shone bright as a polished trophy. It was a kiss that left me weak with the wonder and the power of it.

"Darling...darling..." She kept repeating it, over and over, her voice unrecognizably hoarse.

My mouth descended to her breast and lingered over a nipple that hardened anew under my oral caress. She was moaning and squirming. I nibbled experimentally and her body heaved as in a spasm. Her hands were busy too, sliding tentatively over my rigid prick, hovering there, then, as if she had come to a major decision, grasping firmly and pumping away at it. My tongue trekked downward over her ribs to explore her smooth midriff with its deep navel and continued on toward the thatch of crispy curls, last defensive line before the zone of pleasure. My lips rested on her pubis, kissing lightly, tugging the hairs with my teeth before venturing southwards. Her legs were locked together, but they yielded to my persuasion and unclenched with tantalizing slowness, the inner thighs trembling and dewed with sweat. Her vaginal lips parted, like foliage at the entrance to a secret cavern. The unforgettable smell of woman aroused was released: piquant, slightly musky, inflammatory. I kissed the intricate folds of skin and she cried out harshly, an alien sound.

"Do it, darling." It was almost a sob. "Oh, God, do it now...*now!*"

I was ready. Boy, was I ever ready. I went up on my elbows and entered her, a flowing, coordinated incursion. A few savage thrusts had her panting, her breath coming in little screams, underscoring every stroke. It was as violent a coming together as I had ever experienced.

We had too much pent-up restraint to release to make a marathon session of it. By the time it was over, I was a condemned man. Committed totally and unequivocally to this woman. The debauchery of the past blasted away, as if it had never been more than a chimera. As deeply, possessively, insanely in love as it was possible to be.

Dear God, I've denied you often enough, I said in silent prayer, *but if you exist, let this be my end as an assassin. Let this be my re-birth as a man.*

PART 2

JUST ONE MORE HIT

CHAPTER NINE

ELEVEN YEARS as an assassin and forty deaths lay at my door. Was it possible to break the sixth commandment so often and for so long, and still qualify as a paid-up member of the human race? If my old SIS buddy, Tony Dimeloe, hadn't encouraged me to fly to Egypt to meet a man with a certain need, I might today have been a company executive, living in London's West End or Toronto's Lawrence Park district. Maybe with a wife and kids and the trappings of respectability.

Indirectly and ironically, it was on account of the referral from Tony that I wound up at the Aubergine Club in downtown Cairo the same evening as an American contract killer.

For the best part of a week I had been kicking my heels at the Gresham Hotel, a few doors away from the Aubergine. Tony's contact, Karim Mahfouz, had fixed me up with a room there, when I called him after blowing into town.

"Wait there until you hear from me," was all he said after I introduced myself.

So I waited, and waited. Days crawled by. During my wait, out of sheer boredom, I did the usual touristy stuff: a boat ride on the Nile, a bus ride to the pyramids, a walk around the shops, and a crawl around the bars. I also bought a car; a VW Beetle of years gone by, true retro, not the current fake retro model.

The first time I parked my heap outside the Gresham, the wind-shield wipers went walkabout. Next day the hubcaps, then the VW badge. After that, while the car still had wheels, I found a ramshackle garage to rent just off Talaat Harb Street. The garage roof was full of holes, but as it almost never rains in Cairo this was no handicap.

So there I was, on that fateful evening, at the Aubergine. Slightly smashed, not quite down and out, but running short of cash and credit, waiting and hoping that the man who wanted someone with a gun would contact me. The portents were not promising. A shriek of female laughter had dragged my eyes from the dregs of my beer to where a husky guy with pepper-and-salt hair, probably Anglo-Saxon, was giving Fawzia the chat. Fawzia, the resident belly dancer, was narrow of waist, buxom of hip, with a belly built for wobbling. She was also an inveterate flirt. Her new friend spotted me watching them and beckoned me over.

This so surprised me that I mouthed, "Who *me*?" After all, my butting in wasn't calculated to enhance his prospects with Fawzia. When he nodded, I went over. Maybe he would stand me a beer. Crossing the cracked tiled floor, I exchanged glances with Hashim, the bartender. His impressive eyebrows contracted into a heavy frown.

"What?" I snapped at him with a frown of my own, though I couldn't compete in the eyebrow stakes.

He made a gesture with his head toward Fawzia and her admirer. Sober, I might have heeded the reminder that Fawzia was the personal property of Bakhoum, the club's owner. But I wasn't, so I didn't.

With a dismissive wave of my hand, I joined the happy couple.

"Hello there," I said, banging my empty glass on the counter as a hint.

"Hi, fella." The husky guy grinned, exhibiting a small fortune in gold-capped dental work.

The girl looked a bit startled at my intrusion on their cozy chat. I had exchanged greetings with her once or twice on previous visits, but we weren't even on flirting terms. Back then, still pining for Marion, I was at best a half-hearted seducer.

"It's okay, Fawzia," the guy soothed. He had a Deep South drawl. "This is an old friend of mine."

"Am I?" Beer made me slow on the uptake. "Oh, yes, I *am*. Hi,

Fawzia, I'm André." The intro was as much for the American's benefit as hers.

"Yeah, André," he said, catching on quick to my name. "Good to see you again. You remember me, huh? Ken Collier."

"Sure, I remember." Hands were shaken under Fawzia's scowling gaze. Fortunately, her English was rudimentary, so a lot of the banter passed her by.

"What'll it be, André?"

I'd thought he'd never ask. "A Fosters."

"And I'll have champagne," Fawzia trumpeted. She wasn't amused by our little pantomime.

"No you won't, you minx. You'll have beer." He leered at me. "It makes 'em fart, did you know that, Andy?" He roared with laughter.

I hadn't known. A demonstration I could live without.

The beers came, Hashim still wriggling his brow foliage. He smelled trouble, that much was obvious to anyone whose mind wasn't saturated with booze. Collier, Fawzia, and I raised glasses to mouths in unison, the girl finishing ahead of us males. She didn't fart. Not audibly or even odoriferously. Another round was ordered. Collier and I got to talking about places we both knew. They were numerous. Apparently, he was a well-travelled man, like me. I asked him, in all innocence, what he did for a living.

His chunky face closed up. He didn't look friendly any more.

"It's kinda confidential," he said at last.

Hmm, interesting. As much as I found anything interesting these days, outside of the thinness of my wallet. I didn't probe. So long as he kept setting up the beers, his credentials were fine by me.

We were steering the conversation back to non-confidential topics when Bakhoum strolled in, the usual convoy of hangers-on in tow. The club's owner was an enormous blimp of a man, his body a perfect sphere surmounted by a pointed bald dome. His cream suit looked as if it had been fed through a wringer and left to dry in the sun, and his tie was twisted back to front with the label on display. Not sartorially inclined then. The hangers-on, bees around a honey pot, were to a man, scrawny, facially-challenged runts.

From Collier's point of view, it was unfortunate that his decision to grope Fawzia's comely backside coincided with Bakhoum's entry.

The Egyptian, advancing ponderously toward the bar, did a classic double-take and let rip a squeal of fury. For a big man he had a high-pitched voice. Absorbed in each other, Collier and Fawzia appeared not to notice. Perhaps they thought it was a kettle coming to the boil. He just carried on kneading her butt and she carried on relishing it.

Flicking aside some reeling drunk who happened to cross his path, Bakhoum came thundering down on us like a stampeding elephant. I moved in his path with some ill-thought-out scheme about reasoning with him before he ploughed into Collier. This was a mistake. A smack to my head almost removed it from my shoulders.

Up to that point Collier had remained unaware of the developing drama. My abrupt change of stance—from vertical to horizontal—in company with several chairs, a table, and two customers, alerted him to the wrath about to descend. As I slithered to the floor amid the debris, Collier turned, releasing Fawzia, and collected a punch in the nose that made mine look like a fond caress.

My new friend was projected over the bar, glass flying from his hand. The crash of his landing set the bottles tinkling on the shelves. I heaved aside a foot that was exploring the contours of my face, and went to Collier's aid. Not by tackling Bakhoum—I wasn't *that* tired of living—just checking to make sure the poor bastard was alive. By this time Bakhoum had transferred his attentions to Fawzia; the poor kid had fallen to her knees, wailing, and was tugging plaintively at the cummerbund that had the job of holding that gross midriff in check.

Bakhoum wasn't having any truck with forgiveness or compassion. Nor was he deterred by the local wife-beating laws, if any existed. The cuff he dealt her was enough to send her cartwheeling, arms and legs flailing, and she screamed prettily as she went.

I picked up a chair and shook it at him threateningly; Sir Galahad to the rescue. He stared at me as if I were mad.

Bakhoum on his own versus me made lousy odds. Not lousy enough to satisfy him it seemed: his entourage had formed a ring around me and the hands of some of them had grown knives—long, thin-bladed shivs, designed for penetrating between the rib bones. The club had emptied. Only Bakhoum and his private army, Collier, Fawzia, and Sir Galahad remained. Oh, and Hashim the barman, the top of whose head was just visible behind the counter.

Maybe if I explained to Bakhoum that I was just an innocent bystander.

"Look, Mr. Bakhoum..."

He made a chopping motion with his hand. The hangers-on closed in, knives to the forefront. Maneuvering room was becoming restricted.

It was Collier who bailed me out. Quite properly, since he started it. He rose up behind the bar, nose flattened and gushing gore, right arm dangling uselessly by his side, surely broken. Damaged but not downtrodden: with his good arm he launched a liter bottle of what looked like quality Scotch straight at Bakhoum's head. It slammed into the guy's left ear with an impact that would have killed your average man. Bakhoum, being Bakhoum, just shook his head, and emitted a two-hundred decibel roar. Moving faster than I would have believed possible for someone the size of a hot-air balloon, he went for Collier.

Collier didn't run away. From inside his baggy windbreaker, he pulled a gun.

My four years with the British Secret Intelligence Service had acquainted me with most marketable handguns. Collier's was a hefty Browning GP-35 9mm, with the 13-round magazine. Thirteen rounds would put a strain on any digestive system, even Bakhoum's.

Collier's play had brought everyone to a standstill, the elephantine one included.

"Right, fatboy," the American said, grinning now, lips drawn wolfishly back over his rather prominent gold-capped teeth. "You wanna play games, huh?"

"Collier, let it go—" I began, but he silenced me with a hard glance.

"This pumpkin busted my arm. Now I'm gonna bust something of his, so's he won't forget me in a hurry."

"Wait, you bonehead! This guy's Mister Big around here. He'll have you boiled in oil, or skinned alive, or something."

"You will be well-advised to listen to this gentleman," Bakhoum said to Collier, in that reedy voice that sounded like a choirboy's. "You will never leave Cairo alive if any harm comes to me."

Collier sniggered nervously. His fixed stare subsided and he gave a jerky nod.

"Okay, blimp, maybe you got a point. But you and your play-mates..." His eyes roved over Bakhoum's seedy crew. "...better keep from under my feet. Next time, I won't be so forgiving."

Bakhoum didn't respond but his eyes were twin pebbles of hate. A lot of malice was stored up inside that mountain of flesh. Maybe I wasn't so smart aligning myself with Collier.

"Come on, Ken," I urged. I didn't rate his chances of holding Bakhoum at bay for long, even with a gun.

The hangers-on fell back, opening up like the petals of a flower as Collier and I made good our retreat, him with his gun, me flourishing my chair. His broken arm flopped like a puppet's and he kept emitting little snorts of pain.

At the door, I unloaded the chair. He stashed the Browning out of sight, and we ran for it.

"Where to?" Collier asked, as we shoved through the street crowds. "I'm staying at the Gresham."

"Me too. But first we need to get you to a hospital."

He pulled up short, grabbing my sleeve with his good hand.

"No way, brother. No hospital. No doctors."

"Why not, for Christ's sake? You need to get that break set."

"I gotta steer clear of hospitals—let's leave it at that." The snarl he used on Bakhoum was back in place. He was an intimidating guy, even with a busted wing. "You can set a break, can't you? It ain't mega science. We'll use your room."

"Look, Collier," I said heavily. "You can forget it." I needed him as a room-mate-cum-patient like I needed green skin.

"Goddam it, Andy, or whatever your name is, do I have to shove a gun up *your* nose now?"

Coming on top of my upset with Bakhoum, I wasn't exactly desperate for a showdown with a gun-toting Collier.

We darted into the hotel, trying to behave like normal guests, collected our keys and took the stairs to my room on the third floor.

His wasn't the first broken limb I had set. In Afghanistan, on my first tour of duty abroad, I had to fix a broken leg and ankle for an Afghan colleague. By comparison, Collier's upper arm fracture was a walkover. Two handy lengths of wood, filched from my so-called closet, served as splints, and he was a ninety-per cent going concern again. His bent nose was probably best left to heal itself.

Letting him use my room for convalescence was not an option as far as I was concerned. His room was three doors along the corridor and the layout identical: two single beds with rust-colored throws, en-suite bathroom alcove, bare light bulbs, and a hanging space without hangers for clothes. The floor didn't look as if it had been cleaned lately, if ever, same as mine.

I tucked him up in one of the beds, heavily dosed with aspirin, and hoped that was the end of his part in my life.

———

OVER BREAKFAST, consumed standing at a mobile sandwich bar near the hotel and shared with my personal retinue of blowflies, Collier and I bumped into each other. Call it serendipity.

"Thanks for the nursing," was his opening salutation as he pitched up beside me at the bar counter.

The tone was grudging but I didn't let it rile me.

"You're welcome," I said, breaking a chunk off an over-baked roll and spreading it with honey. "But don't you think you owe me an explanation?"

His look was blank. "Explanation? What the fuck for? Nobody asked you to stick your snout in last night. I didn't need your help."

"Not at the club, I grant you. But if I hadn't stuck my snout in, as you delicately put it, you would've spent the night in a police cell, having your other arm broken. Bakhoum pulls weight here, including with the law. Aside from that, who else would have fixed your arm and kept quiet about it?"

"All right, all right," he growled, flapping at one of my blowflies. "You want me to grovel? You want dough? I don't mind paying, just tell me the going rate for splinting an arm." He reached inside his jacket, awkwardly left-handed, and drew out a roll of money fat enough to block a sink.

The money would have been useful, but I let the opportunity pass. "Put that away, this place is teeming with pickpockets. Just tell me one thing, Ken: why wouldn't you let me take you to the hospital? What are you up to in Cairo?"

Unable to tear his croissant one-handed, he took a bite from it whole, his close-set eyes boring into me. He made me feel he could see inside my skull.

A babble of voices, raised in argument, wafted over us. It was all Egyptian Arabic, but insults were clearly being exchanged.

"That's two things," Collier said, after a lengthy deliberation. "I guess I gotta tell you anyhow. This arm is gonna give me a king-size problem."

I sipped coffee. It tasted vile, which was the norm in the places where I could afford to buy refreshment.

"What do *you* do, Andy?" The sun was on his face, highlighting deep rifts around his nose and mouth. Daylight had put ten years on him. I doubted he'd see fifty again.

"Me?" I was unprepared for the question. I'd thought I was conducting the interrogation. "Nothing much. I came here to meet a guy, see about a job. He fixed me up at the hotel, and I'm supposed to wait for him."

"You don't say. Me likewise, though I saw the guy yesterday and got the job already."

Coincidence? If so, pursuing it with Collier wasn't likely to produce results. He wasn't the kind to open up to a stranger. Well, that was my impression, until he suddenly said, "I need to talk to you someplace more private. Let's go up to my room."

I fluttered my eyelashes. "My goodness. This is so unexpected."

"Oh, for Christ's sake."

Up in his room he sat on the edge of the bed and, using an old-fashioned wick lighter, ignited a cigarette from a pack of Lucky Strike Export. I plunked on the straight-back chair. It shuddered and groaned.

Without preliminaries, he said, "How'd you like to earn thirty grand?"

"Thirty grand?" I said stupidly. "You mean thirty thousand dollars?"

He unleashed a snorting laugh. "What else?"

"Thirty *thousand* dollars," I repeated, tasting the numbers. They were succulent, all right.

"In cash."

Even better.

"Thirty thousand in cash?"

He lifted a buttock and broke wind extravagantly. "Look, quit saying it over and over. I'm offering you thirty big ones for maybe a couple of hours' work. Now, are you interested or not?"

Having finally adjusted to the amount of money involved, I became wary. "What do I have to do for this thir—What's the job?"

"Kill somebody." He said it quickly but matter-of-factly. "A policeman, sort of."

"Kill a policeman?" There I went again. Then it penetrated. "Are you out of your fucking skull?"

He got up and walked to the open window. The argument down below was still in progress and escalating. A yelp of pain was followed by shouting. The empty right sleeve of Collier's shirt flapped in the breeze. He stood there for a while, stirring restlessly at intervals. Half of me hoped he would let the matter drop. The other half was already hooked. Or let's just say I was curious. But to *kill* a man? Having done it before, albeit only with Government sanction, didn't mean I wanted it to become a habit.

Or a living.

Breathing out hard through his nose, Collier came back into the center of the room.

"I'm here on a...contract," he announced. "You know what that means, I figure."

"A contract?" I made a small giggle in the back of my throat. "Sure. You're going to kill someone on behalf of a third party and be paid for it. No mystery about that."

It explained his practiced handling of the gun at the Aubergine Club. Also his refusal to go to hospital. A professional hit man needed to stay away from officialdom in all its shapes and sizes.

"That's exactly right." He ran agitated fingers through his grey-flecked hair. "Say, were you ever in the army? Ever shoot a guy?"

"Not exactly in the army. But, yes, I did do a stint for the government in a semi-military capacity." More than that I was averse to making public. The Official Secrets act has a long reach.

"That a fact? And did you go to go bang-bang with a gun?"

My hesitation-cum-reticence was all the answer he needed.

"So you did shoot somebody, huh?"

"Leave it alone," I grunted. "It's not a topic for discussion."

More finger-combing was followed by more pacing.

"Hell, Andy, I wish I was sure you could be trusted."

"Come off it. If you had any doubts, you wouldn't have told me in the first place."

"Yeah." Slowly, reflectively. "Yeah, I guess that's so." He sat on the bed again, drawing hard on his cigarette. "What about it then? Will you do it?"

"What makes you think I'm capable of it, Ken? You're talking about a capital crime, also known as murder."

His face fell then, as if it hadn't occurred to him.

"Yeah, well, if you ain't, you ain't. It'd bug you, huh, wasting a guy, just like that, cold?"

"Tell me some more."

So he talked and I listened. He talked about the time, the place, and the target, a high-ranking police officer who doubled as a vicious thug. Collier's paymaster—paymistress, rather—was the widow of a political dissident who died under torture, presided over by said police officer. If true, he deserved to be put down. If it wasn't true...Funny, but the moral aspect didn't trouble me as much as I would have expected. It was a job. It was a purpose. It might even have been a vocation-in-waiting. You might say I needed it more than it needed me.

When Collier was done talking, he lit another Lucky Strike and focused his gaze on me.

"Well?"

"Make it fifty thousand."

———

ULTRA-HIGH TEMPERATURES WERE of course the norm for Egypt in June. I just wasn't in the habit of exposing myself to them. It was too hot even for sweat: all moisture simply evaporated. The rocks on which I sprawled were plenty hot too, which was fine for the basking lizard community. So there I was, gently cooking. At least I had known enough not to wear shorts and short sleeves, and to bring a hat and a flask of chilled juice.

It was ten to three: ten minutes to go if the hit—I still didn't know his name—was punctual. Part of the plan was that Collier would call me on my cell phone when the subject set off. I wasn't hopeful he would succeed in making contact. Reception out here would be weak at best. No need to answer it, he told me. If I heard a ring, it would be him and the hit would be on the road.

I took up the rifle. It wasn't new, not by a few decades, but it had been well cared for along the line. The walnut stock was oiled and unmarked, the metal parts free of rust. The words Weatherby Mark V were etched along the top of the barrel, beyond the Weaver V8 tele-scopic sight with its neat hinged covers. It was a bolt-action piece, five-round magazine, .300 caliber. A quirky choice for an assassination. My own preference would have been a Belgian FN 7.62mm or an M14; both semi-automatic, allowing me to squeeze off three or four shots while I'd still be operating the bolt of the Weatherby. It was accurate enough though. At a practice session near the remote Lake Qarun, west of Cairo, I placed all five rounds in an inch group at a hundred paces. Then, as today, I wore surgical gloves to handle the gun. The only fingerprints on it would be Collier's. Impromptu contract though it was, I was taking all the right precautions by instinct.

The minute finger of my watch was hovering over the hour when my cell phone trilled feebly. I flipped it open, put it to my ear. Static was all I heard. No sweat. The call alone was enough to tell me that the hit had started out from Sinnuris, twenty minutes' drive distant.

All was quiet, the road evidently seldom used. Even the flies dozed. On a flat stone, just beyond arm's reach, a sand-colored lizard, about a foot long from tongue to tail, regarded me with an unblinking eye. It was motionless, prostrated by the heat, which made both of us. I changed my position and in a blur of movement it was gone.

The vista before me, from my perch above the road, was unre-lieved ochre with a solitary splash of green at the limit of my vision.

Fayoum Oasis, according to my map. I wished I was there, under the swaying palms, scoffing dates, with a bevy of Fawzias fanning my over-heated brow.

A puff of dust rose from the road out by the junction with Route 2, the Cairo to Luxor highway. It grew into a long brown pennant with a boxy vehicle at its head. Land Rover or Jeep. My watch said twenty-five past two. Sure to be my man. The vehicle was about a mile away now, travelling fast for the rough terrain. Three minutes at the outside and he would be here, making the hairpin turn at the end of my escarpment, slowing to a crawl. A perfect sniper's target. Three minutes left for me to reflect, to return to sanity, to pack up and scuttle off back to the hotel. To wait for the mysterious Karim, who also needed a gunslinger.

To hand back to Collier the advance payment of twenty-five thousand US dollars.

No thank you, not today. I lifted the Weatherby, cuddled the rubber recoil pad into my shoulder, lined up the crosshairs of the scope on a pair of boulders at the curve of the hairpin. Made a last-minute adjustment to the focus. Worked the action, a series of satis-fying metallic clunks, shunting the topmost bullet into the firing chamber.

The dust trail was much closer now, under half a mile. The vehicle was temporarily screened by some low dunes alongside the road. When it came back into view I saw it was a Willys military jeep. Well-worn with beige paintwork. The faded canvas top was raised to keep the sun off. Just two occupants. The driver wore a short-sleeved beige tunic and fez. His passenger similarly attired apart from his peaked cap and epaulettes. Through the flat windshield I could make out the latter's features: swarthy, moustache like a hairy caterpillar on his top lip, hooked nose. He would make a first-rate Hollywood villain.

The crosshairs cantered on his chest. Still I held my fire. They were doing about forty, though the driver was coming down through the gears now as they entered the long, looping curve before the hairpin itself. My chosen killing ground.

All emotion fled from me. I was now no more than a machine. Press the starter button and off I would go, like an electronic toy. Nothing existed outside me, the gun, and the target. It was not necessary to think. Only to follow a sequence of prescribed functions. It was just a job. It was business.

That afternoon, lying there on a rocky escarpment in the Egyptian wilderness, I discovered my true métier.

The rifle barrel was as steady as if mounted on a tripod. The sun flailed the skin of my wrists, the only exposed part of me. I scarcely noticed. All that registered was the hard outline of the edge of the escarpment where it came down to meet the road, the air above trembling in the heat, the arid, tree-less backdrop, the unreal blue of the sky.

The jeep crept around the hairpin, filling the scope, and I fired. Just two shots, fast as I could work the action and aim.

The first bullet smashed through the windshield and struck the officer in the chest, plumb center, bending him backwards over the seat back. The flowering smudge of red provided an aiming point for bullet number two, though my aim was spoiled by the jeep's sudden swerve. It careered off the edge of the road, into a draining ditch, pitching the driver from his seat. As it toppled onto its side, I fired twice more, at front and rear tires in succession. Collier had urged me to eliminate the driver too, for my own safety. Faced with the decision, I copped out. The flat tires should slow him long enough to see me back in Cairo and off the streets.

While the dust was still billowing around the overturned jeep, I was up and sliding down the hillside to the Beetle parked in the shadow of an overhanging crag. I shoved the Weatherby in the front end trunk and, with a muttered prayer, turned the starter key. The engine spun, faltered, died. Don't let me down now, you bitch! I repeated the process—whirr, burp, whirr, cough, and with a lusty *vroom* she fired in traditional Beetle fashion, a sort of controlled explosion, settling down to a ragged beat.

I took off from under the crag as if I were piloting a Formula One racer instead of a weary jalopy, bumped across the rock-strewn ground that lay between me and the road. Nothing in sight in either direction. I turned right, away from the hairpin, and made that Beetle perform miracles of acceleration that in theory it was not capable of, even when new. In the mirror, a receding ribbon of empty road, tapering to nothingness.

My nerves quit fluttering and I began to believe I might actually have gotten away with it. For now.

THE ASSASSINATION WAS ANNOUNCED over *Nile FM*, the English-speaking radio, that evening. That was when I learned that my victim was a police Brigadier-General by the name of Rehab Iskandar. The 'Rehab' made me smile to myself. At the time of the broadcast I was in Collier's room, the two of us making short work of a bottle of *zibib,* the schnapps-like local rotgut. To give Collier his due, he handed over the rest of the cash without any prompting.

"Well?" he said, staring at me when I finished counting those crisp, crackly hundred-dollar bills. "How does it feel?"

I riffled the wad before tucking it in my hip pocket. "Like money."

"Not that, asshole," Collier said in exasperation. "To kill somebody. Don't tell me it's an everyday event for you."

"Not quite. But it's not the first time."

Collier had been balanced on two legs of a chair; now he rocked forward, his eyes locked on mine. "So you *have* been in the killing business. Goddamnit, I knew it!"

"Not as a living. As a by-product."

Though he pressed me to elaborate, I clammed up. We said our goodbyes. I settled my hotel account and moved to the other side of town, where I had set up a hideaway with an Egyptian contact from my SIS era. Ten per cent of my wages from Collier bought me a month in a top floor apartment with full room service, even female company, if I were so minded. I wasn't. I was still in love with my dead wife.

My plan was to stay indoors until the heat died down. A daily delivery of the English-language *Cairo Times* was included in the facilities, and this kept me abreast of developments in the slaying of Iskandar. The day after the killing I read that a certain American citizen, name of Kenneth Collier, 49, had been arrested at Alexandria airport, attempting to board an Olympic Airways flight to Athens. He was now being held for questioning on suspicion of having committed the crime. Broken arm and all.

Poor Ken. The irony of it.

It didn't worry me that he might talk. When I was ready to move out, my beard and moustache would be in full flourish, my hair reduced to a buzz cut, and the bogus passport, filched from my SIS collection when I quit, would guarantee my fake identity. Plus, I would cross into Libya via a stretch of frontier in the middle of the desert that wasn't even marked, let alone patrolled. Onward from there would be courtesy of another contact from the recent past. A couple of thousand dollars would see me safely on a plane to Italy.

The Iskandar contract came to me by serendipity. Its follow-up came by recommendation—ironically from my former employers, on behalf of another country's government who needed a job done in a faraway place and were short of recruits with the right skills. Thereafter the grapevine took over. Word got around in the right quarters and people began to approach me, eventually in such numbers that I was obliged to turn work down. I never had to place ads in the personal columns.

CHAPTER TEN

WITH OUR NEW status as committed lovers, it would have seemed odd to Gina if I were to ban her from my jaunt to Annemasse, where I was due to meet Bonhomme. It was a rendezvous I still meant to keep, despite my change of heart about returning to the assassination game. If I stood him up he'd be on the phone demanding to know why, and I couldn't risk another of those 'Mr. Townsend' calls.

Nor could I risk causing a rift between Gina. I wasn't about to make the mistake of shutting her out again.

"I'll do some shopping while you meet your investment guy," she said, when I explained the ostensible reason for the meeting. So it all fell into place very neatly.

All morning and through lunch my mind had been full of the assault at the P'tit Vegas. As we filtered through Customs and entered France in a hired Merc C-Class, it was still plaguing me, representing as it did a major upgrade from surveillance to attempted abduction. But of inspiration there was none. My vital anonymity had been blown, that much was clear. The motives and identity of my enemy remained unknown.

"Penny for them." Gina roused me from my brooding as we turned off the *route nationale* to head into Annemasse downtown.

"Sorry, love. If you want to know, I was bending my brain over last night's fracas at the Vegas club."

"You ought to go to the police."

Such sweet innocence.

"It's not that simple."

The subject rested there while I piloted us into town. Just off the circular Place de l'Etoile, I spotted a car reversing out of a parking slot and nosed the Merc into it, a bumper's width ahead of another applicant. The deprived driver saluted me with an upturned finger in the time-honored manner as he roared away.

Gina stifled a giggle. "You upset him."

I grunted and lined up, nice and neat so as not to give a traffic officer an excuse to slap a ticket on me.

"To get back to what I was saying..." Gina began, looking at me.

"Go to the police? I don't think so. Partly, because I don't have much faith in their competence, and partly because I prefer to take care of it in my own way. But mostly because I'm still bound by the UK Official Secrets Act."

She turned to stare at me. "Official Secrets Act? What's that?"

"It's a long story and I can't tell you all that much anyway, or it won't be a secret any more, but...well, I used to work for the British Government. In a certain, shall we say, hazardous capacity."

Gina continued to stare and her skepticism was plain to see.

"I'm intrigued. Tell me more."

"That's just it, I can't tell you more. Although I retired a long time ago the Act has a long arm, and people have disappeared in the past because they didn't respect it."

It sounded melodramatic, yet it was true and entirely in context with recent events. Somehow though, it struck a wrong note with Gina. Maybe it smacked too much of James Bond and an overactive imagination.

I touched her arm. "Hey, I love you." Saying it already felt natural.

"Oh, darling, I love you, too. So much."

So that was all right then. We still loved each other.

"Shall we go?" I said and opened my door. She slid out, and my eyes were involuntarily drawn to her derriere in those almost indecent sprayed-on jeans. That's love for you.

In the tourist attraction stakes, Annemasse doesn't amount to much. It has a few tree-lined boulevards, the usual square in the center with more trees, a sprinkling of historic architecture, and is infested with traffic. A cross it has to bear owing to its location by the Franco-Swiss border.

By the covered market, Gina and I prepared to part company with a kiss that revved up my motor beyond the red line.

"Call me when your meeting's over," she said. "You have my cell phone number, right?"

"You bet. Tell me though—how come you never seem to get any calls? Are there no girlfriends wanting to yakety-yak about the shoes they just bought or describe how their new boyfriend is *the* one?"

She tapped me on the nose in mock admonition. "Cynic. The reason you think I get no calls is that I keep it in silent mode all day and pick up messages in the evening. Satisfied? Frankly, I wish the bloody things had never been invented."

For a woman to shut down her cell phone of her own volition was unheard of in my experience. Commendable though.

"You know, love, it could be that you're just too perfect."

Another kiss was called for. It went on for a while. After it was over she went off with a finger wiggle of farewell. I lingered to watch her go with a blend of possessive pride, genuine deep affection, and a healthy dose of desire. My woman.

No post-mortem had been held over our night together. When I awakened she was already up and dressed, percolating coffee in the kitchen. The dialogue over the breakfast table had been banal, the tone light and convivial. I understood that, for her, our lovemaking had represented a giant stride and that she had to come to terms with it at her own pace. That was okay by me. The covenant had been made. Going back was not on the agenda.

I came to the square, the Place de la Liberation, just as the nearby church clock struck three. Bonhomme was there, a dapper figure: slim, greying, not a lot older than me; thin and hawkish, with a pointed chin and a mouth like a steel trap, and an indefinable aura of ruthlessness about him.

As I greeted him in front of a war monument that paid homage to the Glorieux Enfants of Annemasse, Mort pour la Patrie, my private dislike stayed under wraps. After all, it costs nothing to be courteous.

"How are you, Mr. Townsend?" he said in his precisely enunciated French, that trap-like mouth barely opening. His left cheekbone was decorated with an angry red pimple. He was rubbing it with the tip of his finger.

Salutations done, we waded through an army of hopeful pigeons to an empty bench under an oak tree. Bonhomme lit a cigarette and let the smoke trickle from of his nostrils. They were overdue for a trim, I noticed.

"You rendered an excellent service for me last year, Mr. Townsend," he murmured, looking not at me but at the passers-by, especially the young and pretty girls in their short summer dresses. I imagined him watching Gina, imagined his slimy, reptilian gaze tracking her along the street. It was not an agreeable vision.

"Kind of you to say so."

His mouth writhed in the Bonhomme version of a smile.

"I'm told the Thomashoff woman is still alive." It was stated without emotion, as were most of his utterances. I wondered at the fount of his knowledge, but kept my curiosity to myself.

"It needn't concern you." I was equally flat. I wasn't about to make excuses over my failure to finish off the woman. He wasn't the one in jeopardy from two directions.

"True. You eliminated Tillou. You did what you were paid to do. I have no complaints, Mr. Townsend, even though you were also paid for her elimination."

A pair of lovelies strolled by with identical hair styles and identical tight shorts and halter tops. Not a patch on Gina for looks and style.

"Glad to hear it," I said mechanically.

The sun went behind a cloud and the air became chill, the branches overhead flailing in a sudden flurry of wind. The two girls squealed in concert as their coiffures were rearranged.

"You implied you need my services again," I said, when Bonhomme seemed in no hurry to get down to the real nitty-gritty. "You realize I'm no longer active."

"Yes, I'm aware of that. But there is more to it than a simple contract." He slid along the seat toward me. "First, I think there is something you should know." His voice had dropped to a whisper.

"What's that?" Now he had me whispering, too. I cleared my throat. "Contracts are never simple anyhow."

"Tillou, the father, seeks to avenge his son's death."

"So? Let him seek."

"But don't you understand? He *knows* it is you who killed him."

Tillou, a gang boss with plenty of manpower on tap. Manpower the likes of Harley Boy, Bambi, and Blackie. Standard hired muscle. Suddenly, I understood a great deal. Mysteries were unraveled and answers to questions clicked into place like the tumblers of an old-fashioned one-armed fruit machine.

I asked Bonhomme about Schelling.

"Yes, I know Carl Schelling very well. He's in charge of the Cannes end of the organization, a trusted lieutenant. Why?"

"Never mind. What about a big fellow with eyelashes to die for?" I described Bambi.

"Ah. His name is Malpont. He is just a strong-arm man, a persuader." He eyed me, frowning. "You know these people? Have you met them?"

"In a manner of speaking. They and others have been tailing me on and off for the last couple of months. Last night they tried to hijack me."

The clouds directly above us had thickened. A few spots of rain fell; beyond the umbrella of the trees, the sidewalk acquired a rash of dark blots.

Bonhomme stared down at his elegantly-shod feet, his brow corrugated. "I see," he said slowly. "This is very serious, my friend. I was not aware that he had embarked on a vendetta." He was nodding as he spoke, and a wayward lock of hair sprang up on his crown. "This means he is no longer taking me into his confidence. It may even mean he suspects me of having a hand in his son's murder. *Merde*, this is bad news."

Vendetta, he had called it. It had a chilling ring: Mafia, the kiss of death, and all that stuff.

"Let me get this straight. Tillou is on to me and he's going to kill me if he can, to avenge his son's death. Have I understood you correctly?"

"I regret so," Bonhomme said, not sounding regretful at all. "He will not rest until family honor has been satisfied. This means he must kill you—*personally* kill you. That is the way these things are done, you understand. And that will be the reason why he is trying to kidnap you, instead of having you assassinated."

Chewing my nails wouldn't help. I needed to make a plan.

"So what's the next move?"

"Obviously, we must work together on this. Our interests intersect, so it is good that we have met. First, allow me to explain. Since the death of Tillou's son I have been number two in the organization. Frankly, I had expected Tillou himself to be dead by now. He is over seventy, and two years ago he suffered a stroke, and now he cannot even walk. He is permanently confined to a wheelchair."

"One thing's for sure, I'm not going to sit around and wait for him to send his goons after me," I said. "He's tried once already. I got lucky. Next time, *he* might get lucky."

The rain was coming down harder now, pattering against the leaves of the giant oaks, which, for the time being, kept us dry. Most of everyone else had dispersed in search of shelter. We had the square to ourselves.

"Where do you stand in all this, Bonhomme?" I asked.

"I? My position is rather ambiguous." He paused, kneaded his hands agitatedly. "As I told you, since the death of his son, I am number two. I wish to be number one. This is normal, no? However, as long as the *patron* lives, I must appear to give him my allegiance. But it worries me that he has not informed me of this vendetta."

"What's your role specifically?"

"I'm in charge of business operations. The *patron* leaves everything to me. In an operational sense, I am already the top man, but I still receive only a salary, plus a pittance of one percent of the profits." His eyes blazed with resentment. "After fifteen years of loyal service, fifteen years of kowtowing to him and his pig of a son, all I get is a *putain* one percent." His voice shook, as did his hands when he lit another cigarette. He dragged hard on it and puffed out the smoke in quick bursts like shellfire.

"So you've got a grudge. It still doesn't tell me where you stand regarding Tillou's vendetta against me."

His answer, which was slow in coming, was oblique. "For your problem, there is only one solution."

I didn't need to be told what it was. "Kill Tillou, you mean."

"Quite." The trap of a mouth undulated at the edges. "You're not stupid, Mr. Townsend."

Not stupid, but until this meeting perhaps a little blind.

"Let's assume then that you decide to kill him," he went on. "In effect, it will be self-defense. It's a powerful incentive of its own, is it not? Even so, in case you need another more material incentive, I can give you one. As well as a certain amount of practical assistance; inside information, for instance."

I speculated idly how Bonhomme came to be in such a sordid line of work. His phraseology was that of an educated man and he didn't have the look of a stereotypical hoodlum. Smart crooks made me uneasy; too tricky, too full of wheels and cogs turning. You had the feeling they'd stab you in the back as a matter of principle, rather than for reasons of security or economy. For the present though, it suited me to string him along.

"The other incentive you mentioned. What is it exactly?"

He came closer. His hot thigh pressed against mine, which of its own free will retreated crabwise.

"My proposition is this. Three quarters of a million in US dollars, twenty percent now, the rest on completion, to kill Tillou and anyone else who sticks his neck out. Big wages, *hein*?" I nodded at the under-statement. "And at the same time, you will have saved your own life. A double incentive. When Tillou is dead, the vendetta will die with him. There will still be Fabrice's widow, of course, and his sister, but they don't count. They have no power, no connections, and the organiza-tion will not follow them, they will follow me."

"You mentioned inside information."

"You accept then?" He spoke with affected indifference. His inner agitation was betrayed by the tremble of his hand, as he took several pulls on his cigarette in quick succession.

"Where does he spend most of his time?" I asked.

"At his villa on the island of Porquerolles, near Toulon."

Some years ago I had vacationed there. A wooded, tranquil back-water, free of traffic and still undiscovered by the tourist stream. A place to lighten your load, if you have one.

"Does he ever leave it?"

"Seldom. Travel is not easy for him. Twice, perhaps three times a year, he visits a neurologist in Toulon for a check-up."

"How does he travel to the mainland? By boat, I suppose."

"By private helicopter."

I mulled this over.

"I assume he's well-guarded, and being on an island makes it even more hazardous. If I hit him there, my escape route options are down to two: by air, which would mean hiring my own helicopter plus pilot, or by sea—" I stopped in mid-sentence. By sea, of course, in *Seamist*! The perfect escape vehicle. Just sail away south and get lost in the Mediterranean.

Bonhomme regarded me, his eyes narrowed to slits. "You have an idea?"

"A germ of one," I said cagily. "A lot depends on how much inside help you can give me."

"As much as you need. I can supply details of the villa and its grounds, Tillou's daily routine, the number of bodyguards and their routine. I can also keep you informed of developments concerning his vendetta against you."

All useful things, indispensable even, for a hit as fraught with prospective pitfalls as this one.

A large spot of rain splashed on the back of my hand and rested there, a shimmering pearl. I shook it off absentmindedly. My brain was ticking like a time bomb. If Tillou was set on killing me, sooner or later he would succeed. I couldn't dodge his army of hired thugs forever. Beating him to the punch made every kind of sense.

"It's a workable proposition," I conceded. "Though I wouldn't normally accept a contract on someone as well protected as Tillou."

"Which is why I am offering considerably more than the going rate."

"*Touché*. Assuming the fee you propose is about right, apropos the risks involved, what I don't like are the terms of payment. My usual is half when the contract is made, the other half forty-eight hours before execution." I gave him a meaningful look. "Like last time."

Bonhomme sucked hard on his fast-shrinking cigarette as if it contained oxygen and he was starved of it.

"I regret I cannot pay so much in advance. The money comes from my personal funds and I have already handed most of them over to you. Afterward, when I take over the organization, it will be different. This is the reason I am offering only twenty percent now."

In truth, the money was a secondary consideration, though I wouldn't turn my nose up at it. Self-defense, as Bonhomme had observed, was the prime motivation. Put simply, I wanted to live. For myself, for Gina. Incentives don't come more powerful than that.

I came down off my fence. "I'll do it. And I don't want a down payment, just the full fee on completion."

He goggled at me like a startled fish. "That's very generous. How can I ever—?"

"The full fee *being*," I continued, chopping him off in mid-gratitude, "one million dollars by irrevocable letter of credit, post-dated to first of September, to be held in a mutually approved escrow account. *D'accord?*"

He gagged. The cigarette was back in action, the tip glowing furiously.

"All right," he said, a few drags later. "Agreed. One million dollars on completion."

I'd expected more resistance. His almost meek capitulation roused my ever-present suspicion about his good faith. All the more reason to make sure the terms of payment were as tight as a whore's skirt.

"Get the letter of credit prepared, drawn on the Schweitzerische Kreditanstaltbank in Zurich. I'll let you know when I'm ready to set up the account."

Bonhomme actually managed to look hurt. "Don't you trust me, Mr. Townsend?"

Instead of answering, I asked him why he specially wanted me for the job. "Why not some other hit man, someone with no baggage?" I prodded. "There's no shortage of candidates among your own countrymen: Vigneron, or Lopez, for instance. I happen to know they would come cheaper, too."

He chain-lit another cigarette. "You're supposed to be the best," he said stiffly.

I nodded. "Good. That's what I wanted to hear. You just go on believing that, Bonhomme. Roger Townsend *is* the best. Believe it and remember it when Tillou is meat on a slab and you're the top dog, with all that money and all those musclemen dancing to your tune."

I whipped the newly-lit cigarette from his mouth, reversed it and held the glowing tip close to his right eyeball, simultaneously forcing him against the back of the bench with my other arm. He didn't resist. Physically, he wasn't resistance material.

"Remember it, if ever you get to thinking about carrying on Tillou's vendetta and saving yourself a million bucks."

He cringed under my restraint, wriggling as he tried to put space between his eyeball and the heat of the cigarette.

"You can trust me, Mr. Townsend," he said in a falsetto squeak. "I won't try to cheat you. I'm a man of honor." The suave exterior had been stripped away like paint under a blowtorch, and the fear in his face made him uglier than he was naturally.

Satisfied that he was as scared as I dare make him in a public place, I jettisoned the cigarette.

"No hard feelings, Bonhomme?" I said to smooth his ruffled feathers. "Trust is a precarious commodity, especially when it's one-sided."

"Yes...yes." Still squeaking. "I understand."

I pulled my notebook and pencil from my shirt pocket like a police detective about to question a witness.

"I'd like some of that famous inside information right now. The exact location of the villa for starters."

He recovered some of his lost aplomb, and extracted a small but bulky envelope from inside his jacket. "It's all here, including a cell phone number where you can contact me."

"Well, well. You came prepared. You expected me to do it."

His mouth contorted into a smirk. "You really had no choice."

A tepid sun was peeping coyly through a break in the clouds. A minute later, I started back to meet Gina, leaving Bonhomme still sulky over my demonstration. Still thinking he was a step ahead of me.

Maybe he was right at that, the bastard.

———

LYING IN BED THAT NIGHT, replete from the dinner party chez
Jules and ever so slightly under the influence of a twenty-three year-
old Burgundy, Gina and I discussed the past and our future.

She was relaxed and bubbly, as she had been all through the meal
and afterward. Displaying her outgoing, gregarious side and a
penchant for bawdy humor, she had completely won Jules over. Even
the ultra-cynical Nellie visibly warmed to her as the evening
progressed. Seeing us to the door, she had whispered in my ear, "She is
good for you, André. Take special care of her." It was unusual for
Nellie to be so charitable about another woman. All too often she saw
them as potential rivals for Jules' affection. I was mildly touched.

"Are there really no dark secrets you want to confess?" Gina asked
lightly during our *tête-à-tête* between the sheets. "I half hoped there
were, I quite fancy you as a man of mystery."

"Cross my heart," I lied, because a big lie is no different from a
little one, and how could I tell her my secrets were numberless,
beyond reckoning? "I'm in a lily-white vestal state."

It was a good thing the lights were off.

"Nice for you. I wish I could say the same."

"Honey," I played lightly with her breast, heard her breathing
instantly quicken, "if you ever feel inclined to bare your soul...don't.
As far as I'm concerned your life started about eight weeks ago at a
hotel in Digne. What came before is ancient history and nothing to do
with me."

She sighed. "That's broadminded of you." Then she chuckled. "I
might be a murderess, or a drug addict."

"Yeah, sure. And I might be Jekyll and Hyde."

Even as I made that crack, it struck me that it contained a stratum
of truth.

She went quiet then and rolled away from me. I could just distin-
guish the line of her shoulder against the window's pale rectangle.

"Gina?"

"Mmm?"

"Anything on your mind?"

"No, nothing except you. In any case, you said no baring my soul...

so, no baring my soul." Her hand came scuttling across my stomach. "I love you very much, you know. I can't tell you how much. Nothing must ever spoil it." She gripped my hand fiercely. There was a lot of strength in those long fingers.

"Gina?" I said again.

"Yes, darling?"

"Marry me."

Was that me? The André Warner I thought I knew so well, actually proposing *marriage*? Incredible. And I wasn't even drunk—not legless drunk at any rate. Goddamn it, I must *really* want to marry the girl!

If my own recklessness left me stunned, it was Gina who landed the knockout blow with her unhesitating, unconditional, "Yes."

CHAPTER ELEVEN

IN MY ABSENCE the Monaco skyline had sprouted a few more skyscraping cranes, skeletal dinosaurs looming over the wealthiest square mile in the world. They call it progress in those parts. I call it ugliness. And for that and the noise and dust, we have the Great God Property Developer to thank.

Disembarking from the taxi on Quai Antoine that hot Saturday afternoon, I almost collided with Dru, she of the liner-sized yacht and the obliging husband. Pleasing to behold as she was, I could have wished for a less awkward moment. That well-loved, well-kissed, scarlet mouth parted in a smile of invitation, which I couldn't help returning, my friendly nature getting the better of me.

By then, Gina, having exited on the opposite side, was rounding the rear of the cab. I hastily lowered the temperature by shaking Dru's hand, a style of greeting that would surely be totally foreign to her.

"You haven't met Gina, have you, Dru?" I said, glowing with sweetness and innocence.

The two girls exchanged conventional platitudes, accompanied by sizing-up looks that made me feel like a boxing referee at the start of a grudge match.

I rubbed my palms together with an exaggerated briskness that would have kidded neither woman.

"Gotta go. We're late for an appointment."

The cab driver dumped my valises at my feet. I shoveled euros back at him in some haste.

"Get me to the church on time?" Dru hazarded, with a knowing chuckle.

Gina reddened, which just served to confirm her suspicions.

"So long, Dru," I said firmly.

"Anytime...lover," was her parting bombshell, thankfully delivered *sotto voce*. "Before *or* after."

"An old school crush, darling?" Gina wondered aloud when Dru had receded from earshot.

I grabbed the valises and planted a quick kiss on her cheek. "One of those dark secrets we agreed not to tell each other about."

"You're not getting away with that pathetic excuse for a kiss." She hooked an arm around my neck for a lesson in how grownups do it. More for Dru's benefit than mine, I figured.

"Let's get aboard," I growled when she released me. That kiss had my red corpuscles whizzing round like the Paris rush-hour traffic around the Arc de Triomphe.

On board *Seamist*, we swapped kisses and cuddles of the platonic kind with Jean-Pierre and Pascal, and the next day the four of us sailed for the Ile de Porquerolles.

As far as my fellow travelers were aware it was to be a lazy cruise westward along the coast, calling in at such ports as took our fancy. Porquerolles was destined to be our first stopover, though as yet I hadn't mentioned it. It lay on our planned course, I made sure of that, and was a natural port of call: the largest of a group of three islands, it lies south of the Giens peninsula, not far from Toulon. Roughly crescent-shaped, it measures seven kilometers from east to west, and only two kilometers at its widest point, with a few pimples that might generously be described as hills. Trees from oak to bamboo cover half its surface, and the rest is densely packed scrub.

So much for the travelogue. My priorities lay elsewhere. While posing as a camera-toting tourist I would reconnoiter behind enemy lines, part of my plan to remove the threat posed by Tillou Sr.

Late in the afternoon on the second day at sea, I casually floated the idea of a visit to the island. Gina's initial reaction was to grumble about the lack of shopping facilities.

"I've seen it twice already," she complained. "There's nothing to do there."

I turned her objections into a gag. "Hey, we're having our first spat. A little bit of history in the making."

If she was amused, it wasn't reflected in her face.

"Anyhow, you haven't seen Porquerolles with me," I persisted. "Love makes you view things in a new light."

Corny stuff, but better than disclosing my true intent.

She stared at me. "You're quite a romantic, aren't you?"

"You bring it out in me."

Jean-Pierre was no happier about my choice, grousing about lack of opportunities of the nubile kind. Only Pascal was in favor. As skipper and owner, I had a casting vote, so to Porquerolles we went.

On the assumption that *Seamist* was known to my enemy, I planned to steer clear of the marina, adjacent to Porquerolles village, and anchor instead in a nearby bay known as the Plage d'Argent— Silver Beach. We approached the island from the east. While sailing parallel to its coastline, we intersected the wake of one of a fleet of small ferries that plies between Porquerolles and Giens. Pascal chortled with delight at our porpoise motion, while Jean-Pierre, for whom sail was all and steam was naught, glared after the receding vessel.

"To Jean-Pierre, motor powered vessels are a blight on the oceans of the world," I explained to Gina.

She smiled and tucked an arm in mine.

"Perhaps he was born a century too late."

She was less talkative than usual, more introspective.

"Cheer up," I said, pulling her to me. "You can shop another day."

She mock-punched me. "You make me sound like a shopaholic." She touched my cheek, the green eyes under their slumberous lids meeting mine, and what she felt for me was writ large there. "I really love you, André. Whatever happens, I'll always love you."

"Whatever happens?" I echoed. "Wow. Sounds like the knell of doom. Nothing is going to happen except good things. Believe me."

She sighed and leaned into my embrace, gazing toward the buildings of Porquerolles village with their pink roofs behind a cordon of palm trees on the foreshore. On the hill behind the village, the grey turret of the Tour St. Agathe fort was just visible above the huddle of greenery. It was a vista more in tune with the tropics than the south of France, and the impressive heat churned out by the sinking sun enhanced the illusion.

"I believe you," she said, gnawing her lip. "I trust you to make it all come right, really I do."

Her somber mood bothered me. From her various dropped inferences, it was apparent that her previous marriage had been going wrong for years before the actual split. Did its failure sour her view on the institution? I was prepared to work overtime on restoring her faith as well as my own. Whether I was the right material for such delicate reconstruction was a moot point. Perhaps she shared my lack of conviction.

At the Plage d'Argent, where an assortment of small craft bobbed and tugged at their mooring ropes, we found an anchorage next to a down-at-heel sloop with a crew chiefly consisting of rowdy kids.

Before I started trampling all over Tillou's territory I needed a progress report from Bonhomme. For that, I needed privacy. That's the trouble with a boat the size of *Seamist*. No part of it is beyond hearing range. Whatever medium I used, contact with Bonhomme had to be accomplished without arousing Gina's curiosity.

We went on walkabout to the town. It was only a short distance to its hub, an open square named Place de l'Armes. There, olive trees with sun-bleached bark grew in the hard packed earth, their slender leaves wilting. The heat and dust of the dying day cloaked the place in an invisible nebula, muffling the chatter of the promenaders and the squeals of children. Just as we entered the square, the streetlights came on, the lengthening shadows retreating under their haloes.

As we meandered across the square, I spotted a public payphone. It was occupied, but I could wait. A game of *pétanque* was in progress under the olive trees, and we joined the scattering of spectators. The players were mostly bereted veterans in checked shirts and gaudy suspenders that hoisted their pants to chest height. Ancient or not, they still had the strength to lob the heavy steel balls and the finesse to place them accurately.

When next I looked, the payphone cabin was vacant. I touched Gina on the shoulder.

"I need to call my broker about I some stock I want him to unload. Cell phone reception's unreliable on the island, so I'm going to use that payphone over there."

"A bit late, isn't it? Won't the stock market be closed?"

Some people are too well-informed for their own good.

"Not on Wall Street, my sweet. They're six hours behind us."

"Ah." She puckered her lips at me. "Kiss me, then I'll let you desert me."

It was no hardship. I let my hand drift over her behind as I turned away and left her watching the game. Her suspicions not at all aroused, as far as I could tell.

The glass cubicle was stifling. I shut myself in and made my call, keeping a wary eye on Gina. Without preamble Bonhomme confirmed that Tillou's spies had lost my trail, though they were aware *Seamist* had put to sea. A watch was being mounted at all main ports along the coast, an operation that must have stretched even Tillou's manpower to the limit. He was no fool. He must realize his chances of spotting me were slim. And here I was, parked in his backyard, the last place he would think to look, unless he was smarter than me.

Bonhomme briefed me on the strength of the garrison at the villa: five armed men, two of whom were always on duty, plus a large and vicious guard dog. Tillou's daughter and her husband, and a small number of non-combatant houseguests, were also in residence.

Bonhomme tried to pump me as to my whereabouts and my next move. I deliberately misled him, implying I wouldn't be going to Porquerolles for several days yet. With that, I hung up.

As I left the cabin, Gina joined me. "Everything in order?" she asked, coupling my arm to hers.

"Everything's cool." I elaborated on my story about a precarious stockholding that urgently required dumping, as we set off back along the road to the Plage d'Argent.

"After being cooped up in *Seamist* with J-P and Pascal, it's nice to have you to myself," I said.

Her head snapped round. She scrutinized me for a long moment, then said, "I wish I could figure what goes on inside your head,

André." The wistful note was not lost on me. "I can't always tell whether you're being sincere or cracking wise."

"Cracking wise?" My astonishment was real enough.

We had reached a point where the asphalt surface ended and a dirt track, concrete-hard and lying under a thick patina of dust, took over. Most of the pedestrian and cycle traffic was going in the opposite direction, into town. Families in the main, loaded up with cool-boxes, beach bags, buckets and spades, weary from their day's endeavors. On our left, a forest of bamboo chattered in the breeze.

"What's going on?" I said, stopping and placing my hands on Gina's shoulders. "All these doubts and suspicions. Is it about that woman we bumped into in Monaco? You think just because I've had a girlfriend or two or maybe two hundred, I can't possibly love you and be satisfied with just one woman? Say it if you think it, goddamnit!"

She shook her head, but it wasn't convincing. Her eyes glistened with restrained tears.

"You've got to quit doubting me," I growled. "I already admitted when we first met that you were no more than a beautiful face with a beautiful body, a desirable object to be laid, then discarded. Cynical, sure, I know. I'm not proud of it. But I can say it without embarrassment, because I fell in love with you and everything changed. Especially me. I changed. It was like...how to describe it? Like coming out of a room full of smoke into the fresh air. Can you relate to that metaphor? Now, you're all that matters in my life." She continued her teary scrutiny as I spoke. It was disconcerting. "I'm making no promises, love, and I'm giving no guarantees, except this one: as soon as this jaunt is over, we'll put a legal stamp on it."

"And live happily ever after," she agreed, though the quaver in her voice belied the sentiment.

We kissed. As always with Gina it was a kiss that triggered other desires.

"We'd better go," I said, breaking away with an effort that tested my will power.

She was trembling, and not from fright. She nodded.

We went on and returned to the bay where *Seamist* rode at anchor, her silver anodized mast glowing red in the sunset's dying embers.

"You need a bigger boat," Gina said.

"Do I? Why?"

"Or fewer guests."

"Oh." Then I got it. "Ah!"

She had a point there.

————

THE NOISE WAS A SHATTERING, rippling blast. It penetrated my brain with the shock of an explosive-tipped harpoon, catapulting me into instant and total wakefulness.

I was on my feet, heart pounding like a dinner gong, staring wildly into a solid wall of darkness, sweat streaming into my eyes and down my cheeks. Still it went on, a crashing bombardment as if the earth, sky, and the universe were ripping apart.

I was vaguely aware of Pascal shouting in his cabin. Then the light came on behind me, and Gina called my name.

On the deck above my head, I heard a pattering like tiny feet— rain. The wind had got up and *Seamist* was rolling, a docile enough motion, not enough to drag the anchor.

"André!" Gina called again urgently. "It's only thunder. It's only a storm."

The rain came down harder, more insistently, sounding like a truck dumping a load of gravel. I turned toward Gina and she caught her breath, her eyes widening in fear.

"Don't...don't look at me like that, darling," she said, her voice uneven. "What is it?"

It was only then that I realized I was holding a gun—the Korth, always under the edge of the mattress when I slept. The hammer was cocked. All it required was a little more pressure from my forefinger. I shivered, but not with cold. How close had I come to pulling the trigger?

Recovering rapidly, I rendered the weapon safe and sat on the edge of the bed, my back to Gina, my head bent over my knees, my guts threatening to erupt. Minutes passed. The feeling of nausea eventually loosened its grip. My heartbeat slowed, and the sweat was already cooling on my skin. Pascal had fallen quiet, as the noise dwindled to a rumble.

"I didn't mean to frighten you," I said, my breath sawing. "I guess I was dreaming."

Her arms went around me and she leaned against my back. "It's all right, darling. It was just that you looked so...murderous. As if you were going to kill somebody. It was kind of terrifying."

I twisted around and held her tight. "You need never be frightened of me, love. You're the last person I would harm. I love you more than life."

"I love you, too."

We lay down and she snuggled up to me as another thunderclap barreled across the sky. Though loud enough, it was a pale imitation of its predecessor. I reached out and switched off the light.

Gina went to sleep almost at once. I lay awake, staring into nothingness, listening to the rain. Occasionally a flash of lightning illuminated the cabin, throwing the fixtures into glaring relief.

I was remembering my dream. It had been shattered by the thunderclap, but it was with me still, the images sharp and clear, in widescreen, 3-D Technicolor. It was my wedding day, *our* wedding day; mine and Gina's, or so I assumed. I was as I am, down to the last detail. But my bride, when she turned to me, was not the woman who slept beside me, her breathing slow and even. She was blonde, good looking, but the similarity went no further. Her face was that of a certain German woman whose shooting might yet cost me my liberty —the lovely but decadent Frau Ingeborg Thomashoff.

As we stood before the altar and faced each other to make our vows, I drew a gun and for no apparent reason shot her in the neck. Blood gushed, staining the lapels of my beige suit and vest and the white carnation that sprouted from my lapel. But she didn't die. She didn't even fall. She just stood there laughing, her teeth stained pink with her blood, as I pumped five more shots into her at point blank range...

————

BY MORNING the storm had passed, leaving no aftermath other than a choppy sea that slapped against *Seamist's* hull. Unsurprisingly, I overslept. It was long after nine when I separated my carcass from the mattress. All that remained of Gina's presence was an impression on the pillow and the rumpled sheet.

Sheepishly, I pressed my hand on the place where she had lain. I could smell her perfume and I breathed it in as hungrily as any cocaine snorter. Jesus, had I got it bad.

I greeted Jean-Pierre in the galley and came upon Pascal fishing from the cockpit with the new rod Gina and I had bought for him in Geneva.

"*Bien dormi*, André?" he asked.

"Not so good, *mon petit*. The storm woke me. You, too, I guess."

"*Oui*. It frightened me, but only for a little while."

I peered over the side. Nothing swam in the keep net. "How's the rod?"

The rod it seemed was *fantastique*. The fish just weren't cooperating. Too dumb to recognize a tasty morsel dangling under their idiotic gaping mouths. Or too canny.

"Seen Gina?" I asked, squatting beside him.

"I nearly landed a little mackerel just now," Pascal said, lost in his angler's world, single-minded like most children, then as my inquiry filtered into his busy brain, "*Mais oui*. She went ashore. Look, there's the dinghy." The inflatable was on the beach and a couple of toddlers were playing by it, building sandcastles, overseen by a woman in a faded bathrobe.

While I was still wondering where Gina had gone, she came into view between the trees. She was wearing a striped shift and carrying a bag from *Seamist's* inventory. The snouts of several baguettes protruded. Relief washed over me like a line of breakers. Coming after my disturbing dream, her absence had vaguely troubled me. Especially here on Porquerolles, infested as it was with my enemies. Not that she would be aware of their proximity, but I wasn't complacent about the danger to her by association with me.

"I went for some bread," she called across the water. Two toddlers on the beach broke off from their construction work to stare at her.

I took up a position on the cockpit surround ready to help her aboard. She propelled the inflatable with powerful strokes that fairly shot her across the fifty or so meters of water.

"Why didn't you wake me?" I said as she came nimbly over the side, accepting my proffered hand out of politeness rather than necessity. "I'd have come with you."

She deposited a kiss on my nose. It tickled.

"You had a bad night and you were sleeping so soundly, I didn't like disturbing you. Don't you think I'm considerate?"

"I think you're magnificent," I countered and earned a long, loving look that made me want to carry her off caveman-style. As I relieved her of the bread and turned to go down into the saloon, she caught my hand.

"André..."

"Yes?"

"Why do you keep a gun in the bedroom?"

I was hoping she'd written that off as a bad dream.

"Oh, that," I stalled, thinking fast. "I'm sorry, sweetheart. Old habits die hard."

Her expression formed a question mark. "Old habits? Are you in the habit of shooting people in the middle of the night?"

I forced a laugh. "Of course not. But in the spy business you make a lot of enemies, and you never know when one might come looking to square accounts. When I left the service, I hung onto the gun."

"Oh." She looked thoughtful. "Yes, I see."

She seemed satisfied with my explanation. It made me wonder though, how long I could go on inventing stories to explain away the quirks of my lifestyle.

Our breakfast consisted of bread, butter, *confiture*, lashings of freshly percolated coffee, and lots of laughter. In between the merriment, plans were made for the day. Jean-Pierre was going to work on the bow pulpit, which had been buckled in the Cap Ferrat storm, while Pascal reckoned on hiring a bike to explore the island. Gina and I would behave like tourists and explore the village, followed by a restaurant lunch. Afterward, I aimed to take off for the western side of the island and assemble a composite picture of Tillou's villa and its surroundings, while pretending to photograph the scenery.

We took Pascal with us into town. I hired a bike for him, and we saw him off on his travels with a picnic lunch stuffed in the panniers.

"A great kid," Gina remarked as his bare brown back was absorbed into the general swarm of humanity. "Jean-Pierre must be proud of him."

"You can say that again." I didn't mean to sound grudging, but some nuance must have given me away. Gina glanced sharply at me, clearly surprised.

"You're envious of Jean-Pierre? Because of Pascal?" I didn't answer and she took that as confirmation. "Maybe we'll be able to do something about that," she said with endearing coyness. "If you're really sure you'll want to."

I felt choked. Behind my eyes, a burning sensation. In that instant I would have given all I owned to be able to turn the clock back a decade, to wash the bloodstains from my hands and start afresh. A pointless wish that fell to earth even as it left the launch pad. The past would forever remain past, immutable and unforgiving. I must do what I could to atone for it by creating a worthwhile and selfless future. Was it possible? Or would the slime of death cling to me as long as I lived?

I tried to suppress this morbid train of thought and dragged Gina off to see what few sights there were.

We finished our tour at the Hotel de la Poste where, under riotous flowering creepers, we drank black coffee, mine well laced with *eau-de-vie* in the hope of chasing away the blues that had beset me. I was keeping Gina entertained with a long drawn-out tale about a monk who succumbed to the temptations of the flesh, when a woman sat down at the table beside ours. Vaguely, it registered that she had very dark, very straight hair and was probably about my age. Beyond that, she made no impact.

Having wound up the story, to much amusement from my beloved, I ordered more coffee and went in search of a washroom. When I returned the coffee had arrived. So had the dark-haired piece, who was now installed at our table and chattering away in French to a rather unresponsive Gina.

Gina saw me coming and flashed me that ravishing smile of hers that never failed to rock me back on my heels.

"This lady lives on the island," she explained in response to my questioning look.

"*Enchanté, madame,*" I said, resuming my seat.

"So...you are both English," the woman said. She had one of those mouths that naturally curve upward at the corners in a ready-made smile. Her looks were dramatic, with twin drapes of black hair descending from a ruler-straight central parting. She had good skin, if on the sallow side, and was only lightly made-up. In ages not so far past I might have devoted some time to cultivating her. How times had changed.

"We're on vacation," I said. "It's a lovely place."

Madame agreed. "Have you visited the Plage de Notre Dame yet? Or the Fort de la Repentance?"

I raised a restraining hand. "Not this trip, *madame*. We only arrived last night. However, we've both been here before, separately, so we know most of the beauty spots."

"Ah, *bon*. Then you will be able to enjoy your stay all the more. Personally, I have always found that at least two visits to a place of interest are necessary, if one is to appreciate all its virtues. Do you not agree, *madame*...er...?" She was inviting Gina to introduce herself, but Gina was lost in an introspective huddle, a tiny frown grooving the bridge of her nose.

"Mademoiselle Gregg," I said on Gina's behalf, shooting her a glance of reproof. She looked away. Not another dose of rivalry, surely.

If the woman noticed or cared, it didn't affect her demeanor, which remained pleasant and friendly. "And you, *monsieur*...you are...?"

"Warner," I said, not without trepidation. Giving my real name to a complete stranger in the heart of Tillou country went against the grain. In front of Gina, though, I could hardly trot out an alias.

"I am Madame Sabourin."

"It's a pleasure to meet you," I oozed.

"Likewise," she oozed back.

"You were born here on the island?" I asked, to keep the conversation moving.

Madame Sabourin whinnied mellifluously. "No, Mr. Warner, I am Parisian by birth. I live there still. Like you, I'm on vacation."

She was now disregarding Gina completely to concentrate the full wattage of her brown eyes on me.

"How long will you be staying on the island?"

"We're leaving tonight," Gina blurted, suddenly reentering the conversation.

I gaped at her. We hadn't discussed the length of our stay, though I needed another day at least to complete my reconnaissance.

"Where did you get that idea, love?" I said, stifling my irritation.

She was suitably nonplussed. "Oh, I thought we were only staying for the day. I was hoping to do some shopping in Toulon, darling. I did tell you." She put on a reproachful pout, which, if it added to her allure, didn't help lessen my irritation.

I reminded myself it wasn't her fault she was ignorant of the true purpose of our visit.

"If it's all the same to you, sweetheart, I'd like to stay on a couple of days."

A group of mostly blond teenagers, unisexually attired in T-shirts, jeans, and sneakers, came wandering in off the street. Madame Sabourin, raising her voice over their chatter, said, "I'm actually staying at my father's house. He's resident here."

"Well, I hope you enjoy the rest of your vacation." I drained my cup. "We'll have to say *au revoir*, Madame Sabourin. It seems like we have less time than I thought."

"Before you go..." She rummaged in her purse. "We're having a barbecue tomorrow evening at the house. As well as French, there will be some German people, some Italians, a Spanish family...but no English. Would you like to come and represent your country?" She slapped a notepad with a tooled leather cover on the table. "Please say yes." She smiled winsomely at Gina then at me.

While Gina hesitated, I stepped into the breach. "Thanks very much. We'd love to. I'll bring a Union Jack."

Madame Sabourin scribbled away on her notepad. "Here's the address. It's at the western end of the island, by the Souterrain des Pirates." She ripped the page out and passed it to me. "Do you know it?"

I nodded abstractedly. I was deciphering her bold script, a jumble of loops and whorls: Villa du Langoustier, Plage du Muso. It was an address instantly and shockingly familiar. It was, so she said, her father's house. It revealed Madame Sabourin, sitting there so cool and serene with her ever-smiling mouth, in her true colors as Bernard Tillou's daughter.

CHAPTER TWELVE

AT SIX IN the evening it was still scorching hot, the cricket orchestra in full chorus, the beach still littered with sun-worshippers. I lay among them, my skin damp and cool from a dip in the bay. Beside me Gina dozed on her tummy; the expanse of her bronzed back spattered with globules of seawater. Farther south, the triangle of her bikini pants clung lasciviously to the furrow of her behind. I forced myself to look away, damping down the reaction inside my swimming shorts. The beach was too crowded for amorous activity. Later though, I'd teach her not to be so desirable.

Another glorious day in our relationship was drawing to a close. A day when another nail had been hammered into the edifice of togetherness, notwithstanding the distractions. After a restaurant lunch we had cycled across to the lighthouse on the south side of the island, returning to town by a tortuous route that enabled me to scout the all-important lie of the land. Gina had been penitent over her attitude toward Madame Sabourin.

"I didn't mean to be rude," she said as we walked our bikes along the cliff top. "You may find this hard to believe, but I was actually jealous of that woman."

It was hard for me to believe she could be jealous of any woman.

"Jealous? You have to be joking."

"Oh, I know you didn't lead her on, but women just seem to be drawn to you and you can't help kind of playing up to them. Like a peacock displaying its tail fan."

"Look, love, was it my fault you started chatting to her? I didn't instigate it."

"Neither did I!" She sounded indignant. "She opened the conversation, asked if I was on vacation. She was just being friendly. I could hardly give her the cold shoulder."

I grunted. "What's all this peacock stuff, anyway?"

"Oh, it's probably just force of habit on your part, and I don't believe you were genuinely attracted to her. I'm just not used to the feeling, that's all." She had taken my hand in both of hers and pressed it to her lips. "I couldn't bear to share you, not even just a little bit. I've gotten all possessive, you see, darling. When we're married, I'm never going let you out of my sight."

"But, mommy," I said, in a childlike voice. "Can't I go to the john on my own?"

Entering into the spirit of the game, she patted me on the head.

"When you're all grown up."

We laughed as one, touched lips, made serious eye contact.

My mind shifted to Madame Sabourin and her invitation, as I watched a mainland-bound ferry scooting past the nearby promontory, her bows leaping the waves, a line of pure white foam flashing the length of her hull. I was still wrestling with the dilemma of whether to go or not to go. It was an opportunity that had much to commend it. To stay away would leave unfinished the task I had come here to perform. I smeared Ambre Solaire on my legs, gazing thoughtfully out to sea. I was not credulous. The meeting with Madame Sabourin was surely a setup. Ditto, the invitation. Which meant that Tillou was aware I was on the island before we 'chanced to meet' his daughter. He couldn't be sure that my visit wasn't innocent, unless he didn't trust coincidences either. If the Sabourin meeting *was* an arranged one, I had to assume he would have made defensive preparations, too.

Running for it was not the answer either, tempted though I was. Now that I was on his home territory, Tillou would never stand aside while I cruised off into a golden sunset. He would try and preempt my plan of action, keep the initiative that he'd assume Mme. Sabourin had gained for him, with her baited-trap invitation. Plus, he had a score to settle with me as much as I with him.

Supposing, just supposing, I did go to the barbecue, sticking my neck in the noose Tillou had knotted for me. I still held two aces. Bonhomme, my cuckoo in the nest was one. The other was that Tillou wouldn't know I had seen through his ploy with Mme. Sabourin.

Taking the supposing a stage further, how likely was it that Tillou would be receptive to a trade-off? The identity of his real enemy, Bonhomme, in return for a ceasefire. Such a betrayal would be a contravention of professional ethics—even hit men have a code of conduct—and if it ever got out, I would be washed up in the assassination game. But being retired, I could afford to abandon my principles. To secure my future with Gina I would have committed deadlier sins.

The risk to Gina had also to be factored into the scheme. The prudent option would be to leave her on the boat, assuming she would agree to that. A hell of a big assumption. But, arguably, she was almost as much a target as I. Even if they wouldn't go so far as to kill her, she was a sure-fire abduction target, a means of putting me under duress. If I went to the *soirée* alone—and how the hell would I get her to agree?—Tillou might attempt to snatch her in my absence. If that happened, I might as well stick a gun barrel in my mouth and save him the trouble. On balance, I preferred to keep her under my wing.

My game plan for confronting Tillou on my terms was a wash-out. That said, my best chance for removing the threat he posed still lay in cornering him. That much hadn't changed. His barbecue party, with its protective screen of guests, hopefully law-abiding, was therefore the logical time and place. Actually, it was the only time and place.

———

BONHOMME'S LACONIC "*OUI?*" came halfway through the telephone's opening bleep.

"Townsend," I said. I could be laconic, too.

"Ah...Mr. Townsend. You have not been entirely truthful with me."

"You don't say?"

"You are on the island, are you not? On Porquerolles."

"Okay, smart Aleck. I don't have to tell you everything. Do you want the job done or not?"

A pause. "Can it still be done? Tillou also knows you are there."

"It can be done, possibly as soon as tomorrow night. I've been invited to a barbecue at the villa, but I suppose you know that, too."

"Yes, I know, Mr. Townsend." Another pause. "Or would you prefer to be called Mr. Warner from now on?"

So my real name had percolated through already, courtesy of Mme. Sabourin. After this business was over and done with, I might have to take care of Mr. Bonhomme.

"Will you be there, at the *soirée*?" I said, ignoring his question.

"I? Alas, no."

"Then who will be that matters?"

"The bodyguard arrangements will be unaffected. The guests will be mostly professional people: lawyers, bankers, industrialists, one or two from the entertainment profession. Respectable people. Only a handful from inside the organization."

I fed my last 50-cent coin into the slot. "Anything else I need to know? I'm out of change."

"Nothing of importance," he said. "Oh, yes. There is one minor matter. It was only brought to my attention last night after you called." The warning light was blinking and cut-off was imminent.

"Yes...quickly!"

"It seems that Madame Tillou—" Bonhomme's voice was transformed into an unbroken, electronic bleat, cutting him off in mid-sentence.

Mildly exasperated, I hooked the receiver back on its mount. I had no more coins and wasn't minded to trudge back to *Seamist*, then back into town again. Whatever Tillou's wife had to do with anything, she was unlikely to influence my plans. A minor matter, Bonhomme had said. Okay, so let it keep until tomorrow.

————

THE BARBECUE WAS ON SUNDAY. It dawned cloudy with a light drizzle, but this cleared after breakfast. Gina and I took advantage of the drop in temperature for a knockabout on the tennis courts at the Terrain de Sports.

Gina looked pretty spectacular in her tennis garb, the short red skirt setting off her tanned legs. She played an embarrassingly good game, too. It was years since I had picked up a tennis racquet and my technique was rusty. She won two straight sets, at which point I cried quits.

"I'll get my revenge on the squash court," I grumbled as we sank cold beers at the sports center bar.

Her eyes sparkled. "We'll see." Becoming serious, entwining my fingers in hers, she said, "Do we really have to go to this barbecue thing? Can't we just spend the evening alone?"

If only.

"We'll have hundreds of evenings alone," I said, leaning forward to kiss her. "Come on, where's your party spirit?"

She succumbed with a pretend scowl and dropped the subject.

Apart from that, our day was carefree and full of magic. We were together every minute. In the afternoon, we went for a ramble round the island. I had shelved my reconnaissance of the Tillou property. If the reckoning were to take place at the barbecue, it would serve no purpose.

In the course of our wanderings, we happened on a lonely spot on the rugged south shore. It overlooked a lagoon where broken-toothed slabs of rock, black and smooth as gunmetal, were washed by the swell. It was custom-made as a love nest. In no time, Gina was naked in my embrace, and my hands were roaming over gentle undulations and in soft moist valleys.

When I entered her, she became as if possessed, thrusting against me with such violence that we slid backwards on the sparse grass. Her breasts danced under my chest, the nipples titillating my flesh. We climaxed as one, so perfect was our synchronicity; with the climax came first a sensation of falling, then of floating, and finally of coming back to earth with a teeth-rattling bang.

Afterward, we lay there, sapped, and I marveled that notwithstanding all the years of debauchery I could be moved again by the love act. That it could lift me to such soaring heights, as it had years before with my then wife.

"I can't believe this is happening." Gina murmured, her lips against my cheek. "I can't believe it can be this good. It's too much." She jacked herself up on one elbow. "It makes me afraid of losing it, of losing *you*."

"Hey, come on," I said and kissed her. "Nobody's going to lose anything. You're always so full of doom and disaster. Your bad past is history. Don't go checking off the days like a condemned prisoner in a cell. Just live and enjoy. Love me and let me love you."

She hugged me tightly then, nuzzling against my chest.

Around us the shadows closed in. Below, the sea washed over the rocks, a soothing whisper. Above, seabirds wheeled, uttering little cries not unlike the yapping of a small dog. Nature, pure and untainted. It would have been no hardship to linger in that spot. The temptation was strong, but duty called and the pro in me rejected all distractions. My resolve to beard Tillou in his lair, with or without deadly force, was not for deferring.

Our return trek to *Seamist* was conducted mostly in contented silence, just the occasional stop to kiss or merely embrace. To enjoy the close contact, the molding together of body and mind. To listen to the sound of each other's breathing, feel the pulses beating within. In such simple yet complex ways was love weaving its tendrils around us, binding us as one.

It was Pascal who rowed out from *Seamist* to collect us from the deserted beach. Jean-Pierre was out shopping. Not for groceries, I guessed.

Privacy is hard to come by on a forty-foot boat and I needed some on two counts. When Jean-Pierre rolled up not long after, I button-holed him in the cockpit while Gina was below decks. With the aid of our map of the island I filled him in on my contingency plans for a tactical withdrawal. He took it all in his stride. His few questions concerned only the mechanics of the operation.

"To be clear, if you have not returned by 0600 hours tomorrow I am to sail around the Petit Langoustier." He tapped the islet, located off the western tip of Porquerolles. "Then I moor here, at Port-Fay."

Port-Fay was a horseshoe bay that formed a natural harbor, close to Tillou's villa at the Plage du Muso but screened from it. It was as close as I dared let Jean-Pierre bring *Seamist*.

"If I don't show up until after you've moved, it's likely we'll have to leave very quickly."

"*D'accord.*" Jean-Pierre was still engrossed in the map.

"Very, very quickly," I said with emphasis. "I want you to put Pascal in a hotel for the night."

His eyes swung from the map to me. "If you advise it."

"More than just advise, Jean-Pierre. He must *not* be on the boat."

My line of retreat secured, I nipped down into the master cabin while Gina was in the shower and satisfied my other need—firepower. The cream checked sports jacket I had chosen to wear with my beige chinos was fairly loose fitting and absorbed the bulge of the Korth in the clip-on holster in the small of my back. I also took a fistful of spare shells, distributing them about my pockets. I could have used an update from Bonhomme, but my cell phone was still a no-go area for security reasons. Maybe an opportunity would arise to make the call on Tillou's land line phone. The idea piqued my sense of brinkmanship.

Presently, Gina joined me on deck and paraded for my inspection. She had pulled her hair back over her ears, leaving a long tendril on either side. In a simple cream dress with a swooping V-neck and a swirling knee-length hem, she was more than merely desirable. For the twenty-minute walk to the villa, she was wearing practical flat-heeled sandals.

"I'll change into my heels when we make our grand entrance," she said.

"If you're ready, we'll get started," I said. I was equipped with a flashlight, as it would be dark before we got there.

Ferried by Pascal, we made it ashore without getting our feet wet. It turned out to be a pleasant stroll along a winding road to the villa, the crickets creaking away in the bushes and an occasional bat flicking past. It wasn't quite dark, but we couldn't have managed without the flashlight.

A few minutes before ten, we strolled under a stone archway that provided the only landward access to Tillou's villa. The only access, that is, short of climbing the high steel-netting fence that lurked behind a double line of cypresses, and was probably infested with alarms. It was also electrified. I had spotted the spaced porcelain insulators along the top strand of wire; a literal nasty shock for intruders.

Most of the guests had checked in ahead of us, by sea to judge from the several big outboard launches tied at the floodlit private jetty. They were milling about on a terrace the size of a tennis court, lit up brighter than Broadway. At the end of the terrace was a kidney-shaped swimming pool. A group of people were splashing about in it and generally creating a lot of noise. Some of them were patently naked.

Looming over the festivities was the villa, a cube with an acutely angled roof, the high apex fusing with the darkness above the illuminated area. An extravaganza of climbing roses in full bloom covered the side wall that faced us, and an integral first-floor balcony ran along the seaward side of the building. I had frankly expected something more ostentatious, more Mafioso. Maybe crime wasn't paying so well these days.

Gina changed her shoes and, going forward into the light, we were met by the whiff of barbecued steaks. The barbecue itself, coming into view beyond a barricade of laurel bushes, was an enormous stone-built affair with a tiled roof round a coned central chimney. Three chefs in traditional headgear toiled over the grill. A fourth was operating a giant bellows. At every downward stroke, sparks shot from the glowing charcoal and burst out of the chimney like a Roman candle going off. Julien Doré was chanting *Kiss Me Forever* from overhead speakers, competing with the nonstop swell of conversation generated by fifty-plus sets of voices.

We reached the edge of the terrace before we were spotted. A middle-aged man, dressed young in jeans and T-shirt, separated from the throng and strode purposefully toward us.

"You must be the English persons," he said in Gallic-accented English. "I am Yves Sabourin. Jeanne, my wife invites you."

We went through the usual preliminaries. His English was so halting I let him off the hook by swapping to French.

"We don't know anyone, I'm afraid," I said. "Apart from your wife, that is."

"Don't worry, don't worry," he said soothingly. "I will introduce you. Come and have a drink." In his native tongue he spoke so rapidly I had to stay alert to follow him. I couldn't help wondering what his wife, a good-looking woman from every angle, saw in him. He was balding, wore pebble-lens glasses, and had bad breath. Unless all the propaganda about bald men was true and his principal attributes weren't on display.

Gina's hand and mine acquired flutes of champagne, and we met a lot of people in a short space of time. Only a small percentage of faces stuck, and an even smaller percentage of names. We renewed our acquaintance with Jeanne Sabourin, petite and tipsy, wearing a flame-colored dress that was more gaps than material. Then there was Belanger, a smooth, dangerous-looking character about my height, but a bit younger. His handshake was a finger masher. We also met Sabourin's daughter: eighteen or thereabouts, thin as a walking stick, with spiky black punk hair, yet feminine with it. She shared her mother's good looks. She inspected me with a blatant lack of inhibition that, with Gina standing at my elbow, was embarrassing. Gina picked up the vibes and snuffed them out with her full weight on my toe.

We moved on, me limping, Gina smiling sweetly.

"Which one of those was our host?" I said afterward to Yves Sabourin.

"The *patron* is indoors at present. He is not a well man. But don't worry, you'll see him later." He slapped me on the back, in the manner of an old buddy. "He especially wants to meet you, Mr. Warner."

I bet he did. "I'm flattered. But he doesn't know me."

"My wife has told him of you." Sabourin put his head close to mine as though about to impart some juicy item of gossip. "The *patron* has a great admiration for the English as a race."

"I'm only half English," I told him. "But I don't mind reaping accolades on account of it."

"There's someone else you should meet," he said, persevering with his role as a surrogate host. He beckoned to a bull of a guy with no neck, overdressed in a white tuxedo. Gina, who had been waylaid by a burly individual with shaded jowls and an obvious hairpiece, rejoined us as the tuxedoed gorilla swaggered up.

"May I present Fernand Jourd'hui." Sabourin eased the newcomer into our circle. Polite noises were exchanged.

Jourd'hui slurped from a bulbous glass containing a colorless liquid and appraised Gina's modest cleavage.

"And what do you do, Mr. Jourd'hui?" I asked. "Are you in business with Mr. Sabourin?"

Jourd'hui wasn't listening. His nose was all but wedged down Gina's neckline. Fidgeting with discomfiture, she had drawn the material together, pinching it between finger and thumb. As a typical male, I could have told her that was the wrong reaction. It was an attractant rather than a deterrent.

Torn between amusement and outrage, I didn't dare rush to defend Gina's modesty for fear of provoking a brawl and preempting the fracas to come. A waiter arrived with a tray of brimming champagne flutes. Jourd'hui lunged wildly at it, lost his balance and had to grab Gina's arm for support. The waiter, nose elevated in reproof, placed a glass in his hand.

Sabourin and I chatted on, fencing with words, each trying to trip up the other. During this humdrum dialogue, I turned to Gina for an opinion and found only an empty space where she and Jourd'hui had been standing. I scanned the bobbing, jawing heads in my immediate vicinity. No sandy blondes. Well, if she had sneaked off for a necking session with that overdeveloped baboon, I was the worst judge of character since Neville Chamberlain got screwed by Adolf. I was partly reassured almost immediately, when Jourd'hui's profile reeled into my field of view. He was alone and tossed me a boozy grin around the rim of his glass.

"Gina seems to have gone missing," I remarked to Sabourin who cut short a yawn to glance around.

"I don't suppose she's far away," he said reasonably.

A safe enough assumption. If this had been just a harmless evening out I would have thought no more of it. As it was, they could be figuring to use her to pacify me, and I had to track her down fast.

For Sabourin's benefit, I shrugged Gallic-fashion, and knocked back what remained of my bubbly.

"Point me toward the washroom, will you?" I said.

He looked dubious. Letting me roam around unchaperoned wouldn't be part of his remit. He offered to escort me, an offer I politely declined. He finally insisted on taking me as far as the patio door.

"Through the alcove, then first left, first right." He was sure to hang around for my return. Five minutes maximum, and he would come looking for me.

I set off across the brown-tiled floor of a vast dining room. Sabourin's directions led me into an internal corridor with several doors and a curved staircase. Here, the noise of the festivities was subdued, no more than a buzz. The house itself was as quiet as a funeral parlor. I tried a couple of doors: kitchen, laundry-room; both in darkness. A third door was wide open, as if in invitation. It projected a strip of yellow light on to the corridor floor and wall.

I entered cautiously. It was a study-cum-library. A pleasant room, cool, with a restful atmosphere. The furniture was heavy and dark without being somber. Shelves stacked with books lined two walls. The other two contained an imposing traditional *cheminée* and more patio doors, looking out on the rear of the house. External floodlights blazed over another terrace that led to a lawn too lush to have been watered by rainfall in this part of France.

Underfoot was wood not tile, polished block floorboards, laid in a chevron pattern of alternating light and dark. Tasteful. As I ventured farther in, I identified a Picasso on the left of the *cheminée*, and around it a handful of recognizably French impressionists. My gaze alighted on a big, solid desk parked at forty-five degrees to the patio doors, and from there, to a telephone sitting on its corner. It was one of those imitation antiques, all brass and marble, with a dial rather than a keyboard. I hoped it wasn't just an ornament.

My hand was closing around the receiver, when a female voice hailed me from the doorway with a breathy "*Salut*". I whirled round so fast I nearly fell over my own feet.

"I'm Helène. Remember me?"

Sabourin's daughter, the girl with no curves and a punk hairdo. And the sex appeal that was as subtle as a red light in the Reeperbahn.

"Hello," I returned guardedly.

She closed the door and startled me by turning the key in the lock. Oh-oh. I had run into girls like this before. Silly, giggly, rich men's daughters with minds that only functioned at crotch level. Not that the old me hadn't found them useful as bed fodder.

She had a small vampish mouth, etched in lipstick the color of blood. Her smile had all the come-hither you could wish for, plus a bit.

She planted her long, skinny legs on their long skinny heels in front of me and made a gesture with her pelvis that removed any remaining doubt as to her ambitions.

"Hello, beautiful," she said. She had good teeth, straight and very white.

"The same to you."

She was wearing a black mini-dress of a velvety consistency, but not for long. She sort of waggled her shoulders and it slithered down that slender frame to puddle in a heap round her ankles, one of which was encircled by a thin gold chain. What remained of her party attire was a skimpy garter belt and white stockings. Oh, and a necklace with a golden disc that could have passed for an Olympic medal. That was the sum total of her accessories.

Two clear alternatives were available to me. Though it was contrary to my nature, I chose the negative one. I told her to leave the room, only I used stronger language than that. And just in case she felt inclined to persevere, I threw in a couple of insults that even the dumbest streetwalker might have taken amiss.

I thought she was going to slap me. She went white, and the blush on her cheeks stood out like clowns' make-up. Her legs were no longer apart and inviting. The show was over. The old me sighed inside.

"You...you..." She eventually hit on an appropriate French epithet to use on me. I digested it with a polite nod. The dress went back on her body. She unlocked the door and marched out, leaving me trying to recollect when I had last been so iron-willed. It was so long ago, I couldn't.

Hélène had obligingly slammed the door shut on her way out. It was a credit to the builder that the house withstood the shock. I picked up where I left off, lifted the receiver and dialed.

Bonhomme, when he answered, sounded edgy. Probably, I did, too.

"Make it quick," I snapped. "I'm phoning from the villa."

He gave a disbelieving gasp. "You're crazy! Someone might be listening in."

"No, they're not. Everybody's outside having a ball, and I'm supposed to be in the john." Everybody except Tillou, I omitted to mention. If he was eavesdropping on us, the damage was already done. Might as well press on.

"What's the latest?" I said. "Last night you mentioned Madame Tillou. There isn't any Madame Tillou any more, he's a widower."

Exasperation crackled along the line. "Don't be so obtuse. What I can't understand is what you hope to achieve by associating with her. Are you playing some kind of double game?"

I looked blankly into the mouthpiece. "Talk sense, Bonhomme. I haven't associated with Tillou's wife. She's dead! Sabourin told me."

"This conversation is ridiculous!" Bonhomme exploded. "You know who I mean—*Fabrice's* widow, Georgina. According to my information, you've been keeping company with her for days. Is my information incorrect then?"

Even spelled out in plain language, it didn't register. My brain simply rejected the implications.

"Explain yourself, you prick," I said with a snarl. "I've spent some time with a girl called Georgina, yes, but what has she got to do with Tillou, father or son?"

"*Merde alors, quel idiot!*" I visualized him smacking the flat of his hand on his forehead; an emotional race, the French. "Georgina, the girl you've been seeing, is the *widow* of Fabrice Tillou, the man you killed in Munich. Is that clear enough for you? Are you saying you weren't aware of this?"

A grandfather clock stood by the door. It had an octagonal face and intricate Roman numerals. The tick-tock of its mechanism was suddenly very loud, though I had scarcely been aware of it before. My own breathing became audible, a rasping inside my head. I tried to shut it out, to concentrate, to *think*. But I couldn't think. Inside me, pain was blooming and it was no ordinary pain. It was a knife shoved between my ribs, and twisted round and round. It was agony.

"Warner? Warner?" The quacking voice cured my cerebral paralysis. "Are you there, Warner?"

"Yes," I said, a hoarse whisper. "Yes, I'm here."

"Why have you been seeing her?" Bonhomme demanded, like a petulant child. "Don't you realize she's spying on you, reporting back to Tillou, keeping him informed? How do you think he found out you were on the island?"

Shut up. For God's sake, shut up!

I was sweating. This couldn't be happening. Pinch yourself and you'll wake up.

There was nothing more to be said, nothing more to hear. It was finished, all of it. *I* was finished. I put the phone down, and Gina walked in.

CHAPTER THIRTEEN

SHE STOPPED ON THE THRESHOLD, her hand flying to her mouth, consternation written in every line. So lovely, so treacherous.

My she-Judas.

"André?" she said, a tremor in her speech. "What's wrong? Why are you looking at me like that?"

I gave it to her straight, no frills.

"You're his wife...his widow. Fabrice Tillou was your husband." My voice cracked. It didn't sound like me speaking.

Her jaw sagged and she staggered slightly.

"Who—who told you?" At least she didn't try to bluster.

"It's true then," I said needlessly. What a blind infatuated fool I'd been.

She closed the door softly. "I love you. *That's* true."

I dismissed that with a flap of the hand. "Screw that! How can you talk of love? You're nothing but a stinking spy."

"Listen to me, darling." She came to me, pale and so goddamn lovely an unwanted lump formed in my throat. "It's not the way it seems, I swear." Her eyes were moist, tears only a blink away.

"Don't explain, Gina." I felt curiously detached. I still half-wondered if I were imagining all of it.

"But you *must* let me explain." Tears were there, but still held at bay.

I was the one who couldn't meet her gaze. I wanted to run and hide, as I did all those years ago, when Marion died. To lose myself out there in the dark.

"No, Gina," I said, refusing to look at her, afraid of weakening, afraid that if I let her speak, she'd seduce me into forgiving and forgetting. And that would be almost as intolerable as her betrayal.

"But you *must!*" Her agitation burst through now, like a reservoir breaching a dam. She held my arms, willing me to acknowledge her. "You don't know the full story. It wasn't for me. It was Fabrice's father...he..." She broke then, succumbing at last to a torrent of tears, her body against mine, clinging. My arms stayed by my sides. Sympathy was out. Compassion was out. I was a block of ice: hard, cold, and pure.

"Darling, please." She emitted a groan of anguish. "Don't reject me, I beg you. I love you, I *love* you."

Then the door was thrown back. Two men came in: Belanger and Jourd'hui.

Jourd'hui wasn't drunk any more, if in fact he ever had been. One more phony act amongst many.

Behind them came a man in a wheelchair who needed no introduction. Bernard Tillou bore little resemblance to the image in the fuzzy, out-of-date photograph supplied by Bonhomme. The present-day Tillou was a shriveled leprechaun of a man with fine, aristocratic features and brilliant blue eyes, unusual in that the whites showed all round the irises, giving him a startled look. He had a thatch of yellowish-grey hair, thick and dense, and somehow dead-looking, like grass in need of watering. His nose was an eagle's beak, his mouth rosy-lipped and pursed.

At his age—rising seventy-two—and given his poor state of health, some physical attrition was to be expected. But the ravaged, crumbling contours of his face, and the folds of skin that flapped beneath his eyes and along his jawline like drapes, were repellent to put it mildly. His hands resembled mechanical claws grafted on to the arms of the wheelchair.

"It gives me great pleasure to meet you at last, Mr. Warner," he said in a breathless wheeze that seemed to come from some remote, external source. His rosy lips formed a travesty of a smile. "Your arrival here is long overdue."

His right claw moved, operating a diminutive joystick set in the chair arm. The contraption glided forward, Belanger and Jourd'hui gliding with it as if attached. A third member of the team, tall, slim, young, and clad in faded blue jeans with designer rips, slid round the doorpost.

Tillou braked to a standstill. He was studying me earnestly, the ruined face blazing with gleeful malice like a Halloween mask. His disciples, in contrast, were impassive. Belanger flexed his knees, caricaturing an English bobby, while Jourd'hui flicked imaginary specks off his immaculate lapel. Blue Jeans rested against the door, arms folded. Surprisingly, no guns were in evidence.

It was left to Gina to break the silence. "Bernard...let him go... please!" She went down on one knee beside the wheelchair.

Tillou was outwardly unmoved. He had eyes only for me.

"Leave us, Georgina," he said tonelessly.

"No, I'm staying."

"Leave us!" The tone hardened.

"I'm staying!" she almost yelled. "If you want to get rid of me, you'll have to carry me out."

Tillou's lips set hard. He continued to stare at me in a sort of fascination. It was mutual.

"You don't have much to say, Mr. Warner." He paid no further attention to Gina. She got up slowly, flung a defiant stare at the men and came to stand beside me, making a statement. I was acutely conscious of her nearness, her perfume, the warmth of her body—and her treachery. I banished a million racking memories. She was nothing to me now. Nothing.

"Aren't you curious to know what all this is about?" When Tillou spoke, only his lower jaw moved. In poor light, it would be easy to mistake him for a ventriloquist's doll. "If you were an innocent man, you would think our behavior very strange, would you not?"

"The world's full of strange people," I said.

Tillou gave me a sly look. "Are you armed, Mr. Warner?"

That was my cue for a gunslinger-style fast draw before they searched me and relieved me of the Korth. Except that Blue Jeans was even faster. A long-barreled revolver materialized in his hand and I stared into the black hole of its muzzle.

"You killed my son, Mr. Warner," Tillou said, his tone flat.

"True. Why do you think I'm here?" I bent toward him, bringing my face to within a foot of his. At such close range he was like a character from a horror comic. "Why do you think I came to the island in the first place, if not to see you? Christ, man, I've been wise to you for months."

This news patently displeased him. The Halloween mask frowned, augmenting the grooves and trenches.

"How can this be?"

"You use monkeys as employees."

He grunted and snapped fingers at Belanger, who came and frisked me thoroughly. He sneered when he found the Korth.

"Nice gun," he remarked.

I sneered back, maintaining my hardboiled veneer. "Too nice for you."

"Did you also know about Gina?" Tillou asked me, gesturing irritably at Belanger.

I looked at Gina and couldn't help hurting her. "No, I didn't. She was a juicy piece of bait, I'll admit, but she didn't influence my plans at all. As a plant, she was a failure. I've enjoyed screwing her though."

Gina flinched, drawing away, her face flaccid with shock. Distress flowed out of her in almost tangible waves. I felt no remorse. The bitch deserved it and more.

Tillou ignored the slight on his daughter-in-law. He rotated his wheelchair and detoured round me to get behind the desk. Once there, he positioned himself to face me, like an interviewer questioning a job applicant.

"Monkeys, you say." He tapped his lips with a fleshless forefinger, regarding me thoughtfully. "Explain yourself. How did you learn of my interest in you? Through Gina?"

"Not through Gina. I told you, she did good work for you. Very discreet." This brought a whimper of distress from Gina. "No, I had other sources."

"Other sources?" he queried, the second word sounding like the hiss of escaping gas. "What other sources?"

"Have you asked yourself who wanted to kill your son? Or did you think it was personal between me and him?"

"Yes, to answer your first question, and no, to answer your second. I have made inquiries about you. You're no more than a hired gun. I assume you're going to tell me who hired you."

"In return for my life?" I raised a cynical eyebrow. "In a manner of speaking. I came here tonight to propose a deal."

Tillou smiled, prompting smiles all round. I wished I were in on the joke. I had a feeling it was at my expense.

"You're not in a position to bargain." His hooked fingers drummed on the desktop. "The information can be extracted."

"You don't need to extract it. Give me safe passage, and I'll give you the name you want."

Belanger jingled coins in his pocket—or maybe he had steel balls. He was growing restive, constantly shifting his stance. Probably couldn't wait to be turned loose on me.

"Let me deal with him, *patron*," he wheedled. "Five minutes and he'll sell out his own mother." He sounded confident; he sure convinced me.

"You see, Mr. Warner," Tillou said with an apologetic spread of hands. "Why should I bargain with you? Léon here could make a mummy talk."

Belanger grinned delightedly, an ear-to-ear split. "Do you remember that Corsican, *patron*? The one we stuffed into the furnace feet first?"

Distaste twisted Tillou's features. Evidently a man of some sensitivity.

"He talked before the skin on his feet had even begun to scorch," Belanger carried on. "But we finished the job anyway, just for the hell of it. We fed him in a little at a time. It took half an hour to get to his balls." Gina shuddered beside me and I felt slightly sick. "He croaked before that, though. Well, he stopped screaming anyhow."

"Must you recall the incident so graphically, Léon?" Tillou reproved mildly. "We don't want to give Mr. Warner a heart attack."

He eyed me speculatively. "I'll make you an offer. Give me the name right now, and I promise you a quick, clean death."

My bark of laughter was all bravado and no joy. "This isn't a fairy story, Tillou. People don't make deals like that, except in fiction. Sure, you can put this ape to work on me and cause me a lot of pain, and if I die before I talk, what then? You'll never know who wanted your son out of the way, will you?"

"Please don't hurt him, Bernard," Gina said before Tillou could reply.

He looked at her with a show of irritation, the electric-blue optics filmed over, appearing sightless.

"I understand Georgina has formed an attachment to you, Mr. Warner. Naturally, I disapprove. It shows remarkable disloyalty on her part, not to mention lack of taste." That was rich, coming from a mobster. "However, I am rather fond of her and I'm prepared to over-look her wayward behavior. Regrettably, whatever pain it might cause her, I cannot make a similar concession for you."

"Bernard, *please*. It's all in the past." Gina was pleading hard for me. I'll grant her that. I didn't want her contribution. I especially didn't want to be in her debt. But it bought a few precious seconds while I considered Tillou's Freudian slip. He was fond of his daugh-ter-in-law, he claimed. Fond enough to baulk at harming her? It was a possible soft spot and I had to exploit it. Short of suicidal heroics, I had nothing else to exploit.

Gina was still pleading for me when I swung her round, pulling her tight against me. With a single, practiced movement, I stooped and ripped the automatic knife from the masking tape that secured it to my ankle, while pressing the button that shot the blade out frontwards from the handle. I used my free hand to twist her arm up her back, forcing a cry of pain from her, as I touched the point of the blade to her throat.

She squirmed, trying to break free. "André...let me go. Don't do this."

"Shut up, bitch," I snarled, my mouth against her ear. "Unless you want to bleed to death."

"Let her go, Mr. Warner," Tillou said, unflappable as ever. "What-ever you do, you can't possibly get away."

Blue Jeans' gun was still covering me. Belanger and Jourd'hui were looking at Tillou for guidance.

"Don't shoot while Gina is in danger," he ordered. The glare he directed at me was straight from Siberia.

"The first wrong move and this blade goes in all the way." I injected a vicious note into my voice.

Gina struggled anew. To discourage her, I pricked her skin. She yelped. A bauble of blood oozed, shockingly red against the paleness of her throat.

"Keep still, Gina. I've no choice."

"He won't do it, *patron*," Blue Jeans said with a nervous snigger. He advanced, gun extended, hammer cocked. In appearance, he was more college boy than thug, but there was nothing juvenile about his handling of that long-barreled revolver.

"Back off, sonny boy," I warned, tightening my hold on Gina. "She's nothing to me, now I know she's on your side." She had ceased to struggle. Her body was relaxed now, molded to mine as if she suddenly knew that, even if my life did depend on it, I wouldn't hurt her. I was aware of the smell of her, a heady drug in my nostrils. Not enough make me weaken, only to remind me of what I was going to miss from now on. If I survived to miss anything at all.

Tillou flicked a finger at Blue Jeans, who halted reluctantly.

"Now," I said. "My gun, or you lose a daughter-in-law. And don't think I won't do it. What's another death on my conscience?"

For emphasis, I repositioned the knife to place its edge instead of its point against her throat.

"No...please!" Her body writhed.

Tillou, to give him his due, showed real concern. "Very well, very well. You've made your point, Warner."

"Let us take him, *patron*," Jourd'hui urged. He was doing a sort of sidewinder shuffle, working round behind me.

I stepped back, dragging Gina with me, hugging her tighter than I ever did in bed.

"Don't be stupid, asshole. I'm not playing games!"

"Nobody move!" Tillou snapped.

Jourd'hui obeyed with palpable reluctance, like a dog straining to be let off its leash.

"The gun—quick!" I snapped.

Everyone's attention, including mine, was on Tillou. The balance of initiative still lay with him. My rough treatment of Gina was all bluff and he only had to call it.

"André—my arm," Gina whimpered.

"Shut up," I growled in her ear.

Then Tillou said resignedly, "Give him his gun."

I experienced a passing flare of triumph. Passing, because even as he uttered the words, he conveyed an unspoken message to Belanger. It was no more than a contraction of the eyebrows. I nearly missed it. It was a silent command that countermanded the verbal one.

The only course open to me was to move first and move fast. I gave Gina at shove in the direction of Blue Jeans, the most immediate threat, and went for Belanger with my head down. He was quicker on the draw than on his feet. A gun appeared from the depths of his jacket. If he'd been a shade nimbler, he would have stepped aside, leaving me to plough into some very solid pieces of furniture. As it was, I connected with him at waist level. He deflated like a burst paper-bag, crashing to the floor with me on top of him. His head cracked on the parquet, making a sound like a sledgehammer driving a stake. The only downside was, I lost the knife.

"Get away from him, Léon!" Tillou shouted. "Don't kill him! Don't kill him!"

Belanger was in no position to kill me. He was out and beyond. As I got up on my hands and knees, slightly winded, a shot was fired. I swear the bullet parted my hair. I heard a grunt of pain as I dived for cover behind the couch. From floor level, I looked back over my shoulder. Jourd'hui was on his knees, eyes turned up, his dazzling white shirt blooming blood from the bullet that had been meant for me. He toppled in slow motion, like a felled tree.

"Blanc!" Tillou's voice came as a raucous screech. "*Lachez-la!*" Let her go.

But the choice wasn't Blanc's. Gina was all wrapped up with him, her limbs coiled round his, both her hands gripping his gun-wrist. She had guts.

Tillou was left to face me on his own.

I needed a gun. Belanger's was someplace around, but out of

reach. Temporarily hidden from Blanc, I delved inside Belanger's left jacket pocket and struck gold, or rather steel, in the shape of my faithful Korth. A second wild shot from Blanc's gun brought plaster down on the coffee table. I executed another barrel roll to fetch up against the front of a couch. I hauled myself up onto one knee, my finger curling round the trigger, my thumb crunching back the hammer. My priority target was Blanc. The problem was, he and Gina were still entwined, denying me a clean shot at him. So I straightened up and instead drew a bead on Tillou, who was gabbling into the phone. Even as I sighted the gun a hammering on the door prompted a change in priorities.

"What's going on?" a loud male voice demanded. Reinforcements had arrived.

"Everything's cool," I shouted back. Not that I expected them to believe it.

A speedy exit was now my priority. Forget Tillou. First, I had to deal with Blanc who had forced Gina to the wall and was poised to restructure her face with his big butch revolver. A couple of strides took me within striking range. When I brought the barrel of the Korth down on the top of his skull, the force of it reverberated all the way up to my shoulder. Once was enough. He subsided in a graceless slither.

I grabbed Gina's wrist. "Come on. It's not healthy here for either of us."

The hammering had ceased. In its place, a lot of shouting and running feet from the corridor. We went out via the patio doors onto a small floodlit terrace, empty of people.

"This way," Gina said as I took a fleeting breather to sort out my bearings. Her knowledge of the layout reminded me anew that she was a member of the Tillou family, though she had done plenty in the last few minutes to prove she wasn't my enemy. We ran past a pond that was more floating lilies than water, and across a parched lawn. We were still under the floodlights, when a jubilant "*Le voila!*" shattered my hopes of escaping unseen.

I took a snap shot toward the house and glass shattered. Nobody fired back.

Darkness absorbed us. In the moment of self-congratulation at our successful escape, they played their final card by setting the dogs on us

—well, one dog. "Big enough to ride on," was how Bonhomme had described the hound in question. It was no exaggeration. One glance over my shoulder was enough to freeze the blood in my veins. White with black spots, it was a monster of a dog, easily bigger than a Shetland pony. It pounded across the lawn, the floodlights playing across its flanks, accentuating the effortless, elastic flow.

Trying to outrun it was hopeless. I stumbled over my own feet as I positioned myself to shoot. I got off a single unaimed round, that went nowhere. The canine monster steamrollered me to the ground, pinning me beneath a hundred and fifty pounds of muscle and bone. Gina screamed a command, but it had no effect. I hugged the dog's huge head to mine in an effort to neutralize its bite. Saliva dribbled from its jaws onto my cheek. My gun offered the only hope, but it was crushed against my ribs by the dog's weight. If I used it, I was just as likely to shoot myself.

For the second time that night Gina was my salvation, hauling on the hound's tail. It was a brave act. Even big dogs don't like their tails pulled. This one let go a howl and aimed a vicious snap over its shoulder at her, which, showing excellent reflexes, she managed to avoid. In retaliating against Gina, the dog's weight was shifted away from my trapped gun hand. I fired upward twice at the brute's chest. At this point blank range, I couldn't miss. Both bullets emerged via its backbone in eruptions of flesh and gore. It swayed from side to side, its moaning almost human, before crumpling to the ground, air escaping from its jaws in a terminal sigh. I wriggled from under it and got to my feet; dazed, bloody, but still battleworthy.

Gina tugged at my sleeve. A gun cracked and something zinged past my nose. More to deter than to injure, I pumped my remaining ammunition at a group of advancing figures bunched together on the lawn. One of them went down clutching his stomach. The group scattered, firing arbitrarily. They weren't aimed shots, but no less lethal for that. As their guns emptied, the shooting dried up.

I fished around in my jacket for spare cartridges. I found five in all and thumbed them into the Korth's cylinder. Holding Gina by her hand, I used the lull to put some distance between us and them. We stumbled on a path that she was sure led down to the beach. To the rear, flashlight beams began probing the night. By then we were a good two hundred meters from the floodlit area, screened by a morass of shrubbery.

The sea came into view, black like sludge under the moonless sky. Visibility improved as the vegetation receded. We hit sand, firm as asphalt, and Gina kicked off her high heels.

"Be careful," she cautioned. "There are rocks just ahead."

She was calm, as if battling with a monster hound, being shot at and pursued, were all in a day's work. She had guts, all right.

We made it gingerly over the rocks and struck out inland, the blackness enveloping us again. Bushes and thorns whipped us as we stumbled along. Eventually, scratched and bruised, we came to the shore at a tiny sheltered cove.

"Should we stay here or move on?" Gina asked in a whisper.

"Better stay here," I said. "Crashing around in the bushes will just give away our position. Not to mention inviting a broken ankle. We'll wait until first light."

She didn't dissent. We flopped down between a pair of rocks, close yet not quite touching. It was a balmy night; the earlier breeze had tailed off, and the tree foliage overhead was at rest. Only insomniac crickets, sawing away nonstop, held the silence at bay. I was still on the alert for sounds of pursuit. We had gained a reprieve, a stay of punishment only. They weren't finished with me yet, nor I with them come to that.

As the immediate danger receded, Gina stirred restlessly, before blurting out, "I'm sorry, darling, truly, truly sorry. But, you know, I'm glad as well. We would never have met if I hadn't done it."

There was truth in that. The things I wanted to say were stuck like a fishbone in my gullet.

"Thanks for the help back there," I mumbled. It sounded insincere. Relenting further, I added, "I wouldn't have made it without you."

Beside me, an impatient movement. I figured she wanted the air cleared between us, not platitudes.

"So go on, tell me the whole story," I said, when she didn't follow up.

She bent forward and her hair hung down between her knees. Her shoulders shook. She was crying, a silent, heart-wrenching weeping. I wished I could comfort her. She needed it, even deserved it, but I had no compassion to draw on. I was still reeling from the concussive shock of her betrayal.

When she finally lifted her head and spoke again, her tone was even and controlled. "I'll only tell you if you really want to hear it," she said with a sniff. "If you've already made up your mind, if you've already judged me, I can see no point in going over the whole rotten mess. Much as I love you, André, I'm not going to let you put me in the dock."

The wound she had inflicted on me wasn't healed, but she was making me think again, making me want to understand. I hadn't stopped loving her. Trust was the issue.

"Tell me, then," I said, with all the simpatico I could muster. From the telling would perhaps come the understanding that would lead to forgiveness.

She wiped her cheek with the back of her hand. "Shall I go back to the start when I met Fabrice, my husband, the man they say you killed?" She paused, inviting confirmation or denial perhaps? When I didn't speak, she continued, "I'll take that as a "yes". Well then, I met him when I was eighteen. I already told you that, didn't I?"

I gave an affirmative grunt.

"I was silly, immature, and a virgin. He swept me off my feet with his Latino good looks and athletic body. I knew zilch of his criminal background, nothing about his parents. We got married against both our parents' wishes, though opposition was much stronger from mine. They felt I was too young and much too immature. They were right on both counts. But Fabrice was so glamorous and persuasive and such fun, you can't imagine. We honeymooned in Thailand, and his parents bought us a sumptuous villa near Marseille. We lived high, mixed with the cream of Marseille society, and travelled just about every-goddam-where. We had a private yacht, a private plane, and expensive cars. Oh, we had a *swell* time.

"It was several years before I found out how his family really made their money. I'd thought it all came from the nightclubs and casinos they owned—still own. I didn't realize these were just window-dressing for drug smuggling, prostitution, and other lucrative shit. When, eventually, the odd whisper began to filter through to my giddy brain, I was shocked. But Fabrice was such a plausible charmer, he convinced me that what he was doing wasn't so bad. That he was just supplying a service, meeting a demand." In the starlight damp patches glistened on her cheeks.

"So help me...so *help* me, I shrugged it aside. I was still madly in love with him and I was estranged from my own family by then. They refused to have Fabrice in their home. Maybe they had suspicions about the business he was in, but preferred to keep me in the dark. Who knows? The upshot of their hostility was that I was drawn closer to Fabrice's family. His parents—his mother was still alive then—came to accept me as their own daughter almost, and I grew kind of fond of them. In my preoccupation with *la dolce vita*—you know?—I shoved the unsavory stuff into the background. Nothing was allowed to intrude on my fairy tale existence. God, I am so *ashamed*."

She broke off and lifted her face towards the starry sky.

"What went wrong?" I probed. Hints she had dropped over the past week or two made me sure weeds had sprouted in her rosy garden.

"Wrong? How did you know?"

"I now know the divorce never happened, that it was just part of your cover. That aside, I'm just guessing that it all went sour somehow. Maybe it didn't."

"No, you're right." A bitter laugh. "I got pregnant, that's what went wrong."

"You didn't want a baby?"

"What? Oh, you fool! You've no idea how much I wanted it. I was unbelievably happy. Fabrice was just as thrilled. He became even more doting. Everything was perfect." Her voice faltered. She took a long, shuddering breath. "Then, at five months, I miscarried. Nobody's fault except my own, playing tennis like a schmuck. I avoided straining myself, no running, no reaching for difficult shots, and still I miscarried. I couldn't believe it. Anyhow, that was it, my dream shattered."

"Did it have to be the end of the world? You were still young, still are. Why didn't you try for another?"

"I was twenty-five, and we didn't try for another because I'd become sterile, or so I was told. Some complication with my Fallopian tubes. The doctor explained it all to me, but..." Her hand brushed against my knee. "To me, it was all highfalutin Hippocratic cant. I suppose I could have learned to live with it, given time. It was Fabrice who really took it hard. No babies equaled no sons and heirs to the Tillou Empire. He went off me immediately and totally. I scarcely recognized him as the attentive, loving man I'd married. He was still polite, still considerate, but it was all superficial, for appearances' sake. We continued to live together in the same house. We even slept together when he came home, which wasn't every day. Now and again, when he was in between mistresses, he condescended to screw me. And I do mean screw."

She stopped talking abruptly. I guessed she was reliving those times when, in the knowledge of her husband's infidelity with who-knows-what brothel flotsam, she gave her body to him, let him use her as a convenience.

I didn't regret killing him.

She expelled a sigh that came from the depths. "Incredibly, pathetically, I still loved the creep. For nearly four years, we lived together like that, pretending to the outside world and ourselves. Right up until his death, I still loved him." Her head turned toward me. "And do you know, André, I was never unfaithful to him. Not once, not so much as a bloody one-night stand." She punctuated the words by banging her clenched fists on her drawn-up knees. "That's what I meant when I said to you in Geneva about wallowing in pity for myself and contempt for all things male. You remember, don't you?"

"Oh, yes." I remembered too much, that was the trouble. I remembered all the loving declarations and all the loving deeds, and asked myself how many of them, if any, had been sincere. How many of the scenes we played out had been orchestrated? How much of the dialogue was written and rehearsed in advance?

"How did the family treat you? After the miscarriage, I mean."

"They were fine, really supportive. Fabrice's mother died the same year from a brain tumor. For Fabrice, that just piled misery on top of misery. They were very close. But Bernard and Fabrice's sister, Jeanne, were always there for both of us. Of course, Fabrice didn't let on to them how he felt. Like the cold, calculating shit he became—or maybe that was his true nature all along—he pretended that everything between us was cool and he didn't mind a bit that we couldn't have kids." She gave a snort. "He was a hell of a fucking actor, my husband. And do you know, the irony is, I wasn't sterile after all, not permanently. I had some tests done earlier this year and it seems I'm okay now. What do you think of that for a sick joke?"

"What do I think? I think shit happens, and it happened to you with compound interest."

I linked fingers behind my neck and leaned against a rock. I loved Gina; I couldn't help that. Yet I hated her for her deception. Neither emotion was controllable. I hated her deception all the more because I loved her so much. My commitment had been absolute. Now, my torment was absolute. Even Marion's death had barely hit me this badly.

"André...I need to ask you this: did you really kill Fabrice?"

The question was inevitable, I supposed. Should I have cared about confessing to the murder of her husband? With justification or not, I did.

"Yes," I said gruffly. "Yes, I killed him."

"I hoped you didn't, that it was all a mistake." She sounded unhappy, fighting a private battle no less bloody than mine. "I hoped you really were a retired spy after all. Not that it makes any difference now. To how I feel, I mean. My marriage died long ago, even though my feelings lived on. It could even be..." She laughed shakily, joylessly. "...it could be said that you were sent by divine intervention to rescue me from my miserable state."

"Like Rapunzel being rescued from the tower."

"Yes, something like that." She gave a tiny chuckle.

"One thing, though, I wasn't lying about what I did. I really am a retired spy, a sort of spy anyway. That's how I got into my current profession. I killed a couple of guys for Queen and Country." My brutal frankness was intentional. "I've killed more than a couple for profit. It's how I earned my living these past ten years."

Bring out all the dirty washing. Get it over with.

She nodded slowly. "Ten years ago, I would have been horrified if someone had said that to me," she said. "Being married to Fabrice and hearing about things I thought only existed in the movies, I guess I've gotten hardened to the scummier side of life. If I'd learned about the goings-on in the Tillou organization all at once, I might well have walked out. As it was, I was drip-fed the details, which gave me time to absorb and adapt. Eventually, each new discovery ceased to shock me. I became blasé about it all." She wrung her hands. "You must think I'm a pretty worthless sort of person."

"Misguided, not worthless. A bit naïve, too, maybe."

"Agh, it makes me sick to think about the stuff I turned a blind eye to." She pounded her knees again. "So you see, compared with the things I've condoned in the name of love, what you've done doesn't seem so terrible at all. I've tried to convince myself the people you... you know...killed, that they'd gotten their comeuppance. That they were nasty people themselves. Like..." She drew a breath, deep and scouring. "Like Fabrice."

I guessed it cost her a lot to say that.

"You're not far wrong," I said. "Believe this or not, from day one, I only ever accepted contracts on known criminals. I needed some kind of standard, I guess. I'd gotten used to being on the side of the good guys. Not that I'm seeking absolution, no need to let me off the hook. It's all history, in any case. I can't put the clock back and purify myself."

Her hand caressed my thigh. "Neither of us can. It's just as you said. Our life together began when we met. Anyhow, I can't even plead ignorance about your profession, though I kept hoping it wasn't true. I knew all about you before I met you. Before I fell in love with you."

"So that much is true?"

"That I love you?" She seemed startled by the implication. "Do you doubt it?"

"I did. For a little while back there. Now..." I hesitated.

"Now?"

"I...I'm not sure. Was our first meeting accidental, at the Hotel in Digne?" I answered my own question. "No, no, like hell it was." Blind I had been; gullible I was not.

"Let me explain about that," she said. "When Fabrice was killed, Bernard went bananas with grief; only son and all that. I looked after him, which also helped to keep my own blues at bay. When he started to think rationally again, he was determined to track down Fabrice's killer, though at that time he had no idea who it was. Family honor was at stake, and all that jazz. It took the best part of four months. I was never told the details, but I understood the lead came via someone in Germany. Bernard planted one of his trusted lieutenants in an apartment near you, a man called Carl Schelling. He was supposed to check you out, to make sure you really were the man they were looking for. They were very thorough. Bernard didn't want to get the wrong guy. I don't know how Schelling set about it, but he came up with enough evidence to satisfy Bernard that you were the guilty party."

"He posed as a criminal, suggesting he was in the market for a hit man. It was a ruse to get me to admit that was my profession." I smiled inwardly at the memory. "Like the game kids play: you show me yours, and I'll show you mine. It almost worked, did work in fact, I guess. It must have, because Tillou acted on what Schelling relayed back to him."

"Oh, Bernard's a smart cookie all right. And Carl really is a criminal. He was jailed in Austria for messing with kids." She made a sound of distaste. "He gave me the creeps."

"After Schelling reported back, what then?"

"Then Bernard thought of using me to entrap you."

"Entrapment," I said expressionlessly. "Smart move."

"Mmm. I was to lure you into the spider's web, to get you to come here, to Porquerolles. Another sick joke; you came of your own volition! I actually ended up trying to dissuade you, because by then, I'd switched sides. I couldn't be too insistent about it, otherwise you'd have been suspicious, but you might recall I tried to get you to change your plans and go to Toulon instead."

That was true enough. Coming to Porquerolles was my call, not hers.

"Originally, when Bernard asked me to do the entrapment thing, I told him where to stick it. But, well—like Fabrice—he can be very persuasive. He bullied and cajoled and ranted about obligations and family honor, and generally used every subterfuge under the sun. I still held out. So he reverted to type and started behaving like the gangster he is, threatening me if I didn't cooperate. I'm a coward, so I agreed. I became part of the team that had you under observation and

I was supposed to enter your life at a propitious moment. Bernard was confident you'd fall for me."

"Who wouldn't?" I conceded sourly.

Not far away an engine sputtered and fired, unmistakably an outboard. Was it a search getting under way, or just guests returning to the mainland? A second engine crackled, and a third. Throttles opened, and a boat came flicking round the headland, skimming the water. It headed out across the channel, away from the island. I realized I had been holding my breath. I let it out raggedly.

Two more outboards emerged, shark-like shapes, travelling so fast they seemed to aquaplane over the water. The combined snarl of the three engines burst across the millpond surface, amplified in the predawn stillness. While it lasted, we made no attempt to speak.

"Guests being taxied home," Gina observed when peace was restored.

"Not looking for us, at any rate." Then, picking up the threads of Gina's story, "As I also recall, you turned me down when I proposed dinner, the day before I drove you to Monaco. Was that because you changed your mind about helping Tillou?"

"No, at that point, I was still committed to his side. It was simply part of Bernard's master plan, to keep you dangling. "Play hard to get," he advised me. "Don't be a pushover." So I played hard to get, or overplayed. You went away after that on your Mediterranean cruise, as I now know. At the time, it was as if you'd gone for good. Bernard was furious with me for screwing up."

"You certainly fooled me. You deserved an Oscar for the way you played Miss Hands-off-me."

"You're so kind." The sarcasm came over strong. "In truth though, André, I was just relieved to see the back of you. By then I wanted out of his crappy scheme. Vengeance for Fabrice's death was never in my makeup." She paused, rocking back and forth, hugging herself and sighing. "Then you came back. Bernard had stationed someone in Monaco and your return was reported. I was dispatched at no notice to the Hotel de Paris, which is where you saw me and dragged me away from my breakfast. I acted cool to discourage you, yet I was beginning to be drawn to you in spite of myself. In spite of your having apparently killed Fabrice, though at that time, I wasn't hundred per cent convinced you'd done it. I didn't think you were capable of killing someone, that it was a case of mistaken identity."

"I wish."

"My conscience gave me a real bad time at first, when I started to care about you. But because of how things had been between Fabrice and me, I didn't feel entirely disloyal. He'd been disloyal to me many times over when we were married. I thought I was about due for a new and better deal."

"Amen to that."

In the east, the sky was lightening, indigo giving way to slate blue above the treetops. It was after four o'clock I discovered, to my surprise. I was instantly uneasy. Daylight spelled danger. We would have to be ready to move on as soon as there was light enough to see by.

"I almost killed you myself, you know," Gina said, her voice subdued. "On your boat, on *Seamist*."

"What are you talking about?" I said, puzzled.

"When Pascal fell overboard and you dived in after him, I was going to let you drown. That's why I stayed out of sight when you were trying to get back on board. I heard you calling. I thought, as long as I couldn't see you, as long as I didn't have to watch you drown, I could do it, leave you there."

It all came back to me now. Splashing about in those plunging seas and calling her, wondering why she didn't throw me a line. Now, all was explained.

"But you weakened," I said, and even raked up a grin. "You didn't leave me there after all."

She shook her head, setting the sandy blonde tresses swirling. "When I looked over the side and saw you, I couldn't let you die. Especially as you'd been so brave." She laughed softly in the back of her throat. "That sounds corny, doesn't it? But you *were* brave. And in a way, even though I'd been ready to abandon you only minutes before, I was proud of you."

"Some Mata Hari you were," I said. "Not to mention mixed up!"

"You're so right. That was me, mixed up and ambivalent. On the one hand, I wanted you dead, on the other..."

"Why did you come to Geneva? That was one hell of a step; into my camp and out of Tillou's."

"Good question," she said, hugging her knees. "Bernard wanted me to. I resisted at first, and then I discovered I wanted to go anyway. Not for revenge, his or mine. I just wanted to see you again. Maybe I was already in love with you by then, but wouldn't admit it. Even without the Fabrice thing, I was still anti-male. That much of what I told you was true."

An early rising seabird drifted across the empty vault of the dawn sky, wings splayed, describing circles at random. Once in a while it sent out a squawk, a lonely sound in the stillness of the coming dawn.

I lobbed an aimless pebble toward the water. "Okay, but that still doesn't explain why you told Tillou we were on the island. I'm guessing you phoned him that morning you went to buy the bread, didn't you?"

"That's right, but not to inform on you. My God, *please* don't think that. By then, I was totally committed to you." She made a helpless gesture. "I loved you. I couldn't have purposely done anything to harm you. No, I was trying to persuade him to back off, to call off his vendetta. You see, I was certain he already knew we were here. He has spies everywhere. Half the island's population is probably in his pocket, one way or another. You might have been able to hide yourself, but you couldn't hide the boat. I thought I might be able to reason with him." She paused. "So I told him how I felt about you."

"And?" I prompted when she lapsed into silence.

"He hung up on me."

No surprise there. "What did you expect?"

"I'm not sure." She scuffed her bare heels in the sand. "It was worth a shot. Anything was better than just waiting for Bernard to pounce. For all I knew, they might have been preparing to gun you down or blow up the boat."

She had meant well. It had made no difference to the outcome.

"And Madame Sabourin? Was she part of the setup, too?"

"Well, she was obviously sent to make contact after my telephone call to Bernard. But I had no hand in that. She brought me a message from Bernard, which was that he wanted you to come to the barbecue, but only to talk to you, to find out who employed you to kill Fabrice. Through Jeanne, he gave me his word that it wasn't a trap. I wanted to believe him, yet I didn't trust him. When she invited us to the barbecue, I tried to wriggle out of it—don't you remember? Without giving away my identity, which by then I was afraid to do, I couldn't simply warn you off. I just had to hope Bernard was genuine in wanting only to negotiate. I thought that with all those respectable people at the party..." She fiddled with the hem of her dress. "I should have told her to go to hell."

"Visiting the island was all my own idea," I reminded her. "No need to beat yourself up about that. Without your help I'd never have escaped. And while we're on the subject, I'm sorry I had to hurt you back there, and the things I said. I was pretty upset. How's your neck?"

"It's nothing. I can't even feel it." She touched the spot with a fingertip. "I don't hold it against you, not the words or using me to get away. You had to do it."

Her generosity made me feel humble. "I wouldn't have harmed you," I insisted. "Not really harmed you. I was pretty upset, sure. I even hated you a bit, but that was mostly hurt pride. I wouldn't have—"

"Killed me? I know that, really."

I kissed her, a nominal meeting of lips. Neither of us were in the mood for real passion.

She cupped my cheek. "What about us, André? Where do we go from here?"

"Well, where *do* we go?" I retorted lightly.

She stared at me, round-eyed.

"If you mean, do we still have a future?" I went on. "An hour ago I'd have trashed the idea. Now...I stand by what I said before. Do you remember what I said to you that night at my apartment, after we dined with Jules and Nellie?"

She nodded. "Something about my life starting at a hotel in Digne, and what came before is ancient history and no concern of yours. Is that what you mean?"

"There you go. Maybe I was prescient. You know, sweetheart, I believe that what's happened has made us stronger. We've confessed our sins, now we have nothing to hide from each other. Love is blind, isn't that what they say? I'll go along with that."

Her fingers inserted themselves between mine and squeezed.

"Oh, darling."

"Nothing has really changed when all's said and done," I went on. "Except that from now on we can be completely honest." I placed an arm around her shoulders. Her skin was clammy. "I'm hooked, love. I'm a junky. I need my daily fix of Gina Gregg, Gina Tillou, or whoever she is, and I'm not interested in kicking the habit. You're a virus in my blood."

"You don't know, you can't possibly, possibly know how happy it makes me to hear that." She snuggled up to my bloodstained shirtfront with a murmur of contentment. "I do love you so, André."

"And I you."

I lay back against the rock, still embracing her. The stars were gone. Sunrise wasn't far off. Soon, we would have to leave, but not just yet. Not for an hour or so.

Tiredness settled on me, light and gentle as mist, and I surrendered to it.

CHAPTER FOURTEEN

THE SUN WAS high when I was roused from my sleep by the pulsations of a helicopter prowling along the foreshore. Only semi-awake, I watched it swoop over the headland, a bright yellow machine with a Perspex cabin like a goldfish bowl, and torpedo-shaped floats. It dropped down behind the old fort at the western tip of the island and was lost from sight.

"That's Bernard's," Gina announced, yawning and rubbing sleep from her eyes. With her hair tousled and her makeup mostly worn away she looked like a teenage urchin. There were superficial scratches on her forehead, cheeks, and arms from our safari through the undergrowth. I was similarly scarred about the face; my jacket had protected my arms. That particular garment was a write-off, thanks to the quantities of canine blood and goo deposited on it. That made two suits and a jacket Tillou owed me.

I stood up, stretched, and checked my watch. It was 10:20. Unprofessionally, I'd overslept by a wide margin. My mouth tasted like the bottom of a primeval swamp.

The helicopter was a rude surprise. High time I stopped underestimating Tillou. High time I got my brain into gear, too. I totted up my assets: a gun with five shells and a boat. Not much to pit against Tillou's private army, with his helicopter and all.

"Here's what we do," I said to Gina, and it was instant improvisation. "I have to meet up with Jean-Pierre in the bay by the Pointe Grand Langoustier."

"Port-Fay, you mean?"

"Right. Now, whatever happens, I don't want you hurt, and that means we have to separate."

She stood up, too. "Fuck you, bonzo, if you'll excuse my French. From this day forward, till death do us part, whatever we do, we do together."

"Be sensible, love. Tillou isn't after you. He's not best pleased with you, but he's not out for your blood. If you stick with me though, sooner or later, you could stop a bullet. You can see that, can't you?"

Her silence was answer enough.

"You're to go into town and take the ferry to the mainland." I pulled a handful of hundred euro notes from my wallet and wrapped her fingers round them.

"Shove it, André. I can't just run away. I can't desert you."

"You can and you've got to." I struggled to unclip the key to the apartment from my key ring, cursing when a fingernail ripped. "For our sakes."

Her eyebrows rose. "For *our* sakes?"

"Yes, you stupid broad. What future will we have together if you get killed?" I gripped her shoulders and shook her. "What use will all your support and loyalty be if you're dead?"

Again, she had no answer.

I gave her the key and sucked at the split fingernail.

"Okay," I said roughly. "This is how we'll play it. I'm going to meet up with Jean-Pierre. You get off the island, take a train or plane to Geneva. Go to the apartment and just sit tight."

She clung to me. "Sit tight, he says, while he's being hunted down. How can you ask it of me?"

I blew my stack. "Christ, Gina! Haven't you done enough damage already, even if it was well-intentioned? Don't make things worse than they are."

She recoiled as if I'd slapped her, her eyes bright with pain. It was on the tip of my tongue to recant, then I thought better of it. Angry, she was less likely to press me to relent.

"I should be there by Sunday. That's four days from now. If you need money, there's about three thousand Swiss francs in the wall safe behind the Manet painting. It's a combination safe." I reeled off the numbers and made her repeat them twice, which she did sullenly.

I stuffed the Korth in the belt holster. "I'll say *au revoir*, then."

"Right now? Oh, fuck it!" She coiled her hands into fists and beat them gently against my chest. "All right, I'll do as you say, you bastard."

"That's my girl. I'm going now. The longer I delay, the more likely they'll catch up with us. Call me on my cell phone when you arrive."

"Yes. Well, good luck. Don't do anything silly."

"Count on it, sweetheart."

"Goodbye then." The kiss she planted on my cheek was cool. "Take real care, my beloved."

My beloved. Two simple words that moved me beyond measure. I hugged her so tightly she squeaked.

"Give me half an hour to get well clear before you move from here."

Another kiss, lips to lips this time, and I took my leave. I ran lightly up the short slope that led from the beach. At the top, I pivoted round. From twenty meters away she was watching me. Even at that distance, the lines of strain etched on features were visible.

"Be there when I arrive," I called. "I love you."

The impact of those three words was immediate, like switching on a light in a darkened room. She blew me a kiss, and her smile was as dazzling as a small sun.

"Come back to me soon, darling."

I gave her a last upbeat salute, before setting off at a lope with a dry mouth and thudding heart.

———

AT THE OUTSET my progress was rapid. The Ile de Porquerolles is networked with narrow, tunnel-like footpaths, primarily for tourist use. They guided me where I wanted to go. I headed more or less south, taking my bearings from the sun, reinforced by occasional glimpses of the sea. Once, I caught sight of the rooftop of Tillou's house. No activity from that quarter, as far as I could tell. Maybe they'd given up. More likely they were out combing the island for me.

As long as I kept to the footpaths, I was relatively safe. Even from above I'd be invisible. The wide dirt tracks posed the greatest danger. I crossed several, but apart from a family of cyclists, I saw no one.

As I came to the crest of a hill, the small closely packed trees thinned out in favor of equally dense shrubbery, tough and wiry, with treacherous scree underfoot. I was able to see right across to the peninsula that curved protectively round the Port-Fay cove. And—God bless Jean-Pierre—there was *Seamist*, anchored just inside the rocks that acted as a breakwater, like talons reaching out to sea. A figure, adult size, was bent over the bow pulpit.

I blundered on down the far side of the hill, fighting the shrubs that seemed reluctant for me to leave, and sliding on loose shale. Pretty soon I came to the brink of the low cliffs that edged the bay. The scene was picturesque. Foaming rollers charged up a wide sandy beach, under an array of date palms. A scattering of vacationers huddled beneath colorful parasols or frolicked in the surf. The sea within the bay was a deep ultramarine, changing dramatically out beyond the rocky spit where two currents clashed. *Seamist* was bucking somewhat, white tipped combers breaking against her bow. Wind was about force four from the south-west, I estimated. Near-ideal conditions for sailing.

Following the line of the cliffs, I bypassed the Hotel du Langoustier, its red-tiled roof alien in the profusion of green. The most direct route from there to *Seamist*'s anchorage required me to leave the protection of the shrubbery and take to the beach. I stripped off my bloodstained jacket and shirt and parted with my holster; I bundled them together and stuffed them down a crack in the rocks. The gun went into my pocket where it made a bulge. Couldn't be helped.

On the beach, I attracted less attention than a taxicab in Times Square. The only second glance came from a lithe African girl reclining alone on a rush mat. She checked out my pecs and I'd like to think she approved. I tossed her a cordial *"Bonjour, mademoiselle,"* which had her raising her pink-framed sunglasses for a more searching appraisal of the rest of me.

My saunter carried me to the far side of the bay in a few minutes. This brought me within hailing distance of *Seamist*, except that there was no longer anyone on deck to hail. With the approach of midday, chances were Jean-Pierre would be preparing lunch. My stomach growled, a reminder that I hadn't eaten since scoffing a couple of canapés at the Tillou bash.

Just as it was beginning to look as if I would make it to the boat unobserved, the yellow helicopter came hammering over the trees behind me, overflying the ruined fort atop the peninsula and making a beeline for *Seamist*.

I ducked down in a cleft between some rocks and watched it bumble off over the bay, silhouetted briefly against the sun's glare. It was impossible to say if they had spotted me or identified *Seamist*. Their flight path hadn't deviated by so much as a degree, so I guessed I was still in the clear.

I got moving again and tried a yell. "Ahoy, Jean-Pierre!"

Only when I reached the edge of the beach, the smell of cooking wafting tantalizingly across the intervening water, did I get a response: Pascal burst out from the companionway with the velocity of a popping champagne cork.

"André!" he shouted, arms windmilling.

I stiffened in dismay. What was Pascal doing on board when he was supposed to be safely in a hotel?

Suppressing my fears for now, I waved back.

Jean-Pierre came up on deck, hailed me with a nod and set about lowering the inflatable. I kept ears and eyes cocked for the chopper while he rowed across for me.

His handclasp was perfunctory. No questions were asked. My appearance must have told its own story.

Once on board *Seamist*, we secured the inflatable, and I sent him to start the motor. After his usual effusive welcome, Pascal rushed off to raise the anchor. While Jean-Pierre was getting us under way, I flopped exhausted on the cockpit seat. The Korth slid out of my pocket, falling into the cockpit-well with a clatter. I was too bushed to bother with it.

"How come Pascal's still aboard?" I snapped at Jean-Pierre as he took the wheel. I was angry out of fear for the boy. Tillou's mob were unlikely to make distinctions between adult and child if it came to a clash of arms.

Jean-Pierre juggled with the throttle, getting the revs to his liking before he replied. "The hotels were all full on the island. I telephoned several in Giens and in Hyères, but they were also full. It's the height of the season." He shrugged. "What else could I do?"

Abandon me, you bone-brained Frog bastard, that's what. Though I was glad he hadn't. I squeezed his shoulder. "Thanks for being here, Jean-Pierre. But now, we've got to get the hell out."

"I know." He looked me up and down. "The *soirée* was fun, *hein?*"

"Of the wrong kind."

A hail from Pascal meant the anchor was up. The wind was already nudging the bows to port, toward the open sea. Jean-Pierre took a stance behind the wheel, applied throttle, and *Seamist* came obediently round into the wind, south-by-south-west. With an effort I bent and retrieved the Korth from the well-deck.

"Where is Gina?" Jean-Pierre asked, a parental eye on Pascal who was scrambling back along the cabin roof.

"She's safe." I wondered, even as I spoke, if that were true. "She should be on her way back to the mainland by now."

He studied me, nakedly curious. "Do you want to tell me what's happening? Perhaps I can help, perhaps not. I'm willing to try."

"You're doing all you can. Maybe when it's all over. But to be fair to you—and especially to Pascal—I should tell you that someone wants me dead and he happens to be a big chief in the rackets, with a troop of armed goons at his disposal. They won't make special concessions for you and Pascal. Do you understand what I'm saying?"

He understood well enough. His countenance was sober as he glanced at Pascal, now sitting next to me, watching the wake. The boy seemed unconcerned by talk of armed goons.

"I'm worried for Pascal, not for myself."

"That goes double for me. Look, Jean-Pierre, you must get away from me. You and Pascal take the inflatable. Now, right away."

"Let me think about it. Do you want to head out to sea?"

"No," I said with emphasis. "I'll head for the mainland, but not to a port. This man, this big boss, has spies everywhere. I'll find a cove near Hyères-Plage, that'll be safer."

"Are we going ashore?" Pascal asked. "I need to buy some fishing hooks."

Prosaic Pascal. In spite of our mutual fears for the boy, Jean-Pierre and I grinned at each other over his dark head.

"Now," I said, "get the hell off this boat, will you?"

"Actually, no, I won't," Jean-Pierre said. "It seems to me that we will be safer in *Seamist*. Shall we go via the Petite-Passe?" The Petite-Passe was the smaller of two channels into Hyères Bay.

"No. We'd have to pass the boss's house and they probably know the boat. Better to go the long way round, through the Grande-Passe." I planted myself in front of him. "But look, Jean-Pierre—"

He made a slicing motion with one hand. "It is decided. We stay."

I opened my mouth to take a stronger line, but he looked away from me, rotating the wheel to bring us round on a south-easterly course. The wind was now on our starboard beam and blowing steadily. I surrendered. You can only go so far with persuasion. The alternative, getting physical, was more likely to end up with me in the drink, not him.

"We could put some canvas on her," I mused aloud, listening to the strum of the rigging.

"Leave it to me." Jean-Pierre inclined his head toward the companionway. "Would you like some pizza? We were preparing lunch when you arrived."

"I'll get it!" Pascal cried, jumped down into the well and thence through the open hatch. The clatter of plates rose from the saloon.

Running beam on to the seas, *Seamist* was rolling a bit. The waves were more vicious than they looked and fairly thumped against the hull, even slopping over the gunwale occasionally. I was soon soaked, but since all I had on was a pair of ruined pants I could afford to be philosophical about it.

Summoned by Pascal, I went below. He and I dined together on pizza and salad, with a rough *vin de pays* to wash it down, his ration diluted with water as always. While we ate, Jean-Pierre engaged the Autohelm and raised the mainsail. Presently, the engine died. The crackle of canvas took over, the deck canting as *Seamist* responded to the power of the wind like a wild animal freed from a cage.

After a badly-needed shower I changed into shorts and T-shirt, and went back on deck to watch the pale cliffs of Porquerolles recede. Wise sailor that he was, Jean-Pierre was steering away from the island, opening up sea room to leeward. Though benign weather conditions were forecast, he was always ready for the worst.

We were fairly ripping along even with only the mainsail set, the wind freshening as we cleared the southern tip of the island. Other sailing vessels were sharing our stretch of water that afternoon. The seascape was speckled with white deltoid shapes, darting back and forth in apparent disorder. Powerboats were out in force, too, from tiny outboards to stately cruisers.

A red-hulled launch off our port quarter stood out from the rest. It was bow on to us, throwing up a geyser of spray on either side, closing rapidly.

Jean-Pierre followed my gaze sternward. "What is it?"

"Maybe nothing."

The glasses brought the launch up close. It was a spectacular sight as it hurdled the waves, the hull sometimes leaving the water completely. A Starcraft Islander—fiberglass construction and an inboard motor, Canadian-built. It was capable of twenty knots or faster. I concentrated on the crew, which consisted of four males, all strangers to me. Or were they? A fifth figure in a sleeveless black T-shirt emerged from below: burly, near-black hair. Belanger—or just my overactive imagination?

"André?" I detected a note of anxiety in Jean-Pierre's voice.

"I can't tell." I lowered the glasses. The launch was about half a mile away, say three or four minutes to come alongside. If those guys had been sent by Tillou, we were in big trouble. I cast around for the nearest other vessels. Two yachts to the east, sailing in tandem, were closer than the launch, but on a course away from us. Not a hope of catching them. Nor would it have been fair to involve innocent parties in this unequal contest.

"More sail?" Jean-Pierre suggested.

"Too late. In any case, they'd still catch us."

I focused on the launch again and my stomach lurched. It was Belanger, all right. For him to be back in action so soon after that fall on the floor was a tribute to the bone density of his skull.

There was a tug on my arm. A solemn-faced Pascal held out the gun I had left in the saloon.

"Thank you, Pascal," I said, matching his solemnity.

I crouched to put my eyes level with his and gripped his shoulders. "Now listen to me, Pascal. Some men—bad men—are chasing me. They won't harm you or your father if they can help it. But if they shoot at us, which is likely, you may be hit accidentally. So I want you to go below, lie down on the saloon floor, and stay there until either your father or I tell you it's safe to come out. Got it?"

He nodded trustingly with no sign of fear. He was too young to know the ruthlessness and the degeneracy of man; too young to comprehend the finality of death.

He looked toward Jean-Pierre. "Papa? Are you coming down, too?"

Jean-Pierre's grim visage softened. "No, Pascal. I must stay and help André."

"You don't have to—" I began.

But his retorted "I'm staying!" killed my objections. The true depth of our friendship had never been more apparent.

The launch was no more than a quarter of a kilometer behind us, battering through the waves, its sleek prow glistening with spray. It was traveling too fast for the conditions, pitching badly in the longer troughs. It might even yet hit a freak wave and bury its bow or capsize.

Wishing for it wouldn't make it happen.

I propelled Pascal down the companionway and went after him. When I rejoined Jean-Pierre, complete with a box of .357 magnum cartridges, Belanger and company had been reinforced by the yellow helicopter. It swooped in astern, a persistent glass-eyed bug we couldn't swat away.

With so many other boats on all sides, presumably crewed by solid, law-abiding citizens, it was hard to believe they would actually attack us, actually open fire on us, unless, in his blind quest for vengeance, nothing mattered to Tillou except my demise.

The chopper's speed bled off and it took up station to port. A man leaned out, armed with a megaphone.

"Ahoy, *Seamist*," came the metallic boom. "Heave to or we'll sink you."

Sink us! My God, no half measures. What with, I wondered. Torpedoes?

I stuck up a defiant middle finger.

"You have one minute," the megaphone blared. "One minute. There will be no second warning."

I raised the gun, using both hands, and let them have six rounds. Glass starred, but didn't shatter. They made a fast, straight-up getaway. For all the effect my shots had, I might as well have been throwing pebbles.

A squall would have been timely. I did a three hundred and sixty degree scan, hoping for signs of one. The sky had never been bluer. No meteorological assistance then. We were on our own.

The sixty-second period of grace was just long enough for me to cram six more bullets into the Korth.

"Keep your head down," I cautioned Jean-Pierre as the ultimatum ran out. "War is about to be declared."

He was tense and grave, but summoned up a ghost of a grin.

The launch was to starboard on a converging course. I expected them to try and board us like pirates of old, minus the grappling irons and cutlasses between their teeth. But I had it figured all wrong.

No further warning, they said. It wasn't an empty threat. The helicopter's nose dipped and it flew straight for us, floats skimming the wave tops. A head and torso protruded from the side opening of the cabin. Beads of orange sparkled round it like firecrackers. I was slow to comprehend. Only when holes began to appear in the mainsail and splinters of fiberglass whizzed past my ear, did I realize they were using a machine gun! Now its stutter reached me over the clamor of the engine.

I returned their fire ineffectually, crouching behind the cabin for protection. Jean-Pierre had already dropped below the gunwale, still hanging onto the wheel. His face was as white as the mainsail, fear and rage mixed up together.

The machine gun fell silent. The chopper's engine note rose, as it zoom-climbed over *Seamist*'s mast, whirling away to port. The lull was likely to be brief. I reloaded the Korth fast, spilling several shells on the well-deck in my haste.

Jean-Pierre set the Autohelm and crawled toward the cabin hatch. "Pascal!" he called out, his voice off-key. "Are you all right?"

"*Oui*, papa," came the tremulous response.

A peek at the launch told me they were now keeping station to port. Watching and waiting, like vultures preparing to dine off a corpse. Then back came the chopper, full tilt. Now that I was listening for it, I detected the stutter of the machine gun at once. It sounded so distant and puny that I was unprepared for the veritable blizzard of bullets that ripped into the hull and cabin. Over the noise of the helicopter, the gunfire and the splintering of fiberglass, I heard a wailing cry from inside the cabin. A stricken Jean-Pierre dashed bent-double toward the hatch and took a header down the companionway.

Let the boy be all right, I pleaded to the God I denied. Don't let him be hurt, or worse.

I fed more shells into my gun and yelled down the stairwell for Jean-Pierre.

"Is Pascal all right?"

No answer, but I could hear a new ominous sound—the gurgle of water. Not hard to guess the cause. In the last attack *Seamist* had been holed below the waterline.

"Start the pumps, Jean-Pierre!" I would have done it myself, but the chopper was commencing another run. This time around, I was going to hit them hard, even if it cost me my life.

I scrambled up on the cabin roof and adopted a classic sideways-on gun-at-arms-length pose. It made me a juicy target, but when that machinegun opened up the shots went wide. They were still out to take me alive, to shoot the boat from under me and trawl me out of the water for delivery to Tillou.

And the way they looked at it, if innocent people died in the process that was just too bad.

The helicopter was less than fifty meters away, the orange sparks still dancing a demented jig when I opened fire. I placed my shots meticulously, aiming for the pilot. I actually saw the second and third strike the Perspex bowl, starring it, but not shattering it. The helicopter wobbled—maybe the pilot flinched—and lost a meter of height it couldn't spare, just as it passed over a leaping wave. The front end of the floats kissed the water and the helicopter flipped over. It was as instant and undramatic as that. Rotors flailing, the machine performed a complete somersault. The slender tail sliced through *Seamist*'s sail, through the boom, and through the cabin roof, which I had vacated, propelled by survival instinct into the cockpit. I landed in a sprawl, lost the gun, and made painful contact with the steering control. Behind me, flames erupted.

I got to my feet, staggering, and shook the fog from my brain. What was left of the helicopter was a blazing tangle of metal. A column of oily smoke spewed upward to stain the sky's flawless backcloth. From somewhere came screaming, a high, thin ululation.

"Jean-Pierre!" It was supposed to be a shout, but it came out a rasp. "Jean-Pierre! Pascal!"

The screaming stopped, cut off in full flow. I moved toward the companionway. Everything was enveloped in black smoke. *Seamist* was a smashed shambles. She was also settling by the bow.

The helicopter's fuel tank went up, sounding exactly like a gasp of breath amplified a thousand times. Scorching air slammed into me. I went over the gunwale, limbs gyrating like a broken doll. I entered the water feet first and went under so quickly I had no chance to inflate my lungs. Fortunately, my angle of entry being shallow, I bobbed to the surface at once, coughing seawater, my legs pedaling of their own volition. I was off *Seamist*'s port beam, on the opposite side to the launch and screened from it. It was a strictly temporary refuge. *Seamist*, a dismasted wreck with the remains of the chopper embedded amidships, was well and truly ablaze, her foredeck already awash. Her life could be measured in minutes.

I tried not to dwell on Jean-Pierre and Pascal. They were gone. Nobody could have survived that holocaust. They were dead, and I was as much to blame as if I had been firing that machine gun myself. Sick at heart, I trod water, staying alive but wishing I was dead, too. My burden of guilt was so huge I would gladly have sacrificed myself to bring Jean-Pierre and Pascal back to life.

Instead, I carried on treading, just keeping my head above water, no thoughts about my next move.

Seamist was foundering. Most of what remained above sea level was helicopter wreckage. The fire continued to burn, but only feebly now, steam merging with the tower of smoke that spiraled skyward.

Through the smokescreen, I glimpsed the red hull of the launch. Deciding that I ought to make myself scarce, I took a deep breath and dived.

As an accomplished underwater swimmer, I could stay down for up to three minutes at a pinch. While I swam I had a fish-eye view of *Seamist*'s final plunge. She went down in a leisurely, even graceful manner, descending through that milky-blue world, the detail blurring as she slid towards the sea bed. The helicopter tail broke loose and tumbled off the cabin roof. Being metal, it sank faster than the boat, dragging with it the broken mast and boom. No bodies floated free of the hull. A tiny consolation, for which I was thankful.

The wreck merged into the opaque depths, spectral almost. Then it was gone completely. Smaller pieces of debris spiraled downward in her vortex, following her to the bottom. It had not been an ignoble demise. She would make a fitting resting place for my friends. Only the cause was ignoble.

More wretched than I could remember ever feeling, I swam on, setting a punishing pace, swamping my remorse in physical self-chastisement. When at last I was forced to the surface, the launch was nowhere to be seen. I couldn't believe it; couldn't believe they'd given up so easily.

They hadn't. A wave lifted me, another conveniently parted, and there was the red hull cruising through some flotsam, the profile of Porquerolles island forming an almost surreal backdrop. I hoped they would presume me killed in the explosion, though Tillou wouldn't be best pleased to hear it. It wasn't personal enough.

I stayed on the surface, swimming more slowly now, conserving my strength. I didn't stop until, eons later and still going strong, I ran into a solid object and knocked myself out.

———

"*M'SIEU.*" The voice rattled around inside my skull like a marble in a can. "*M'sieu!*" More insistent now.

I wished he would fuck off, whoever he was. My head was hurting and he wasn't making it any better.

"*M'sieu!*"

Then memory exploded with the impact of a highway pile-up. I sat up quickly—too quickly. My head protested, dragging an involuntary groan from my lips. A circle of anxious faces blotted out the sky. Two men, two women; all elderly, all wrinkled. Nobody of my acquaintance.

"You swam right into us," one of the men said wonderingly. He was tall and bony and sported a dark blue baseball cap. "You hit your head on our hull."

"That'll teach me to look where I'm going." I squinted at him. "So you picked me up?"

"Naturally," he said with a chuckle. "You'd have drowned if we hadn't."

"Well...thanks." I made an effort to rise and failed in my enfeebled state.

"Here." The man with the baseball cap offered me a glass. I sniffed at it. Cognac, what else on a French boat? I downed the lot in a single swallow. Nor had he been stingy.

"I had an accident," I said. How much had they seen? "A helicopter..."

"We saw it," one of the women said. "What happened?"

I thought fast. It was a strain.

"Hard to say exactly. I was out sailing alone. The helicopter pilot must have been either drunk or crazy in the head. He kept flying over my boat very low, then he collided with the water and *pouf!*" I pantomimed an explosion with my hands.

"Some people in a red launch searched the area for a long time afterward," the second man said. "I'm surprised they didn't see you."

I was also surprised. Even more, I was relieved.

"You are English?" the second woman asked.

"Dutch." Dutch and English accents are all but interchangeable when speaking French.

"Monique, my wife." The man with the cap pointed at the second woman. "Monique thought...I know it sounds silly, but she thought she heard, well, shooting." He looked uncomfortable and scratched his chin where a couple of days' growth of bristle sprouted.

"*Shooting?*" I said, and my incredulity brought a flood of relief to their creased faces. "You mean...shooting with guns?"

Four heads jerked up and down like a music hall act.

"No kidding." I forced another grin. "Shooting, eh? I think it must have been the helicopter noise."

Acting innocent came naturally to me. It seemed to convince them that the shooting had been the product of Monique's faulty hearing aid. Even Monique herself didn't press the point.

With some assistance from my rescuers, I managed to stand upright. I was now able to look about me properly. The boat was a cabin cruiser, rather long in the tooth, with a large stern cockpit. Designed for fishing. Rust stains and cracking paintwork abounded. She was hove to, her engine ticking over, and tossing badly as power-boats tend to do in all but the most tranquil seas.

"Would you like some dry clothes?" someone asked.

"No thanks. Mine will dry soon enough in this heat."

"The accident must be reported," Baseball Cap said primly. "Unfortunately, we have no transmitter."

I silently cheered. Dealing with officialdom was a complication I didn't relish.

I agreed the accident had to be reported without delay and I was the man to do it. All they had to do was put me ashore so I could inform the local police. My virtuous tone met with approval. To cast out any lingering doubt about my good faith, I asked them to write down their names and addresses on a slip of paper in case the police wanted to contact them for statements. That would also make it unnecessary for them to accompany me to the police station. No sense in disrupting their vacation if it could be avoided.

My consideration earned me an approving beam from Baseball Cap

"We'll get going right away," he announced.

"Great." I returned his smile and hoped I wasn't overplaying my role. "Better head for Hyères. This will be a bit too big for the Porquerolles police."

"You're right. Hyères-Plage is the nearest harbor."

Hyères-Plage, a small seaside resort on the mainland proper, suited me fine. Nice and discreet.

"This is pretty nice of you. I haven't even thanked you for saving my life."

They lapped up this smarm. They helped me below to a bunk, where I remained, recuperating and plotting, until we entered harbor.

They dropped me at the landing stage. I waved and thanked them on their way. Watching the boat head off back to sea, I tore the list of names and addresses into confetti and scattered them in their wake.

Since I had no cash, my first objective was a bank. My credit card wallet was still in my button-down back pocket. One of those little scraps of plastic would serve to conjure up the price of a train ticket to Marseille, where all wishes, especially the illegal variety, can be made to come true.

CHAPTER FIFTEEN

DARKNESS, the rustle of foliage, and the sound of the sea advancing and retreating on a shale beach, regular as the breathing of a sleeping person.

Standing there, gazing up the short incline toward the cube-shaped dwelling that was Tillou's Porquerolles retreat, I recalled a different time and another place: a day in November last year on the banks of Lake Ammersee near Munich. A routine, straightforward contract that had descended into a farrago of persecution and pursuit. A deadly hide and seek that had led indirectly to the death of a good and faithful friend and his son, whom I loved almost as much as if he were my own.

Until now, all I had wanted was to be left in peace. The deaths of Jean-Pierre and Pascal had created new demands. Yes, my ultimate desire was still to be left alone to marry Gina and start a new life, cliché though that was. But peace, love, and marriage, and a new life were no longer enough.

Now, I had a score to settle and an account to square.

Now I wanted blood, pure and simple.

I'D SPENT a day and a night in hot, smelly, noisy, bustling Marseille. To keep my profile low and avoid providing ID when checking in, I bedded at a squalid no-questions-asked hotel near the Old Port. I killed the evening in my room, surrounded by peeling wallpaper and a smell akin to dead fish too long in the sun. My only companion was a bottle. It was many years since I'd been on a solo binge. While the effects lasted, they anaesthetized guilt, sorrow, rage, and all the emotions that were tossing and turning inside me like washing in a tumble dryer. I expected to pay for my overindulgence next morning, and I did pay—with interest.

By mid-afternoon though, the hangover kept at bay with doses of paracetamol, I was kitted out in new clothes, a French Identity Card and driving license in the respectable name of Marcel Laroche. The decision to go to Marseille had not been a random one. It was the home of one of my two suppliers of false documentation. Working ultra-fast and ultra-expensive, Thierry Marceau had produced the necessary documents inside two hours. They wouldn't stand scrutiny by the electronic scanners they use on international frontiers nowadays, but they were good enough for a roadside check, which was enough for me. Now, I was ready to face the world and all it could throw at me.

Armed with my papers, I hired a nondescript white Peugeot from Hertz. I paid for two days in advance, in cash, qualifying for a wide smile from the pretty male clerk. In my temporary transport I dawdled down the six-lane Avenue de Prado to the principal shopping area, where I made a number of purchases. Some were innocuous, such as a dinky unbreakable flashlight, a canoe paddle, and a capacious carryall. Others were less innocent. Mazé had recommended an illegal arms merchant operating circumspectly out of basement premises, behind the Muse de la Marine. At prices well above those recommended by the manufacturer, I became the strictly temporary owner of a small arsenal. The principal component was an Ithaca Stakeout twelve-gauge riot gun, fitted with a sling. Designed mainly for police and prison work, it has a pump-action four-round magazine and a pistol-type handgrip instead of a wooden stock. Compact, utterly lethal, as nasty a killing machine as ever devised by man.

The dealer was unable to replace my lost Korth. In any case, I needed a silenced gun, which ruled out a revolver. With the exception of the obsolete Russian Nagrané, sound suppressors do not function well on revolvers. From what was on offer I settled for a Beretta Px4 Storm automatic .40 caliber with a fourteen round capacity. Plus two spare magazines, a quantity of ammunition for both guns, a cartridge belt, and a Horseshoe fast-draw shoulder rig.

It was a complete Action Man kit for anyone with ambitions to start a war single-handed. Arnold Schwarzenegger used to use similar hardware on most of his screen outings.

My cell phone had gone to the bottom of the seas with my boat. I would buy a burner phone as soon as I had a minute to spare. Meanwhile, down the road from the arms dealer's troglodytic premises was a grubby telephone booth. Inside it stank of sweat and urine but, miraculously, the phone worked. With the door wedged open to facilitate breathing, I phoned my apartment in Geneva. It rang but nobody picked up. It was by then over thirty hours since Gina and I parted. If she had travelled by plane, she ought to have been there. Or she might have arrived, but be out shopping, or having a meal. Or she might have gone by train or rental car.

Or she might have changed her mind.

At about 11:00PM I left Marseille and took the *autoroute* to Toulon. Three hours later, I drove onto the Giens peninsula, the nearest mainland point to the Ile de Porquerolles. Leaving the car in a pull-out just outside the town of Giens, I proceeded cross country to the harbor on foot, aided by my flashlight. Within minutes I had selected a suitable craft for crossing to the island: a tough-looking inflatable, equipped with a hefty Johnson outboard. The starter key was missing, but that wouldn't inconvenience me above a minute or so. Short-circuiting ignition systems was another of my more dubious talents. I lowered the carryall onto the wooden main thwart and lowered myself after it and paused to listen. Nothing stirred, apart from water slapping against assorted hulls. Owners asleep or absent.

I had one nasty moment when, as I unhitched the mooring line, a light came on in a yacht berthed at a neighboring jetty. Bad language carried clearly across the water. Under cover of a rising storm of vituperation, I paddled the inflatable clear of its berth and got the hell away before the rest of the marina woke up. The slanging contest faded into the night. Once out of earshot, I rested briefly from my labors.

Only when I was well beyond the headland of the peninsula did I start up the outboard. I gripped the flashlight between my teeth while I rearranged the ignition wiring. The motor fired as soon as I brought the two bare leads into contact. A twist of the throttle grip and I was on my way.

My arrival off the Ile de Porquerolles was timed to coincide with first light. At that hour, the new dawn's eastern glow would take the edge off the darkness, guiding me in to a safe landing place on that rocky shore. Navigation was simplified by the beacon located on an islet to the west of Porquerolles. I kept it to starboard, taking a fix from it and another islet lying close in to the shore, just down from Tillou's beach.

Coming ashore at the Plage du Muso's northern end, I dragged the inflatable clear of the water. It wasn't easy to do quietly on the shale. Around my black-clad body, I distributed the tools of my trade. The flashlight went into my pocket, the jimmy in my belt, the shoulder holster where shoulder holsters usually go, pulled extra tight to eliminate swing. The cartridge belt, with its forty filled pockets, went round my waist. In my hands, where it would do most good—or harm—the Ithaca riot gun.

I had no alcoholic anesthetic within reach now, nothing at all to distract me, to dull the pain of the loss of my friends. All I had to drive me on to finish this thing I had never wanted to start was a cold, calculating hatred.

The light was just enough to grope along by if you didn't mind the odd stubbed toe or barked shin. I suffered these minor hurts with no more than the occasional muttered curse as I ascended the slope from the beach, on the alert for patrolling bodyguards. Nothing was stirring. Before long I reached the terrace, well-remembered from the BBQ bash two evenings ago, and came under the shadow of the house, black against a lightening sky.

As it turned out, I didn't need the jimmy. All ground floor and basement windows were either shuttered or had vertical bars set in the recess. Upstairs, they were laxer, height tending to induce a misplaced feeling of security. Some windows had their shutters open and neither of two smaller windows was barred. I singled out what was, to judge from the adjacent pipe work, either a washroom or a powder room, and shinned up a handy drainpipe, the Ithaca slung across my back. Weighed down as I was with hardware and thirty-eight years, it was no mean accomplishment. The pipe's wall fixings were well spaced to serve as footrests, which made it easier. Even so, the climb left me huffing and puffing like the big bad wolf who blew the little pigs' houses down.

The window was made to open inward, French-style, the way they do things in France. In expectation of it being securely latched, I gave it a gentle push and nearly fell off the drainpipe in surprise when it swung open. All was dark within. I took a firm hold of the window sill and swung the top half of my body toward it, still hanging onto the pipe with my right hand and legs. The pipe creaked under the unaccustomed stress. I pretended not to hear—too late to back out. I had both hands on the sill and was able to relinquish my foothold. I went in over the sill. Gravity took charge and I made an inelegant landing— in a bathtub.

The clatter of the gun barrel on enamel was as loud as a hammer drill in that still house. I crouched in the tub, ears pricked for sounds of movement, the Beretta drawn in readiness. A road drill thudded away inside my chest. Far off a dog yapped, regular as signals from a satellite. The Tillou household slumbered on, unhearing and unheeding, or so it seemed.

Somewhat reassured, I clambered gingerly out of the bathtub onto a tiled floor. I snapped the flashlight on and off, noting the geography of the room before tiptoeing past a bidet to the door. The next phase was crucial. The upper floor of the house was virgin territory to me. Obstacles would be encountered. I listened again, my senses tuned to a fine pitch. Peace still ruled. I moistened dry lips, twisted the doorknob, pulled and stood aside, flat against the wall. Not so much as a dripping faucet broke the absolute stillness. It was almost too still. My heart started doing its road drill thing again.

My every move felt clumsy and uncoordinated as I groped along the wall of what I supposed was a landing or gallery. I came to an alcove, only it wasn't an alcove, but a short passage, a dead end. I was tempted to use the flashlight again, but was averse to destroying my night vision. I shuffled on and eventually came to a handrail, ornately carved from the feel of it. At last I had something solid to guide me to the stairs.

Stairs, even in new houses, have a tendency to creak. By placing my feet at the extremities, I avoided this pitfall. A phantom couldn't have done it with less disturbance.

Reaching ground level was like emerging from a fog into brilliant sunshine. The layout was lodged in my subconscious, a skill developed through years of housebreaking practice. I intended to beeline for the study, there to lie in wait for the man who declared war when he could have had peace. It was not a plan as such. When I saw him, I would terminate him, speedily and without the last rites. In the courtroom of my mind, he was already condemned to death.

At the foot of the stairs I turned right, crossed a narrow corridor, and—ouch!—flattened my nose on the study door. It was a heavy door, but it swung freely on its hinges. The Beretta was still in my hand. Racking the slide produced a metallic double click that made my nerves jangle like wedding bells.

I eased the door shut behind me, leaned against it and exhaled a pent-up breath.

That was when the lights came on.

I was momentarily dazzled. If they'd been smart, they would have blown me away there and then. It was probably the Beretta that made them hesitate: cocked, ready to go off, and pointing, quite by chance, at Bernard Tillou. A classic stand-off.

Huddled behind the desk in his Rolls-Royce wheelchair, was the wizened homunculus himself. Beside his master stood the faithful house-trained lapdog, Herr Carl Schelling. In his pudgy hand a revolver of uncertain make and caliber.

"Good morning, Mr. Warner," Schelling said. He fought with a smirk and lost. "As you observe, we have been expecting you."

"It was very kind of you to drop in," Tillou said.

I shrugged. "I was in the district. It seemed the least I could do."

He was toting iron, too, in the form of a dainty automatic. From the look of the muzzle diameter, it fired a round no bigger than an orange pip. But even an orange pip makes its presence felt when it runs into you at 600 mph. Forty-eight hours earlier, I had faced a similar stand-off. Only this time around Gina wasn't here to plead my case.

"Put the gun down like a good fellow," Schelling said coolly. His gun was as steady as if it had been grafted onto the end of his arm.

I wasn't about to make them a gift of myself. I grinned. "You first."

Tillou shifted restlessly. They didn't quite have the whip hand over me. They could shoot and I might still get one or both of them in return. My gun was bigger than theirs, too. Judging Schelling's piece to be more likely to do me damage, I angled the Beretta's barrel away from Tillou toward his lackey, too quickly for them to react.

"We have two guns," Schelling pointed out, as if I had voiced my thoughts. "Even if you succeed in disabling one of us, the other will kill you. So...drop your gun and you live."

"How did you know I was coming?" I was stalling, buying time to calculate my next move.

"We have men posted in the grounds," Schelling said and smirked again. "We were sure you would be back. That is why I did it, to make sure you came."

"Did what?"

"Enough of this banter!" Tillou snapped. He pressed a button on an intercom next to the phone.

"*Oui, patron?*" the tinny acknowledgement was immediate.

"Belanger? We've got him. *Viens toute de suite.*"

For a fraction of a second, Schelling's attention was distracted from me to his boss. It was less a window of opportunity than an arrow slit. The blast of my Beretta shook the room as, simultaneously, I dived behind the couch. My two hasty shots smashed into Schelling and hurled him against the wall. He worked the trigger of his own gun as he toppled, but it was no more than a muscular reflex: the bullet buried itself in the floor. By then I was concealed behind the couch. History was repeating itself.

That left just me and Tillou; the arch-villain and instigator of my woes. Considering his age and physical handicaps, he put on a good show. The moment Schelling went down, he banged off at me. The couch was no protection. A bullet plucked at the upholstery centimeters from my nose, then another and another, missing but not by much.

I flattened myself against the boards and slithered toward the end of the couch, where I risked a peek. Gun arm extended, Tillou was looking for me at the opposite end. Even as his eyes swiveled away from there and toward me, the pistol close behind, I got off two quick shots at his head, the only part of him I could see properly behind the desk. His face disintegrated into a pizza of blood and shattered bone as he rocked back in the wheelchair. The little automatic hit the floor with a clatter.

Elation surged through me as I got to my feet. I had done what I came to do. Mission accomplished. Enemy destroyed, though I was far from being in the clear. Belanger and company could be expected to join the party.

My smoking Beretta was still at action stations, my finger still hooked around the trigger, when the door crashed open. I fired blindly, defensively, at a human outline in the lighted oblong of the doorway, a spontaneous reaction to a dimly perceived threat. Even at that, my aim was true.

For once, all too true.

My victim was a woman in a red and cream kimono-style robe. Like Schelling, she took both bullets in the chest and spun round, arms thrown outward, falling heavily against a bookshelf, dragging a row of leather-bound volumes to the floor with her. Jeanne Sabourin and her daughter were the only women staying here that I was aware of. Only neither of them was blonde.

The woman came to rest, face-up in an attitude of crucifixion. What my appalled eyes registered at the very instant of firing was confirmed: the woman I shot, almost certainly fatally, was Gina.

On feet weighted with lead, I ran to her and knelt beside her. I watched the color bleach from her face, even her full lips becoming pale and bloodless. She was dying. The human body isn't made to take so much punishment. I couldn't bear to look at the wounds. At the back, where the bullets had exited, would be bloody craters big enough to insert a fist.

Her eyes flickered open. Those green eyes with their lazy lids that normally sparkled with vitality, now dulled as death drew its veil across them.

"You're not real," I gabbled, pain tearing me apart inside. "You're not here." My voice cracked. "You're not *here*!"

"André?" Her pallor was grey-green under a sheen of perspiration. "André...I...thought it...was you."

"You're not here, you're not here!" I sobbed, unable to believe the evidence of my own handiwork. "You're in Geneva."

God, let her be in Geneva! Let this be a nightmare, let me wake up.

A scarlet pearl oozed from the corner of her mouth, that same mouth I had tasted so often and with such desire.

"They...caught...me. I..." She broke off with a groan of such agony that I felt as if my own guts were being ripped out.

"Don't talk. Don't talk."

She pawed feebly at me. "It hurts. Hold...me...darling."

Darling. Her life was about to end at my hands and still she called me 'darling'. A long sigh escaped her and her body seemed to deflate. Her eyelids slowly closed with the finality of a curtain ringing down on the last act of a play. A convulsive shudder ran through her frame, her limbs went slack, her head lolled sideways and her lips parted slightly, a sick parody of a movie starlet publicity pose. The trickle of blood slowed as her heart ceased to pump.

I didn't need a degree in medicine to diagnose death.

I straightened up and kicked out savagely at one of the books that she had dragged off the shelf as she fell. It shot across the room, pages fluttering. I was numb, beyond feeling. I gazed down at her, drinking in every facet of her beauty: the sandy blonde hair that now formed a bouquet about her head, the finely sculptured features that mere words could never do justice to. Without the sparkle in those green eyes, she was merely a mask, lifeless as an alabaster bust.

Gina was no more. Stolen from me by my own hand, a victim of my vaunted lightning reflexes. How pathetic these attributes looked now.

Running feet in the corridor brought home to me my still precarious situation. The old survival senses were still functioning. I rammed the Beretta into the holster and had the riot gun off my shoulder and targeted on the doorway in a flowing movement born of long practice.

The feet were no longer running. Through the still-open door came a mutter of voices. Impelled by nine-parts blind fury to one-part common sense, I ran to the door, silent in my sneakers, and burst into the corridor, seeking absolution through confrontation.

They were about where I expected them to be. Belanger and two underlings in a huddle only a meter away from the doorway, and all armed. I blasted off a single shot from the hip, missing on purpose—though my mood was murderous enough—to cleave the air centimeters above their heads. The cartridge pulverized the green *crepi* wall covering and flung fragments of plaster along the corridor to patter on the floorboards. The three froze into immobility. Only a man with no nerves or no imagination faces down a shotgun. Pistols crashed to the floor and hands rose shakily.

"Don't shoot, Warner," Belanger quavered. His eyes were bright with fear. Some bodyguard he was.

Smoke hung suspended in wreaths above them, and the tang of cordite stung my nostrils. It was suddenly as quiet as the inside of a monastery.

"Kick the ironmongery over here," I said at last, resisting the impulse to kill them as I had killed their master.

The three pistols skidded across the floor. A revolver and two automatics. As I used my toe to shovel the weaponry behind me, Belanger's name was called from the direction of the kitchen.

"Answer," I ordered.

Belanger dredged up a croaky "*Oui?*" Then he turned to me. "It's Blanc. He has two men with him."

"Two men with him, eh? Now I'm really scared."

"What's going on?" Blanc demanded loudly, wisely keeping the stout kitchen door between us.

"This is Warner!" I called back. "It's finished, Blanc. Tillou and Schelling are dead. Belanger is here and I have a gun on him."

A muffled expletive was followed by whispers that degenerated into a dispute. Blanc again, "*Merde!* Are you crazy, or what?"

"Come on out, Blanc. I've no quarrel with you."

"The *patron* is dead? Truly?"

"Come and look for yourself. He's in the study. Him and Schelling." My thoughts drifted to the other body lying in the study, and hot tears welled. I blinked them back, raging inside at my weakness and even more at my guilt.

"We're not afraid of you, Warner," Blanc said. "We're three against one."

"Tell my shotgun that. It's loaded with solid. Do you know what a solid cartridge does to a man?"

Evidently, he did. More cursing and more whisperings, terminating in "*Allons-y!* I'm out of here!"

Sounds of hasty departure: feet on the move, a door crashing back, voices fading.

Silence. But silence, like running feet, is easy to fake.

"They've gone," Belanger ventured.

"You say."

If their departure was faked, if they were still lurking behind the door with three guns ready to open up, there wasn't a lot I could do about it. A floorboard creaked upstairs. I was so wound up I nearly squeezed the trigger.

"Who's up there?" I demanded of Belanger.

"Monsieur and Madame Sabourin, their daughter...and Sabrier."

"Sabrier?"

"Our..." Belanger faltered. "Our new boss, I suppose. Now that Monsieur Tillou is dead."

Sabrier, alias Bonhomme? It was a fair supposition. If Sabrier and Bonhomme were the same, at least he was a potential ally.

"Fetch him," I ordered Belanger. "Fetch them all, but stay in sight unless you want an enlarged asshole." I gestured at his two henchmen. "You, face down on the floor!"

As they complied, I backed against the wall. From here, I had an unobstructed view of the whole landing and most of the doors leading off.

Belanger sidled toward the stairs as if reluctant to present his back to me, then went up them at a run. He beat a tattoo on the first three doors in turn, identifying himself with, "*Ici* Belanger. *Déscendez.*"

Monsieur and Madame Sabourin came meekly enough. He was fully dressed, but for his shoes; calm as a lizard on a hot rock. She, pale and trembling, wore a white toweling robe and unflattering hair curlers. Daughter Helène, next door, was quite the opposite. Indignant and brash, she was sporting black leather pants and a black shirt. As she descended the stairs behind her parents, her icy glare swept over me like a searchlight. One-handedly, I checked the three of them for weapons.

That left just Sabrier. He was slow to answer Belanger's summons. Repeated assurances from Belanger, prompted by me, finally enticed him out, blue pajamas under darker blue robe. It was the man I knew as Bonhomme, all right. Hair ruffled, chin shaded with overnight growth, far from the spruce and dapper image I carried in my mind. Now promoted to Mister Big. Long live the king in the blue pajamas. I giggled and they all gaped at me as if I'd grown a second head. In that instant I wanted to kill Sabrier-Bonhomme even more than I had wanted to kill Tillou. I felt my lips draw back, baring my teeth. Without him, without his imperial ambitions and his resentment of Tillou's son, none of this would have happened. His was the responsibility for Tillou's vendetta against me, for the deaths of Jean-Pierre and Pascal—and above all, for Gina.

My finger tightened on the trigger with no conscious input from me. My hands shook with the effort of holding my fire, my teeth grinding as I struggled to contain the urge for retribution. Reason won over emotion, but only by the slimmest of margins. My madness ebbed, wiping the red mist from my vision. To get clear of the island, I might need Sabrier's cooperation. In return...in return, I could waive my fee, a million dollars in exchange for a period of grace. It was either that or kill him, and not just him. If he went, the rest would have to go, too. Wholesale slaughter, in other words. Mass murder.

I wasn't capable of it. Surely. Not even to avenge Gina.

"Mr. Sabrier, I presume," I said. "Come on down, Mr. Sabrier. You, too, Belanger."

They descended the stairs side by side, slowly and warily. Sabrier was wearing backless slippers that flip-flopped as he walked. He looked faintly ludicrous and he was aware of it. Bad for the image; not at all gang boss-like. Belanger joined the line-up. Sabrier was set to do likewise when I beckoned him over.

"Is there a cellar under here?"

"Naturally. Where else would they keep the wine?"

But of course. After all, this was France.

I addressed my captive audience. "All right, now listen to me. You're going to be locked in the cellar. That's the worst that can happen to you, a few hours of discomfort, provided you don't do anything rash, such as trying to escape."

Helène spat at me. Literally spat. Happily, her aim was lousy.

"Lead on, Sabrier," I said, ignoring her. "The rest of you, follow in single file, hands on heads."

Helène naturally declined on both counts, until I jabbed her backside with the gun barrel. The look she gave me over her shoulder was neat venom.

The cellar was accessed from the kitchen through a recessed door and down narrow stone steps.

"Where's the key?" I asked Sabrier from the top of the steps as he hauled on the heavy door.

"In the lock." He pointed.

"Lock them in, then come back up here with the key."

Helène was last in line. As the others filed submissively into the cellar, she hung back. I prodded her with the gun.

"Get on down there."

She pivoted around with the grace and coordination of a ballerina and came at me, fangs gleaming, claws unsheathed, and with what I guessed was a nail file growing from her fist like a dagger. Her intentions were clearly hostile.

The riot gun was pointing down the steps therefore awkwardly placed for fending her off. She hit me in a sprawling leap and sank the nail file into my shoulder below the bone. I let out a yelp that was more shock than pain. Then we were rolling on the tiles and she was punching and scratching, her spiky hair filling my mouth. I drove my knee up between her legs and into her crotch with a force that jarred my whole body. Her eyes bulged and her mouth opened to scream, but only managed a gurgle.

I pushed her aside and struggled to rise, as Belanger moved in to join the party. I lashed out with the riot gun and he dropped as if hit by a runaway bus.

I swung the gun's blunt snout to threaten Sabourin and the two goons bunched behind Belanger's comatose form. Sabourin managed a strangled "No!" before the gun crashed and hurled a solid cartridge past his ear. I pumped the slide and another round clunked into the firing chamber.

"Right, back off!" I gasped, using the wall for support. Several centimeters of steel were still embedded in me and it hurt just to breathe. "Get down to the cellar," I ordered the petrified Sabourin. "And take these two."

Belanger was out cold. A thin trickle of blood, dark as treacle, wormed from his hairline and across his forehead. Helène was writhing beside him, alternately whimpering and moaning, nursing her groin. I was sorry for her, but she'd picked the fight, not me.

My immediate concern was the nail file in my shoulder. It had to come out. It would hurt like crazy, but it was hurting anyway. I braced my back against the closed door, gritted my teeth and gave it a sharp tug. Easy, really. Yeah. I nearly fainted as it slid out of my flesh, the coarse blade dragging on the lips of the wound. Blood spurted and was mostly soaked up by my T-shirt. Stop the bleeding, my brain commanded, and the other parts of me reluctantly obeyed.

A hand towel from the kitchen served as a pad. While I was trying to position it inside my T-shirt, Sabrier reappeared.

"Help me fix this." I covered him with the Beretta, while he found some surgical tape in a cabinet and secured a makeshift dressing.

"The gun isn't necessary," he remarked as he worked on me. "You and I are on the same side."

I gave a sardonic grunt. "You sure about that? And where's the goddam key?"

He handed me a strictly functional hunk of metal with a plastic tag on which was written *Cave*.

A thought struck me. "The servants. Are they in the basement? They must have heard the shooting."

"Don't worry, Warner. Three of them live in town. They're not due until seven o'clock. As for old Thomas, he went to the mainland yesterday to spend some time with his family and will not be back until the weekend." Sabrier finger-combed his hair, his actions nervous. "Tillou and Schelling, you killed them, yes?"

Boss and chief rival both eliminated. This was a great day for him.

"They're dead. So is...so is Gina."

"Ah." He peered at me and comprehension came gradually, like sunrise peeking over the horizon. "*Ah*. Now it is clear. She is—was—important to you? Did Tillou kill her?"

"Never mind that! It's none of your fucking business." I reined in my temper and made an effort to speak evenly. "I'm leaving. This minute."

He gesticulated with the shoulders, French-style. "So, leave."

"I need time to get clear. I need forty-eight hours."

"You think I will inform the police?" The question was accompanied by a mocking smile.

I had the riot gun barrel wedged under his chin so fast, the smile stayed in place for several seconds afterward. It became fixed as I gouged into his bristles.

"You think I'll kill *you*?"

His face bled of color.

"You motherfucker," I mouthed and some of the madness came surging back. "I'd as soon blast your head off your shoulders as do a deal with you. But, rot you, I need your help."

"My help?"

"I'll explain in a minute." I lowered the gun. "First, the deal. Cover up for me, don't squeal to the *flics*, and I'll forget about my fee."

That appealed to the right instincts. Above all, he was a numbers man.

"Leave it to me, *mon ami*." Suddenly, we were *amis*. The way to Sabrier's heart was through his bank account, all right. "I will conceal all evidence. Nothing will incriminate you."

"You needn't worry about evidence. There won't be any."

His narrow brow creased. "*Comment?*"

Instead of enlightening him, I said, "Find me some gasoline or kerosene." Which, I suppose, was an explanation in itself.

He goggled. "You're going to burn down the house?"

"Just find it. Move!"

He scuttled off. I sagged against the kitchen sink, mentally and physically sapped. My shoulder throbbed, but compared with the other, inner pain, it was a pinprick.

Gina, Gina, I moaned inside my head. How could I have done such a thing? Was it divine retribution for my misdeeds? The rational part of my mind rejected such sanctimonious bullshit. Quit passing the buck, I ranted to myself. *You*, André Warner, killed Gina and you're stuck with it for as long as you live.

The kitchen shutters were not properly closed, and through the gap the sky was lightening. The dawn chorus, previously unnoticed, was gaining momentum. I was running late. I had planned to be away from here before daybreak, if only get clear of the Giens area before the inflatable's disappearance was noticed and the police summoned.

A light footfall sounded in the corridor. I didn't even have the energy or the will to defend myself. If it turned out to be Blanc...

Sabrier entered, carrying a five-liter plastic container. I smelled the gas fumes.

"Here you are. It was in the garage."

It was becoming an effort to speak, so I didn't.

"Why are you going to burn the house?" he queried.

"I like fires."

In fact, the fire was for Gina, her Valhalla, and my farewell gift. The house just happened to be there. I wasn't leaving her for others to maul, cut up, or eviscerate. A shudder wracked my body. I pressed the tips of my fingers against my temples and they came away slick with sweat.

"What is it, Warner?" Sabrier took a step toward me.

I waved him away. "Give me the gas."

From down in the cellar came a thumping noise. "Hey! You up there. Let us out!"

"Glad you reminded me," I said softly and tossed the key to Sabrier. "As soon as I start the fire, release them. If anyone comes after me, I'll hold you personally responsible. Likewise, if you sick the law on me, I'll come looking for you, just like I came looking for Tillou."

His color had returned, now he lost it again. Yet his voice was steady as he replied, "You worry needlessly, Warner. We have a bargain. I'm very happy with my side of it." He stuck out a hand. "Start your fire. I will deal with everything else."

I took the proffered hand, bounced a grin off him and went to the study to sit on the floor beside Gina. I stroked her cheek. Was it my imagination or was she already growing cold? I wanted somehow to convey to her my regret, my grief, and above all, my love. But there was no spark. She was just a collection of dead organs. I was but a step removed myself. Dead in all respects but the physical.

I unscrewed the cap of the container and got busy. My nostrils dilated at the sickly-sweet fumes that rose from it. Half of the five liters went to soak the furniture, drapes, rugs, and the floor, but not Gina. The other half I doled out among adjacent ground floor rooms.

Returning to the study, I happened upon Sabrier, who was rummaging through Tillou's desk drawers. He just nodded and smiled nervously.

On Tillou's desk was a heavy table lighter that had the feel of gold. As I flicked it experimentally, my gaze alighted on its late owner, slumped in the wheelchair, held in place by the arms. The shattered features seemed to jeer at me, with reason. Although technically I was the victor and he the vanquished, I had lost much more than I gained.

Never was a victory more Pyrrhic than mine.

Lighter in hand, I went again to Gina, drawn by invisible strings. I knelt, bent over her and pressed my lips to hers, wishing her alive, wretchedly, uselessly.

I touched the lighter to the doused couch. A wall of flame instantly bloomed, singeing my eyebrows. I retreated in haste. I went out through the patio doors and across the terrace at a trot without a backward glance. The fire crackled and popped, already taking hold.

It was light enough to see the path and, following the route Gina and I had taken during our flight two nights ago, I was soon at the beach. The inflatable was where I left it, the empty carryall lying on the bottom. The relief I felt proved all too premature.

The first shot, a whip-crack from the bushes on my right, went wide, whining off a rock. The second scored my right thigh, and the impact was enough to tip me over. I never realized sand was so unyielding. With a triumphant rebel yell, Blanc leapt out of the shrubbery, flourishing a machine pistol. As a souvenir of our previous encounter, he had a bandaged ear, but his trigger finger was healthy enough. He opened up, firing as he ran at me. Belly down on the beach in the semi-darkness, I made a poor target. Light automatic weapons have a tendency to climb his, and the bullets flitted by overhead. The short curved magazine emptied in about two seconds. And that was just too bad for him.

Now came my turn. I used the Ithaca, firing only once, and transformed his head into a bloody, featureless stump. He kept coming on though, a headless chicken, crossing the strip of sand in a totter. He finally pitched into the water, raising a splash that spattered my face.

I got up on my knees. That was as far as I could manage for the moment. I was swaying like a poplar in a hurricane. Blanc floated face down by the inflatable. He, too, had had it coming.

My stomach churned. Vomit bubbled geyser-hot in my gullet and gushed out over the sand at the water's edge. I spat weakly, wiped goo from my chin and sweat from my eyes. Bile drooled from my slack lips and dripped down my clothing.

If Blanc's buddies were out there waiting for an opportunity, here it was. I was theirs for the taking.

Behind me the roar of flames intensified as something caved in with a crash. Incandescent reflections danced and shivered on the water. What remained of the night had been banished by a fiery aura that shimmered and pulsated. I heard, or imagined I heard, shouting.

My leg was paining me. Yet even in my battered, weakened state, my self-discipline continued to power me. I lurched to the inflatable, hoping it wasn't full of the bullet holes intended for me, and more or less fell into it. I stuffed the riot gun, shoulder rig, jimmy, the lot, into the carryall.

Nobody took a shot at me. Blanc had been on his own.

The outboard fired at first go when I jiggled the wires. I steered out of the bay, leaving a jagged wake, then piled on the revs, accelerating across the red-tinted water. Flames leaped skyward on my left, but were soon behind me. Across the channel, I saw the lights of Giens. They were my aiming point. The open sea, dark and silky, that most capricious of elements, rolled beneath me in a blur. It would leave no trace of my passing. It would also hide the material evidence of my crimes. The sea was my accomplice.

In mid-channel, I heaved the carryall over the side. I had left it partly unzipped to prevent an air pocket from forming inside. It sank quickly with only a solitary burp of protest. My exertions brought twinges from my thigh. I knelt and lowered my jeans and examined the wound as best I could in the pale light. It was hardly more than a graze. The skin around it was tender to the touch, but it wouldn't slow me down. That was all that really mattered.

I pressed on at flat-out speed between the ragged islets of Grand

Ribaud, presently coming ashore in a narrow V-shaped cove. The surf swirled about the inflatable like lather as I nudged it up a steep pebbled beach. Ordinarily, I would have sunk it offshore to further cover my tracks. That now seemed a rather superfluous precaution. Whatever I did, I was finished in France.

The sun was just coming up, diffusing the sky with a saffron fan. Another, different glow drew my eye back toward the island. Orange shot with red, Gina's Viking valediction.

"Goodbye, sweetheart," I whispered. "Safe journey."

I scrambled to the top of overlapping rocks that bordered the cove and set off, favoring my injured leg and nursing my perforated shoulder, across a flat grassy terrain toward the Giens highway.

CHAPTER SIXTEEN

BEFORE THE SIRENS started to wail, I was on a slow train back to Marseille. trying to stay awake. By the time I disembarked at St. Charles Station, in the city's downtown, it was late morning. My shoulder was stiff and sore, and my thigh was throbbing. Medical attention was first on my must-do list. Thierry Marceau proved his worth all over again by drumming up a disbarred quack who, for a consultation fee that would have represented a week's income to legally accredited members of his profession, treated my hurts and left me strapped up and stinging.

Collecting the Aston from Monaco was next on the agenda. Unwise though it was to prolong my stay in France, I was not about to abandon that expensive piece of machinery. I took to the train again, bound for Nice.

At Nice-Ville Station I had a twenty-five minute wait ahead of me for the Monaco connection. I crossed the Avenue Thiers to a bustling snack bar and ordered a Pernod. The TV was on, tuned to an F2 news program. As my drink was pushed across the counter toward me, a newsflash popped up. In reverential tones the female newscaster announced a mass murder. Ten bodies had been discovered at a house on the Ile de Porquerolles, nine of them burned beyond recognition. A

Toulon-based gang was suspected. Stay tuned for further developments...

The bar erupted into an excited babble: stupefaction, horror, disbelief. Each to his own reaction. Mine was a combo of all three, with a sizeable dose of impotent fury. By my reckoning there should have been only three bodies in the house, plus Blanc on the beach. Sabrier must have left the Sabourin couple, Belanger, and the other bodyguards to burn to death in the cellar. Eliminating all witnesses and rivals at a single stroke, without the need to dirty his hands or his sensibilities. All he'd had to do was walk out, a gloriously classic crime of omission. After all, the fire was my doing. That meant that, technically, those deaths were murder. All of them now laid at my door. I downed my drink, tossed a five-euro note on the counter, and went to catch my train.

At the station my papers were perfunctorily checked, the first sign of abnormal police activity. My false identity card raised no flickers of suspicion. At the Monaco end, also nothing. A couple of taxis were waiting outside the entrance. In a straight line, the port was three hundred meters from the station. It took twenty minutes to get there through streets that were clogged with tourists.

At the Bar du Port, Victor welcomed me effusively and sold me a Pernod. No messages. I relieved him of the keys to the Aston and went to fetch it from the rented lockup garage on Avenue John Kennedy. My bona-fide papers, hidden in the front passenger seat squab, were undisturbed. I now reverted to my true identity, to conform to the car ownership documents. Additionally, my Swiss resident status and British passport would ensure more respectful treatment from the police. In theory. I ripped the bogus papers into tiny pieces and sprinkled them down a drain in the garage. Goodbye Marcel Laroche. It was my shortest acquaintance yet with a false identity.

Travelling under my real name carried certain risks. Sabrier in particular knew who I was. By his treacherous actions in letting the prisoners in the cellar burn to death, he could no longer be considered a reliable ally. In some respects, it might even be to his advantage to tip off the law about my part in the killings. Since I wasn't in a position to shut his mouth—if it wasn't already too late—my only course of action was to flee France by the fastest means and the most anonymous route. By Aston Martin, by country road.

So it was back on the well-trodden highway, through Nice, Castellane, and Digne. The last-mentioned was a bittersweet reminder of the day I met Gina. I shut out the memories and focused on my driving. Speed was a kind of antidote. On twisty roads that teemed with vacation traffic and swaying, overloaded Italian trailer trucks, I averaged 100 kph. Maybe I had a death wish.

No police vehicles appeared in my rear-view mirror and no road blocks through the windshield. North of Digne, in the village of Lajaire, I snarled past a solitary *gendarme* in debate with a man in a butcher's apron outside the La Poste building. Farther on, as I accelerated out of a bend, I encountered a *gendarmerie* van. The heads of the two blue-uniformed occupants swiveled my way but they didn't have the horsepower to pursue me. In my mirror they dwindled to insignificance.

I drove through the night with only two short breaks: once to refuel the car and grab a pack of sandwiches, and once for a short nap. Grenoble, hushed and lifeless at three in the morning, came and went. I was into the final lap, all *autoroute* now, sacrificing the anonymity of the lesser roads, for speed. I whipped the Aston up to 200 kph and more. The necessary high level of concentration helped keep my black mood at bay.

At last, the frontier, the illuminated *Douanes* sign welcoming me like an old friend. On the other side was Geneva, my refuge. If Gina had been waiting for me, asleep in my—our—bed, as she should have been, it would have been a true homecoming. But Gina had ceased to exist, except as ashes. And that special loving she introduced into my loveless existence had also ceased to exist.

Ceased. To. Exist. The words punished me, punching home my guilt and my anguish.

There are no French Customs for vehicles entering Switzerland at the Thonex checkpoint. On the Swiss side though, the entry protocol remains as you were. Decelerating for the border post, I crossed the invisible line and entered my adopted country. I had made it! I was back in my zone of immunity, safe for a while at least.

"*Bonjour, monsieur.*" The Swiss Customs officer in his sludge-colored outfit bent to peer inside the car, his bright suspicious eyes roving. At this hour of the day, they would be short of trade and therefore in the mood for mischief. "Are you carrying any goods?"

I shook my head.

"Your identity papers, please."

I offered my Swiss residence permit and my UK passport. He went off through a door marked POLICE in the long, low building at the roadside. A second officer stayed with me. He was young and therefore not yet dehumanized. We chatted about this and that, until the first officer reappeared on the heels of a blue-uniformed policeman. They approached the Aston. The policeman was still adjusting his peaked cap, but managed a curt nod, followed by a request to accompany him.

I stiffened inwardly. "Is there some problem?" I asked, tendering a fixed, meaningless smile.

"A matter of identification."

It was only then that, like a shockwave, it hit me. Engels, Inspector of Police, would still be bent on handing me over to the German police for the killing of Fabrice Tillou. Recent traumas had all but wiped it from my memory. Had I escaped justice in France only to be confronted with it in Switzerland?

The only alternative to complying with the cop's request was to put my foot down and trust to the Aston's acceleration to extricate me. Without papers, I wouldn't travel far. Tight-lipped, I got out and walked beside him to the office.

Inside, it was uncomfortably warm. At a desk against the wall, a young police officer, his shirt armpits damp, pecked painfully at a computer keyboard. Engrossed in his toil, he didn't look up.

A seat and coffee were offered. I declined the seat—I'd been sitting for most of the night—but accepted the coffee. The customs man went out of the office through a swing door. I glimpsed a stark white-walled corridor before the door flapped shut. The police officer remained, rocking slightly on his heels, hands clasped behind his back. We ignored each other politely.

The customs man returned with two steaming plastic cups, which he deposited with haste on the corner of the nearest desk, licking spilt coffee from scalded fingers.

The policeman at the keyboard glanced up and laughed unsympathetically. "That machine makes very hot coffee," he observed.

The other swore good-naturedly at him and handed me a cup. It was too hot to drink, so I left it to simmer on a shelf behind me.

"What's this all about?" I said with a show of part bafflement and part vexation.

"We're waiting for a telephone call, *monsieur*," the police officer said, his smile flashing on and off. "Just a routine inquiry. Nothing to worry about."

He didn't know what I knew.

I tasted the coffee. It was drinkable in an emergency. This wasn't an emergency, not yet. The clock on the wall said 03:27. It was a hell of a time of day to be cooling one's heels in the can.

The minute hand edged onward in staccato jerks. I fumed and fretted. I held my tongue with difficulty.

The clock hands had travelled round to 3:50 when, preceded by a gust of self-importance, in breezed Inspector Klaus Diethard Engels, scourge of the Geneva underworld. In his wake, naturally, came Sergeant Maurer, aglow as ever with goodwill to all mankind, especially me. My lingering hopes that all this was just an administrative screw-up evaporated.

"So you have returned to us, Mr. Warner," Engels said in his impeccable English. His fake smile was broad and his teeth boosted to maximum candlepower.

I shrugged. "Why shouldn't I? I live here, remember?"

He turned to the policeman. "Have you searched him?"

"Er..."

"*Quel idiot!*" A gun sprang into Engels' hand, fast as a conjuring trick. Maurer was a fraction slower, but then his gun was bigger. "Do it now!"

The policeman grimaced and ambled over, not hurrying. "*Vous permettez, monsieur?*"

I reached for the sky in classic Western fashion. The frisking was proficient, but unproductive. I wasn't carrying as much as a nail clipper.

The policeman stepped back. "Nothing, *monsieur l'inspecteur.*"

"This is a very dangerous man," Engels told him sternly, as if lecturing a refractory child. "You should not be so lax." His attention swung back to me. "Now then, Mr. Warner. If you would be so kind as to accompany me, I have a car waiting outside."

"Before we leave," I said, "I'd like to know what's going on. I'd also like to call my lawyer."

At four in the morning—Jules would love me.

"You will not need a lawyer, Mr. Warner. Not where you're going. As for what is going on..." He stroked his elongated chin reflectively. His gun still covered me. I'd looked down a lot of gun barrels lately. I was getting pissed off with it. "Shall we just say it's a continuation of the unresolved matter we discussed during our last meeting? In fact, one might almost say we're bringing it to a satisfactory resolution."

Had new evidence come to light? According to Jules, I couldn't be extradited without incontestable proof. And even then, the procedure would be lengthy and subject to appeal. How then to explain this Gestapo-style arrest?

"Shall we go?" Engels backed away from the door.

Maurer came alongside me and took my arm. I shook him off. My blistering glare dented his casehardened exterior about as much as an arrow on armor plate.

We went: Maurer, me, and Engels, in that sequence. The police officer bade us a courteous goodnight. Nice guy.

My car had been moved and now stood in a rank of more modest conveyances at the end of the building. A white Opel with police markings and uniformed officers in the front seats was waiting, engine running, muffler dribbling blue smoke. As we moved toward it, a German-plated Harley, groaning under two beefy riders and enough camping gear for a troop of boy scouts, pulled away from the checkpoint. They rumbled past, helmets turned inquiringly toward us.

Then I was sliding along the back seat of the Opel, Maurer nudging me from the rear. Engels entered from the other side. I felt the clasp of cold steel around my right wrist—handcuffs. The snap of the ratchet had a chilling finality about it.

"Are you arresting me, Inspector?" I asked, watching Maurer attach the other cuff to his own wrist.

Engels took his time about replying as he got settled.

"You are in custody," he said at length. "Let's leave it at that." He leaned forward. "The airport, Sergeant."

The airport!

The car accelerated smoothly down the divided highway and through the suburbs of Chêne-Bourg, toward the city. I was frantically assessing my situation. I had two facts to grapple with. One, Engels was still pursuing the Munich killing. Two, I was going for a plane ride. Conclusion: extradition without the usual judicial process. Thus, *illegal* extradition. Not that pointing it out to Engels would cause him to perform a U-turn. He would be better informed on Swiss law than I was. In any case, he was not the instigator, merely the instrument. Unless the Inspector was gambling with his career out of spite or financial gain, my hijacking had been authorized at a far more exalted level in the chain of command.

I looked sideways, past Maurer's unlovely profile at buildings flitting by, bathed in the pale orange of the streetlights. We were fairly rocketing along the empty road. Dawn was still an hour ahead, and Geneva, sensibly, was not yet up and about. The stop lights were with us: green, nothing but green. A privilege only the police seem to enjoy. On either side were endless multi-story blocks, the sidewalks lined with trees. Finally, we did hit a red light. The car shuddered as we came down from 120 kph to zero in a space of fifty meters.

A city garbage truck lurched out of a turning, grinding across the intersection in low gear. Rue de Malagnou, I read off the corner of an apartment block, one of the main thoroughfares into the city from the east. It was also a short walk from my apartment; any right turn along here would do. Funny how nostalgic you can get about a place you never really cared for, when it seems likely you've seen the last of it. It prompted flashes from the recent past, like images projected on a screen inside my skull. The few, all too brief days when Gina, by her very presence, had transformed my apartment from a collection of rooms into a home. The images were infinitely painful. The most painful image of all was only twenty-four hours old.

The lake, black and glossy like spilled ink, opened out on our right as we sped across the Pont du Mont Blanc toward the north side of the city. It was a dry night—or, rather, morning. No rain, except on me. I had my own private cloudburst.

An *Aéroport* direction sign glowed from an overhead gantry. We rumbled over the cobblestones of the Place des 27 Canons and down into an underpass beneath the railway, then out onto the long straight of Rue de la Servette. The airport beacon was in sight, suffusing the night with an alternating white and green corona.

Not far now. My hours on Swiss soil were numbered, with precious little prospect of a miraculous escape. I wasn't Houdini and the handcuffs weren't made for slipping out of. Even if they were, that still left me in a four-to-one minority. Lousy arithmetic. Forget it. Apathy and weariness were weaving their insidious spells. Notions of escape faded.

Up ahead, a row of illuminated letters became visible above the rooftops: GENEVE AEROPORT. One after another, the sodium lights appeared along the road to the airfreight terminal. At a T-junction, where the road joins the RN1 autoroute to Lausanne, we went left and slowed. Engels was on the edge of his seat, directing the driver in an undertone. We swung into the Route de l'Aéroport, then left it almost immediately for a narrow road hemmed in by high concrete walls.

"You just took a wrong turn," I pointed out. "The air terminal's back there." I jerked my thumb at the lit area receding behind us.

All I got for my whimsy was an elbow in the ribs from Maurer that jolted my wounded shoulder. I gritted my teeth and imagined him spit roasted over a barbecue. It didn't make me feel any better. Or him feel any worse.

The walled road led directly onto the airport apron. The blank wall of a vast windowless building overshadowed it, probably the freight terminal. Assorted aeronautical hardware stood around, and I guessed we were in a maintenance area. Just a kilometer away was the French border. A five-minute jog, say. I was in no rush to cross it, though. Right now, France was as hot as Switzerland.

We stopped. The uniformed policeman in the front passenger seat got out. So did Engels. As Maurer followed suit, he wrenched my arm so badly that the nail file wound reopened. Warm blood trickled behind the dressing.

"Take it easy," I protested. Predictably, he ignored my plea. I seethed

quietly and stuck close to him to avert further damage. Then I saw the helicopter and stopped thinking about how I'd love to stake Maurer out on an
anthill. The machine was parked between two single-engine aircraft and
the main rotor over the cabin was revolving lazily. The fuselage was white
and egg-shaped, with a black stripe running the length of the tail rotor
boom. It had skis instead of wheels. Apart from the D-HXVC registration
letters along the lower fuselage, it was undistinguished by any markings.

D for Deutschland.

Engels and Maurer frog-marched me towards it. We were perhaps
thirty meters away, when a man jumped down from the open cabin
door and called a monosyllabic greeting. The turbulence from the
rotor tossed his hair about and, though there was ample clearance, he
ducked and came forward at a crouch. A second man, plump and
wearing a pork-pie hat, stepped down from the helicopter, but stayed
by the door, arms folded, his features in shadow.

"*Wie geht's?*" Engels queried as the stranger came up. Hands were
shaken. Not mine, though. I was nobody's friend. The stranger gave
me a flinty appraisal and spoke to Engels in quickfire German, of
which I understood less than one word in ten. Engels answered in the
same lingo, drawing a grunt from the stranger. He was about my age as
far as I could tell in the indifferent lighting, and clad in a well-cut grey
suit. His hair was thinning on top, and the skin of his narrow face
looked as if it had been stretched to fit his skull.

"So you're the famous Mr. Warner," he said in halting but gram-
matical English. "My name is Vogel. *Bundestaatpolizei*."

A kraut cop, as I suspected. The bastards really were going to
airlift me to Deutschland. It wasn't a prospect I relished.

"This is illegal," I said to Engels, without much hope.

"I suggest you complain to the authorities when you arrive in
Germany."

"I'm complaining to the authorities in Switzerland, while I'm still
here. This is illegal."

Engels remained unmoved. "So is murder, Mr. Warner."

"You've got the wrong man, I already told you."

Vogel snapped handcuffs on my right wrist and stood aside while
Maurer removed his. I was glad to be shot of him anyway.

Engels gave me a pitying look. "Don't waste your protestations on me."

"Condemned without a trial, eh?" I said, my lip curling. "You can't do this, Engels, you bastard. Switzerland is supposed to be a democracy. Christ, man, I've lived here for seven fucking years. I pay my taxes. I've got rights!" I was shouting.

"Mr. Warner," Vogel said, as calm as I was agitated. "You gave up your rights when you killed in my country. When we prove that you are..." He appealed to Engels for help. "*Schuldig*. How do you say it in English?"

"Guilty?" I hazarded.

"Yes. When we prove you are guilty, it will do no good to speak of rights."

Another brief exchange in German between Engels and Vogel, a spate of "*Auf wiedersehens,*" and I was towed toward the helicopter where Vogel's teammate hooked a second set of cuffs on me.

We sat behind the pilot on the passenger seat, which had three sections, separated by armrests. Vogel fastened my seatbelt; considerate of him.

The pilot, youngish with blond cropped hair, turned his head sideways. "*Alles in ordnung?*"

"*Ja,*" Vogel said. "Let's go."

The pilot spoke into his mouthpiece, got the go-ahead from the control tower, and proceeded to wind up the rotors. Standing by the Opel, Engels, and Maurer looked as if they were in a wind tunnel, their clothes molded against their bodies, their hair tossing crazily.

Our ascent was fast and steep and left my stomach on the runway. Voices crackled through the R/T set, sundry radio traffic. The sky was clear and growing light in the east. I had seen dawn break three mornings running now. It was a lovely and often dramatic sight, but I'd willingly have exchanged it for a decent night's sleep in my own bed. Or even in someone else's bed.

Engels and Maurer were now gnomish figures beside the runway, several hundred meters below. There were no farewell waves. The helicopter slanted across the sky, flying parallel to the northern shore of Lac Léman, and the two cops and their car were lost from sight.

Geneva, a panorama of twinkling lights fused into a mass at the center, fell away. As we picked up speed, the noise and vibration escalated in roughly equal amounts.

Only the empty spread of the lake lay below. Beyond it the mountains and valleys of Switzerland. Viewed from up here in the half-light of the approaching dawn they were just bumps and hollows, vague and amorphous. A Switzerland that would soon be of the past. My future lay outside its borders. A future as vague and amorphous as the landscape, and guaranteed bleak.

CHAPTER SEVENTEEN

WE FLEW TO MUNICH. Back to where the chain of events had begun, that transported me first to heaven, now to hell.

My expected final destination was the *Polizeipräsidium*—Police Headquarters—a fortress-like building in Ettstrasse. As it happened, my expectations were wide of the mark by half a city. We landed on a soccer pitch in the suburbs, to be whisked away in a black Mercedes with tinted windows. We proceeded along a ruler-straight highway, through an industrial zone, and ultimately to the last house in a tree-lined dead end, a typically modern-traditional private residence, five stories high. Steep terracotta-tiled roof, beige stucco walls, all the windows evenly spaced. Very geometrical, and harmonizing to perfection with its neighbors.

My quarters were on the top floor, hot and airless, an angled section of ceiling where the slope of the roof encroached on it. Bars on the inside of the window with a narrow, prison-issue bed, and a table with a laminated top peeling away at the edges. It was bracketed by two upright chairs that looked ready to fall apart if you so much as flashed your backside at them. On the vinyl floor, a rectangle of pink carpet with a burn hole in its middle. I was deprived of my watch, shoelaces and belt.

Leading off behind a sliding door was a washroom. I visited it and pissed long and loud into stained ceramic. I flushed it noisily, not quite drowning the doom-knell of a nearby church clock. Very fitting, considering my circumstances.

Too tired even to agonize over the disturbing turn of events, I flopped on the bed fully dressed, shoes and all, and the lights went out all over me.

When I awakened, it was not because I had slept my fill but on account of some thoughtless bastard shaking my shoulder. As I came to, he quit shaking me and stepped back from the bed in haste. The haste of vigilance, not panic. He was tallish and bald. He wore a beige suit with a maroon handkerchief stuffed artlessly—or arranged artfully —in his top pocket, and a wide tie of the same color.

"Schmidt," he said by way of introduction. His top lip had a kind of built-in sneer, lifting crookedly when he spoke, and he had a slight lisp. And he was seriously bald; I'd seen more hairs on a ping-pong ball.

"Hello, Schmidt," I returned, my vocal cords still furred with sleep. "What time is it?"

"A little after twelve," he replied, without consulting his watch.

The sunlight suffusing the room made it noon not midnight. I'd slept for just two hours. I felt used up and wrung out. Grubby, too, on account of not having washed since...I couldn't remember when. My chin, when massaged, sounded like a saw cutting wood. And my wounds were sore and throbbing.

I wanted to ask for a drink, but my tongue was stuck to the roof of my mouth.

"Would you like a drink?" Schmidt enquired, reading my mind. His English was effortless and natural, the opposite of my German.

When I nodded, he fetched water in a tooth glass. I had never realized water was such amazingly drinkable stuff. The thought raised a hollow internal laugh. Water would likely form part of my daily diet from now on, along with dry bread.

"Come." Schmidt backed toward the door. Not once did his incisive blue eyes leave me. Under his armpit the line of his well-cut jacket swelled revealingly. These days, police usually wore their hardware in the small of the back, where it was less obvious. Schmidt was either independently-minded or high enough in the law enforcement strata to play by his own rules. My money was on the latter.

"Come," he said again. "There is a person downstairs who wishes to meet you." He flung open the door and barked a command at two hunky plainclothes men lounging there. Guns were displayed, and not the kind you keep under your armpit either. These were mean-looking Ingram machine pistols, fitted with sound suppressors. More than anything else, they impressed upon me the deadly seriousness of my predicament.

The four of us descended by a succession of right-angled staircases to the first floor, where I was shown into a room at the back of the house. It faced a large and unkempt yard with a cluster of mature conifers at the end and a double row of the same species along either side. It was an effective natural screen.

Schmidt left me standing in the center of the room, which contained only a long oval table encircled by six matching chairs. The walls were painted insipid green. I dwelled listlessly on the view beyond the yard. The dominant feature was a grey shoebox of a building, topped by a pair of tall metal chimneys that vented plumes of brown smoke, the only blemish on a picture-postcard spread of blue. My thoughts were drifting back to the day I first saw Gina, that evening in Digne, when she brushed me off so ruthlessly. The tattoo of high heels on wood intruded on these bittersweet memories. Simultaneously, Schmidt spoke my name.

I turned slowly through one hundred and eighty degrees, my gaze passing over Schmidt, then Vogel, coming to rest on the woman. A woman I last saw comatose, with a life-threatening neck wound, at Schloss Thomashoff half a lifetime ago. A ghost of my unlamented past, risen from the grave to condemn me.

She wore a summer dress, abounding in feminine frills. A very short summer dress. On some women legs are just a means to support their bodies. On Frau Ingeborg Thomashoff, they were lethal weapons, invitations to check them out all the way to heaven. The ivory sling-back shoes added several centimeters to her height and coordinated with her ivory purse. The ensemble shouted money and sex. In daylight, without the hooker makeup, she was a natural beauty.

Much improved, too, without the bullet hole in her throat. If there was a scar, the black choker concealed it.

Under my scrutiny, she first paled then reddened. Neither of us spoke.

"You know each other, I think," Schmidt said to me.

"Do we?" I clung onto my innocent stance to the last. In the true tradition of my father's race, I was going down with flags fluttering from the masthead, guns booming a final defiant salvo.

"Frau Thomashoff?" Schmidt said, his voice a confident purr. "*Kennen Sie oder nicht diesen Mann?*" Do you know this man or not? Even my German was capable of unravelling that sentence.

Her eyes were blue-grey, widely spaced below blue tinted eyelids, the only makeup she sported, other than a subtle shading of blush along the cheekbone. She looked younger than I remembered. Maybe it was the absence of cosmetics. She would be what, thirty-four, thirty-five?

As we stared at each other a spark leaped across the gap, a telepathic linkup that brought a hot flush to my body and fomented a wild, unreasoning, surge of hope.

"Frau Thomashoff?" Schmidt was tapping his foot ostentatiously.

Vogel, more perceptive perhaps, glanced from the woman to me in puzzlement.

"So!" she said, tilting her lovely head. "Mr. Warner himself." She chose to speak in English, which I appreciated.

"Hi," I said, keeping it noncommittal, awaiting developments.

"Do you recognize him?" Schmidt demanded, also in English, forcing the pace in his impatience.

Without removing her gaze from mine, she nodded. "Of course I recognize him."

Schmidt's grin of triumph almost split his lower face.

As for me, I resigned myself to the inevitable.

But Schmidt, like any good cop, wanted his i's dotted and his t's crossed.

"Do you identify him as the man who shot and killed Fabrice Tillou at the Schloss Thomashoff, in November last year?"

I held my breath, awaiting my death sentence.

"What!" She seemed taken aback by the idea. "*Gar nicht!*"

I goggled at her. If I had translated that correctly she had just said "Not at all."

Schmidt looked shaken. "What do you mean by that? You just identified him."

"So I did. But not as the gunman, you fool." She stretched out an arm and touched my cheek. "This is my old boyfriend, returned to me. Where were you, my darling? They said you'd had an accident."

Hopes soaring, I played along. "It's wonderful to see you again, Ingeborg."

"How long has it been?"

"It must be almost ten years," I replied, unable to grasp what was happening, but signing up for the fun just the same. Was she really going to double-cross the police and save me? Or was she toying with me, like a cat with a mouse?

Schmidt was perplexed. "We have proof that this man killed Fabrice Tillou. All we need is your physical identification."

"This is not the man, I tell you."

"You described the killer. This man fits the description exactly."

She had an answer for that, too.

"He is blond, yes, with blue eyes. But the gunman's hair was receding, and straighter, and his nose was crooked, as if it had been broken sometime. Also, he was shorter and more thickset."

"You never mentioned that," Vogel accused her.

She disregarded him and dipped into her purse, dug around and produced a card.

"Here, darling. When these cretins set you free, as they must, call me."

As I tucked the card in my shirt breast pocket, she turned and walked to the door, letting herself out.

One of the Ingram-wielding sentries thrust an inquiring head around the door as Frau Thomashoff clip-clopped past him. Vogel telegraphed a resigned gesture. Schmidt was oblivious, giving a fair imitation of a pressure cooker on the boil. Any moment now he would go off.

I was no less mind-blown. I had accepted as inevitable that Frau Thomashoff had been primed by Schmidt and co. to identify me. Now my thoughts were a writhing snake pit. Why had she let me off the hook? Never mind debating the point, my pragmatic side snapped back. Just be grateful and accept the gift.

The same head was back at the door. "*Sie ist gegangen.*"

Schmidt was cooling to a gentle simmer. "*Scheisse,*" he said without emotion. He glared at me. "She is lying. I know it. You certainly know it. If only I knew why."

He pounded a fist into his palm over and over, and then stormed out, still pounding away, leaving Vogel to escort me back to my room.

During the rest of the day I was fed and watered and provided with the means to remove my facial fungus. A handful of ragged paperbacks in English was dumped in my lap, and, most welcome of all, a two-day-old *New York Times.* At my request, a doctor came to change the dressings on my wounds, no questions asked as to their origins. Though it still hurt to move my arm, both wounds seemed to be healing cleanly.

The next morning, as I was polishing off my third cup of breakfast coffee, Schmidt came in. He crashed down on the spare chair to the accompaniment of ominous creaking. Without so much as a "*Guten Morgen,*" he pitched into me.

"There is something that puzzles me."

"Me, too," I interrupted. "Like what am I doing here? Like, who the hell are you? Not the police, that's for sure."

"Never mind who I am. I have all the authority I need under German law. Just tell me this: why did you shoot Mrs. Thomashoff with a different gun from the one you used on the Frenchman? He was wearing an empty shoulder holster. Did you kill him with his own gun?"

"All this talk of guns! You're crazy."

The lips formed a sneer. "Which movement are you working for, Warner? The Turkish Army Faction?" He proceeded to reel off seven or eight meaningless titles and sets of initials. I acted dumb. Not that acting was necessary.

"Is it the Greens then?" he said finally, with a hint of desperation.

"If you're asking am I a terrorist, the answer is, don't be so bloody stupid."

His face clouded. "Careful, Warner, careful. I could easily get nasty with you."

"You've been nasty enough already by holding me here illegally. Face it, Schmidt, you've fucked up big time. I'm no terrorist, never have been, and never likely to be. Furthermore, you heard your star witness. I'm not the guy who shot her boyfriend."

"She was lying," he said slowly and with certainty, and departed without another word.

It was two days before I saw him again. Two monotonous, dragging, solitary-confined days. It was an occasion for reflection. When I wasn't sleeping, reading, or doing press-ups and jogging on the spot, I reflected and I grieved. With so little to keep my mind busy, it was permeated by images of Gina and the highs of our days together, all too few as they were. The lovemaking above all, but also the moments of magic aboard *Seamist*, and wandering the pathways of Porquerolles, arm-in-arm like teenagers. A good friend and his son gone, too—that hurt almost as much. Other regrets crept in, over the many deaths laid at my door and thirty-eight wasted, self-destructive years.

Inside my head, I was much changed. Even to save my own skin I doubted I was capable any longer of dispensing death. I'd had my fill. Since I couldn't actually go back and make myself virgin pure again, I would have to compromise. Settle for the retirement I once coveted and latterly came to despise. Climb right out of the cesspool. Maybe find some good works to occupy me. A lot of shit would still cling to me, but eventually...

If Gina had lived, I would have done it for her. Why not do it for her memory? I owed her that much. God knows, I owed her infinitely more.

These private vows would amount to jack shit unless I succeeded in prizing Schmidt's grip from my short hairs. Despite Frau Thomashoff's best efforts to get me off the hook, I was still locked in my attic prison under armed guard, with Schmidt determined to punish me for my crime.

On my fourth morning in custody, Schmidt delivered my breakfast in person. A hardboiled egg, various meats and salamis cut thin, and coarse-grained brown bread, also cut thin. I wasn't hungry, but I managed the egg and a couple of circles of salami. While I ate, Schmidt stood with hands clasped behind his back, a plain pink folder tucked under his arm, gazing out at skies that were still cloudlessly blue. It reminded me of the old standard "Blue skies, nothing but blue skies, from now on". Yeah, sure.

When I had clearly eaten my fill, he came and sat across from me. The chair bore up manfully.

"Do you find Frau Thomashoff attractive?" was his initial ranging shot.

"Sure. You heard her. She was my girlfriend once."

The pink folder was in his hand. In a fit of pique, he lashed me across the face with it.

I jumped up, sending my chair spinning, instinctively preparing to meet violence with violence. But a gun had popped up between us, and I was at the wrong end of it. My temper plummeted from boiling point to deep freeze as Schmidt flipped the safety catch to 'fire'.

"Come on, Warner." He was ready to let me have it. His finger was curled round the trigger, the skin taut over the knuckle. All he wanted was an excuse, and I would be meat on the mortuary slab.

"What are you waiting for, Warner? Come on! Save us the cost of keeping you in prison for the rest of your life."

Had he been unarmed, I would have accepted his invitation. The gun made all the difference. Self-immolation wasn't written in my tealeaves. I backed off.

As the heat went out of the atmosphere, he covered up his overreaction with the nearest I ever saw him come to a grin. He waggled the gun in semi-apology and slid it back behind his lapel.

"Sit down," he said.

I fetched the upended chair and did as I was told.

"We have talked again to Frau Thomashoff. She now confirms you're the man who shot her."

The big bluff. I didn't believe him for a second.

"So you might as well confess," he said stolidly. "It may help lighten your sentence if you are cooperative."

My snort of disbelief didn't please him. He shifted position and was caught by a sword of sunlight slicing through the window. His bald head glowed like a light bulb.

"It is possible you will be sent to an open prison," he battled on. "The conditions there are..." He scowled. "Well?"

"Confront me with Frau Thomashoff again. Let me hear it from her."

"You *filth!*" The table jumped under his balled fist. The guy had a short fuse. "You think you're so damn smart! We know all we need to know about you." As suddenly as he'd lost it, he calmed down. "Unfortunately, what we can prove is another matter. If you were not an *Auslander*...if you were a German, we would very quickly make you confess. Very, very quickly."

"The old Gestapo instinct dies hard, eh, Schmidt?"

He didn't react to that jibe. He got to his feet slowly and wearily, like a man carrying the troubles of the world on his shoulders. Though he was probably a year or two younger than me, right now he could have passed for fifty.

"In one hour from now, you will be released." He stood, very erect, looking straight past me. "Where do you wish to be taken?"

I blinked at him, too stunned by the unexpected about-turn to reply.

"Where do you wish to go? Geneva?" His eyes lowered and focused on me.

"I...nowhere," I gasped. "Just open the door and I'll walk away."

Fast.

"Very well. Please be ready in one hour."

I was ready there and then but spent the allotted hour as fruitfully as I could making myself presentable. Not easy in a shirt that hadn't seen the inside of a washing machine in six days. At the appointed time, I was taken downstairs by a member of my guard detail. No machine pistol in attendance. I was officially a law-abiding citizen again.

Schmidt and Vogel awaited me in the entrance hall. Vogel returned my wallet and other personal belongings. No receipt to sign, this wasn't a police station. The front door was open. Sunlight streamed in, symbolizing freedom.

"Before I leave," I said to Schmidt, "there's something I'd like to know."

"Yes?" His manner was frigid and unresponsive.

"Who, or what, are you exactly?"

His mouth turned down. "One day, Warner, one day, I think you

will find out. I think we shall meet again, you and I. *Sie sind dreck!*"
Spittle flew. "Scum!" he obligingly translated. "And scum always rises
to the surface. Next time when you rise to the surface, I shall be there
to scrape you off."

I was too exhilarated to take offence. "Not this scum, Schmidt. No
rising for me. On the other hand, should you happen to cross my path
without your army of goons to back you up, I might—just might—be
tempted."

The corner of his mouth lifted, exposing his teeth. We had perfect
mutual understanding. I winked back, conveyed a nod to Vogel, and
strolled out into the warm morning air. Its sweetness was perfume to
my olfactory senses.

The door shut behind me. I had a feeling that, if I were to return to
the house tomorrow, I would find no Schmidt, no Vogel, no goons, no
trace in fact of their ever having occupied the place. Nor even that I
had spent the best part of a week on the fifth floor.

It was a spooky feeling.

On the sidewalk, in the shade of a sycamore tree, a woman.
Standing very still, hands interlocked before her. The dress was different. This one was frothy and white, the neckline plunging toward a
soaring hem, the twain not quite meeting, but having a bloody good go.

She was typical of the sort of woman who, pre-Gina, had represented my staple diet: sensuous, highly sexed, with a penchant for
perversion, including a touch of S and a dab of M. With the coming of
Gina, I had forsworn the type, in fact all other types. Did I want to
retrace my steps? Well, no. And yet, yes. People have to be true to
their instincts, and although unlucky in love, I wasn't ready to give up
on lust.

She smiled nervously to begin with, then easily, boldly, a smile of
invitation.

I strode down the short paved path and joined her in the shade.

"Frau Thomashoff," I said and executed a stiff little Prussian bow.
"What a pleasure."

The smile softened. "Mr. Warner," she acknowledged, extending
her hand. "I hope you are well."

"Very well, thanks to you." I took the proffered hand and held onto
it. Neither of us was quite at ease in these unusual circumstances.

Maybe she was remembering what I did for a living, and the bloodletting that brought us here.

"Quite near here is the Englischer Garten. Shall we walk there? Perhaps you will feel at home. We have much to talk about."

"We do?" I said, wondering what was in the "much".

She chuckled, a delicious babbling brook sound. "You and I must get to know each other properly," she said, as we moved from under the tree. She took my arm. "Tonight, we shall dine and drink champagne at the best restaurant in town, the Käfer-Schänke. Do you know it?"

"Only by repute."

"You will be the handsomest man there, I'm quite sure of it."

"And you, Frau Thomashoff, are surely the loveliest lady in all of Munich."

"So gallant! And, please, call me Ingeborg, or if you prefer, Inger."

"Inger is better. More intimate," I added, testing the temperature. "And afterward? After the meal?"

We hurried across a busy road. Ahead was a bridge over a canal.

"We go that way, over the bridge. The gardens are on the other side." Then, with a hint of coyness, "Afterward? Afterward we shall see. Perhaps I will take you to my home. Since I divorced my husband, I'm living permanently near München. I have this small house beside the Ammersee, which is a large lake to the west of the city." Her eyes found mine and a galaxy of promises sparkled in them. "But why do I tell you this? You have been there before. You must remember?"

————

AFTERWARD...

Lying next to her, sated, the sweat on my body cooling, my heart ceasing to thump. Darkness was relieved only by the green display of the digital bedside clock and the glow of her cigarette. Her right leg made a bridge over my left. Our breathing was the only sound in the bedroom. Mine was harsher. We were out of sync. Outside, absolute quiet.

"You're pretty fucking hot, you know, darling," she said, her voice throaty and seductive. From the position of the glow of her cigarette, I could tell her face was turned toward me.

Darling. How trite it sounded from her lips. Cheap, tawdry and meaningless, a whore's endearment.

Like the good reliable stud I was, I had done what was expected of me, though she had made all the running. A woman like her—a total lack of inhibition and a figure fit to arouse a eunuch—was hard to resist. But I wasn't proud I had succumbed. I told myself I did it out of gratitude.

"Thanks for the compliment. You didn't do badly either." An understatement, really. I groped for the glass of Scotch on the night table, almost upended it in the dark. "A couple of weeks ago, I had a dream about you."

"You *did?* I'm flattered. Was it a good dream, or just a wet dream?"

"A bit of both." No point telling her I'd killed her. "We got married."

The bed creaked; I sensed her shrinking away from me.

"Married? Why the rush? I only just got divorced."

"It was just a dream, Inger, not a prophecy, and even less of a proposal. Who knows what dreams mean? If they mean anything." I sipped my Scotch. The rocks had long melted, the diluted Scotch insipid.

"Just as long as you don't have ideas about making me Mrs. Warner."

Even as a joke, the prospect of exchanging vows with Fabrice Tillou's former mistress wasn't funny. Just sick.

She stubbed her cigarette in the ashtray by the clock. "It's almost three. I'm going to sleep now."

"Me, too. Goodnight, Inger."

"Goodnight, darling."

There it was again. *Darling.* Not "darling" the way Gina said it. After Gina, I never wanted to be called "darling" again, especially not by this woman. At least she hadn't called me beloved. I couldn't have borne that.

Within a few minutes she had slipped into a deep slumber. It took me a while longer, but eventually I drifted off, too.

While I slept, even as I lay next to her, it seemed to me that she entered my dreams again.

——————

IT WAS MORNING, a bright summer morning, the kind that comes after a rainstorm when everything smells of plant life growing. It was a domestic scene. We were in her kitchen. I was seated at an island bar, on a high stool with a backrest. On the counter before me lay a dusting of crumbs and a half-drunk glass of juice. Inger was standing at the sink, rinsing our breakfast dishes. Barefoot, in a white kimono robe of fine silk, a suspicion of pink buttocks beneath. All her clothes had a sensual element. Her hair was caught carelessly in a clip from which a few strands had escaped, dangling down her cheeks like yellow lianas. She looked younger than her years. Her skin was wrinkle free, her eyes clear, her lips plump. She was a fake blonde with fake boobs, but the rest was authentic.

"You want anything else to eat?" she asked over her shoulder. Standing there, clattering dishes, she stirred memories of Gina, memories of that first day of our life as a couple, in the kitchen of my apartment. It was a painful image.

"Not a thing, thanks. German breakfasts are enough to keep a guy going all day."

From where I sat, facing the wide window, I could make out the far shore of Ammersee and a triangle of water. It was very blue, reflecting trees and buildings, the inverted images three-dimensional.

Inger moved from the sink, dried her hands, and headed for the living room. As she passed she bestowed a faint smile on me. I returned it. Both smiles meant nothing. It had been a strictly one-night stand. I got up and went to the window. The door to the terrace stood open. The bolt I had sawn through last November had been replaced, I noticed.

Behind me, I heard her pad back into the kitchen. A drawer opened, then closed.

"Tremendous view," I remarked.

"That is why my husband buy it." She didn't often get it wrong in

English, just the odd syntax error, letting slip that it wasn't her native tongue.

She came to stand by my side. I smelled the shampoo she used. It smelled of jasmine.

"I've got something for you."

As my mouth opened to ask what it was, a hard cold object was pressed into the side of my neck.

"There. Can you feel that, *darling?*"

Her voice was different from before. No longer warm, the "darling" overdone, jeering.

Intuition warned me that to move might be a mistake. So I froze.

"What is it?" I said stiffly.

"Can't you tell? You're supposed to know all about guns."

My brain locked solid for a few endless seconds. A gun at my neck. Work it out, schmuck. It wasn't all that hard to figure out why I was here, what she meant to do.

"You remember where I was shot, darling? Hey? In my *neck.* As you've seen, I have a neat little scar to prove it." She sniggered. She was strung up, nervous, which didn't make her any less deadly. "And another scar, not so neat, at the back. This is your *Handarbeit.* So now I'm going to give you a dose of the same. Not because you disfigured me. Oh, no, I can live with that." She gave a longer snigger, with a hint of hysteria. The pressure from the muzzle increased almost to the point of pain. "I'm going to shoot you because you killed Fabrice. Does that make sense?"

I made spit to lubricate my throat. "To you, I guess. Not to me. If you just wanted revenge, why didn't you identify me to the police?"

"Because it's a personal matter. I wanted you all to myself. Not rotting behind bars for a few years, where I can't see your suffering."

Her inexperience with guns had led her to a classic error of coming too close. She couldn't resist the personal touch, I guessed. People who know guns stand out of reach from their intended victim. It was a weakness I could exploit, the only one, in fact; a chance to deflect the gun barrel before she fired. With the muzzle gouging my neck and my side vision limited, I couldn't tell if the hammer was cocked. If it was, the prospects of success were at best fifty-fifty.

Her lips caressed my cheek, light as a butterfly settling.

"Goodbye, darling, and thanks so very much for the fuck. It was your last, so I tried to make it memorable."

Waiting wasn't an option. I rammed my elbow into her midriff, ripping a gasp of pain from her lips, and simultaneously slapped the muzzle away from my neck. The gun went off, the heat from the blast searing my ear. I heard the bullet smack into the wall. It had been cocked after all. Before she could get me back in her sights for a second go, I bulldozed her toward the nearest stretch of counter.

When she crashed into the counter rim with my weight propelling her, she screamed. Hurt, but still not ready to quit. She tried to hit me with the gun—it was a short-barreled revolver—but I intercepted the down stroke of her arm with my left hand and grabbed her wrist with my right, smashing it down on the granite counter. More squeals. The gun flew out of her fingers and shot across the black tiled floor.

She raged at me as we struggled, a flood of German that included the word "*Schwein*". Now she was really fighting me. There was nothing of the weaker sex in the whirl of punches she landed on my face. Surprise slowed my reactions. When her knee came up, searching for my crotch, I realized I had to take her seriously, quit handling her as if she were an antique vase. I hauled off and socked her on the side of the jaw, putting a lot of force behind it. The one punch was enough. Her eyes swiveled up. She would have crumpled to the floor if I hadn't caught her.

As I lowered her onto the black tiles, I was already plotting ahead. The logical next move was to walk out. Even better, to drive out. Take her car and hoof it for the Austrian border, less than a hundred kilometers and two hours from here. To hang around was to invite retribution; when she came to, she would regret letting me off the hook with the police. A word from her would put me back in that grubby little room with the stained toilet and creaky chairs, en route to a real prison.

Sprawled on the tiles, still unconscious, mouth agape, she began to snore. Her robe had come open at the front, exposing a breast. It didn't flatten like a natural breast.

Under her neck, a pulse fluttered. It was a skinny neck. With my two hands, I could easily encircle it. It sure would simplify matters. That old taboo about killing women was what held me in check. Plus, it would be an overkill. Immobilization for a few hours was enough for my purposes.

I went through the drawers in the kitchen cabinets and eventually came across a roll of black insulating tape. Impossible to break by pulling or stretching it. Just to be sure, I bound her wrists both above and below the wrist bone separately, winding the tape round a dozen or more times. For good measure I did likewise with her ankles, and across her mouth, dragging her lips back over her teeth in a rictus-like grin. She didn't mind. The cleaner was due tomorrow, so she wouldn't have more than twenty-four hours of discomfort.

Her bag was on the counter. The keys to the house and her car lay beside it. I scooped them up. She was still out, but her chest was doing a regular rise and fall. The snoring had petered out. I finished off my juice. It was grapefruit, fresh from the juicer. Shame to waste it.

I went out through the front door to the driveway. Her Merc, the sports model, was carelessly parked, with a wheel in a flowerbed. Collateral of last night's carousing: too many schnapps and too many lines. My memory of it was hazy. It could even have been a dream.

None of that mattered anyhow. It was all over. This was the end of a saga that began in this exact same spot, nine months and several millennia ago. Really the end. *My* end, too, as an assassin, if not quite yet as a man.

A PSYCHOLOGICAL THRILLER THAT FOLLOWS AN UNCONVENTIONAL HITMAN WHO'S TRAPPED IN THE KILLING ARENA.

Racked by guilt over the accidental killing of a young Italian girl, contract killer André Warner has effectively retired himself from his 'profession'. But when a contract in Tangier to assassinate an Arab drug trafficker lures him out of retirement and self-pity, he encounters an attractive American widow, Clair Power, and her precocious sixteen-year-old daughter, Liza.

As he embarks on a fling that brings him into conflict with a mysterious Dutchman—who also seems to have eyes for Clair—it appears that his budding romance is destined to fail. Even more so when Clair disappears, and Warner is landed with the role of de facto guardian to Liza.

In an attempt to track down his latest love interest, Warner crosses a line that brings him into conflict with the local police and sees him returning to Andorra with a distraught Liza in tow.

And when the enigmatic Dutchman pitches up in Andorra and begins to take an interest in Liza, too...Warner is forced to get possessive the only way he knows—retirement be damned.

AVAILABLE JANUARY 2023

ABOUT THE AUTHOR

A reluctant businessman is how Lex Lander describes himself.

British by birth, he is a true cosmopolitan, having lived and worked in France, Spain, the Netherlands, New Zealand, and latterly, Canada. He began writing fiction at an early age, but his literary bent always had to take a back seat to the need to, as he expresses it, 'put bread on the table'.

Nevertheless, in spite of a sporadic output, his books have enjoyed modest success over the years—in hardback, paperback, and e-book formats. His genres are crime thrillers, with the occasional foray into psychological/political/spy thrillers.

He is looking forward to working with Rough Edges Press, who will initially release three titles from his backlist, and he is committed to upping his game, with three completely new titles to be published over the next twelve months.

CPSIA information can be obtained
at www.ICGtesting.com
Printed in the USA
BVHW050204051222
653455BV00004B/18